THE
DEMONOLOGISTS'
LEGACY

Book Two of The Demonologists Trilogy

K. SCOTT CULPEPPER

Jacket art: Brandi Doane McCann
Author Photo: Josiah Culpepper

www.kscottculpepper.com

Hardcover ISBN: 979-8-9916850-3-0
Paperback ISBN: 979-8-9916850-5-4
Ebook ISBN: 979-8-9916850-4-7
Library of Congress Control Number: 2025921704

Minneapolis, Minnesota

Dedicated to two men who left an enduring positive legacy. They made the world a better place and me a better person.

To Kenny Culpepper, world's greatest dad and papa. I miss you every day and will always be thankful for the honor of being your son.

To Grady Culpepper, world's greatest papaw and World War II veteran serving in the U.S. Army, 90th Division, 357th Infantry. Thank you for your service and sacrifice in the cause of protecting human freedom and flourishing. May we continue to honor your legacy by cherishing those freedoms and working with renewed commitment toward the day when all people will be truly free.

CHAPTER ONE

LUCILLE'S PAST SLAMMED INTO MY PRESENT, accompanied by the roar of a racing engine and a woman's piercing scream. I saw her reflection in the window while I was waiting for Trey outside Landry's Seafood House. Standing across the street near the corner of Jackson Square, her gray mane hung loosely down her long-sleeved red blouse, which combined with her long black skirt, seemed unseasonably warm for the sweltering Louisiana summer heat.

I turned and met her eyes. Even across the street, I could see the uncertainty registering on her face. She hesitated, and for a moment, I thought she was about to turn and dart the other way like a spooked deer. It wasn't the first time we'd done this awkward dance. I'd noticed her earlier that morning while I was presenting my paper at the Hilton and again while I was signing books in the exhibition hall afterward. She listened with rapt attention while I spoke; I thought for sure she would approach me during the signing. Instead, she hung around the periphery of my line for a while and then disappeared only to reappear now across the street.

Her eyes held mine as resolution settled on her face. She took a step off the curb and smiled as she walked toward me. A spark of light hit my eyes as she stepped forward, temporarily blinding me. I shielded my eyes. Looking through my fingers, I realized that the light was reflecting from a silver pendant dangling around her neck. It looped in a perfect circle and held a pentagram at its center. I recognized that pendant. I'd seen one just like it a few months ago. She noticed me looking at it and reached down to lift it slightly so I could see it better. Something about her tugged at the back of my mind. A phantom of familiarity floated around her, but the ghost wouldn't take form. She was walking slowly across the intersection, still only about halfway, a slight limp slowing her progress.

While waiting for her to cross, I watched a few cars heading down the cross street to my left, and then in my peripheral vision I noticed a gray BMW passing a car, and I heard its engine roar. It accelerated faster than I thought possible. The tires shrieked. I looked back at the woman still in the intersection. She had also noticed the BMW, but it was too late. She had just enough time to turn and scream before it plowed into her. That piercing wail ripped through me. A sickening thud followed it as her body flipped over the hood into the windshield, forming a nasty spiderweb where her body struck the glass. She ricocheted off the windshield and came to rest in the middle of the street. The driver was unable or unwilling to regain control after their sudden burst of speed. I jolted into full awareness. The car was heading straight for the sidewalk where I stood and going fast enough to jump the curb.

"What the hell?" I heard Trey say behind me. I spun around and tugged at his arm, hoping he could read the urgency in my eyes and voice.

"Move!" I yelled.

Acting on pure instinct, he grabbed me and launched us both as far to the right as he could lunge. I felt the bottom hem of my skirt rip and a sharp pain in my left knee as we hit the pavement. Trey grunted beside me. His landing hadn't been any softer. His arms stayed around me, leaving no support to stop his face from grazing the concrete.

The BMW's brakes squealed. Two of its tires jumped the curb right where I'd been standing. The driver was correcting now that we were out of the way. All four tires hit the pavement again, and the BMW roared down the street away from Jackson Square. Pedestrians jumped aside and shouted at the rogue driver. Miraculously, the car avoided hitting anyone else as it raced down the street and out of sight.

I fought to catch my breath. People were screaming and pointing at the motionless form lying in the street. So far no one had worked up the courage to approach her. I pushed myself to my feet and stumbled that way. The voices started raging in my head before I knelt beside her.

Shouldn't we keep her on her back? I fought desperately to keep the memories at bay. *Don't think. Just focus on what needs to be done.* I reached for her shoulder to roll her over.

She wasn't as old as I'd first thought when I saw her earlier at the conference. I judged her to be in her mid-to-late sixties. *Close to the same age as . . .* I pushed the thoughts away again. Blood oozed from several little cuts on her face. More blood dribbled from the corners of her mouth. Despite the gore on her patrician face, I could tell the straight angular lines of her chin and cheeks were once full and youthful, the ghost of the beautiful young woman she'd once been lingering.

"Ma'am? Can you hear me?" someone said behind me.

Two women in blue scrubs appeared at my side. Nurses taking time out for lunch only to find there was no rest for essential workers. I heard one of them calling an ambulance on her cell. The woman's eyelids fluttered. She looked up at me through piercing green eyes filled with fear and confusion.

"You've been in an accident. We're calling for help now," I said. One of the nurses knelt beside us and checked her pulse. When she turned the woman's arm, I noticed a small pentagram tattooed on her wrist. The nurse looked at me with a sorrowful expression and shook her head. I could tell the woman was fading fast even without the professional diagnosis.

Help me, Debbie! Please! They're killing me!

"Is there anything we can do for you?" I gritted my teeth as I asked the question. My lunch lurched in my stomach on the verge of making its way back up my throat. *What's wrong with me?*

My question brought clarity for a moment. Her eyes focused on me. Confusion melted into urgent desperation. She grasped my hand.

We can't give up on her! Stay with us.

My ears rang. Sweat poured down my face and matted my dyed blonde hair. I felt my chest heaving. She was trying to talk to me. Her lips were moving, but the words weren't coming out.

Momma! Don't leave us, Momma! You're going to be okay.

My vision was swimming.

Don't leave me, Debbie!

"Are you okay?" It took me a moment to realize that the nurse was talking to me.

"Diana!"

"Trey," I mumbled.

"Is she okay? I need her to move so I can try to make this woman comfortable."

"She's experiencing post-traumatic stress," Trey explained. "She lost her mother a few months ago."

"I can help," I said.

"Diana, it's too soon. You're having flashbacks. Let the nurses take her."

"I'm not . . . flashbacks . . . having," I could barely get the words out between breaths. My vision continued to blur. He was right, of course. I'd jolted awake so many times over the last few months with milder but similar symptoms.

I felt Trey's arms around me. Just like that night. I could smell the hardwood floor of our old school gymnasium. My senses took me back there. I shivered as if still wrapped in the cold December air of the unheated gym. That night I held Lucille in my arms and begged her not to leave us. The night I called her "Momma" for the first time in twenty-five years. The night she died so that I could live. The gunshot exploded behind me again. My body poised for an impact that never came because of her body stretched across mine. The images clicked back and forth like erratic slides on a deranged View-Master. Lucille. Dinah. Lucille dying in my arms. Dinah bleeding on our kitchen table. My mother. My sister. Gone.

I heard Trey's voice whispering in my ear. "You've got this, Di. Come back."

I fought my way back to the present moment with sheer determination. The voices didn't disappear, but they did start to fade. My vision slowly came into focus. Identifying the monster, knowing what was happening to me, gave me the clarity to lift myself above it.

"I'm okay. Help me up." Trey released me, stood, and offered his hand. I took it and was just about to slide out of the nurses' way when the woman seized my other hand.

"Deborah . . ." she gasped.

Trey and I both froze.

"Lucy . . . wanted . . ."

"Ma'am, you need to move so we can help her."

"That's my name," I said.

The nurse gave Trey a confused look. This time, Trey offered no help. He was just as surprised as I was. She glanced skeptically at the conference name tag I still wore with DIANA CHAMBERS clearly spelled out in bold black letters.

"Deb . . . Deb."

"You really shouldn't talk, Ma'am."

She ignored the nurse and stared straight into my eyes. Iron settled into her pupils as the will behind those eyes marshaled every particle of her remaining strength for one final effort. As more words escaped her dying lips, I could hear traces of her rich French accent even in that broken stream of words.

"Lucy . . . Broussard. . . took the list. Key . . . chest. Warn them. Save them..."

Trey shook his head. "Lucy Broussard? Who's that?"

I started to answer him, but she spoke again.

"Save our children. Save yourself . . .Deb . . ." Her head slumped back onto the pavement.

"Okay! Everybody, move!" The two nurses bent over the woman as I stumbled backward. The piercing siren of an ambulance resounded in the distance.

"Who is Lucy Broussard?" Trey asked again.

I couldn't take my eyes off the woman's inert form as the nurses performed their futile task. "Broussard was Lucille's maiden name. I've never heard anyone call her Lucy."

Paramedics arrived and loaded the woman into the back of the ambulance. One of the nurses insisted on going to the hospital with her. As she climbed in, I pushed forward. I noted the erratic rise and fall of her chest. She was holding on, but barely.

"We'll do everything we can to make her comfortable," the nurse promised.

"Could you please let me know how she's doing?" I asked. The nurse nodded and took my cell number.

New Orleans police officers dispelled the crowd of onlookers and settled us into chairs outside the restaurant to take our statements. There wasn't much we could tell them. Neither of us caught a clear look at the driver due to the sunlight glinting off their damaged windshield and our rush to escape their sidewalk incursion.

"I think this was intentional," I insisted.

Officer Burton, with his chiseled dark face cut straight from police procedural central casting, raised a skeptical eyebrow and glanced at his partner behind me.

"I appreciate your opinion, Ma'am. But this just looks like another out of control French Quarter drunk driver to me."

"They weren't out of control," I said. "At least, not in the beginning. The BMW was creeping down the cross street when I noticed it, and then it accelerated. They intentionally rammed into her."

Trey nodded. "She's right. It looked like they were aiming the car at her when I walked out. The driver wasn't even trying to make the turn." He was holding an ice pack supplied by the Landry's hostess over his left cheek. It was swelling into an ugly black knot after his contact with the sidewalk. The ache in my knee had ebbed, but I didn't want to think about what it would feel like tomorrow.

"I assure you we'll check every possibility, of course," Officer Burton said, but his tone didn't assure me.

I prepared to argue, but my phone started playing "We Are Family" by Sister Sledge.

"Haven't heard that one in a while," Burton said.

"Sorry. I have to take this," I said. I rose and stepped a few feet away while Trey shook Burton's hand and gave him our contact information.

"Hey," I said, trying to keep my voice from trembling.

"Are you okay?" Dorcas asked. I obviously wasn't succeeding. My little sister could read me too well.

"It's a long story, but we're okay. Tell you more later. We're going to be late getting to the house."

"About that. Daddy and I just got back from a deliverance trip. We were in Bogalusa and . . ." Dorcas' breathless delivery promised something important at the end, and as usual, it was taking a while to get there. I suspected her story had something to do with chasing or expelling demons since they were fresh from a "deliverance" trip, code for exorcism counseling.

"Dor, can you please just give me the short version today?"

"We caught somebody breaking into the house! They went through Momma and Daddy's room and the artifacts room!"

I snapped to attention.

"Are you two okay?"

"Yes. We're fine. We ran them off. They jumped into a red pickup parked out behind the barn and drove away."

"Did they take anything?"

"No, but they left something. I think they found it in the house and dropped it when we chased them out. Two white guys in jeans and flannel. Redneck home invasion."

"Left something? What did they leave, Dor?"

"You need to come see for yourself," Dorcas said. "I've never seen it before. Daddy said it belonged to Momma, but he's never seen what's inside."

I was intrigued.

"We'll be there as soon as we can. Have you heard from Delilah?"

"She was supposed to be landing around three."

"We'll pick her up and head your way. Love you."

"Love you too, Diana," Dorcas said. "Be careful."

"Always."

"Well, you've sure let this place go to hell," Delilah observed. Our living room was a maze of overturned furniture and scattered papers. Dorcas had obviously minimized the damage report over the phone. The intruders had particularly selected several of the oldest pieces of furniture in the living room. They cut into the lining with a sharp object. Stuffing spilled out of several ugly wounds. Delilah raised her baseball cap to tuck a loose strand of emerald-green hair, her color for the summer season, underneath before glancing at us to see if we appreciated her dark humor.

"We can't all have your dedication to clean living," Dorcas said.

"Wow! Kitty has claws after all!" Delilah said.

"How did you manage to stop them?" I asked my dad.

Denny Hebert stroked his gray beard and said matter-of-factly, "I spoke to them like a gentleman." His rakish grin revealed there was more to the story.

"And . . ." I prodded.

"Tossed a little lead at them."

"That's interesting," I said. "You got the gun out pretty fast."

"Well," he said, "it helps if you're already packing."

"I seem to recall a conversation with Deputy Gorman about you not packing for a while after all the excitement last fall."

"Well, sure," he said, "but nobody said anything about Dorcas packing."

"Are you prone to packing, Dor?" I asked.

She tried to suppress a grin that slipped through anyway. "Habitually."

"So, Dorcas chased them off with the gun?"

"Yep," Denny confirmed. "Good thing too. The police will have a better chance of finding them with their back window blown out."

I rolled my eyes. "Dorcas shot their back window out?"

"Yeah. Dorcas is sweet, but she gets overexcited with firearms."

"I bet she does," I said. Dorcas widened her already saucer-round brown eyes, swept her long black hair over her shoulders, and gave us her best Charlie's Angels pose.

"So," he continued, "the police should look for the shattered back window."

"Shattered window," I noted.

"And Dorcas may have shot out one of their taillights."

"Should we be dragging their bodies out from behind the barn?" I sighed.

"Next time," Dorcas said.

"Butch and Sundance here will both be in jail by the end of the summer," Delilah said. "And Princess Di will inherit the kingdom while I slum it on the road."

"The kingdom is in disarray," I noted.

"That going to make our job easier or harder?" Delilah asked. We had all agreed to meet at our old house in Picardy in these early days of summer to finally do the heartbreaking task of going through Lucille's things. None of us had been up to it in January; then Delilah and I both had work commitments for most of the spring. With Delilah's tour and my semester both done, we'd planned a couple of weeks to focus on boxing her things up and rearranging the house.

"Nothing's going to make it easy," Daddy said as he bent over to straighten our overturned coffee table. "If your momma saw this, she'd . . ." His voice caught for a second. I could see the slightest shudder ripple through his big solid shoulders. Dorcas and I both reached out to take a hand. He smiled gratefully and squeezed both of our hands with his massive paws. Even in the gentle touches he gave his girls you could feel the tremendous power he was holding in reserve. Our intruders were lucky they had received a bullet to their window instead of Denny Hebert's foot to their asses.

"Maybe I can make you a sandwich and you can rest a little while," Dorcas said. "That exorcism was long and hard."

"Thank you, Angel. We need to get started cleaning this up."

"Delilah and I can start on it," I insisted.

"We can?" Delilah mouthed silently.

"You just got here," Daddy said. "You're tired, too. I've got some catfish out back we can fix."

"Let's do the catfish tomorrow night when we have more time," Dorcas said. "You need to rest, Daddy. And you're overdue for your meds."

He shook his head and started for the bathroom to wash up. Dorcas hurried to the kitchen and made all of us ham sandwiches with chips and water. She settled Daddy in the living room to eat in his recliner. The recliner was newer than some of the other furniture. It had escaped desecration by our intruders, a fact which sparked my curiosity. There seemed to be an age bias in the furniture our callers had chosen to vandalize.

Delilah and I ate our sandwiches quickly and started picking things up. Nothing but the furniture was damaged. The rest was disorderly but intact. Trey and I had told Delilah about our tragic afternoon on the way home, and I was still shaken when Trey dropped us off. He hated to leave us to deal with the aftermath of the home invasion, but the accident had delayed us so much he was late to meet his kids and ex-wife at his house. The kids were coming to stay the weekend, and he'd already lost his grocery time. Having a different emergency at our house and sliding back into the complicated familiarity of our family circle helped ease the lingering horror. Delilah aided the cause by dwelling on the happiest of topics.

"At least, when you die, we can just donate all your books to Vanderbilt and your schoolmarm wardrobe to Goodwill. Be done in one afternoon."

"Who says I'm going to go first? You're the ancient one. I take care of myself."

"I'm only older by one year," Delilah said. "And I take care of myself too. I dance. I sing. I exercise."

"You vape."

"Clears the airways, my dear. So, based on visual analysis, you probably won't have much lipstick or mascara to donate to the Goodwill?"

"Some of us don't need to show solidarity with the raccoons in our mascara application," I said, tossing a stray rag at her head. She dodged and grinned.

Dorcas joined us once she was sure Daddy was settled.

"How's it going?"

"Long," I said. "On the bright side, we're getting a good workout."

"What are we even supposed to do with all this crap!" Delilah complained as she pulled her green hair out of her face and bound it back with a clip. She had started to let it grow a little over the last couple of months and was regretting it in this stifling Louisiana summer heat. Sweat poured down our bodies and made our hair stick to our necks despite the ceiling fans swirling furiously at their highest settings throughout the house.

"It's not crap," Dorcas said. "These things all meant something to Momma."

Delilah shook her head at our younger sister and pointed at a stack of *Life* magazines in the corner.

"Those are not heirlooms. That is clutter."

"She didn't like to throw things away."

"Clearly," Delilah huffed as she picked up the enormous stack of magazines. "You care to help, Princess Di?"

"You're out of breath picking those up, and you think I'm about to jump in and throw my back out?"

"We can't risk damaging your delicate physique," Dorcas teased. "How will you ever set up your Powerpoint slides if you can't stand straight?"

"She's not worried about her classroom agility," Delilah said as she tossed the magazines into our recycle can. "She's afraid she won't be able to twist into all the weird sexy positions Trey likes if she injures her back."

"My ability to . . . do that . . . is not a problem and not your concern," I said, surprised to feel my cheeks burning as they blushed a bright red. *How old do you have to get before you're done feeling awkward discussing your sex life with family? Obviously older than forty.*

"Hear that, Dor Dear?" Delilah said, her bright blue eyes gleaming like a cat with its prey in reach. "Prowess is not a problem for De-Bore-A. Not so vanilla these days, huh?"

"Anyway . . ." Dorcas said. Her face flushed a deep crimson. Eager to change the subject, she said, "Come take a look."

Dorcas led us into the artifacts room. I felt a chill as we stepped into the scattered assortment of creepy relics. Gratitude washed over me when I remembered that the leering face of Christine, our allegedly demon infested doll, had been obliterated forever by Crissy Dixon's wild gunshots. At least she no longer lingered here to torment me. I took a breath, closed my eyes, and imagined the moment Trey's lips first touched mine in this very space when we were just thirteen. The image helped dispel the sense of dread that always seized me when I entered that place.

The curiosities in my parents' artifacts room were strewn in a disorderly pattern that would have driven even Lucille to un-Hebert language. Tarot cards, allegedly cursed voodoo dolls, and the miniature iron maiden were pushed out of their usual places. The iron maiden was tipped on its side.

"Here," Dorcas pointed and knelt in one corner of the room. A china cabinet filled with voodoo dolls of various kinds usually stood there. It was lying on its side, tossed over by the intruders. The wall space it covered was splintered and torn from the baseboards to the middle of the wall. A gaping hole had been ripped by a sledgehammer, exposing the musty skeleton behind our walls. The space wasn't huge, but it looked like the studs and supports were strategically placed to create a pocket about three feet deep and four feet wide.

"What the hell!?" Delilah said.

I was too stunned to speak.

"Before you ask," Dorcas said, "I had no idea this was here."

"And Daddy?" I asked.

Dorcas glanced toward the living room. Satisfied Daddy was settled there, she whispered, "He said, 'That's your Momma's place, Angel. Not our business.'"

"What is that supposed to mean?" Delilah said.

Dorcas shrugged.

"So why were they tearing into our walls, Dor?" I asked.

Dorcas stood and motioned for us to follow her. We walked into the kitchen, which didn't look disturbed by the thieves. Dorcas pointed down.

"Daddy and I found this in the yard near the barn when we were chasing off our intruders," Dorcas explained. "They dropped it and ran when Da... I started shooting."

An antique chest made of solid oak sat under the table. A band of burnished silvery steel wrapped around it. The steel frame gripped an impressive iron lock on the front of the chest. Even without measuring the chest, I could see that it was a perfect fit for the space behind the ugly scar in our wall.

I looked at the ornate lock at the center of the chest. The past beckoned from the calligraphy emblazoned around the oddly shaped keyhole. Nobody took the time to make their containers works of art anymore. We just drive down to a container store or Walmart to buy a mass-produced clone with no personality or originality to hold our stuff. Before Henry Ford, before assembly lines, before industrialization, every piece of furniture and every scrap of clothing bore uniqueness and character like this chest.

"That is a beautiful piece," I said.

"Looks like something you would like," Delilah said.

"You can tell it's antique?"

"Well, it looks old, and you do too, so I thought you could empathize."

"You're thirteen months and three million hangovers ahead of me in our march to the grave," I said, bending over the chest. I ran my hands along its dusty surface, savoring the tactile contact with an object forged centuries before me. "I'd love to get it appraised and see how old it really is."

"There's an inscription on the top," Delilah said. She pointed to an area just above the locking mechanism. I pulled my phone from the back pocket of my shorts and shined the light across the lid. *L'obscurité fuit devant l'aube* was carved in old style cursive script across the surface.

"Darkness flees before dawn," Dorcas read behind me.

"Glad to see you're still keeping your French fresh, *ma chère*," I said with a smile. "Generations of Heberts and Broussards would beam with pride."

"*Merci, ma sœur*," Dorcas replied.

"Haven't you people heard of Google Translate?" Delilah moaned.

Before I could answer, a wave of memory washed over me. I paused, pushing Delilah's and Dorcas' voices out of my head as they continued to trade jokes about language translation. *Something caught my attention. What was it?* I ran my fingers back over the lock. The shape of the keyhole and its size dated it as much as the inscription or anything etched on its surface. *I've seen this before.* The sounds of our old outboard motor echoed in my memory along with the smells of our Aunt Etta's kitchen. My own voice rang in my head from the distant past. I said the same thing back then. "It's so beautiful. No one takes the time to make things this nice anymore." I remembered that look on Lucille's face when I said it. The mixture of astonishment and something else I couldn't identify. I would have almost called it pride, but Lucille Hebert never admitted to harboring human passions like pride in those days. That day was the closest I remember feeling to her even in those early years before we lost Dinah.

My mental gears whirred, and a newer memory surged to the surface of my consciousness. I saw Daddy handing me a brown envelope at the cemetery.

"She left this for you, Angel."

I still felt the cool metal of the key as it slid into my palm on that chilly day six months ago when we laid Lucille to rest. Ornate and beautiful like this chest, without doubt it was born in a different, more elegant time. I'd known then that it probably opened a chest or antique door. Now, I knew which chest. The mysterious words of her note resonated with a new urgency given the strange events of the day.

"You will know what to do with these if the time comes. Protect them all if I can't. You may not believe me, but there is no one besides your daddy I trust more than you. You are the one most like me."

Protect whom? How will I know? I shivered despite the humid summer evening. The words the woman gasped lying in the street resembled Lucille's message. *Save whom? From what? Or whom?*

"I think Luci . . . Momma . . . left me the key to this chest."

"It's okay if you call her Lucille, Diana," Dorcas said. "We know you loved her. More importantly, she knew you loved her."

"Thank you, Dor," I said with genuine gratitude. "It's hard to break old habits."

"You have the key to this?" Delilah asked, sounding uncharacteristically intrigued.

"I think. Daddy gave it to me at the funeral along with a note from Lucille."

"What did the note say?" Dorcas asked.

"She said I would know what to do with the key if the time came."

"What time?" Dorcas' brow furrowed as she asked the question. There was something I couldn't identify behind her big dark eyes. She was struggling to suppress it, or at least to hide it. But whatever it was surged too strongly to be easily dismissed.

"I don't know. She was vague and mysterious, as usual," I shrugged.

"Why did she leave it for you?" Dorcas pressed. There it was. Dorcas had always been the faithful bearer of the family legacy. She never wavered from that path like the rest of us had. She'd earned my parents' absolute trust. My heart broke a little, sensing the growing ache behind her questions.

"She left it for me because it was a historical artifact," I said quickly, "something in my wheelhouse." I realized how flimsy the excuse was even as I came up with it on the fly. Dorcas had her own historical interests. She maintained her French so well because of her interest in genealogy. She knew the history of the Heberts and Broussards from Louisiana to their migration from Acadia and all the way back to their origins in France. But I couldn't hurt her by telling her the full contents of Lucille's note. *You are the most like me. You may not believe me, but there is no one besides your daddy I trust more than you.*

"So, go get the key and let's see what's in here," Delilah insisted.

"I don't have it here."

As if on cue, my phone buzzed. I flipped it over and saw Jasmine Pike's name insisting that I take her call.

"It's Jasmine," I said.

"From Vanderbilt?" Delilah asked.

"Yes. She's watching over my apartment this summer."

"Your soon to be vacated apartment?"

"Yes. I think so," I said a little too fast. "She'll manage it while I'm on sabbatical."

Delilah pursed her crimson lips, causing her nose stud to glint in the fading light of the setting sun. She wanted more details, but even she realized now wasn't the time.

"Jasmine?"

"Diana! So glad I caught you! Are you where you can talk?" Her crisp Brazilian accent flowed through the speaker like melted butter. Jasmine kept the religious studies department at Vanderbilt solid and sane as our administrative assistant while also working part-time on her own graduate degree.

"Sure. Everything okay at Vandy?"

"We're all fine here," Jasmine said. "It's your apartment."

I knew what she was going to say.

"Someone broke in?"

"Yes." We could hear the astonishment in her voice. "How did you know?"

"We've had a similar problem down here. Is anything missing?"

"Not as far as I can tell. Just a lot of things out of place. They rummaged through your closet and shelves."

Anger burned in the pit of my stomach at this further violation of my space. Eric Dixon had helped himself to my living room last fall to plant a recorded exorcism, paint a warning on my door, and scare me with a fake ghostly apparition of my dead sister. People really needed to stop breaking into my apartment.

"I'm handling it with the police. I'll let you know if anything comes to light," Jasmine said reassuringly. "I locked it back up and will go by to check on it as often as I can."

"Thank you, Jaz," I said. "So sorry it's turning into a headache."

"You're my favorite headache, my friend. Glad to help. By the way, Pedro stopped by looking for you. He heard about the break-in somehow."

"That's sweet, but Pedro Silva needs to remember it's not his job to worry about me anymore."

"Be nice, Diana. You were together for five years. It's a hard habit to break. I wouldn't mind someone worrying about me like that."

"I worry about you twenty-four seven, Jaz," I said with a grin echoed by my sisters.

"I guess that will do for now," Jaz said. "Tell your sisters and Brandy 'hello' for me."

"Will do. Thanks, Jaz."

We stood in silence for a moment after I ended the call. Before anyone could speak, my phone buzzed. I didn't recognize the number, but the message contents revealed the sender.

SHE DIDN'T MAKE IT. DIED AN HOUR AGO. NO ONE HERE FOR HER YET. SORRY. U DID ALL U COULD. WILL LET U KNOW IF ANYONE CLAIMS HER.

"It appears we have a situation here," I finally said.

"You think what happened to that woman has something to do with these break-ins?" Dorcas asked. I could tell she did too. She was hoping I would dismiss her fears.

"I can't be sure, but it's hard to believe it's all random," I said. "She wasn't just some random bystander. I'm sure she followed us from the Hilton. It was like she'd been working up the courage to talk to me, choosing her moment. I can't place her yet, but there was something so familiar about her."

"I'm guessing that key was in your apartment?" Delilah asked. Her tone conveyed she didn't think she wanted to know the answer.

"Actually, no," I said.

They both looked surprised.

"Where is it?" Dorcas asked.

"Not far," I said. "Keep this safe, and I'll go get it."

CHAPTER TWO

"I DON'T SEE WHY YOU CARE! It's not like we'll be keeping you up tonight! Dad said it's fine."

"Dad doesn't know about your little stunt last week."

I'd slipped through Trey's front door quietly, hoping to avoid the crossfire I'd already overheard. I was tiptoeing through the living room when my cover was blown.

"Diana," Brandy called, "tell her Dad said we could go tonight!"

I sighed and turned toward the kitchen reluctantly. Brandy was planted firmly beside the island at the center of the kitchen with her hands on her hips, chestnut brown hair hanging loosely down her back. Erin, her mom and Trey's ex-wife, was leaning against the sink. Her frustrated expression shifted for a moment to offer me a welcoming smile and an eyeroll.

"Trey stepped out to get some groceries," Erin said.

"Are you driving back home tonight?" I asked.

"Yes," Erin said. "I've got a work thing this weekend."

"You heard Dad say we could go to the party tonight, didn't you?" Brandy asked me again.

"I heard him say if it was okay with your mom," I said carefully.

"See, I told you so," Brandy said, ignoring like a skilled attorney the "okay with your mom" part.

"Maybe you should tell Diana how you and Amira decided to detour from the library to the Downs without asking," Erin said, her auburn eyebrow raised.

Oh boy. "The Downs" lived down to its melodramatic S. E. Hinton name. The area served as the scandalous playground for the youth of Covington, the town about two hours northeast of Picardy, where Brandy lived with her mom and younger brother Chip.

"I wasn't doing anything wrong!" Brandy insisted, her voice in danger of rising to shouting levels.

"I know what you were doing." Erin was making a supreme effort not to look accusingly at me. I wanted to melt into the wall. I knew what they were doing there too. "You're not a cop or a counselor. You are fourteen years old. That place is dangerous. You can't just go off on a whim without permission."

"It wasn't on a . . ." Brandy's sentence ended with a frustrated groan. "I can't with you. I'll talk to Dad when he gets home." She looked at me imploringly, shook her head, and stomped out of the room.

Erin and I stood in awkward silence for a beat too long.

"I'm sorry, Diana. You shouldn't be put in the middle."

"It's okay," I said. I didn't want to bring it up, but we were both thinking it. "You know she was there to help. Maybe I shouldn't have told her about the police reports."

"Maybe not," Erin said. She was trying to be gracious, but I could see the frustration bubbling in her eyes.

"Erin, I . . ."

"Diana, I love you," Erin said tentatively. "Trey loves you, and I understand why. I've never seen him happier."

"You don't have to say that. I know it can't be easy."

"It's true, and I'm secure enough to admit it," Erin said. "We never made each other as happy as you two do. My kids love you too. Hell, Brandy wants to be you."

"I sense a but is coming," I prodded.

"Diana, I'm just . . ." She gazed into my eyes. I was surprised to see a tear trickle down her face. "I'm scared. I'm terrified, Diana."

I wanted to ask why she was scared, but we both knew. There was no point trying to pretend.

"Erin, I never encouraged her to investigate that group. No one is even sure it's real."

"I know," Erin said, wiping her eyes and brushing her curly auburn hair out of her face. "You don't have to encourage her, Diana. You've become her hero. She wants to be a hero too."

"She cares," I said, trying to keep my tone even despite the passion behind the words. "She cares like few people I've ever known. You have an amazing daughter, and she's going to change the world for the better someday."

"I know, and I want her to," Erin said. "But she has to grow up first. She needs to make it to adulthood. Your life is so dangerous. Your family. Your mom's death. That poor woman today. It's all so scary! I just worry."

"None of those things are Diana's fault." We both jumped at the sound of Trey's voice. We were so focused on our conversation that we hadn't heard him enter through the garage door. "And you don't have to worry. She's careful. We're careful."

Erin's eyes widened in astonishment. She shook her head in disbelief. "Have you looked in a mirror, Trey?" The ugly black swelling on Trey's cheek told a different story.

"Well, I . . ."

"Are you aware that your fourteen-year-old daughter is chasing alleged cult masterminds in the Downs at midnight?" Erin asked.

Trey's expression revealed that he was not aware.

"We really don't encourage people to call them cults until . . ." I trailed off at Erin's withering look.

"Really? I don't care what we call them these days so long as my daughter stays far away from them."

"I'll talk to her, Erin," Trey promised.

"Thank you," Erin said.

"I don't want to punish her for good intentions," Trey said. Sensing

Erin's pending response, he quickly added, "but I'll be sure she knows she can't just go off like that. We'll present a united front."

Erin's expression softened. "Thank you, Trey."

I hated feeling my outsider status at times like this. The conversation was all about me and yet at the same time, it wasn't. I felt like an intruder standing in the middle of two people who'd shared a life and still shared experiences, memories, and priorities I never could. They held in common the two most important people in their lives. They always had to set aside their own needs to nurture the two lives they had brought into the world. I would always be an honorary member of that exclusive club.

"Di," Erin said. "Please don't think I'm trying to be a bitch. I meant what I said. I'm so glad you are part of our lives. Just, please, think about Brandy."

"I do, and I will," I promised.

Erin glanced at her watch. "I need to start back before it gets too late."

"I'll walk you out," Trey said. He reached over, squeezed my shoulder, and winked reassuringly at me as he followed her to the front door.

I decided to let them have a few moments alone to talk. Climbing the stairs, I took a right and followed the sounds of Beyonce down the hall to Brandy's room. Brandy was lying across her bed staring at the ceiling, wearing a black Bon Jovi t-shirt untucked from her khaki shorts. We had a conversation on one of our early outings with Trey about all the eighties and nineties band shirts she and her friends wore without even knowing what songs the bands sang.

"The designs are cool and vintage," Brandy insisted. "It's not important what they sing."

"Not important!" Delilah had shouted through Facetime when I told her. "You need to educate that child now. Plus, why are they not wearing Delilah shirts?"

The musical education of Brandy Laurence and the transformation of our relationship had begun when she came back with me to Vanderbilt over spring break. Trey had suggested it.

"Brandy has spring break next week. Why don't you take her back with you? I can come up and get her next weekend."

"Are you serious?" I sputtered, my wine threatening to slide down my windpipe instead of my throat.

"Sure," Trey said. "It would be great for her to see a big city besides New Orleans. She loves music and is already talking about going to college."

"Maybe she should hang out with Delilah if she likes music," I said.

Trey grimaced, "I want my daughter to get a little culture and see the big city. Not dye her hair purple and hook up with a roadie named Gremlin."

"Gremlin's always a perfect gentleman," I said. I stretched my hand across the table to dangle my fingers in his. The candlelight flickered over his chiseled face and wavy brown hair. It amazed me every time I looked into his eyes how certain I was that I would do and give anything for him.

"Do you really want me to take her back? I don't know anything about fourteen-year-old girls."

"You were the greatest of fourteen-year-old girls," Trey said with a wink.

"You know what I mean," I said. "I love her. I do. But she would be bored hanging out with me. I'm not even sure she likes me some days."

"She'll love you like I do when she gets to know you," Trey said.

Two days later Brandy and I were driving in my Corolla back to Nashville. Our conversation was polite but very awkward. I started her musical education with Bon Jovi and a little Nirvana. The music helped to fill the silence in between bursts of strained conversation. We shared the same dynamic once we got back to my apartment. She went to the library the first two days while I taught courses. I met up with her in the afternoons, and we toured the city in the evenings.

The choreography shifted dramatically on day three when she came with me to my office. We entered the outer office to find a sobbing young woman seated next to Jasmine's desk. Between sobs, she shared that her name was Elise, she was a junior at Vanderbilt, and she believed her roommate was trapped in an abusive high demand religious group meeting near campus. Drugs were involved and loads of emotional abuse. Elise feared physical and possibly even sexual abuse would follow if someone didn't intervene soon. I caught Brandy watching me closely a couple of times during the interview. Once, I noticed that her own eyes were misting as she listened to Elise.

After hearing her story, I comforted her and called my colleagues, Mason and Tyra, to tend to her while I followed up on her story. When I finished, I returned to my office. Brandy was sitting in the chair across from my desk reading a book on her phone. She looked up expectantly.

"Can you help her?"

"Maybe. But I'm going to have to go visit a couple of people first."

"Can I come with you?" she asked. Her earnest face and probing eyes reminded me so much of Trey.

"It could be dangerous, Sweetie."

"I want to come," Brandy said again. "Please Diana. I'll be safe with you."

Three incredible things happened that week. My colleagues and I faced one of our most interesting cases so far. Elise's roommate escaped the tentacles of a very dangerous group. And, in the course of our adventures, Brandy and I bonded deeply.

We were sitting on the couch in our sweats the night before Trey came to pick her up, our hair back in ponytails and a tub of Rocky Road Bluebell ice cream between us, when the realization struck me that I loved her like my own child. The closest I had ever come to having a daughter was taking care of Dorcas when we were young. The realization was surprising, overwhelming, and just as sure as my love for Trey. Chip was always easy, and I knew that we would grow close. But I had never been sure it would click with Brandy until that night. Brandy seemed to feel it too.

"Dad just sat down and offered you a pack of M&M's?" Brandy asked.

"He offered me two as a gateway drug before producing the whole pack," I said, smiling at the memory. "He's a skilled enabler."

"How old were you?"

"Third grade. I felt so plain and unlovable sitting in that cafeteria. Staring at my food while some girls a few tables away made fun of my clothes and my hair. He sat down, offered me some M&M's, and the rest was history. We were inseparable. Best friends."

"Sounds like something Chip would do," Brandy said. "That's why you guys always share M&M's. That's cute."

I felt relief that she thought it was cute. Cute was better than cringy.

"I'm glad you found each other again," Brandy said. There was no hint of sarcasm. "He's always been the best, but he's so happy when you're around."

I felt a catch in my throat. Before I could reply, she reached out and hugged me for only the second time since I met her. The first time was at Lucille's funeral. Delilah liked to kid me about becoming an "S-Mom." That night, I knew I was up for it. Looking at Brandy now and hearing Erin's voice in my head, I wasn't as sure. *Do I pose a danger to them?* Shame filled my head and heart as I remembered why I'd come up here.

"Hey, Diana!" Brandy noticed me and sat up.

"Hey, Brans. Are you okay?"

Brandy sniffed and made a sweeping motion across her shoulder to signify shaking it off.

"She's just being a drama queen. Dad will calm her down."

"She's worried about you, Brans," I said. "And she's not wrong. You need to be careful."

"That's her talking, not you," Brandy said.

"It's all of us talking," I insisted. "We want what's best for you."

Brandy grimaced and raised her hand like someone swearing an oath in court. "I promise I will not take any unnecessary risks and always get my mommy's permission before I go out."

"Thank you," I said.

"For at least the next two hours," she smirked.

"Brans," I groaned, fighting hard not to smile. "Don't put me in the middle here."

"Are you going to stay over tonight?" She asked, eager to change the subject.

"Probably not. Delilah's here, and we're going to work on putting my mother's things away. I'll probably sleep there so we can get an early start."

"Bummer. We'll miss you tonight. Chip has some new amateur radio thing he's working on with Dad. Amira's parents are bringing her by later to stay the weekend."

"I'll probably stay tomorrow night," I said. "It'll be good to see Amira again. Brans, do you have that key I gave you?"

"Sure." Brandy rolled over on her stomach and leaned over the side of her bed. She rummaged around beneath the bed for a few minutes and emerged with a pink caboodle. Her fingers popped the lid. The antique key lay nestled at the bottom of the caboodle. She plucked it out and handed it to me. Guilt gnawed at my gut. I fought to remind myself that I'd had no idea what was coming when I gave it to her. I thought the key was just an interesting curiosity. Lucille made everything dramatic. Who could have known lives could be endangered by the secrets it held? *Good one, Chambers. You read the message. You should have known.*

"Amira researched it a little," Brandy said as she watched me examine the key. "But she never found anything about it online or at the library."

"I may know what it fits now."

"Really?! A door?"

"An old chest. One that belonged to Lucille. I'm going to try it tonight and see if it fits the lock."

"Wow!" she said. "You have to let me know what you find."

"Definitely!" I felt a twinge of guilt. Erin's words came rushing back. *Think of Brandy.* I'd entrusted her daughter with an object that caused two break-ins and possibly a hit and run in the span of twenty-four hours.

"Diana! Come check this out!"

I grinned, and Brandy rolled her eyes at the sound of Chip's voice booming from across the hall.

"Coming!" I called. I patted Brandy's knee and gave her my most reassuring smile. "Thanks, Brans. I hope you have a great night with Amira. And please cut your mom some slack. She loves you."

"I know," Brandy said grudgingly.

"And I love you too."

"You better," she said, her gruff pretense betrayed by the smile that slipped out.

I crossed the hall to find Trey and Chip bent over a miniature audio device crackling with frenetic static. The sound assaulted my sensitive ears. Involuntarily, I reached to cover them. Chip, a perfect gentleman even at nine years old, noticed. He clicked a button on the front of the device that reduced the volume.

I smiled gratefully. "Thanks, Chip. What are you two up to?"

"We're setting up my shortwave radio," Chip said with barely suppressed excitement.

"You've got to check this thing out, Di." Trey gushed as he turned toward me. I suppressed a laugh. Trey was bouncing off the walls as much as Chip, maybe more. Moments like that made it seem like no time had passed at all. We were twelve again, and Trey was itching to show me some new thrilling gadget or TV show that was going to change our lives forever. Or at least fill the time for the next day or two before a new rad fad came along. I loved the boyish look on his face and the excitement in his eyes.

"Which one of you is getting the toy?" I teased.

"Ain't no toy," Trey said in his spot-on Humphrey Bogart impersonation. "Communication is serious business for real men, Sweetheart."

"Yeah, for real men," Chip said, trying a cute imitation of Trey's Bogart that fell far short of the original.

"Please forgive me," I said. "I don't want to cast shade on two communicating studs like yourselves. So, you're introducing this to a new generation?"

"You know you loved playing around with the shortwave back in the day." Trey and I had read through the Hardy Boys mysteries together when we were eleven and decided we needed to equip ourselves like Frank and Joe if we were going to fight any criminals lurking in Picardy. I guess Trey's parents decided the shortwave radio would be cheaper and easier than listening devices or spy cameras. Those amateur detectives stockpiled James Bond level tools without the backing of any government. Trey's parents, also lacking funding from any major international power, bought the shortwave and prayed it would satisfy us. It did for one summer. Then we moved on to Dungeons & Dragons. D&D gave us a chance to interact with people in person and was at the top of Lucille's list of banned activities. The thrill of rebellion overcame the quaint charm of talking to strangers in Portugal.

"It was spending time with you that I loved, but I did enjoy it for the summer. Aren't there other ways to do the same thing now?"

"What other ways?" Chip asked.

"Like using a phone, Goofus," Brandy said from the doorway.

Chip gave her a dismissive snort and said, "Everybody uses phones. Shortwave is different, and different is cool."

"Chip can't have a phone yet. Therefore, it makes sense for him to try an alternative form of long-distance communication." Amira's clipped and matter-of-fact tone left no room for argument or debate. Just stating facts. Her brain was incredible, but her social cues didn't always hit the same level.

"Hi, Amira," I said. "I didn't hear you come in."

"No one ever does," Amira said. "That's why I'm secret agent material." She adjusted her red-rimmed glasses as she spoke. I noticed her glistening black hair wave across the tops of her shoulders as she shook her head. *It's so beautiful. How much longer will we see it?* At fourteen, she was nearing the age where many Muslim women started wearing a hijab. Amira's parents were very traditional and broached the subject often since she entered puberty. She'd asked me about it last time she stayed with Brandy. She listened intently as I explained what I knew of the practice from both my studies and personal relationships with Muslim women around the world. I'd felt very inadequate trying to explain something a little beyond my topical comfort zone. Seeing her reminded me that I'd made a note to contact one of my friends with more expertise in Islam to correspond with her. Like so many things, that task was still piled in my "to do" stack. As always, Amira remained unreadable during our conversation, processing the information with her superior brain like a supercomputer and giving no outward tells to indicate her emotions.

"You're buzzkill material," Brandy said, giving Amira a playful punch on her arm, "You're not supposed to take his side."

"She's smart, so she takes the right side," Chip proclaimed with a hint of smugness.

"Whatever," Brandy sighed.

"Take my side, Brans," Trey said dramatically, wrapping his arm around her. "This set will provide hours of fun talking to fascinating people."

"My phone does that just fine," Brandy said.

"It does as long as you stay away from the Downs," Trey said with a raised eyebrow. "Phones tend to disappear when we don't listen to Mom."

"Message received," Brandy huffed with a mildly irritated look at Trey. Moms really had a raw deal when it came to dealing with daughters. Trey could get away with saying things to Brandy that would provoke a shouting match if Erin said them. I thought about how unfair that was. Then I was surprised to find myself wondering how often Lucille felt that way about Daddy's relationship with us.

"See?" Trey said, spreading his arms dramatically. "Successful communication all around!"

"I'm going to set up every night from seven to ten," Chip said. "Dad said you have to get on at a regular time, so people know how to find you."

"Seven to nine and only when homework is done," Trey said.

"Seven to nine," Chip corrected.

"That sounds awesome, Chip," I said, patting his shoulders.

"You should get one too, Diana," Chip said excitedly. "We could talk when you're in Nashville."

"Or you could just borrow someone's phone," Brandy said, unwilling to accept total defeat.

"You going to loan him yours?" Trey asked.

"Enjoy the little radio," Brandy said.

Brandy and Amira headed for Brandy's room.

"We'll see, Chip," I said. "I don't know that I'm much of a shortwave person anymore." *And I'm not sure how long I'll be in Nashville.* I avoided looking at Trey. I sensed he was trying not to react too. We'd been circling the question of how to make our relationship work given our jobs and family commitments. I had a nice deal at Vanderbilt. I didn't want to give it up for a lesser role somewhere else. The academic job market was tough and was getting tougher with each passing year. Securing a place as a full professor with tenure and a funded chair was enjoyed by only the most fortunate and hard-working academics these days. Too many gifted and disciplined faculty were trapped in perpetual contingent status, stuck doing course overloads on temporary contracts that offered low pay and no benefits. Trey could get another job teaching English almost anywhere, but his family was here. The sabbatical I'd secured from Vanderbilt, one that was long overdue, gave us more time to figure things out before making a permanent change. So, we were procrastinating, hoping things would clarify with time.

"If you do get one, my handle is 'Nighthawk,'" Chip said with pride. "I'm going to use 14.0 to 14.35 MHZ for my frequency."

"Wow!" I said, genuinely impressed. "You know your stuff."

"Dad set it up for me."

"Of course he did," I said, ruffling the back of Trey's hair. "He's just a big kid."

"Never growing up, and I'm sticking to it," Trey declared. He grabbed me and twirled me in a spinning dance move that ended with our faces centimeters apart. He closed the gap and gave me a deep kiss that I returned with enthusiasm.

"Can you guys take that stuff outside please?" Chip said, mimicking his sister.

We parted and smiled.

"Sure, Buddy," Trey said. "Let me know if you need any more help."

We went downstairs. I fished out my keys while Trey circled my waist with his arms and pulled me close.

"Stay," he insisted.

"I'd love to, but you'll have both girls and Chip."

"So," he said with a mischievous gleam in his eyes. "They sleep. And I can be vewy, vewy quiet."

I laughed at his spot on animation imitation.

"Sorry, Elmer. I need to get this key back. Whatever's inside that chest may help us understand what's going on."

He sighed and nodded.

"Okay. Raincheck it is."

I turned to face him and cupped his face in my hands.

"Just until tomorrow."

"Tomorrow."

We exchanged a passionate kiss. I lingered in it as I savored the feel of his lips, his familiar smell, and the comforting nearness of his presence.

As he raised his head, I found myself staring at the ugly bruise on his cheek. The throbbing in my knee had stayed at a low level throughout the day, and I hoped it would be better after I rested it tonight. It would probably take a few days for his bruise to heal though. I reached and touched it gently, careful not to press too hard.

"What's wrong?" Trey asked, noting the change in my expression.

I suddenly and surprisingly found myself on the verge of tears. A delayed response to my emotional conversation with Erin.

"I love you."

"I love you too, Di."

"I never want to hurt you."

"I know that," Trey said. He still wasn't sure where this was going.

"I love Brandy and Chip too."

Trey's eyes registered understanding.

"Di, Erin is just a concerned mom. She didn't mean . . ."

"She has a point."

"She has some legitimate concerns that we will address," Trey said. "That doesn't mean she's right about everything."

"You could have been killed," I said. "That car could have run us both down today. Dixon could have shot you at the high school. In New Orleans, when those guys . . ."

"I'm still here," Trey insisted, holding me tighter. "We're still here. Anything could happen to any of us at any moment. That's life. Yes, you travel some dangerous roads sometimes. And you do it to make the world a better place. I wouldn't trade it for anything because I wouldn't trade you for anything. Who you are is why I love you. You're worth any risk and then some."

I kissed him fiercely, but as I pulled away, a haunting thought pierced the veil of reassurance.

"But do we have the right to make that decision for Brandy and Chip?"

I saw the struggle in his eyes. He wanted to be flippant and breezy. Dismiss the concerns with a wave of his hand accompanied by a witty joke. But his paternal instincts were reminding him of his responsibility for the two lives he'd helped bring into this screwed up world.

"We will do everything we can to protect them. Always."

He pulled me into a tight embrace.

I wasn't in the habit of praying these days like I once had. Still, a thought, a wish, issued from my heart to whatever benevolent powers there might be to keep the ones I loved safe. An image of Lucille on her knees beside her bed slipped into my consciousness. Even before she lost Dinah, her greatest fear had been losing the ones she loved. She fought so fiercely to keep us safe that she pushed two of us away. In the end, keeping her vow to protect us cost her life. *What would it cost me? What would it cost Trey?*

The living room lights were on when I got back to my parents' house. Dad and my sisters were sitting there waiting for me. The ornate chest sat in the center of the room on our rug. I produced the key and wasted no time fitting it to the silver lock. For a moment, I felt resistance. Had the mechanism rusted? Then it gave way, and the key started to turn. A resounding click accompanied the release of the latch. The top of the chest popped free. We all exchanged nervous looks. We were on the precipice of something new. What were we going to learn about Lucille?

"Open it," Delilah prodded.

"What if we don't like what we find?" Dorcas asked, echoing my thoughts.

"Whatever secrets your momma had, we all knew who she was deep down," Denny said.

I wasn't as sure of that knowledge as he was. In so many ways I felt like I may never have really known Lucille at all. What was she hiding behind that emotional armor she wore all those years?

I grasped the lid and lifted it. The hinges squeaked as they performed their assigned task for the first time in decades. A moldy stench rose from within, so different from the rich cedar smell that wafted from Lucille's hope chest when it was opened. All of us leaned in to see what was inside. Delilah threatened to bump heads with me in her haste.

"Old papers?" Delilah said. "I think she left these for you, Professor."

"You don't want old papers to wallpaper your tour bus?" I asked. "This top one is a newspaper."

I lifted it out gingerly and spread it to its full length on the living room floor. The name *Le Monde* was emblazoned in elegant calligraphy across the top. Despite the paper's yellowing with age, the script was still readable. The date in the right-hand corner read *Mardi, 5 Novembre 1974.* A large black and white photo printed above the fold drew my attention. A handsome young man looked back at me. His eyes were clear and penetrating, staring straight at the photographer. His feathery light-colored hair was combed back in a thick wisp so typical of early seventies fashions. His chiseled jawline and breezy expression conveyed easy confidence and personal self-assurance born of privilege. The man may have enjoyed privilege in life, but his death was less fortunate based on the headline.

JEAN-PAUL BROUSSARD EST MORT

Underneath the main headline, a smaller subheading drove the point home with more details.

"Un jeune héritier décède dans des circonstances mystérieuses."

"I remember enough French to know this bastard is dead," Delilah said.

"That bastard was probably one of our distant cousins," I said. "And he looks like a pretty nice guy."

"He looks very nice," Dorcas remarked. She turned red when we both looked at her with raised eyebrows. "What? I have eyes!"

"Just remember the cousin part," I said with a grin. "I may need some help, Dor. I can read 'mysterious circumstances,' but I don't know the beginning."

She crawled closer and studied the page. "The second line reads,

'Young heir dies under mysterious circumstances.'" Her eyes swept the text of the article. We sat quietly, trying to be patient while she read through it. Dorcas whistled when she straightened. Her expressive eyes were wider than normal.

"They found his body on the grounds of his family estate in Brittany. He'd been shot five times."

"Waste of good ammunition," Denny muttered. "It's not worth shooting if you can't do it with one."

"We'll be sure to tell the guys driving around in the red truck without a back glass," I teased with a gentle pat on his back. He grinned.

"They don't have any suspects," Dorcas continued. "At least, they didn't when this article came out."

"When did he die, Dor?" I asked.

"You're going to love this," Dorcas said to our dad. "October 31, 1974."

Denny Hebert loved Halloween. For someone who spent his life chasing scary things, it was amazing how much pleasure he still took from simulated scares.

"Was it some kind of Halloween prank gone bad?" Denny asked.

"Doesn't look like it," Dorcas said. "They don't seem to know a lot. His mother, Madeleine Broussard, is quoted saying they had several guests in town for a reception earlier that evening. None of them saw or heard anything unusual. The guests had all left the estate by midnight. His body was found the next morning. Police estimated that he died around 2 a.m."

"Sounds pretty straightforward to me," Delilah said. "Maybe he ticked somebody off at the party? Got horizontal with someone's wife or girlfriend and paid a price for it? It is France, after all."

"The French have a pretty high tolerance for those things, but I guess you never know," I admitted.

"There's more," Dorcas said, her big dark eyes glittering. The look on her face transported me back in time to those days when she would come running up to us breathlessly with the latest news, her ponytail swinging. I loved those little reminders that the sweet young woman beside me still held inside the boisterous little fireball I helped raise.

"I'm afraid I know where this is going," I moaned. Only one thing got her this excited.

Dorcas broke into a wide grin and lowered her voice to imitate a solemn Vincent Price narration. "Some Belle Plage residents, that's the nearby town, are quoted saying they saw mysterious lights flashing from the grounds of the estate shortly after midnight that night. Others claim they heard screams and wails coming from the estate on a regular basis. Reports of suspicious strangers frequenting the village and random figures roaming the grounds of the estate at all hours of the day caused some locals to believe that the Broussards were hosting some kind of hippie commune or even cult."

"I guess that was the season for it," I said. "Though, again, France was not usually the first place you turned for that sort of thing even in the seventies. And, if you were seeking it in France, you were more likely to find it in Paris or the French Riviera than in Brittany."

"Just telling you what I'm reading," Dorcas said, continuing to scan the page. "Neither the reporters who wrote the story nor the police they interviewed gave much weight to those stories."

"But you'd like to think there's more to it," Delilah said.

"Sure," Dorcas said. "Who doesn't like a good ghost story combined with a hint of true crime?"

"I could do without any more real-life ones for a while," Delilah said. "I had enough of that last fall."

"I second that," I said.

"They were busy people," Dorcas said. "The paper says they ran a small preparatory school on the grounds. When this article was written, none of the students had been seen since the murder. None were made available to talk to reporters despite several requests to interview them."

"That's why your momma was there," Denny said. "She'd been in Los Angeles for a bit and things weren't working out. She heard that Madeleine was looking for teachers to help with the academy. And she'd always wanted to see France."

My dad was so focused on his memories he hadn't noticed all three of us staring at him in shock.

"Los Angeles?" Delilah asked. "She lived in L.A.? All the years I've lived there, and she never mentioned that she had lived in L.A."

"She didn't like to talk about that time," he said. "I don't know much about it myself. Lucille was still wounded from whatever happened in France when we met. She shared a little bit, but I respected her need to keep it to herself. I thought over time she would share more when she was ready."

"And you were okay with that?" I asked.

"There was ever only one reason she kept things from me and that was always to protect me in some way. I loved her and trusted her. We started our ministry, and that took all our focus. Then your sister was born. All of you were born one by one. We lived our lives. The past didn't matter anymore."

Part of me admired that sort of mutual trust in a relationship while the rest of me recoiled at the idea of potential icebergs that could be floating under the surface of your relationship ready to burst into full view and sink your unsinkable bond.

I turned back to the trunk to examine the items stored below the newspaper. A soft square of blue fabric, large enough to cover the items below it, lay across the top. I pulled it out and passed it to Delilah, who ran her hands gently over it. Stacked below the fabric square rested six charcoal drawings done by a skilled hand. They looked like preliminary sketches for a painting. Three of them featured nature scenes with flowery fields, a vineyard, and ocean waves breaking against a steep cliff. A fourth drawing depicted a vibrant yellow rose on a green field. The fifth drawing presented an elegant French chateau with two turrets, an elaborately crafted front door created from a combination of wood with iron framing, and a stone archway spanning the drive that led to the front door. Stained-glass windows decorated the towers while more opaque expansive glass windows rose several feet along the walls of the lower floors. Even in miniature charcoal form, the old Broussard family chateau lived up to the hype bestowed on it by generations of family lore. I'd thought about visiting the chateau several times on my trips to Paris, but I was always too busy to make the side trip to Brittany.

I passed the drawing to Dorcas. She'd finished with the newspaper and was eager for something new to examine.

"I think that's it," I said. I was just about to close the lid when I noticed the tiniest hint of white on one side of the chest. It looked like the corner of a piece of paper. I reached in to pry it loose. Someone had lined the left side of the chest with a cardboard covering painted to match the color of the chest. Not just one, but two papers were concealed behind the makeshift pocket. The first looked like some kind of official document. *Deborah* was written on the back in pencil. My fingers trembled as I unfolded the document.

"What is it?" Dorcas asked.

"It looks like a claim check for a safe deposit box," I said as my eyes ran down the document.

"In Picardy?"

"In Geneva, Switzerland. Banque Genève."

"I wonder if she stored some money there?" Denny said.

I opened the second folded document, hoping it would give me insight into the first. Instead, the open document proved to be an ordinary piece of stationery from a hotel in Geneva. A list of five names and locations were printed in Lucille's precise manuscript handwriting.

GRETA ROSENBERG	MONT	AL
JACOB LE ROUX	HOU	TX
ESTELLE MARTIN	LA	CA
FRANÇOIS MUIR	BOS	MA
SARAH ABRAMS	OM	NE

"Who are they?" Dorcas whispered over my shoulder.

"I don't know," I said. "I've never heard any of these names before." I passed the paper to Dad. He examined the list and shook his head.

"Why would she hide this?" Delilah asked.

None of us had an answer. We poured over the chest for a few more minutes. Nothing new came to light. We'd exhausted its contents but not even begun to plumb its secrets.

Filled with more new questions than answers, we agreed to take a break for the night. Delilah was planning to go clubbing in New Orleans with her friend Tianna. She left to get ready and returned dressed in unseasonably thick leather pants, black leather boots, and a turquoise t-shirt. She'd donned a long red wig in hopes of making herself less recognizable, but I was glad her personal security guards would be going with her tonight.

"Don't wait up, Kids," she smirked. "Tianna's husband has the rugrats, and she's not on call this weekend. We're going to blow wherever the wind takes us."

"Have fun and tell Tianna hi for us," I said. I was glad to hear Tianna wasn't working this weekend. I doubt most Picardy families were gifted with the imagination to picture Tianna, the consummate medical professional, transforming into Tianna, Queen of the Rager, when Delilah had her in tow.

I remained on the couch after Dorcas and Dad went to bed. Just like the new recliner, this newer couch had been left untouched by our vandals. My yawns reminded me that I needed to get some sleep myself, but I couldn't tear myself away from the two documents and the newspaper. I felt my eyelids starting to sag, and my head slowly drifted down to the couch's armrest. My head swam with visions of an elegant party on the cliffs of Brittany, dazzling light surrounding a historic chateau, and multiple gunshots echoing across the waves in the dark. My sleep was fitful. I waded in and out of consciousness, the rough arm of the couch creating an uncomfortable pillow.

As the night wore on, I was aware of a figure sitting in my dad's recliner. Her blue skirt and white button-up shirt were so familiar. Her hair was neatly packed into the bun she wore as far back as I could remember.

"You look so tired," she said. "You really need to take better care of yourself, Deborah."

"Like you always did?"

Lucille's mouth formed the slightest hint of a smile. "You don't want to follow my example. I was always too tired."

"Are you really here?" I asked groggily.

"What if I were? That would cause all kinds of problems for your closed skeptical world if I were really here. Do you think we go on after death?"

"I don't know," I admitted. "Some days I'd like to think that we do. That who we are does survive."

"And other days?"

"I think it would be nice to just sleep. To rest from it all."

She nodded with a pensive look on her face.

"Why did you say her name?" I asked.

"Which name?"

"Dinah's name. Just before you died you said her name," I whispered.

"I did," Lucille said. That was all. She just kept looking at me with that same thoughtful gaze.

"Did I ever really know you?" I finally asked.

"Yes and no," Lucille said.

"Do you have to be mysterious even in my dreams?" I asked.

She smiled a big genuine smile this time.

"You keep asking the wrong questions, Deborah."

"What question should I be asking?"

Lucille rose from the chair and walked over to me. She cupped my chin in her hand like she had when I was little.

"The question you should ask is if I knew you," Lucille said. "And the answer is yes, I did. Through and through. Even when I didn't agree with you. Even when I couldn't follow your path. I didn't make the wrong choice. You are the one to make all this right."

"Make what right?" I shifted my head. The rough armrest had magically softened. I leaned into it, savoring the soft feel of its gentle surface. As the fog of sleep cleared from my brain, I realized that there was a pillow under my head. I'd stretched out across the length of the couch, and a light sheet was pulled up to my shoulders. I rolled over to face the room. It was still dark outside with just a hint of the coming dawn visible on the horizon outside our front window. I noticed a motion out of the corner of my eye. The figure was still sitting there in the recliner.

"Lucille?"

"It's just me, Angel. Try to get a little more sleep."

I could make out his beard now in the semi-darkness. He was sipping a steaming cup of coffee.

"What are you doing up, Daddy?"

"Couldn't sleep. Guess it's contagious tonight."

I burrowed into the soft pillow.

"Thank you for making me comfortable. This couch isn't made for sleeping."

"Always glad to take care of my girl. What's wrong, Angel?"

"Just all these things with Lucille, I guess."

He shook his head with a gentle smile. "You were chewing on something when you came home earlier. What's bothering you?"

I sat up on the couch and looked into his caring brown eyes. I fought to keep the tears back.

"I'm scared, Daddy."

"Scared," Denny said. "You? Of what?"

"I'm afraid I'm going to hurt Trey. Or hurt his family. I don't know if I can go the distance. I never have before. I don't ever want to hurt or endanger them."

My dad moved over to the couch and wrapped his big arms around me. I rested my head on his shoulder for the first time in years.

"Hurt's the risk we run to love somebody," Denny said. "God knows your momma and me hurt each other plenty over the years. But you can't let that stop you from loving. You'll miss all the best stuff in life."

"I've been responsible for leading my students," I continued. "I've been in relationships, but always with a managed level of commitment. This time is the first time I've stepped so close to total commitment. If Trey and I go on, I'm going to have so much power to affect Brandy's and Chip's lives for good or bad. I want to do it. I just don't know if I can."

"You can do anything," Denny said. "I know you can. Your momma knew you could. Those kids are going to be so lucky to have you. Trey is the luckiest man in the world, and he knows it. Nobody will ever be perfect enough for you, but Trey is the best man I know. He's the one thing I've always wanted for you. Someone who knows how wonderful you are as much as I do, Angel."

I felt the tears pooling in my eyes and noticed them in his too through my blurry vision. He pulled me into a tight hug. For just a moment, I felt like I was six years old again and my Daddy's arms could drive all the bad things away.

A creaking sound broke into our peaceful interlude. We both recognized the sound instantly. Several boards on our front porch needed replacing. They announced new arrivals better than a doorbell. Dad and I broke our embrace and sat up, listening. A second board creaked. We exchanged a glance.

As a third board creaked from the porch, we heard another set of quiet footsteps descending the stairs. Dorcas appeared wearing a pink robe hastily thrown over her white nightgown. Her bare feet barely made a sound as she slipped into the living room.

"Did you hear that?" Dorcas whispered.

We both nodded, all doubt removed by Dorcas hearing it too. Dad touched my hand and pointed to the far side of the couch. I slid over, and his hand disappeared into the lining between the horizontal cushion and the back of the couch. It reemerged clutching a .22 caliber handgun. I blinked in surprise.

"I was just sleeping on that!" I hissed.

Denny put his finger to his lips. He rose and exchanged a glance with Dorcas. She automatically fell into line behind him. I envied their wordless perfect connection. I rose and got behind Dorcas. The three of us slowly advanced. My dad slid to the front door like a cat and wrapped his fingers around the doorknob. I marveled at how stealthily he could move for a man his size.

Another board creaked. A hooded silhouette appeared through the living room window. Someone was definitely out there. And it wasn't Delilah or Trey.

Denny gripped the doorknob tighter, looked at us, and darted his eyes toward the door. His message was clear. Dorcas produced a pocketknife from the folds of her robe and flicked the blade open. I reached into my shorts pocket and felt the reassuring bulk of my mace cannister still there. We both signaled Dad that we were ready.

Denny Hebert threw the door open and jumped out onto the porch.

"Don't move!"

A scream echoed through the humid night air. We stepped outside. Denny was pointing his gun at a tall figure wearing blue jeans and a dark green hoodie. The woman underneath the hoodie threw her covering off. Her raven hair unfurled in curly rivulets. Expressive green eyes wide with fear stared back at us.

"*Pardon! S'il vous plaît!*" She cried. Seeing the confusion on Denny's face and remembering where she was, she continued in English, "I'm sorry! Please do not shoot! I did not want to frighten you!"

Denny wasn't convinced. He stepped closer, still pointing the gun at her.

"What are you doing on our property?!"

She was visibly trembling with barely controlled panic. Her eyes darted around the porch until they fixed on us standing behind Dad. She gasped and clasped her hands to her chest.

"Debbie? Is that you? Please tell him who I am. *Ma mère*, she is dead. They ran her down like a dog in the street. You must help me!"

The threads of memory I'd struggled to reconnect all day began to cohere at last. I couldn't believe I hadn't recognized the woman lying in the street.

"I'm sorry," I said. "It's okay. We're not going to hurt you."

Denny lowered his weapon. Her breathing slowed, and the panic seeped from her eyes.

"It's been too long," I said with a comforting smile. "It's good to see you, Angélique."

CHAPTER THREE

APRIL 29, 1995

"Are you going to cast an invisibility spell or attack?"

Trey drummed his fingers along the surface of our kitchen table as he waited for Delilah's response. I looked to my right and caught her staring out the window.

"Delilah!" I barked.

She stirred and shot me an irritated look tinged with a side of bored frustration.

"I'm going to shove a bazooka up his ass and pull the trigger."

"You promised, Delilah!" Trey said.

"You don't think that's a good strategy?" Delilah asked with feigned innocence.

"You know there are no modern weapons in this campaign," Trey said.

"Well, I'll shove the Holy Grail up his ass," Delilah said.

"You said you would help us practice," I reminded her. "Trey wants to be sure he's got his world ready before we bring in other players."

Delilah gave me a pitying look. "Dear innocent little De-Bore-A, you listen and learn from me. I'll teach you much better things to do with a room full of boys. Isn't that right, Laurence?"

"Well, I . . ."

"Oh, that's right," Delilah grinned from ear to ear. "You're a rookie too."

She rose from her seat and stretched, angling her torso so her tight t-shirt rose just enough to reveal her bellybutton. I shot her an angry glance, which she returned before strolling out of the kitchen. Delilah was displaying a newfound reckless disregard for the rules of proper language in the Hebert household. She cursed plenty at school, but she'd always been careful to keep it clean at home. I was waiting for her to slip up in front of Momma.

"Sorry, Trey," I said. "I don't know why she has to be such a jerk."

"It's okay," Trey said. "I'm surprised we got her to play that long."

The front door opened and closed. We both tensed and listened. Trey's hand slid over to the D&D manuals that lay open on the table. We were playing with fire. My parents had been gone for two days, but you never knew when they would suddenly breeze back into town. I reached for the dice that lay scattered around the table, and my heart thumped as I strained to hear movement from the living room. Nothing. Trey and I glanced at one another. We each heaved a relieved sigh.

"What are you doing playing Satan's game! The devil's going to get you both!"

I jumped so high my knee slammed into the table, shaking all our carefully constructed environments and action figures. The voice sounded so much like my momma's. I was too panicked at first to process the slight difference, but then the sound of childish giggles broke through. I wasn't sure whether to be amused or angry.

"Why're you so scared, Deborah? You jumped higher than a rabbit!" Dorcas barely got the words out between peals of laughter. She scrambled around my chair and into my lap like a little black-tailed squirrel.

"Deborah's scared because she knows what happens to girls who play with dangerous games," Dinah said from the doorway, continuing to imitate Momma's voice at almost perfect pitch.

Dorcas stopped laughing and looked over at our oldest sister with wide eyes. "What happens, Dinah?"

"Sometimes their bottoms get all red and achy, Dor," Dinah said with a twinkle in her eyes. "Especially when Momma finds out."

"I told them Momma was going to shut it down!" Delilah shouted from the living room.

"Trey, is it fun being an only child?" I grumbled.

"Some days," he laughed. Trey was just relieved it wasn't Momma.

Dinah laughed and wrapped her arms around me from behind, pulling me in for a tight hug. "Think how empty your life would be without us."

"Oh, I'm thinking about it."

I tried to sound mad, but my irritation was slipping away; Dinah's hugs worked magic.

"I'm sorry, Debbie," Dinah said. "I couldn't resist when I saw you two sneaking game pieces like junior high kids behind the gym puffing a cigarette."

"Exactly!" Delilah shouted from the living room. "It's f . . . freaking lame to get busted for doing something nerdy. At least get caught doing something badass."

Dinah grimaced and shook her head at Delilah's awkward word choice correction.

"Little ears are listening!" She shouted toward the living room.

"I bet you can't guess which finger I'm holding up, Grandma!" Delilah retorted.

"Probably one of the ten I'm going to wring your neck with if Dorcas repeats any of your choice vocabulary."

Dorcas leaned forward in my lap and whispered in my ear conspiratorially, "I think Delilah's saying bad things again."

"Sweetie, if Delilah's talking, she's saying bad things," I patted her on the leg and scooted closer to the table with her still in my lap. "You want to help me beat Trey?"

"Yeah!" Dorcas pounded the table. "You're goin' down, Trey!"

"Wow!" Trey laughed. "We only say that when we're playing other people, Dor. You can't use it on me."

Dorcas mustered all the wisdom of her six years. "It wouldn't be fair if we just did it to other people and not you. Right, Deborah?"

"Right, Sweetie. And try to call me Debbie now."

"Why?" Dorcas asked.

"It's easier to say and it sounds better," I said.

"Momma will shut . . . it . . . down!" Delilah called again.

"You obviously aren't doing anything interesting in there if you're listening to us!" I shouted back.

"I'm watching a car pull into the driveway. That's pretty interesting. Especially on a Saturday."

We exchanged skeptical glances. Dinah shook her head and rolled her eyes.

I turned back to the table and motioned for Trey to continue the game. Dorcas leaned to the edge of my lap and fixed Trey with her version of an intimidating stare across the table. Trey fought to keep from smiling. He tried his best to look afraid of his formidable adversaries.

A fierce rap on our front door startled us again. The panic returned. I shuffled Dorcas out of my lap and furiously started sweeping game pieces into our ziploc bag. Trey tried to pick up three manuals at once and ended up dropping them all on the floor.

"Calm down," Dinah said as she headed for the door. "Momma and Daddy wouldn't be knocking."

Of course, she was right. Still, we picked up the remaining evidence and crammed it wherever it would fit. I heard Dinah talking to someone in the living room while we were stowing the last manual in Trey's backpack.

"No, she's not here right now."

"You must be her daughter; you look so much like her." The voice swelled with a beautifully rich French accent.

"Yes, Ma'am. I'm Dinah."

My curiosity overcame my caution. I stepped around the corner to get a glimpse of our visitors. Two women stood in our doorway talking with Dinah. The woman speaking was close to Momma's age. She had lustrous curly black hair that flowed like a silky river down to the small of her back. Her oval face rounded to a pointed dimpled chin and set into stark relief her bright green eyes. She was dressed in a light long-sleeved red shirt and short black skirt. The skirt was almost short enough to be classified as a miniskirt. That and the knee-high black boots she wore gave the impression of someone whose style was shaped in the seventies and refused to bend to the winds of change. The girl standing behind her bore unmistakable physical evidence of being the woman's daughter. Her curly hair was slightly shorter, but it also boasted the same silky black sheen. I thought enviously of my own unruly long tangle of black hair. Her face rounded in the same oval pattern as her mother's, but her fashion sense differed incredibly. She wore jeans, tennis shoes, and a yellow FIFA t-shirt with Brazil's logo emblazoned on the front. I estimated her age to about twenty or twenty-one. Probably just a few years older than Dinah.

"Ah! *Oui*! You are Lucille's oldest girl!" The older woman clapped her hands together and reached to embrace Dinah. Dinah gave her an awkward partial hug in response.

"And you are . . .?" Dinah asked.

"Oh! *Pardon*!" She said, her hands flying to her face to cover her embarrassment. "I forget myself. My name is Aria, and this is my daughter, Angélique."

"Pleased to meet you both," Dinah said, extending her hand to shake Aria's and nodding to Angélique. Angélique gave her a timid, but sincere smile in return. "You have such beautiful names."

"*Ma mère* said my first cries were beautiful music filling the world and making it a richer place," Aria said with pride. Looking back at her daughter, she said, "And she is my beautiful angel sent from the goddess and the god to bless this earth."

Angélique's cheeks reddened at Aria's effusive praise.

Wanting to relieve Angélique's embarrassment and sidestep tactfully Aria's reference to the "goddess and the god," Dinah said, "My daddy calls us his angels too, but we don't always act like it."

"I'm always a perfect angel," Delilah called from the recliner she'd refused to vacate the entire time.

"Aria and Angélique, this is my sister Delilah in the recliner. She's thirteen. That's Deborah over by the kitchen door. She's twelve. And so is our friend, Trey."

Trey had stowed all his contraband and was leaning past me to see the new arrivals. He waved. Dorcas scurried into the room and positioned herself at Dinah's side to stare up at Aria.

"Are you a queen?" she asked. "You talk different."

"And this is Dorcas," Dinah said, smiling and pulling her close. "She just turned six."

"You are so pretty, *mes chères*! So much like your mother. I am not a queen, *ma petite biche*, but you make me feel like royalty with your warm welcome."

"Please come have a seat," Dinah said. "Momma left me an emergency number to reach her when we need something. I'll let her know you're here."

I exchanged surprised glances with Trey and Delilah. We'd never been told about an emergency number.

Delilah rose to offer Angélique her seat. As they settled into the recliner and the couch, Delilah slid to Dinah's side. I heard her whisper, "Did that French lady just call Dorcas a bitch?"

Dinah looked confused for a minute, then she covered her mouth to keep from laughing out loud.

"*Biche* means deer. She was calling her my little deer."

"Well, good," Delilah huffed. "Only I get to call my sisters that. What's this crap about an emergency number?"

"Something I have that you don't," Dinah said. "Stop whispering and entertain them while I call Momma."

Delilah gave Dinah her "this conversation is not over" look and went to ask if our guests wanted coffee or tea.

I perched on the edge of the couch and listened as Delilah tried to make conversation with Aria. Angélique smiled at me and Trey a couple of times, but she sat quietly while her mother carried the conversation.

Dinah was gone for a while. When she returned, her announcement shocked me.

"Momma said she'll be here in about thirty minutes."

"What do I have to do to get that kind of response time?" Delilah grumbled.

Dinah ignored her. "Can I get you anything?" she asked Aria and Angélique.

"I would like to freshen up if I might," Aria said.

"Of course," Dinah said. "The bathroom is this way."

Aria followed Dinah out of the room. Dorcas had abandoned us earlier to play in her room, leaving me, Trey, and Delilah with a very silent Angélique. We sat in awkward quiet for what seemed like hours.

"Do you like to play games?" Trey asked Angélique.

She smiled and nodded. I noted her response. *At least she can understand English. Can she speak it too?*

"He's just trying to recruit you for his stupid dragon game," Delilah said.

I breathed an inward sigh of relief when Dinah returned.

"Would you like to see our house, Angélique? I'd be glad to show you around."

Angélique nodded and rose to follow Dinah.

We were so focused on them that we didn't hear the door opening. Two loud noises snapped us into awareness. The first was the screen door slamming shut. The second was Momma's bag hitting the floor.

I turned to see my momma like I'd never seen her before. She stood straight and tall with her hair pulled into a tight bun like always, but her penetrating eyes and pronounced nose, which often drew comparisons to the actress Katherine Hepburn, framed a face whiter than I'd ever seen it. Her hands visibly trembled, and her mouth hung open as she stared at Dinah and Angélique standing together.

"Momma?" Dinah said. "Are you okay?"

I was scared. Momma was unmovable most of the time. Seeing her off balance like that was a first. Through illnesses, deaths in the family, and other times of extreme stress, I had never seen her look that haunted. Haunted was exactly the right word. It looked like she was seeing ghosts as she studied Dinah and Angélique.

"The resemblances are amazing, aren't they, *ma chère?*" Aria said softly from the hallway. Her voice broke the spell. Momma blinked and swallowed. She nodded. My breath caught in my throat. I thought I saw glistening moisture in Momma's eyes.

"They are," Momma finally said. Her voice betrayed no hint of the emotions that were tearing through her mind and body. "It's almost like looking in a mirror twenty years ago."

"We were so young," Aria said wistfully.

"We were so naïve," Momma said, a definite edge to her voice. I found that steel oddly comforting. It wasn't attractive, but it was familiar.

"It's good to see you, Lucille," Aria said.

"We need to talk privately," Momma said.

Dinah frowned and gave me a questioning look across the room. I raised my eyebrows as subtly as I could manage. Momma acted abruptly and sharply often with family, but she wasn't usually rude to guests.

Aria took it well. She nodded and called to Angélique, "Stay here, Angélique. We're going to talk a moment." She repeated the sentence in French to be sure her daughter understood. Angélique nodded. Her face mirrored our own confusion. She didn't seem to know any more than we did about the business between Momma and Aria.

Momma led the way to my parents' "office," the room where they handled official ministry business and performed exorcisms on occasion.

We all looked at one another when they were gone.

"Well, great!" Delilah said. "This again."

She didn't need to worry. No silence invaded our living room this time. The murmur of voices filtered through the closed office door. We strained to hear. Occasionally, one of them got loud enough for us to catch a sentence or two. Momma sounded frustrated with the whole situation. She wasn't holding back.

"I've told you over and over again that it's not safe for you to come here!" Momma shouted at one point.

"What did you want me to do, Lucille?" Aria said. Her voice dropped, concealing her next sentence from us.

More murmuring.

"It's safe, and it needs to stay where it is!" Chill bumps rose on my skin, a Pavlovian response to Momma's raised voice.

"We need to check on them, Lucille!" Aria pleaded. "Please! It needs to be guarded closely now."

More murmuring.

"I swear to God Almighty if danger comes to this house or my family because of your careless . . .!" Momma's voice dropped again. The rest of her sentence was lost. Dinah and I exchanged startled looks. Strong language for Lucille Hebert. She invoked the name of the deity only in direct address or highest reverence.

Five minutes later, the office door flew open. Momma stormed out of the office like a swirling tornado. Her eyes scanned the room, noting each of us with our mouths hanging open. They settled on me.

"Deborah, I need your help."

"Uh, okay. Sure."

Her eyes flicked to Trey sitting beside me.

"Mr. Laurence, I need your help too."

"Me?" Trey asked.

"Is there anyone else here named Laurence?"

"No, Ma'am."

"Then I guess I'm talking to you. Dinah, come with me for a minute." She waved Dinah toward the kitchen. Dinah silently followed her.

They returned five minutes later. By then, Aria had emerged from the office and was sitting beside Angélique on the couch.

"How long will you be gone?" Dinah asked.

"Just three or four hours," Momma said over her shoulder. She disappeared into her bedroom, returning a few minutes later wearing jeans and a red checkered button-up work shirt. She exchanged a grave look with Dinah.

"Remember what I told you," Momma said.

"What do you want me to say if Daddy comes home?" Dinah asked.

"He won't. We're in the middle of a case that will keep him a few more days. I'm hoping to join him again after we take care of this. If he calls, tell him I'm busy and will call as soon as I can."

Dinah nodded. Momma's eyes swept to Aria and Angélique. She said to Dinah, "Keep them inside. Don't let them go anywhere on the property or off."

"We are capable of discretion, Lucille," Aria said.

Momma ignored her.

"Stay here," Momma said to Dinah.

"It's what I do best," Dinah said. A steel undertow seeped into her voice that sounded very un-Dinah like. I caught Delilah's eye. She heard it too. We'd been hearing it for a while now.

"Please, Dinah," Momma said, "I don't have time for this now. We can talk more later."

"You know where to find me," Dinah said. She held Momma's gaze for a moment. Then she flicked her eyes downward and moved to join Angélique and Aria in the living room.

A palpable tension stood between Momma and Dinah. It wasn't present all the time. Sometimes it seemed forgotten altogether. Just two weeks ago, Dinah received her blue Picardy High School graduation robe. Just three weeks until she gave her valedictory address and walked across the stage to receive her diploma. She'd gone out with friends to celebrate that night. Dinah told me later they spent the evening at the local pizza parlor remembering their high school years and talking about their futures. When she returned that night, Dinah had strode into the house, gave my parents a devastated look, and hurried to her room. I heard her door slam. I thought I'd seen her lip trembling like she was on the verge of tears before she escaped to her room.

"Is Dinah okay?" I'd asked my dad.

"It'll all be okay, Angel," was all he'd said.

I carried those questions with me now as Trey and I followed Momma out onto our porch. I saw our old brown station wagon, the backup to our big brown truck, parked out front. I expected Momma to lead us to it. Instead, she circled around our house, walked past our barn, and headed for the woods.

"Where are we going, Momma?" I called after her.

"Aunt Etta's," she said.

"We're not taking the car?"

"No," Momma said. "We can't go by the road today." Her tone left no room for questions or arguments.

We climbed the ridge overlooking our house, entered the dense woods, and threaded our way toward the river that ran past our homestead until it emptied into Bayou Mystere three miles south of us. Momma headed straight for our olive-green boat moored by the little makeshift dock Daddy had constructed. To my surprise, she leaped in and clutched the handle of our outboard motor. She looked up at us expectantly.

"Well, come on. What are you waiting for?"

We scrambled into the boat.

"What are you gawking at, Deborah?"

"It's just. You've never driven the boat before. I didn't think you could."

She snorted.

"You would be amazed at what I can do, Child."

I sneaked a cautious look at Trey. He widened his eyes but didn't say a word.

"Deborah, do you plan to untie us, or are we supposed to pull the bank with us?"

"Sorry!"

I clambered ashore and untied the boat. Moving fast, I jumped back in before it slid too far away. Trey and Momma paddled us out until we were far enough for Momma to stand and pull the engine chord. Our old outboard groaned and then sputtered to life. Momma seized the handle and propelled us out into the center of the river. We sliced through the brown water, heading south toward Aunt Etta's house and, further down, the junction with Bayou Mystere.

I savored the wind blowing in my face and scattering my loose hair in all directions. The bright green trees rushed past us in a dizzying blur. Hanging moss dangled from the trees, flashing by us and threatening to smack us in the face a couple of times. Spray erupted on both sides of us as we split the water before us. Droplets kissed my face, banishing the sweat and humidity. We passed several sandbars with olive-colored shapes resting on them. Gators sunning themselves. One eyed us lazily before sliding into the river. I shared a euphoric look with Trey. He was enjoying the sensations of being on the water as much as I was. The high was almost enough to make us forget the weird circumstances of our trip.

Almost, but not quite. Momma sat guiding the motor in solemn silence, her brow knit in a care-laden expression. She seemed immune to the charms of the water, the sun, and the curtains of moss hanging from the majestic bald cypress trees around us. Her eyes were focused on some unseen distant horizon. For her, life involved jetting from one destination to the next. Arrive, see, conquer; then wash, rinse, repeat. I vowed not to let myself be like her. I easily could with my own focused intensity, especially when it came to schoolwork.

I smiled at Trey, relishing his joy as he absorbed every speck of this moment. He was my antidote to the sheer lifelessness of our family "mission." I realized how much he infused my life with personality and meaning. Momma lived her life in battle mode. I admired that she had something important enough to fight for, maybe even die for, but what about all the rest? *Was it worth fighting for life and the ones you loved if you never had time to stop and enjoy either one?*

My swirling thoughts were disrupted by a distinct change in the engine sounds as Momma throttled down. Aunt Etta's own little landing, also built by my dad, slid into view. Momma steered us close. I leaped from the boat with rope in hand and waded to the shore. Trey followed. We secured the boat around Aunt Etta's dock. Trey reached out a hand to steady Momma as she climbed off the boat.

"Thank you, Mr. Laurence," Momma said.

"Wow!" I mouthed silently to Trey. Expressions of gratitude from Momma were as rare as snow in Louisiana.

When she was up the hill and out of earshot, Trey said, "Wow! I don't think I've ever gotten one of those before."

We hurried up the hill after her. Despite the fact that we were both young and in good shape, Trey and I heaved heavy breaths when we finally caught up to Momma at the door to Aunt Etta's screened porch. Momma must have phoned her. She was reclining in her rocking chair, fanning herself with a portable hand fan while an electric box fan blew a steady stream of air. The blast lifted the strands of blonde hair not bound in her tight bun and blew them behind her head like flags waving in the wind.

"Hello, Sweetheart!" Aunt Etta exclaimed as I hurried through the screen door and into her open arms. "Why, you're growin' up so tall and pretty. It's so good to see you. Who's your friend?"

"This is Trey."

"Nice to meet you, Trey. Any friend of Deborah is more'n welcome here. You like cookies, Trey?"

"Yes, Ma'am," Trey exclaimed.

Aunt Etta laughed, her eyes twinkling. Her carefree joy contrasted so much with Momma's dour personality. It wasn't like she hadn't had her struggles too. Uncle Arnold had worked fifteen years for Picardy Power and Light. Last year two young men in yellow hats showed up at Aunt Etta's door to tell her Uncle Arnold had been electrocuted in a freak accident with a rogue power line. I'd heard Momma talking about how she was left with two kids and no steady income. My cousins, who were a little older than Dinah, were hardly ever around anymore. People talked about them both getting into lots of trouble, drinking and fighting. Despite her struggles, however, Aunt Etta managed to exude a vivacity in her tiny slightly plump frame. She boasted a whole litter of surrogate kids from teaching Sunday School at her little Baptist church. Their parents brought them by to see her often. I hoped it lightened the loneliness of her riverside home.

"Hello, Lucille," Etta said, rising to hug her sister. Lucille usually didn't hug. She made an exception for Etta. They said Etta was always the "toucher and hugger" of the family while Lucille tended to be "a little standoffish." I noticed to my surprise that Momma sank into Etta's hug, lingering longer than normal. Etta noticed it too.

"Are you all right, Lucille?" Etta asked.

Momma nodded as if she didn't trust herself to speak.

"You two hit the kitchen and help yourself to anything you find," Aunt Etta said to us. "Your momma and me are goin' to visit for a bit."

Trey and I dived into a cornucopia of sugary delights in Aunt Etta's modest kitchen. I looked over my shoulder a couple of times to see if Momma was watching me devour lemon cookie after lemon cookie. Trey slipped a canned Dr. Pepper out of the fridge and slowly started easing the tab up. I winced at the first pop and release of fizzy air. I glanced over to see Momma and Aunt Etta still sitting on the porch, their heads bent close together in earnest conversation. I nodded at Trey. He quickly raised the tab the rest of the way. The first drink flowed like liquid gold over my taste buds and down my parched throat.

After a while, I heard Aunt Etta and Momma walking back to her sewing room. I waited about ten minutes and then went to find them. Aunt Etta's sewing room was cluttered with both finished projects and works in progress. Her large sewing machine stood near a comfortable red chair, and measuring tape looped over it for easy access. Spools of thread were littered around the table. Aunt Etta had gone upstairs for something. Momma was standing in the room alone when I entered. She was looking down, so intently focused that she didn't hear me come in.

"Momma?"

"Oh, Deborah. You startled me, Child."

"What are you looking at?"

She smiled and moved aside so I could see the ornate chest at her feet. A glistening silver band circled it. Beautiful calligraphy spelled out words in French. I'd seen enough French to know what it was, but I hadn't learned to read it yet. The wood that framed its sturdy structure looked even thicker than the massive shelves Daddy made in his workshop for friends and sometimes extra spending money. It looked so ancient. It beckoned to me in a way I couldn't explain. Before I realized it, I was running my hand along its hard surface.

"What's it for?" I asked.

"Storage mostly," Momma said.

"It's so beautiful," I said in awe.

"It is," Momma agreed.

"Why don't we make nice things like this anymore?"

"What do you mean?" Momma asked.

"Our storage containers are so plain. Well, except for your hope chest. People used to care so much about making beautiful things. Even the things they made to hold things were beautiful. Like everything was art. Imagine the people who touched this through all the years since it was made."

"All the centuries since it was made," Momma said. She sounded lost in thought. When I looked at her, I caught her smiling in a way that she had never smiled at me before. "You're not the first person who's said that."

"Who else said it?" I asked.

A shadow descended across her face. "A young woman I used to know."

"Did this chest belong to her?"

"Once."

"I would love to meet her someday," I said. "I'd like to ask her about the chest."

"She's gone now," Momma said quietly. "But she would have loved to meet you too. You are so much like her." That look and the special smile returned for just a moment. Then something else replaced it. Sadness and, for a frightening instant, sheer terror. Momma's voice trembled slightly when she said, "You must remember that only Jesus can keep us safe, Deborah. All the good gifts we have pale in comparison to the gift of knowing him and serving him."

"Sure, I know," I said, surprised by the abrupt change in topic.

Trey's arrival interrupted our conversation.

"What's that?" he asked.

"The reason I needed you, Mr. Laurence," Momma said. "You and Deborah are going to help me get this down to the boat."

"We're taking this home?" I asked.

She nodded, "I'll let Etta know we're on our way out."

Trey whistled and circled the chest. As he bent closer to examine it, he reached into one of his pockets. I don't know if he was reaching for candy or something else, but when he removed it, he also dislodged one of the twenty-sided die from our game. It clattered along the floor and rolled to my feet.

Momma paused and glanced back.

"What was that?"

I slipped my left foot out of my sandal and snatched the die with my toes.

"What was what, Momma?" I asked, trying to imitate Delilah's "not poor little me" innocent façade.

She pursed her lips, regarded me with a raised eyebrow, and turned toward the door again.

"That looks so old!" Trey said.

"Momma said it was centuries old."

"Wonder what's inside," Trey said. "Maybe gold?"

"The Holy Grail!" I proclaimed in a deep regal tone. "We must make haste to deliver it to Delilah, Queen of Drama!"

We both dissolved into uncontrollable laughter. As I laughed, I suddenly became aware that Momma was still standing in the doorway. I looked in her direction. Once again, I was surprised by the expression on her face. The look in her eyes jolted me. She was looking at us, but it was like she was seeing beyond us. Deep penetrating profound sadness was etched on her face and in her eyes. And there was something else. I was reminded of how Delilah looked when Trey and I forgot to include her in some activity she claimed she didn't want to do anyway. My momma seemed sad, hurt, longing, and even a little jealous all at once.

"Momma? Are you okay?"

She stirred herself, forcing her expression to move back into neutral.

"Of course," Momma said. "I'll be back in just a minute."

As she swept from the room, Trey and I studied the chest. I was sure we were both wondering how much it weighed. Fun time was over. Work time was about to begin.

I looked back over my shoulder again while Trey knelt beside the chest. I felt a dull ache. I'd just experienced one of those rare teasing moments when it almost felt like we were normal. Like she was just my momma. Not some holy warrior on a mission from God. Like I was just a preteen girl learning how to live my life. Not a "good little soldier for Jesus" serving time as an inmate in the family asylum. Those moments came and went so fast. Fleeting at best. Reality always came roaring back, and I would feel the mother-shaped hole in my heart all over again.

Trey was talking, but I wasn't hearing him. My thoughts were swirling. *Did she have any idea what it was like to play and relax? Truly relax. Could she begin to understand what it was like growing up with the shadow of Satan falling over everything? Did she know what her rules were doing to all of us?* I thought of that strange look she directed at me and Trey. *Does she know what it's like to have a best friend?*

CHAPTER FOUR

BANQUE GENÈVE
Reference # 12181991
Manuscript Held In Trust For Boxholder 763

An Excerpt from

DARK CONFESSIONS (1975)
By Lucille A. Broussard

This story begins and ends on a beach, on two beaches worlds away from one another. Those two beaches bookended two very different lives. Those lives are separated as far from one another in tenor and tone as those sandy beaches are in space. Each life is divided from the other by a violent separation point that took only seconds to unfold. May these dark confessions find you a gentle judge and a sympathetic reader. The secrets shared here are heavy to bear. If, someday, the author finds the courage to share it widely, may this book bring justice, hope, and healing mercies to all who read it.

Lucy Broussard sat on the first of our two beaches on a sunny Sunday morning in September 1974. Below her, the Pacific Ocean swelled into powerful waves that rolled over the white sands below like a blue carpet. Foamy suds bubbled around four bodies standing in the shallows of the water. Two young men with long hair stood on either side of a young woman. Another man, a few years older than the rest with a bushy black mustache and Beatles style short bowl cut, stood a few paces away facing the beach. All four participants were balancing waist-deep in the powerful surf.

Onlookers were gathered around the beach watching. Lucy counted about fifty of them. Men and women, mostly in their twenties or thirties, sat or stood on the beach watching with rapt attention. Any casual observer would say it was just another hippie music festival. Those casual observers would be wrong. All the hallmarks were there. The braids, long hair, floral wreaths, bare feet, and even a few guitars were represented in the crowd. But there were no drugs being passed. The only grass at the gathering was the odd patch here or there at the edge of the sand. Lucy was perched on one of these herself. She jotted careful notes about the setting, the people, and the ritual she was witnessing.

The man with the mustache faced the crowd. He raised his voice to be heard over the crashing surf. His words and bearing marked him clearly as the spiritual leader of the group.

"When Jocelyn came to this City of Angels two years ago, she was looking for truth."

The slender young woman standing in the surf nodded.

"This city tried to break her like it has so many before her. Our City of Angels so easily becomes the City of Satan for far too many. The devil and his minions attacked her and abused her in every way. She was so desperate for love and security, she even sold her body."

Lucy inhaled sharply. "Surely he asked her permission before he shared that," she murmured to herself.

Obviously, he had. Jocelyn was nodding vigorously in agreement. She wiped tears from her eyes.

"In her most desperate hour," the man said, "Jocelyn found a better way. Jocelyn found real truth and matchless grace. She found someone who gave his life for her sins. Jesus came to her, and she received him."

Jocelyn raised both her hands high and shouted something that Lucy assumed to be either "Hallelujah" or "Amen!"

"Today, Jocelyn confesses publicly her love for Jesus and the new life she has found in him." He waded further into the surf until he stood beside Jocelyn. The two young men steadying her stepped back. The pastor slipped one hand to Jocelyn's back to hold her while the other rose toward her mouth to cover her nose.

"I baptize you in the name of the Father, and of the Son, and of the Holy Spirit!"

With ease honed by constant practice, the pastor tipped Jocelyn backward and immersed her in the cold waters of the Pacific. He raised her a moment later. Jocelyn was thoroughly soaked and totally enraptured. She waved her hands joyfully. The crowd on the beach erupted in applause and shouts.

"Praise God!"

"Welcome, Jocelyn!"

"We love you, Jocelyn!"

Lucy watched with deep fascination. Something stirred within her. *What would it be like to belong like that? Was it real? Could it last? When the euphoria was gone, would the grace still be there?*

"Your mind is so full, Lucy B! You need to just enjoy life and not chew on everything so much!"

Lucy smiled at Etta's voice in her head. She missed her big sister. She missed her parents too, though she didn't really want to admit that to herself or them. Sweltering Picardy, Louisiana seemed so far from the temperate swells of Los Angeles. She raised her eyes to the horizon as the breeze tossed her wavy chestnut hair. The sun hovered over the ocean, casting sparkling beams of brilliant light into the shimmering waters below.

The meeting started breaking up a few minutes later. Lucy returned the greetings of several people she had come to know well over the last few months. She almost told them she was leaving, but she stopped herself each time. Lucy Broussard didn't enjoy goodbyes. The less fuss, the better. She stood, gathered her notebook, and brushed the sand from her legs and shorts.

"Well, how is the writing today?"

"Hello, Pastor Lindell," Lucy returned his warm smile. "It's going well. Thank you for letting me observe."

"Any time," he said. "We're glad to have you." He hesitated for a moment and then plunged forward. "You know we would be so happy to see you out there too."

She nodded, "I know."

"And?"

"I'm thinking about it."

"Fair enough," Pastor Lindell said. "You know I'm glad to talk more if you want."

"Thank you."

"How are things? Your situation at the university any better? Roommate situation improved?"

So he hadn't heard. Lucy breathed a sigh of relief. There were advantages to losing yourself in sprawling cities like L.A. and busy university campuses.

She shook her head. "No. It's been very frustrating. I'm thinking about a change. At least for a little while."

He saw it. In spite of her supreme effort to contain herself, the pastor knew something wasn't right. Lucy could tell he wanted to pierce the emotional veil she wore. Respecting her boundaries, he opted for a more indirect approach.

"What kind of change?" Pastor Lindell asked.

"Stop bombarding her with questions, Dear." The pastor's wife, a tall woman with long straight black hair, appeared holding some flyers.

"Jan thinks I'm too nosy," the pastor said. "I call it curious."

"It's okay," Lucy said. "I got a letter last week from my cousin, Alex. His mother runs a small boarding school on her estate in Brittany."

"Brittany in France?" Jan asked.

"Yes," Lucy said. "He said Madeleine, that's his mother, needs live-in teachers to help with their lessons and watch over them at night."

"I thought you wanted to be a writer, not a teacher," Pastor Lindell said.

Jan rolled her eyes playfully. "You're taking up career counseling now?"

Lucy smiled. She thought to herself how wonderful it must be to have someone like that. Someone who knew you inside and out, loving even your awkward silly parts. A partner you could trust with every piece of yourself.

"Just asking," he said with a smile. "Curious, remember?"

"I do," Lucy said. "But what better experience to prepare me than teaching? And seeing France! There's so much more inspiration there than in a classroom at UCLA. I'll come back and finish eventually. But I really can't turn it down, can I?"

"You're asking," Jan said. "But I think you already have your answer."

Lucy nodded. "I'm leaving next week. I wanted to stop by and see the baptism and . . ."

"What is it, Lucy?" the pastor asked.

Lucy won the struggle to keep her tone even and continued. "I wanted to thank you. It's been a hard year. You've all been so kind to me. Especially the two of you. I'm going to miss you."

Jan enveloped Lucy into a hug. Lucy willed herself not to flinch. It required supreme effort; she never engaged in physical contact lightly. It took her a while to feel comfortable enough with someone to be that vulnerable.

"Let us know if you need anything, Dear," Jan said when they separated.

The pastor placed his hand on her arm and squeezed lightly. He reached in his pocket and produced a tiny red Bible. Before Lucy could protest, he placed it in her hands and cupped them gently between his large paws.

"Take it," he urged. "It's not anything fancy. Just a New Testament the Gideons pass out at the schools. But maybe God will use it to encourage you when we can't be there for you. Psalms and Proverbs are at the back too. Lots of practical wisdom and encouragement there."

"Thank you," Lucy said.

She looked back once after she climbed behind the wheel of her orange Volkswagen Beetle to see the couple watching her. They waved when they saw her looking back. She waved back, then swallowed the lump in her throat and started the car.

One week later, Lucy clutched the armrest of her seat as the Pan Am

Boeing 747 dipped on its approach to Charles de Gaulle Airport.

"You look a little green in the gills, Dearie," the lady beside her said. She'd kept up incessant conversation for the first four hours of the flight until she'd blessedly fallen asleep.

"I'm not a very relaxed flyer," Lucy said. She gripped the seat tighter as turbulence bumped the plane slightly.

"So sorry. We'll be on the ground soon enough. Sooner if things don't go well." Her cackle confirmed Lucy's earlier suspicion that the lady shouldn't have had that last glass of champagne.

Lucy's heart leaped ten minutes later when she felt the reassuring bump of the plane's wheels on the asphalt. She peered through her window and watched other planes taxiing down neighboring runways as the 747 rolled toward the terminal.

I did it! I'm in France!

Lucy exhaled and clutched her armrests again, this time out of excitement rather than nervousness.

She gathered her bags from the massive carousel in the main terminal and made her way toward the outer drop off area to catch a cab, but all her romantic notions of what it would be like to finally use her French in the wild were instantly challenged. Attendants regarded her with bemused expressions as she stumbled and gestured her way through requests for directions. They took pity on her at last and described the right path in perfect English, but then she heard a familiar voice.

"Lucy!"

Relief flooded her heart. She turned to see a familiar young man with an unruly mop of curly blond hair elbowing his way through the crowd to reach her.

"Alex!" Lucy laughed and beckoned him forward.

"*Ma jolie cousine!*" Alexandre Broussard said when he reached her. "You may wriggle and twist like a rabbit, but I will still hug you!" He made good on his promise with a quick but firm hug. Lucy couldn't help laughing.

"You forget yourself, Sir," she said.

"I never forget you, sweet Lucy," Alexandre said. "I'm so happy to see you! I told *Maman* I could not wait on the train and that I would come to get you myself. How long has it been? *Un, deux ans?*"

"Yes, two years. Two years since I steered you through high school English."

"English is a truly stupid language," Alexandre said with a smile. "None of the refinement of French. I came to your country to study your culture and know my American family. And what do I get in return? I must endure English with your Miss Austen and Mr. Shakespeare."

"Our schools assume exchange students want to learn about English since they took the time and trouble to come to our superior schools," Lucy smiled as he took her bait, shaking his head in exasperation.

"I can forgive your Mr. Shakespeare. He knows how to swing a good sword, like the great Alexandre Dumas. A great French writer with the greatest of French names. But your Mr. Twain? Floating. Always floating. Down the river. Up the river. Are we there yet? No! We are still floating! Always floating!"

Alexandre swept his hands dramatically. Lucy almost lost her hold on her bag in the fit of laughter that shook her body. Seeing her bag slip slightly, Alexandre took it from her. "We will talk the merits of your American authors in the days and nights to come."

"Two of the three authors you assailed are British, by the way."

"You think that technicality will save you when you have Twain floating, always floating?" He shook his head, took her hand, and led the way through the bustling airport. A long black limousine waited for them outside, and a middle-aged driver with two tufts of graying hair poking from under his chauffer's cap waited to take Lucy's bags and stow them. He tilted his head in greeting before sliding behind the wheel of the car.

"Thank you, François," Alexandre said, opening the back door for Lucy and motioning for her to enter.

Lucy's face was glued to the side window as they rolled from the countryside to the bustling suburbs of Paris. Alexandre let her look, talking as they drove.

"I've reserved rooms for us tonight at Robert's favorite hotel. He is in the city attending to business. We can enjoy the city tonight. Tomorrow, we will meet Robert at the station and take the train to Brittany."

"How is Robert?" Lucy asked.

"Insufferable as always," Alexandre said. "He and Jean-Paul believe their little brother is a dreamer obsessed with fantasies. Artists do not qualify as inhabitants of the 'real world' for them. My siblings are all about business, money, influence."

"I'm sure it's not that bad," Lucy said.

"You will see for yourself," Alexandre said.

"Does Madeleine help with them?" Lucy asked.

"*Maman* is grateful I came back to help with the school," Alexandre said. "But she defers to *Papa* in most things. *Mon papa* believes Jean-Paul is the Victor Hugo of international finance and Robert master of the universe. I am tolerated."

"Families are hard," Lucy said with a sympathetic nod.

As the suburbs gave way to the city proper, Alexandre pointed out the sites. He watched Lucy's face with delight when the Eiffel Tower came into view for the first time. She leaned forward, her eyes bright with excitement.

"Paris can truly work miracles if she turns even you awestruck," Alexandre said. "I have never seen you so excited."

"I get excited," Lucy said. "My excitement is just . . . contained."

"Well, prepare to open your container, *ma chère*," Alexandre said. "I have quite the night prepared for us. We will stop off at the hotel, dine at my favorite restaurant, walk up the Champs-Elysées, and end the night at the cinema."

"Are we going to a French film?"

"No," Alexandre said. "It is that new American film that's driving all the priests and bishops mad. It is finally being released in France after nine months of waiting. *Papa* gave me his balcony pass for the showing they are having at the Gaumont Champs-Elysées tonight."

"*The Exorcist?*" Lucy asked.

"Yes! You have seen it?"

"No. I've been too busy to see anything lately."

"Then we must go!" Alexandre proclaimed. "It will be like the scary stories we told around the campfires in Picardy."

"I'm not sure any director, no matter how talented, can do it better than Etta."

"We will see," Alexandre said. "Mr. Friedkin is *très célèbre*."

"So is Etta," Lucy said. "Picardy *célèbre*."

They stopped by their hotel in the Montmartre district. Lucy's room was a luxurious suite with a walk-in closet and large bathroom. She studied the massive tub and promised herself a relaxing bath in the morning. She changed from her travel clothes into an emerald satin blouse and white bell-bottom slacks and ran a brush through her tangled chestnut hair, smoothing it as much as she could.

Lucy studied herself in the mirror. The young woman looking back at her appeared so young for someone who had seen so much. People said she was pretty. Her aunts and even a few classmates said she looked like Katherine Hepburn, but Lucy didn't see it. Boys never seemed seriously interested. She mentioned that to Etta once, and Etta exclaimed, "Because you scare them, Lucy! You're so serious! They think you're the prettiest girl in the room until you fix those killer green eyes on them. It's like you're measuring everyone in the room. They're too scared to talk to you." Lucy remembered thinking she didn't really care to spend time with boys so easily intimidated.

Lucy leaned closer to the mirror. The dark circles under her eyes marred an otherwise flawless complexion, but Alexandre would notice them. How much did she want to tell him? Her eyes flicked to a light blue soap dish sitting beside the sink. A shudder ran through her body. She leaned more of her weight against the counter. *So blue. Her lips were so blue.*

Alexandre noticed the circles an hour later while they were sitting across from one another at *Le Diderot*, Alexandre's favorite restaurant. Lucy was sipping a spoonful of soup when she noticed him gazing at her.

"What is it?" she asked.

"You have not been sleeping well." He said it as a statement, not a question. But it was a statement that demanded an answer.

"No. Not recently."

Lucy left it at that.

"We have some medicines at the chateau that can help with that," Alexandre said.

"That would be nice," Lucy said. "Thank you." She avoided looking directly into his eyes.

"I was surprised you agreed to come so easily," Alexandre said, testing the waters. "Especially only one month into your second year at the university."

"It's an opportunity to see France. And everyone needs a change once in a while."

"Lucy," Alexandre said. He reached for her hand and stared at her until she had no choice but to look into his eyes. "How is Tamera?"

Anger filled Lucy. She ripped her hand back across the table.

"Why do you have to bring her up? We're having a good night!"

Alexandre knew Lucy's fiery temper well. He'd weathered the storms before. He'd served as a living punching bag more than once as she pounded her fists on his chest in frustration. When the calm exterior broke, Lucy gushed forth like raging floodwaters.

"How is she, Lucy?"

Lucy slammed both fists on the table and bowed her head. Diners at neighboring tables stared, giving Lucy concerned indiscreet glances. She glared back at the nearest ones until they returned to their entrees. Alexandre waited. Five minutes passed. Lucy finally looked at him. Alexandre's mouth dropped open when he saw her lower lip trembling. Her eyes opened unnaturally wide to keep the tears at bay.

"Tamera is dead," Lucy said. No inflection. No emotion. Her voice was taught, tense, and level.

"*Merde*!" Alexandre exclaimed. "When? How?"

"I woke up three weeks ago and saw her lying in a strange position across her bed. She was half on with her head and arms dangling off the edge. I knew something was wrong before I checked."

"Lucy, *désolé*," Alexandre whispered. "I am so sorry. Was it drugs?"

Lucy nodded. "She was so blue, Alex. Her lips were so blue. Her skin. Her eyes were open so wide. They were always so blue."

Alexandre started to reach for her hand again. He stopped himself.

"She'd been out partying late," Lucy continued. "Nobody could even tell us how she got home or who got her the drugs. We were going to do it together, Alex. See the world. Write beautiful stories. How can someone destroy themselves piece by piece like that?"

"I do not know, Lucy," Alexandre said.

"How could she leave me like that?" Lucy whispered. "How could she leave everyone who loved her like that?"

"She was trying the rehab?" Alexandre asked.

Lucy nodded again.

"She did not want to go, Lucy," Alexandre said. "Not any more than all of you wanted her to go. There was a monster inside tearing at her, hurting her from within. When we were at the high school, Tamera was fighting even then."

"I was fighting even then," Lucy said, her anger flaring again. "I held her hand so many nights and pulled her hair back while she vomited all over the bathroom. Two separate trips to the hospital to have her stomach pumped. Still, she always went back! I tried so hard, Alex! So hard! I hid the drugs once. She pushed me down and called me vile names. Alex, she actually kicked me in my side! It was like the pressures of college life amplified all her problems. And Los Angeles provided more opportunities for them to consume her."

"Her demons would have found her no matter where she was," Alexandre said softly.

"It's my fault," Lucy said. "We should have stayed in Picardy."

"You don't mean that. She was not your responsibility."

"Then why do I feel responsible?" Lucy asked.

Alexandre slid his hand across the table. This time, Lucy allowed him to rest it lightly on hers for a few moments until their waiter appeared with succulent plates of *coq au vin blanc,* poached chicken in white wine sauce. Steaming seasoned potatoes and green beans complemented the tender chicken. Alexandre clapped his hands at Lucy's enraptured expression when she tasted her first bite.

"You see!" Alexandre said. "I told you!"

"It's excellent," Lucy agreed.

They ate in silence for a few minutes, enjoying the gentle ambience of the restaurant. A fire flickered in an ornate mantle to their right. Soft chords from a piano wafted from the next room.

"Alex?" Lucy asked.

"*Oui?*"

"What did you mean when you said that something was tearing Tamera up from the inside?"

"I guess I just meant that she was fighting with herself," he said carefully.

"Do you believe in demons?"

"You have been preparing for the movie, I see," Alexandre said with a forced laugh.

"I'm serious," Lucy insisted. "I met some people. Very kind people. They believe demons are real. They say demons are working to destroy all of us all the time. They say only Jesus can save us."

"Sounds like my catechism classes," Alexandre said. "But much more talk about the devil. We Catholics believe that St. Michael and the holy angels will defend us from the ways of the devil."

"Where were they when Tamera needed them?"

Alexandre gave her a helpless look. "I so much wish I had answers for you. I am not a deeply religious person, but I do believe in God. I believe there are things in this world we cannot explain. That is why we need God. As Voltaire said, we would need to invent God if he did not exist. Tamera, for me, is one of those many things I do not understand. I just have to believe that there is some reason for all of it."

"Because you trust God?" Lucy asked.

"Because I refuse to exist in a mindless universe," Alexandre said cryptically.

"What about evil?" Lucy said after the waiter cleared their plates and took their dessert orders.

"I highly discourage it at all times," Alexandre said with a smile.

"Do you think it's personal? Malevolent with intentional plans like Satan? Or is it more of a force? A tendency?"

"I think you would give the professors at the Sorbonne a hard debate," Alexandre said. "I do not remember you being this interested in such things."

"Like I said, I've been encountering some new ideas. And we've always attended Picardy First Baptist."

"Of course," Alexandre said. "I know you have always been religious. I just do not remember you being so . . . committed."

"Were you trying not to say 'fanatical' just now?" Lucy teased with a raised eyebrow.

"*Moi!* Never!" Alexandre insisted. Palpable relief flashed across his face. Her levity was returning.

"You ask about evil, whether it is personal or impersonal," Alexandre continued. "I believe it is most often banal like Hannah Arendt writes. You are familiar with her?"

"Yes," Lucy said. "She was the journalist and scholar who covered the Adolph Eichmann trials in the early sixties?"

"Correct. Hannah Arendt was convinced after hearing Eichmann's testimony and conducting interviews with other Nazi collaborators that human banality drove the evils of the Holocaust as much as intentional cruelty. People following orders, using the mandates given to them by others or imposed by their personal need to survive as a shield from personal human responsibility."

"So, you think people are responsible for evil?" Lucy asked. "That there is no devil?"

"I did not say that," Alexandre said with a sly grin, making the sign of the cross. "I believe whatever evil the devil may orchestrate, humans are foolish, vain, and imbecilic enough to do much of his job for him."

They were well into a rich chocolate cake smothered with vanilla ice cream by then.

"I suppose this is French vanilla by default," Lucy said, raising her fork in salute.

Alexandre returned her salute and raised his wine glass.

"To French vanilla, Swiss chocolate, and light dinner conversation."

Lucy laughed and clinked her glass with his.

Content, they stepped into the balmy Paris night. The lights of the beautiful Parisian shopping district produced a healing effect on Lucy. They strolled down the Champs-Elysées until they reached the Place de la Concorde. Lucy gazed at the Luxor Obelisk and the Tuileries Garden beyond. The gentle sounds of trickling water from the fountains tickled her ears.

"Can you imagine the horrors this place has seen? All those heads rolling off the guillotine day after day right here on this very spot."

"You are standing in front of one of the most beautiful gardens in the world and all you see are dead revolutionaries," Alexandre said, shaking his head. They strolled through the ornate greenery of the Tuileries down to the majestic open courtyard framing the entrance to the Louvre.

"It looks a little bare," Lucy observed.

"Bare," Alexandre sputtered. "One of the finest surviving royal palaces in France and you call it 'bare.'"

"The classical architecture is beautiful," Lucy continued. "They just need something to draw attention. It's too plain. You wouldn't even know it was a museum."

"I am sure the finest minds in France will get to work right away! It is a national emergency because Lucy Broussard finds our Louvre bare!"

She shook her head in exasperation. "Wait and see. Just wait and see."

They arrived at the Gaumont Champs-Elysées cinema in time for the late showing of *The Exorcist*, but the crowd stretched around the corner. Alexandre complained incessantly that they wouldn't make it at this rate. They finally settled into a packed auditorium decorated in ornate classical style. Red bunting and draperies framed the screen while gilded gold and brass finishings complemented the framing along the seats and balcony area.

Cheers filled the auditorium as the screen flickered to life. Eager patrons leaned forward in their seats, excited to finally see what all the fuss was about. Opening credits rolled, followed by images of a lone figure in the Iraqi desert.

Lucy sat transfixed for the next two hours. The crowd around her gasped in mingled horror and delight throughout the film. Lucy sat silent, captivated by the suffering of little Linda Blair as she transformed from a precocious child to a raging demon. *Consumed from within.* She felt the helplessness of Ellen Burstyn's Chris MacNeil, battling to save her daughter from certain destruction. *I tried so hard.* Hope surged through her as the two priests made the ultimate sacrifice to defeat the demon Pazuzu. *What is evil?* She heard her own voice in her head asking the question that haunted her nights now that they were no longer haunted by her fears for Tamera. *Is there good strong enough to pull us back from the abyss? To protect us from the darkness?* Lucy thought she had faced evil. Looked death in the face and watched it whittle away a beautiful person bit by bit, piece by piece. That night, it was a small mercy that Lucy had no idea the depths of the evil she would soon face. Or what she would have to lose to stop it.

CHAPTER FIVE

WE WATCHED ANGÉLIQUE SIP A STEAMING CUP of coffee. She lowered the cup and wiped her mouth.

"*Merci*," Angélique said. "I mean, thank you."

"*De rien*," Dorcas said with a smile. "You're very welcome, and you don't have to apologize. I'd like to think I could get by just fine in France with what I know, but I don't think I could do as well as you're doing right now."

Angélique returned her smile.

"Your English has improved quite a bit since we last saw you," I said.

"I've had a few years to practice," Angélique said. "I work as a travel agent now. I can understand and compose in English, Spanish, German, and even a little Chinese."

"Impressive," I said.

"We're very sorry about your momma," Denny said.

She nodded. "Thank you, Mr. Hebert."

"Denny."

"Thank you, Denny."

"I'm sorry I didn't recognize her," I said.

"Don't apologize," Angélique insisted. "It was a long time ago. It comforts me to know that someone she knew was with her at the end."

"It's more than just the years in between," I said. "We lost Dinah shortly after your visit. Everything that happened earlier that year gets overshadowed in my memory by the weeks right before her death."

"I'm so sorry," Angélique said earnestly. "Dinah was such a beautiful person. How could I expect you to remember instantly someone you knew for two weeks almost thirty years ago?"

As if on cue, the loose board on our porch squeaked again. A key turned in the door. Delilah stepped into the room looking like a frazzled parody of the polished partier who left a few hours earlier. Her wig was gone. Her green hair was tossed in all directions. I tried to remember if she'd left with a purse or not. If so, she'd returned without it. She studied us all with a smirk.

"You know, it occurs to me that I might have a slight drinking problem," Delilah said. Noticing Daddy sitting among us, she started to say something. Then she waved her hand dismissively and said, "Nothing you don't already know."

"Know what?" he said, winking at me and Dorcas.

Delilah stared at Angélique.

"Hey! You're the mute French girl. You were like a mime, except taller and less entertaining."

Dorcas was shaking with laughter at my frustrated expression.

"Diana was just telling us how hard it is to remember people," Dorcas said, wiping her eyes.

"You have to have the right blend, De-Blore-Er," Delilah slurred.

"Speaking of blend," I said, "looks like someone else needs coffee."

"I think I might take some too," Delilah announced, stepping past us to stumble into the kitchen.

"You remember . . ." I began.

"Oh, I remember," Angélique said.

"No one ever forgets," Dorcas said.

"I've heard her music," Angélique said.

"You have?" I asked.

Angélique sat silently for a moment. When she realized we were all waiting for her review, she whispered, "It's very loud."

Laughter filled the room. Delilah poked her head out of the kitchen and said, "Keep it down. My head hurts."

"Did they let you in to see your mother?" I asked.

Angélique placed her cup on our coffee table and nodded. "Yes. I identified her for them."

Her voice caught. Dorcas leaned forward to place a hand on her shoulder.

Angélique continued. "The nurse who rode with her to the hospital was there. She told me what happened and that you witnessed it. I am sorry it is so late. Or early. I had to see you."

"I got the impression that your mother was looking for me," I said. "She showed up at my conference and then across the street from where we had lunch. I think she was trying to work up the courage to speak to me. I'm not sure why she was afraid to approach me."

"She was afraid of many things," Angélique sighed. "Her hesitation was probably not about you, but about what she feared their enemies might do to you if they knew you were in contact with her. Your mother made it clear to her that any contact between them or their families could be perceived as threatening."

I suddenly remembered the shouts behind the office door after Aria and Angélique had arrived that day.

"Threatening to whom?" I asked.

"Someone at Chateau Broussard?" Angélique shrugged.

I exchanged a furtive glance with Dorcas and Dad.

"Did Aria still live near the chateau?" Dorcas asked.

"I convinced her to move to Paris with me a few years ago. Brittany is a beautiful region and the people are wonderful, but it is remote. It takes at least four to five hours by train and that is if everything is running on schedule. I felt she needed better medical care than she was getting there. And she couldn't stop obsessing about the past."

Delilah returned with a cup of coffee and a ham sandwich she'd thrown together from the remains of our dinner. She settled into an open chair, kicked off her heels, and rested her bare feet on the coffee table. I could see from her expression that Angélique considered Delilah's behavior a barbaric breach of etiquette.

"What about the past?" I asked. "What was her obsession? Who would be threatened by Aria and me having a simple conversation?"

"Your mother never told you about Chateau Broussard?" Angélique asked.

"I grew up knowing that it existed," I said. "Lucille would tell us stories about the grounds and some of the history, but she never said much about the time she spent there."

"I read a little about it when I was working on our genealogy a few years ago," Dorcas said. "Our great-grandmother's sister, Lillian, was interested in our family history and traveled to Brittany to see the ancestral home. She met and married Henri Broussard. They brought the family lines back together."

"We really are close cousins?" I asked. "It's not just a historic extended family connection?"

"That is correct, Dr. Chambers," Dorcas said, excited to be educating me for a change. "We're third cousins. The man that was killed in 1974, Jean-Paul Broussard, would have been Momma's second cousin. His mother who ran the school where Momma taught, Madeleine, would have been Grandpa Tom's first cousin."

"*La Reine des Glaces*," Angélique muttered. Her expression darkened.

I knew enough French to catch that one.

"The Ice Queen?" I repeated.

"Spend five minutes in a room with her and see if you do not say the same thing!" Angélique spat the words out.

"Lucille probably gave her a run for her money and then some," I said. "She could be pretty frosty herself."

"You can judge for yourself when you meet her," Angélique said.

"Hold on," I said. "Nobody said anything about meeting people. You still haven't said what all this is about."

"Did your mother never tell you the stories about the dark forces that haunt that chateau?"

Great! Here we go again. My head started aching at the prospect of another ghost chase or worse, a demon hunt. Dorcas was radiating the opposite emotion across from me. Family division straight down the middle over alleged demonic activity was the last thing we needed right now. We needed to heal without the rancor of the past tripping us up.

"We've already established that she didn't," I said. "Enlighten us."

"I only know what Maman told me. And that was not much. She said they barely escaped the grounds the night Jean-Paul died."

"They?" I said. "You mean Lucille and Aria?"

"And the students," Angélique said.

"Students?" Dorcas asked.

"Their pupils. They escaped with five students from the school."

Understanding dawned in my weary mind. I looked across at Dorcas and Dad. They were thinking the same thing. Even Delilah grasped the significance despite her hangover. Or maybe because of it. Spinach made Popeye stronger. Alcohol could make Delilah either a Neanderthal or Einstein depending on the day and dosage. Delilah whistled and shook her head.

"The list . . ." I began.

"Those are the kids from their school," Dorcas finished.

"And probably where they settled after they left France," Dad added.

"Yes," Angélique said. "Maman said Lucille had a list. When she heard about Lucille's death, she became obsessed with finding the people on the list and warning them. It was as if she thought Lucille's death triggered something or maybe removed some protection from them. She wanted to come here right after she heard Lucille died."

"Why didn't she?" Dorcas asked.

Angélique blushed. "She was ill for several months, and when she was well, I insisted that she not go. I was afraid."

"Why were you afraid?" I asked.

"Because of the stories she told," Angélique shivered visibly despite the warmth of our Louisiana summer. "And not just her. People in Belle Plage have whispered for years that the Broussards owe their wealth to a deal with the devil. They have spotted processions in robes and hoods walking from the estate to the cliffs above the ocean. They speak of the strange lights that lit up the sky the night Jean-Paul was shot. And how the school disappeared overnight. Shut down."

"We know where five of those students went," I observed.

"But what of the rest? Where did they go?"

I wished I had an answer for her.

"Diana, you know my maman practiced Wicca?" Angélique asked.

I nodded. I'd forgotten I heard that term for the first time when Aria used it in our living room.

"She was not one to feed cult hysteria," Angélique insisted. "It was as dangerous to her religion as it was to anyone's."

"But she did in this case?" I asked.

"Maman believed, and she said your mother did as well, that the Broussards were allowing evil people to hold ceremonies on the estate and to train the children to believe and do terrible things. Violent things! Inhuman things!"

Dorcas and Dad were sold.

"She always had a keen eye for those things," Dad said.

"Because she saw them everywhere!" I moaned. "Angélique, I didn't know your mother well. I did know mine. Have you ever read any of her books?"

"No," Angélique said.

"Let's just say she tends to be an unreliable narrator," I said.

"True story!" Delilah said with her mouth full of sandwich.

I tried to ignore the hurt in Dad's eyes. We'd all done so well since Lucille's death had united us in grief. Dredging up the past was also exposing our family scars. Those scars remained tender, ready to split open again at the slightest scrape.

"Please don't call Momma an 'unreliable narrator,'" Dorcas said. She was trying to stay calm, but I could hear the storm clouds on the edge of her voice.

"You'd rather Diana just called her a compulsive liar?" Delilah asked.

Always depend on Delilah to throw kerosene on the embers.

"I'd rather both of you show some respect for our momma!" Dorcas said. "She was not a liar just because you didn't agree with her beliefs."

"Her spiritual beliefs were not what made her unreliable," I said, trying to sweep in and repair what I'd started. "Her tendency to shape facts and events to fit those beliefs was the problem. She sensationalized so much in her books to promote the ministry and the movies. We're not attacking her, Dor. It's just a fact we need to remember while sorting through all this."

"It sure sounds like you're attacking her," Dorcas said, tears of anger starting to appear in her wide brown eyes. She looked at me pointedly and said, "She's not here to defend herself and maybe you should remind yourself why exactly that is!"

Ouch! Dorcas was formidable when her metaphorical guns were locked and loaded. Her physical ones too. I didn't believe Dad's story about Dorcas firing at our intruders for a second because I know him too well, but the idea that she could have fired those shots was not farfetched at all. If she had fired them, we probably would be dragging their bodies out from behind the barn.

"Don't do that to Diana!" Delilah shouted. She was sobering up fast and forgetting her headache.

"Do what?" Dorcas asked.

"Lay a guilt trip on her like she's responsible for Mom's death. Mom chose to do what she chose to do, and she would have done it for any one of us."

"I'm sorry," Dorcas said more to me than Delilah. "But you can't just say these things about Momma! She's gone."

"That doesn't make the things she wrote in her books any truer than they were before, Sweetie," I said, pleading with her by my tone to understand.

"Hell, we all said these things and worse to her face when she was alive," Delilah said.

"Not all of us," Dorcas said accusingly.

"Maybe if you had, she would have cut the crap and written something entertaining instead of demon porn!" Delilah shouted.

"Please, just stop!" Daddy said. His words came out more as an anguished groan than a shout. Tears were creeping down his rough cheeks and moistening his beard. Dorcas hugged him fiercely. She glared at Delilah, who shook her head at Dorcas in disgust.

I'd almost forgotten about Angélique. She sat staring white-faced at our display of Hebert dysfunction.

"I'm sorry," I said to her. Thinking of one of Brandy's favorite phrases, I continued. "We can be a lot sometimes."

"I am sorry I caused a problem," Angélique said. I could see tiny shades of her old timidity in her apology. The shy girl we met in 1995 still lingered below this confident exterior.

Daddy detached himself from Dorcas and spread his hands toward Delilah and me.

"I love you so much, Angels," he said. "And your momma did too. She had a hard time showing it for reasons none of us may ever understand, but I know she did. Whatever she left behind for us to finish, I believe she had good reasons for leaving it with us. We're not going to agree on everything. Or maybe anything. But we have to do this together."

"Do we?" Delilah said. "I honestly don't feel an obligation to settle some old business Mom started with her friend and five strangers when bell-bottoms were cool."

She looked to me for support. I disappointed her.

"I think we do have to finish it or at least figure out what finishing it means."

"Why?!" Delilah asked, genuinely surprised.

"Delilah, Aria was mowed down right in front of me," I said, seeing images again of her bloody body and hearing the impact when the car struck her.

"So?"

"Whoever did that wasn't just getting revenge," I said. "They were trying to stop her from talking to me. Whatever she wanted to discuss about the past scared someone enough to kill her. They could have run over Trey and me too."

"They wanted that chest enough to break into our house and Diana's apartment," Dorcas added. "That must be linked to Aria's death, which means it's personal whether we like it or not."

Delilah nodded. She didn't want to see it, but she did. She sighed, "So ghost, demon, or drag racing dumbass, we're going to find this person. I guess that's what we do now."

"Wherever it leads," I said, looking at Dorcas. A sad smile dispelled the tension on her face. We'd repeated that phrase to each other several times last fall, pledging to probe the twin mysteries of Dinah's and Mia Jordan's deaths to the bitter end.

"Wherever it leads," Dorcas said. "I love you both. I'm sorry."

"I'm sorry too," I said, grateful to feel the gap between us shrinking.

"If you have to be sappy about it, then me too," Delilah said.

"I guess we'll settle for that," Dorcas said, winking at me.

"Best you're gonna get," Delilah said. Her smile took the sting out of her gruff words. She turned to Angélique and said, "So, our moms were educating the Children of the Damned?"

"What?" Angélique asked.

"It's a movie," Delilah said. "I know you get movies in France."

"I have heard of it," Angélique said. "Sorry. I am just trying to keep up."

"It's not easy on the best of days," I said. "Do you believe the stories, Angélique?"

"I do not know," Angélique said. "I am not . . . How do you say it? A person who is afraid of unseen things?"

"Superstitious?" I prodded.

"Yes! I am not that. But Maman was obsessed and afraid. People seemed to be watching our apartment in Paris. Maman took two trips to Brittany when I was away on business. Both times she was removed by security from Chateau Broussard. I had to go up and bring her home to Paris. The second time, Madeleine called me up to the chateau before I left. She threatened to have Maman arrested and held if she trespassed again."

"Sounds more like she was harassing them than they were harassing her," Delilah said.

"They have opened a new school at the chateau this year to commemorate the fiftieth anniversary of the original school's opening,"

Angélique said. "Maman wanted to see if the school was legitimate. One of the teachers, my childhood friend's daughter, smuggled her onto the grounds. She visited two or three classes before one of the servants noticed she was not a teacher or staff member."

"Can you imagine the recruitment pitch?" Delilah said. "Come study at the latest version of the incredible disappearing school."

"People still go camping at Camp Crystal Lake for some reason," I said.

"And will as long as the tickets are sold," Delilah said.

"Is this camp a local establishment?" Angélique asked.

The laughter felt good and helped to clear the air.

"It's from a horror movie franchise," I explained.

"Based on what our mothers said, Chateau Broussard could be too," Angélique reminded us.

We sat quietly for a while, pondering our mothers' mysterious legacy. What was it? What claims did it have on us? What responsibilities, if any, did we owe to our mothers and these strangers on the list?

"So, what are we supposed to do?" I finally asked, breaking the silence. "Both Aria and Lucille talked about protecting someone. Were they talking about their former students? Us? Someone at Chateau Broussard? Does it have something to do with the murder of Jean-Paul Broussard? Did Lucille save that newspaper clipping because she wanted us to find out who killed him?"

While contemplating those questions, I replayed the day I'd first met Angélique and Aria.

"I remember that Lucille and Aria spent hours huddled in the office talking on the phone after we brought that chest home," I said. "They had to be contacting the people on the list. Maybe Lucille had the contact information hidden somewhere else or had memorized it."

"Finding and contacting them is a good first step," Dorcas said. "It's something we can do from here. I'm not opposed to going to France if we need to, but it would be nice to be sure that's necessary before we rush to buy tickets."

The others nodded.

"Sounds like a smart plan, Angels," Dad said.

"Can you find these people?" Angélique asked.

"Normally, I would have an energetic team of graduate students to help me with that kind of task," I said.

"These students are not available now?" Angélique asked.

"Not reliably. They scatter during the summer to do research, visit family, and write their dissertations."

"Then we must do it ourselves," Angélique said.

"Actually, I have access to the next best thing," I said. Delilah and Dorcas grinned, guessing my thoughts exactly.

"You have graduate students here?" Angélique said.

"You ever read the Sherlock Holmes stories?"

"Of course," Angélique replied.

"You remember how Holmes used the Baker Street Irregulars to follow people and investigate clues?"

"Yes!" Angélique said with a smile. "He sent out the dirty little street urchins."

I laughed and said, "I have some little urchins of my own equipped for the digital age."

"They deploy well as long as they're between pedicures and crushes," Delilah said.

I pulled out my phone and pressed the appropriate contact. My Facetime app made a bubbling sound and then issued a sharp whooshing chord. The window opened to reveal a green face looking back at me.

"Did you Hulk out again, Brans?" I teased. "I didn't think you were that mad at your mom."

"Just for that, you're not going to get one of these when you show up tonight," Brandy said. "Your pores will dry out, your skin will sag, and everyone will call you Dr. Gator Face."

"How do you know they don't already? Did you talk Amira into doing a facial too?"

"Yes," Amira's voice called. "It's actually pretty nice."

"But that's not the best part," Brandy said, her voice brimming with excitement and mischief. "Check this out!"

She swiveled her camera. I heard a groan. Then I saw Trey sitting across the room in his favorite chair. I tried to suppress my laughter but completely failed.

"Brans, you promised!" Trey said. "No videos and no pictures!"

"Facetime generally streams rather than captures video, Mr. Laurence. Brandy is keeping her promise."

"Not helping, Amira," Trey said.

"What did they do to you?" I asked between peals of laughter. I felt my sisters gathering around me. They dissolved into laughter too. I could see Trey's eyes roll even through the small eye holes of his green facial mask.

"Looking good, Sweetheart," Delilah said, mimicking Trey's Bogart impression.

"You're so pretty, Trey," Dorcas giggled.

"Should I show Daddy?" I asked.

"It's okay, Trey," Dad called. "You've seen the crazy stuff these girls have dragged me into over the years."

"Yeah, but we never got to give you a facial," Delilah said.

"I have a face preserver," Dad said. "It's called a beard."

"You're the best girl dad under fifty in the world," I said, blowing Trey a virtual kiss.

"He will be if and when he lets us give him a pedicure," Brandy said.

"I would say don't hold your breath, but you always seem to find a way where there is no way," Trey said.

"Brans, can I ask you two for a favor once you're done torturing your dad?"

"Sure, Diana. What do you need?"

"I'm texting you an image of a list we found in Lucille's box. It's a list of names, cities, and states. We think these people may be Lucille's former students from her time teaching in France. That would make them at least ten to fifteen years older than me. They would be in their late fifties now. Maybe even early to mid-sixties."

"You think they're still alive?" Brandy asked.

"Brans, how old do you think sixty is?!" I asked.

"Older than I want to be," Brandy said. "We'll see what we can find. What do you want to know?"

"Their current place of residence, employment, family, and any publicly available contact information."

"Sounds good," Brandy said, typing a note on her phone. "What's in it for us?"

"My everlasting gratitude."

"That sounds amazing," Brandy said. "But it might sound better with popcorn and a movie."

"Or a snowball," Amira said.

"You're two teenage extortionists," I said. "We can do the movie, and I might see fit to stop at a snowball stand afterward if I like what I get."

"Awesome!" Brandy said. "We'll call you back when we find stuff."

"Thanks, Brans. Tell your dad I'll come rescue him in a few hours."

"A lot can happen in a few hours," Trey called.

Brandy raised her eyebrows and grinned as far as her mask would allow before ending the call.

Angélique eyed my phone with skepticism. "You think those children can handle the search?"

"I do," I said. "If they don't come up with something soon, we can look around ourselves."

My gaze shifted to the ornate chest that still sat in the center of our living room.

"I agree," Dorcas said.

"You agree with what?" I asked. I tried to sound mysterious, but I was secretly pleased that Dorcas knew me so well.

"We need to move the chest," Dorcas continued. "It's too important to leave unprotected."

"We could leave it with Jim Gorman at the police station," Denny said.

"I don't mean to offend . . ." Delilah began.

"When have you ever not meant to offend?" I asked, smiling.

"Yeah, doesn't sound like me," Delilah said, returning my smile. "I saw the Picardy Police Department in action last fall. They didn't impress me."

"Well, where else can we hide it?" Denny asked.

"I think I may have an answer for that one too," I said.

"Well, aren't you just the woman with all the answers?" Delilah teased.

"I'll take a winning streak any day I can get it," I said. "They're too few and far between to turn down."

I pressed another contact on my phone. Aubrey Morris picked up after two rings.

"Diana?" Aubrey sounded surprised and very pleased.

"Yes, it's me. Thank you for taking my call on a Saturday morning."

"Not at all," Aubrey said. "In fact, you were reading my mind. I was planning to call you on Monday. I want to grab some time to talk with you before you go back to Nashville."

"What about?"

"I'd rather discuss it in person."

"Sure," I said, slightly puzzled. I'd just seen Aubrey two nights before when our old graduate school friends met at a Bourbon Street karaoke bar for an impromptu reunion on the last night of the conference. I'd been a little nervous because it was the first time Trey got to meet them. There was no need. Trey charmed everyone as always, keeping the table entertained with his tales of misadventures in the high school classroom. Aubrey sat close to us all night. We'd had several opportunities to catch up. I wondered what was so important she hadn't wanted to discuss it with the group present.

"I have a favor to ask," I continued.

"Anything," Aubrey said without hesitation.

"I need to find a safe place for an artifact," I said. "It's an ornate chest, probably French in origin. Possibly as old as the sixteenth or seventeenth century."

"Sounds fascinating."

"Do you have anywhere at Tulane we could store it? The place needs to be secure." Aubrey had taught philosophy at Tulane University in New Orleans for twelve years before "turning to the dark side" as she put it and accepting an administrative role there as an academic dean.

"Absolutely," Aubrey said. "We have the Latin American Studies Center and the Special Collections. Both are secure. There's always someone at the Special Collections when they're open and tight security when they're closed. I know the archivists well. They're both highly competent and trustworthy. Let me give them a call. When will you be bringing it?"

"Monday?" I said, sweeping the room with a glance to make sure the others were on board.

"Sounds good," Aubrey said. "Do you have time to grab lunch when you drop it off?

"Sure." My curiosity peaked again.

"Excellent! I'll make the arrangements and look forward to seeing you Monday."

I thanked her and wished her well. When I ended the call, Dorcas said, "That's so smart, Diana! Hiding it among all those other artifacts."

"It'll fit in much better at Tulane than in our collection of voodoo dolls and tarot cards," I said.

"The collection seems hollow since you two sent poor Christine to her grave," Delilah said with mock solemnity.

"She is not missed," I said.

Angélique rose.

"I must go now," she said.

"You're welcome to stay with us," Dad said.

"Thank you, but no. I need to make arrangements for Maman."

"Will you fly her back to France?" Dorcas asked.

"No. She has said for years she wished to be cremated. I will have that done here and take her ashes back to scatter along the coast at Belle Plage."

"We're very sorry for your loss," I said.

"And I for yours," Angélique said, placing her hand on my arm. "If we must grieve, at least it is a small mercy that we can grieve together. I will be waiting to hear back from you. When you arrive in France, I will be happy to be your guide in Belle Plage."

"If we arrive in France," I said.

"Of course," Angélique said.

We stood on the porch watching her drive away in her red Nissan Sentra rental.

"She's a blast from the past," Delilah said. "Remember that thunderstorm from hell when she was here?"

I shivered. The rumble of thunder and crack of snapping tree limbs resounded in my mind. The driving rain battered my face again. I heard Dinah calling to us.

"Who's that?" Delilah's question roused me from my memories.

A black Mercedes-Benz passed our driveway and continued down the road in the same direction Angélique had driven just a moment ago.

"Nobody raised in Picardy," Denny said. "Nobody drives a car like that on these roads."

"Definitely a fish out of water," Dorcas agreed.

An uneasy feeling descended on us.

I reached for my keys. Daddy shook his head and reached in his pocket. He produced his key ring and tossed it to Dorcas.

"You're gonna need something heavier than a Corolla," he said.

"And a driver who still knows the back roads," Dorcas said. She was already hurrying to Daddy's old brown Ford F150. I followed, and I sensed Delilah behind me.

"I'll call Jim at the police station!" Dad called after us. "Wait on him before you catch up with them, Angels."

Dorcas threw the truck into gear. The transmission groaned with a screeching sound that unsettled me. We rolled down the driveway and flew down the road well past the speed limit. Delilah and I exchanged a glance. Dorcas ignored us, focusing intently on the road ahead. We finally saw the Mercedes-Benz ahead of us. Angélique's red car was visible just ahead of the Mercedes. The driver was tailgating her. Getting closer every second.

"That bastard is going to ram her!" Delilah said.

"Sorry, Daddy," Dorcas whispered.

"Sorry for what?!" Delilah and I said in alarmed unison.

Dorcas hit the gas and the truck lurched forward, the powerful V-8 engine issuing a deafening roar. The driver of the Mercedes was so focused on Angélique that they didn't realize we were coming until it was too late.

Our truck rammed into the back of the Mercedes. Delilah and I were tossed around the cab like rag dolls while Dorcas clutched the steering wheel to maintain control. The Mercedes veered wildly back and forth before careening off the road into the ditch. Angélique was watching in horror through her rearview mirror. She drove a little further before pulling over to the shoulder when she recognized us. Dorcas drove up to Angélique and slammed on her brakes. Delilah and I reached out to stop ourselves from hitting the dashboard.

"You know this thing hasn't had working passenger seatbelts since 2003," I reminded my little sister.

"Sorry," Dorcas said.

Delilah rolled down her window. Angélique was looking out at us from her own window. All the blood had drained from her face.

"*Mon Dieu*! Who was that?"

"We don't know," Delilah said. "We're about to find out. Keep going. Call us when you get to New Orleans so we know you got there okay."

Angélique nodded. She raised her window, took a deep breath, and drove quickly. As she continued down the road, we looked back just in time to see the Mercedes spin out of the ditch back onto the road. Their trunk was dented, and the back bumper was separated from the body on the left side. Aside from that, our attack failed to damage their operational capacity. They were going the opposite direction this time. Back toward our place. Dorcas threw the truck into gear and executed a perfect U-turn in the middle of Breyers Creek Road.

"These are not the country boys who tried to rob our house," Dorcas said as she sped after the Mercedes.

"It may be the person who ran over Aria," I said grimly. The common fetish for classy European cars seemed too rare to be coincidental.

The Mercedes passed our house and roared toward the McMartin property just beyond it. Delilah was updating Dad on the phone as we passed.

The Mercedes executed a screeching turn at Bellinger Road. Dorcas passed Bellinger and kept going.

"He went down Bellinger," I said.

"Trust me," Dorcas said. She turned right on Murphy's Cross. We bounced over two cattle gaps at top speed. I felt my teeth rattling along with the truck. Dorcas plowed down the dirt road, gravel and dust flying left and right. We swung out onto Peterson Road just ahead of the Mercedes. The driver braked and swerved. Their tires squealed. I thought for sure they were going to hit us. Instead, the Mercedes came to rest about a foot from us. I strained to see the driver, but all I could see was a long black sleeve and a massive white hand gripping the wheel.

The Mercedes peeled out and retraced its path back in the direction it had come. It disappeared around a bend in the road. Our truck stalled when Dorcas tried to follow. She stopped and cranked it again. The engine sputtered and finally roared to life.

"I hope that delay didn't cost us too much," I said.

We rounded the bend to see the Mercedes sitting on the side of the road. The driver's door was standing open. A large figure dressed in a black suit was running into the nearby woods. He held a phone to his ear as he ran. I couldn't make out any physical details beyond the fact that he was bald and one of the most massive men I'd ever seen. Most of his bulk appeared to be muscle from what I could tell. Not someone you wanted to meet alone in a dark alley. He reached the edge of the woods and disappeared.

The reasons for the driver's evacuation were speeding toward us with their blue and red lights flashing. Jim Gorman's and Reggie Colson's squad cars pulled alongside the Mercedes.

Dorcas parked the truck on the shoulder. Delilah and I staggered out the passenger's side.

"That was pretty wild," I said.

Delilah brushed past me, hurried to the side of the road, and spilled the contents of her stomach all over the shoulder. I rushed over to pull back the edge of her green hair.

"She okay?" Dorcas asked in alarm.

"Are you?" I asked her.

Delilah nodded and wiped her mouth with a tissue that Dorcas produced from the truck. She stood straight and took a breath.

Dorcas was reassured enough to have fun at Delilah's expense.

"Looks like somebody's a car chase lightweight," Dorcas said, winking at me.

"It's just the booze, Speed Racer," Delilah grumbled. "Don't get carried away."

We hurried to the Mercedes. Officer Reggie was already inside the car, fishing in the glove compartment for its registration.

"He took off into the woods," Jim Gorman said.

"Did you see him?" I asked.

"Yeah. We had the road blocked up ahead. He stopped and jumped out when he saw us. White guy. Big, ugly, and bald. Dressed really nice though. You can see the broken brush where he went in the woods."

"Car's a rental," Reggie called from inside the Mercedes. "Probably from the airport."

"You think this guy had something to do with the break-in at your place?" Gorman asked.

"Maybe," I said.

"We'll search the car and woods. I radioed Ben to try to intercept him on the other side. If he's on foot, we have a good chance of catching him. But I'm guessing he's got somebody else to pick him up on the other side."

"What makes you say that?" Delilah asked.

"If I was drivin' a Mercedes, I could afford somebody to pick me up on the other side. And he was talking pretty hard on his phone while he was running."

"Can't argue with that," Delilah said.

My phone buzzed. I almost ignored it, but I changed my mind when I recognized the "Livin' on a Prayer" ringtone I'd assigned Brandy after our Bon Jovi conversation.

"Hey, Brans. Can I call you back? I'm in the middle of something."

"Hold on," Brandy said. "I need to tell you about the people we're looking up for you."

"Did you find them?" I asked.

"We confirmed that there are people with those names in all the cities on the list. There's more than one person with that name in some cases."

"We'll whittle them down to the right ones tonight," I said.

"Diana, two of them may be dead," Brandy said, "if the people in the articles we found are the ones from the list."

I swallowed and nodded.

"We had to expect some of them might have died over the years. It has been a long time."

"No, Diana," Brandy said, her voice as serious as it ever got. "They died this week. One was shot and the other drowned."

CHAPTER SIX

LUCILLE ONCE SAID THE HEBERT HOUSE CEASED to be a quiet place the day she first walked into the living room with baby Dinah nestled in her arms. The chaos only got wilder as more baby girls crossed that threshold, but Monday morning surpassed even Hebert levels of chaos at the old homestead.

Dorcas rolled two small suitcases into the living room. She steered around Ramona Dykstra's feet. Ramona was reclining on our couch playing a game on her phone, her purple mohawk waving along with her head.

"Sorry, Ramona," Dorcas said.

The muscular woman looked up and grunted before returning to her game. Rico Sanchez looked over at his colleague, looked up at Dorcas, and said, "Excuse her. She don't have the social skills."

Ramona looked up long enough to give him the finger and returned to her game.

"Not what she pays me for," Ramona muttered.

"That's okay," Dorcas said. She gave Ramona a wider berth. Dorcas rolled her bags beside mine and leaned over to whisper, "Those people are scary."

"That's the point," I said. "Their boss is scarier."

"No doubt," Dorcas laughed.

Their boss entered the room just in time to hear Ramona's comment. Delilah playfully slapped Ramona's shoulder.

"Hey! You got me killed, Delilah!"

"It's about time you do what I pay you for," Delilah said. She leaned closer. "Are you playing freaking Angry Birds! I should give you the bird! How old are you?"

"It's a classic," Ramona said defensively.

"You people need some action," Delilah said. "You're getting too soft sitting in hotel rooms watching movies and playing Xbox all day."

"Maybe you shouldn't leave us in hotels and sneak away to party with normies," Rico said.

"I need you when I need you," Delilah said. "Right now, I need you."

Rico shrugged and popped his fifth Oreo that morning into his mouth. Oreos were considered a breakfast staple in Rico's world. Despite his addiction to cookies, Rico stayed in peak physical condition, evident through his tight t-shirt, black leather vest, and jeans despite the searing Louisiana heat. Ramona projected vintage punk from head to toe wearing a fishnet top with black halter top underneath and dark leather pants. Delilah assured me I didn't want to see their rap sheets. Whatever past misadventures they'd gotten into, they spent their days now as part of Delilah's security detail. Delilah usually left them in New Orleans when she came home, but after the weekend's adventures, we'd decided having them here with us would be a good idea. I wished she'd brought them when she returned to Picardy last fall. I entertained wicked thoughts about how many painful ways Rico could have pummeled Eric Dixon, although Trey had gotten some pretty good licks in at the end himself.

"Are you and Daddy ready?" I asked Dorcas.

"Almost. He's out checking the barn one last time."

We'd spent Saturday night and most of the day Sunday desperately trying to contact Lucille's former students. I left a couple of voice messages for Jacob Le Roux, François Muir, and Sarah Abrams. No response from any of them. Either they were afraid to respond or just ignored me because they didn't recognize the name. I regretted our decision to retire and recycle Lucille's phone; calling or texting from her number might have encouraged them to answer.

I spent Sunday afternoon and evening waiting for responses and staring at the two articles that Brandy and Amira found. RIVERSIDE WOMAN FOUND SHOT IN APPARENT BURGLARY ATTEMPT. My eyes traveled to the text that described how Estelle Martin, aged sixty-two, was found dead in her apartment last weekend. Police were investigating it as a robbery because the house had been ransacked. The second headline screamed DROWNING VICTIM FOUND AT RESIDENCE MONDAY. Greta Rosenberg's son and granddaughter discovered her lifeless body floating in the pond behind her house. Rosenberg was sixty-three and in perfect health according to her family. Her daughter told reporters she had always been a strong swimmer. Police were waiting for the autopsy report to make a final ruling on her cause of death despite the premature diagnosis of the media.

That left three students. Any or all of them could also be in danger. Jacob Le Roux lived in Houston, François Muir in Boston, and Sarah Abrams in Omaha. Sunday evening, we agreed that we had to go to them if they wouldn't answer us. I hurried over to Trey's house, Delilah roused her security detail, and Dorcas started looking for plane tickets online.

I tried to give Trey a pass if he wanted it, but he insisted he was going.

"I'm out of school and you need me," Trey said. "I'll call Erin to come get the kids. She'll understand."

Erin understood just fine. She was glad that we were leaving the kids out of it. Brandy, on the other hand, wasn't quite so Zen about being left behind. She'd already expressed her feelings to Trey and made sure I was aware too when I arrived.

"You may end up in Paris and you're not taking me!" Brandy said. She glanced at Chip's disappointed face and added, "Taking us."

"Sweetie, it could be . . ."

"Dangerous?" Brandy said. "Who found the articles, Diana?"

"Please, Brans. Not now. Someday."

"I will make it to Paris, Dr. Diana Chambers," Brandy huffed. "And even though you're leaving your best asset behind, I will still answer your call when you inevitably need my help because I'm chill that way."

I pulled her into a tight hug and said, "And because you love me?"

"Maybe because I love you," Brandy said.

I hugged Chip too.

"Sorry we're having to bail early, Buddy."

"It's okay, Diana," Chip said. "Mom said I could bring my shortwave to Covington. I'll be on every day if you want to talk."

"Thanks, Nighthawk," I said, ruffling his hair. "I may take you up on it when I get homesick."

All the arrangements were made by Monday morning. Trey arrived around nine, and our strange little convoy of three cars pulled out of the Hebert driveway. Delilah drove my Corolla with her security detail. They planned to board a flight for Omaha to find Sarah Abrams. Dad and Dorcas were flying to Houston. They were driving Dorcas' car because Dad's truck was sorely in need of a new grill and some bodywork post chase. They would find Jacob Le Roux in Houston. Trey and I were booked on a flight from Louis Armstrong to Boston's Logan airport. We hoped to find François Muir alive and well. We were in Trey's car sandwiched for safety between the others because the mysterious chest was in Trey's trunk. We made it to New Orleans and crossed the Lake Pontchartrain bridge with no problems. If anyone was watching, our numbers discouraged them from trying anything.

Once we were in New Orleans, Dorcas and Dad peeled away with waves to catch their earlier flight at Louis Armstrong. We continued deeper into New Orleans, twisting around the magnificent silver Superdome and exiting downtown. Trey drove us through a small business district and picturesque old homes. The residential area gave way to academic buildings without much warning. Our smaller caravan entered the area where the two main campuses of Tulane University and Loyola University nestled against one another. Following Aubrey's directions, we arrived at the twin library buildings near the central quad.

Rico and Ramona picked up the chest like a toy. They carried it up to the richly furnished Special Collections room on the second floor. A blonde graduate student named Linda introduced herself to us and ushered us into the back where all the valuable pieces were housed. Researchers glanced up from their solitary desks piled with folders and documents. A couple eyed the chest with awe, but no one slowed us down as we traveled into the heart of the archive. An archivist named Prentiss was waiting for us in the artifacts room. We chatted for a few minutes, he took down my information, and Delilah's security detail eased the chest into the spot on a lower shelf Prentiss had prepared for it. I breathed a sigh of relief when the door to their secure artifacts room slammed shut with the chest safely inside.

Leaving the others to get lunch on their own, I hurried to the Malkin Sachs Commons building to make my lunch meeting with Aubrey. She was sitting at a table waiting when I arrived. Her ebony skin seemed to defy time. She still looked so much like the introspective young brainiac I met at Princeton all those years ago. She'd traded her frizzy longer hairstyle for a tightly coiled short Afro that complemented her oval face, high cheekbones, and smooth jawline. Aubrey wore a white skirt with a black blazer over her light blue blouse. I felt underdressed in my travel jeans and t-shirt. She shouted my name and rushed to wrap me into a warm hug. The smell of her perfume, which also hadn't changed, reminded me of nostalgic nights studying, stress eating, watching movies, and sharing life in our Princeton apartment.

Aubrey guided me through a buffet with an impressive array of choices. Once we'd fixed our plates, we returned to the table Aubrey had selected. It offered a beautiful view of the green quad beyond through the picturesque glass wall. I savored the sights and sounds, glad to be on a university campus again. The cafeteria food tasted better than average. The succulent roasted chicken, mashed potatoes, and mixed vegetables surpassed our Hebert homestead sandwiches easily. We talked for a few minutes about my experiences since we'd seen each other last week and the mysterious mission I was about to undertake.

"You should literally take a page from your mother's book and write these stories down," Aubrey said. "They'd make a better movie than anything Lucille wrote."

"That's what Salena Malone, the actress who plays Dinah in the

'Demonologists' films, keeps telling me," I said. "I'm still not comfortable with the way they spin things. Though I have to say, the money Dad and Dorcas have squirreled away from the films came in handy when we had to plan these quick trips."

"When's the next one coming out?"

"I haven't heard yet," I said. "They're still deciding what direction to take the film series next. I'm just glad they stopped production on the *Devil's Circle* adaptation. It would have been a nightmare to see Dinah's death reenacted."

Aubrey took a bite of salad and shifted the conversation to a much better topic.

"I enjoyed meeting Trey last week," Aubrey said. "You've built him up as a bit of a legend over the years. It was fun to finally meet him."

"Does he live up to the legend?" I asked.

"Absolutely!" Aubrey said. "I love him! He's hilarious. Smart. And kind. You can see that instantly."

"I think I'll keep him around," I said.

"I'm counting on it," Aubrey said with the slightest hint of a smile. "I always liked Pedro, but you and Trey just seem right. Happy looks good on you, my dear."

"Thanks, Aubs," I said. *What is that mysterious little smile all about?*

We finished eating without Aubrey mentioning her reason for meeting me. When our dessert was done, Aubrey rose.

"Walk with me," she said.

We left the Commons and started strolling across the quad. I checked my phone. Still a couple hours until our flight.

"Do you know why I succumbed to the dark side, Diana?" Aubrey asked.

"They have prettier lightsabers?" I teased.

"They can afford the best lightsabers money can buy. But that's not the reason. I left the virtuous ranks of full-time teaching faculty for the alligator infested world of administration so I could help my fellow humanities faculty from above. Universities are obsessed with football, AI, and STEM while the whole fabric of society is unraveling before our eyes."

"You can take the philosopher out of the classroom, but you can't take the classroom out of the philosopher," I said.

"Damn straight!" Aubrey said. "I could bore you all day with silly behind the scenes stories that would horrify you. Talk about misadventures in missing the point. But I didn't invite you here for that."

We'd arrived outside a beautifully built four-story red brick academic building. It exuded old school ivy league vibes. The sign outside identified it as "Madison Hall" with Tulane's green field and "TU" emblem in the corner.

"Why did you invite me? And why are we at Madison Hall?"

"Because Hebert Hall would be too on the nose," Aubrey said with a mischievous grin. "No relation, I assume?"

"Not that I know of."

We entered the spacious blue carpeted foyer of Madison Hall. Aubrey led me to an elevator. We stepped inside, and she pressed the button for the fourth floor. She turned to face me as we began our ascent.

"I've been able to work some donors over the last year to give funds to humanities initiatives," Aubrey said with evident pride. "It's not an easy sell these days. Lots of other priorities and all kinds of people arguing that the humanities are unnecessary in today's world. I believe they've never been more relevant, and I know you do too."

I nodded as the door opened. We stepped off into an empty office complex. Bookshelves lined the walls. I could see doorways down the long hallway to my right that I assumed led to study areas and seminar rooms.

"The business department just moved some faculty they had here closer to their classroom buildings," Aubrey explained. "It's empty now. Waiting for new occupants."

I examined the varnished wood desk perfectly positioned for an administrative assistant and peered beyond it through the open door of the main office behind it.

"I believe religious studies has never been a more vital field than it is today," Aubrey said. "Radicalized influencers are peddling all kinds of religiously based misinformation about everything from human origins and identity to the American founding. The secularization thesis has folded.

Nobody with any sense or finger on the human pulse believes that religious belief or religious questions are going away any time soon. People like their worlds enchanted. The number of ways they choose to enchant them are diversifying and multiplying."

"You are literally preaching to the choir, Aubs," I said.

"We have some brilliant faculty across several departments who are doing amazing work tackling those kinds of questions in their respective fields," Aubrey said. "They try to work together, but you know how hard it is to coordinate activities across disciplines. Everyone has their own needs and priorities. We only have a minor concentration in religious studies. We need an entity to coordinate and provide focus for exploring religious issues across the curriculum. Given our identity and mission, it would need to be nonsectarian, academically oriented, and inclusive. It's a big challenge. But I have something the humanities don't often enjoy."

"Respect?" I said teasingly.

"Money, my dear," Aubrey said with a raised eyebrow. "I've got three donors with deep pockets and an even deeper commitment to investigating how religious issues impact society and vice versa. They want to open a research and teaching center with a distinguished chair as director and a dedicated group of faculty from across disciplines to provide support."

"That's amazing, Aubs!" I said.

"You think so?"

"Absolutely! New Orleans is a perfect setting for that kind of research center with its culture and religious diversity. And Tulane is well positioned for it."

"Most prestigious institution in Louisiana, with no apologies to our friends in Baton Rouge," Aubrey said. "Nobody in Mississippi and Alabama comes close. You have to go to Texas to find someone in the mid-south who can compete with us."

"All true," I said. "Congratulations, Aubrey! I'm so proud of you!"

"And I am of you, Diana. Always have been."

"You're going to need someone with an established reputation and a passion for both teaching and scholarship to give it the boost and grounding it needs."

"Absolutely."

"Do you have a name for the center?" I asked.

"We're hoping our director can help us with that."

"You have someone in mind?"

"Yes," Aubrey said. "She's brilliant, but she can also be a little clueless sometimes."

It took a minute for her words to sink in. Her smile started slowly and widened as she saw realization finally dawning on my face.

"Me?" I stammered.

"Of course, you!" Aubrey said. "Who else? Nobody can do this like you could."

"Well, there's Walter Treadwell. He's . . ."

"I don't want Walter Treadwell!" Aubrey said, placing her hands on my shoulders and looking straight into my eyes. "I want you! I want your mind, your voice, your experience, your passion, and your heart! I want them here at Tulane!"

My thoughts were swirling in a million different directions.

"I don't know what to say," I managed.

"You don't have to say anything yet," Aubrey said, releasing my shoulders. "That's why I wanted to catch you before you left town. You can take some time to think it over. I know you have a sabbatical from Vandy. Do you have contractual obligations afterwards?"

"No," I said. "They owed me the sabbatical. It was delayed a couple of times by unexpected classroom needs, so they consider my obligations to them already fulfilled."

"I was hoping so," Aubrey said, her eyes brimming with excitement. "So, you could hypothetically start as early as next January?"

"Hypothetically," I said carefully.

"I know we don't have as big an endowment as Vandy and our campus is not as spread out, but aside from that, we compare pretty well," Aubrey said. "And there's one other thing you need to consider."

"What's that?"

Aubrey spread her arms wide to draw attention to the total space around us.

"This center would be yours to build and define as you like," she said. "Even to name as you wish. Think of the legacy you could leave here. Generations of students and faculty."

My imagination was providing images to match her words. Excitement rippled through me. I was struggling to believe it was real.

"This is incredible, Aubrey. I'm definitely interested. I would like the time to think about it if that's okay."

"I already said it was," she said. "Think about it. Talk it over with Trey. Maybe talk to directors of similar centers to get an idea of the opportunities and practical challenges involved."

"Thank you," I said. "I do have a friend and former colleague who left Vandy a few years ago to run a center somewhat like what you're proposing."

"In Tennessee?"

"Minneapolis."

"Did it work out well?"

"I think," I said. "He seems to enjoy it."

"Run it by him," Aubrey said. "Go take care of this business Lucille left behind. You can let me know your decision after it's settled. I want you to do what's best for you, but I also hope what's best for you brings you to us."

We rode the elevator down to the ground floor. I hugged her goodbye in an introspective fog and made my way back to Trey and Delilah. Immediately, Trey knew something was up.

"You okay?"

"Yeah," I assured him. "I'll tell you once we're in the air."

We said goodbye to Delilah, Ramona, and Rico at Louis Armstrong and headed for our gate. After we took off and banked northeast, I filled him in on my conversation with Aubrey.

Trey was stunned and delighted. He took my hand and leaned over in his seat to kiss me.

"I'm so incredibly proud of you, Di," Trey said.

"Thank you," I said. "Who knew?"

"I knew," he said, stroking my cheek. "I knew how special you are the first day I saw you sitting in that cafeteria."

"Can I do it?"

"Hell, yeah!" Trey exclaimed. "There is no question that you can do it. The only question is if you want to do it."

"I think? I don't know. It's a lot. I've built a good home at Vanderbilt. It'll be hard to say goodbye to everyone."

"That's fair," Trey said. "Aubrey gave you time to think about it. Take some time to do that. Contact Aidan like she said and see if he has any advice to offer."

"Do you want me to do it?" I asked.

"I don't trust myself to give you an unbiased answer," Trey admitted. "It's the most perfect answer to our questions about the future I can imagine. It's an amazing opportunity for you. I could get a good job teaching in the city. We'd be close to the kids in Covington. Actually, closer to them in New Orleans than in Picardy. But it's only perfect if it's right for you. If this answer isn't the right one, we'll find another way."

"Are you sure? I don't want to disappoint you."

He gripped my hand and looked into my eyes.

"I want us to have a solid foundation, Sweetheart," Trey said, channeling Bogart but continuing in his own voice. "It needs to be right for both of us. You need to have peace with whichever decision you make. I'm glad to do whatever I can to help you make it, but I will respect whatever you decide."

"Thank you, my love," I said, cupping his face in my hands and kissing him again.

We turned to lighter conversation topics for a while. Then I tried to read a bit. At some point, I slipped off to sleep. I woke to Trey shaking me gently.

"We're descending," he said.

We took an Uber from Logan airport and headed into the city. Our car crossed the beautiful Charles River and cruised into the downtown convention center and historic districts. For all my youthful obsession with Boston, I'd actually spent little time there. There'd been a quick trip for a conference at Harvard that left limited time for sightseeing, and Pedro and

I had done a layover for a few hours three years ago and toured the Freedom Trail before rushing back to the airport.

Our Uber dropped us off on Charles Street in front of a collection of stately brick rowhouses across the street from the Boston Public Garden.

"They call this area Beacon Hill," Trey said. He scrolled on his phone. "I have Muir's address. It's a few houses down."

We strolled down a grassy median with a sidewalk running straight up the middle. Statues greeted us at strategic points along the walk. They portrayed significant individuals and events in Boston's history. With Boston's history being so intertwined with American history in general, many of the figures were familiar to me. I resisted the urge to read the plentiful historical markers, reminding myself of our urgent task. Trey sensed my dilemma.

"This must be killing you," he said with a grin.

"Maybe I can stop and read them on the way back," I said.

"Maybe we'll find another way back, Sweetheart," Trey joked.

Trey's GPS brought us to the steps of a three-story brick rowhouse on the left. It had been converted from the original floorplan to house four apartment units. We stepped on the porch and rang the bell under the name "Muir." No response. Trey pushed the button again. We were debating what to do when the outer door popped open and a middle-aged woman in jogging pants and a t-shirt poked her head out.

"Darren?" she said to Trey.

"No, Ma'am. My name is Trey Laurence. We're looking for François Muir."

"Ma'am!" the woman said in a thick Boston accent. "I'm only fifty-five, Young Man."

"Sorry," Trey said. That bedrock of southern gentility didn't translate well in other parts of the country.

"I thought you were my Door Dash boy, Darren," the woman said.

I could tell Trey was resisting the temptation to tell her Darren might object as much to being called "boy" as she did to being called "ma'am."

"Do you know Mr. Muir?" I asked.

"Frank? Of course, I know Frank. I call him Frank, but he uses the

French form most of the time. Too exotic for me."

"Do you know if he's in?" Trey asked.

"He was this morning," she said. "I went up to have a cup of coffee with him."

She beckoned us to follow her.

"My name is Gladys. You look harmless enough. I'll take you up to him."

We climbed a short flight of stairs and circled around the stairwell on the second floor.

"He must have left his door open because of the heat," Gladys said.

My heart skipped a beat. A door was standing wide open across from the stairwell.

"Frank?" Gladys called.

No one answered.

We walked into the small apartment. The main room was furnished simply with older furniture that included a blue couch, a coffee table, and a couple of brown chairs.

"Let me check and see if he's in the kitchen," Gladys said.

I walked around the room studying the pictures hanging on the wall. They told the story of a full and fulfilling life. A wedding portrait featured a young man standing with his bride outside a gothic cathedral. Their happy smiles warmed me as I examined their hopeful expressions. The couple, obviously François and his wife, aged gracefully over the years as the pictures continued around the room. Their children grew until they appeared with families of their own in more recent photos. I also noticed sadly that the two most recent photos included the family and François, but no sign of his wife.

"What happened to his wife?" I asked.

"Sweetest lady in the world," Gladys said, returning to the room. "She caught Covid early in the pandemic. Nothing they could do. Broke Frank's heart and all of ours too."

"They look so happy," I said.

"I think they were," Gladys said. "Very fine people."

I gazed at the images. A full and fulfilling life. *They would never have lived that life without you, Lucille.* I didn't know how I knew that, but I sensed it was true.

"Why did he leave this?"

Gladys leaned over to pick up a walking stick resting against the coffee table. She examined it, a frown creasing her face.

"Does he usually carry it with him?" Trey asked.

"Yes," Gladys said. "He's got a bad hip. He can't get far without it."

Gladys handed me the stick. I peered down at it, looking for any clues it might offer.

"Diana!"

Trey pointed to a coaster lying on the coffee table. I leaned toward it. The coaster bore a painted image of a beach with waves cresting on the sand and a steep cliff wall in the background. A black cartoon shark was sunbathing at the edge of the beach wearing sunglasses. The glasses were lowered slightly. The shark was winking. The bold letters at the top read *Le Requin Noir.*

"The Black Shark," I translated.

"The letters at the bottom are what got my attention," Trey said.

My eyes focused on them. *Belle Plage.*

"Someone left it beside the walking stick," I said.

"Do you think Frank's okay?" Gladys asked, her voice quavering a little.

"We hope so," I said. I honestly had no idea. "Can you call us as soon as he returns? It's urgent that we talk to him."

Gladys agreed, so I gave her my number, thanked her for her help, and we made our way outside back to the walkway.

"What now?" Trey asked.

I checked my phone.

"Nothing from Dad and Dorcas yet. Delilah checked in about ten minutes ago. She said they're almost to Sarah Abrams' place. She'll let us know when they arrive."

"I guess we have some time to kill," Trey said.

"Until we hear back from them," I agreed.

"You hungry?"

"I could eat," I said.

"Follow me," Trey said, smiling.

"What are you up to?"

"Why do I have to be up to anything?" He asked, feigning innocence.

"You're always up to something. Especially when you smile like that."

We crossed Charles Street and turned left. I studied the greenery of the public park. Teenagers tossed frisbees across the expansive lawns. Young mothers congregated in close circles watching their children cavort in the public splashpads alongside the paved trails. We rounded the corner of the park. A familiar canopy trailed from the doorway of the building ahead to the street.

"No way!" I exclaimed. Trey was watching my expression with relish.

"I checked it out before we left," Trey said. "Welcome home, Dr. Chambers."

Trey insisted we pause under the canopy so he could take my picture with the canopy and sign. We descended the stairs below street level to the front door of the Bull & Finch Pub. A waiter ushered us inside and seated us at a table near the bar. My eyes traveled the walls, soaking in the memorabilia. Memories rushed back to me. Sitting in Trey's living room every afternoon watching television. Watching beloved characters live their lives to the fullest. Free of demons and darkness. Free of fear. Wishing someday I could live to the fullest too. I had found so much inspiration in that imagined world that I eventually chose my name from it.

Trey lifted his water glass the waitress had just left and said, "Cheers! Pun intended."

I laughed and clinked my glass with his.

"They even have food named after the characters," Trey said. He looked up from his menu and smiled at me. My eyes and ears were still soaking up the sights, the sounds, the smells, and the people. "You pull off your makeover well most of the time, but there are amazing moments like this when I see Debbie Hebert in your eyes and all over your face. You look like a little girl in a candy store. And I love it."

I blushed and grinned.

"Thank you, Trey."

"For what?"

"You knew I needed this."

"Needed what?" Trey said, failing again to pull off his innocent act. "Can't a guy just enjoy a hamburger and a beer without ulterior motives?"

"You have the best ulterior motives," I said, "and I love you for it. I understand a little better what Delilah was saying now. I should have been more sensitive to her concerns."

I chose to become the person I became for a reason. I rejected the fear, the paranoia, and the insular smallness of our family home. I pledged to engage with the world rather than run from it. To heal its wounded instead of judging and condemning them. I dyed my hair. I'll never forget the furious look on Lucille's face when I walked out of the bathroom blonde. I got in my little used car, drove to the airport, and flew to Princeton University. I enrolled under my birth name, Deborah Hebert, but, within the week, I started introducing myself as Diana Chambers. It was a new start and the beginning of an incredible journey.

"I can do this without losing who I am," I said.

"You absolutely can," Trey said gently. "Whatever Lucille left done or undone, you are no more obligated to follow her path now than you were before. It's beautiful that she loved you enough to die for you. Remember that she died for you as you are, not her idealized image of you. You have always been better than her ambitions for you."

"You've saved me over the years in more ways than you know," I said. 'I'm so happy to be here with you."

Trey smiled. My phone started playing Pat Benatar's "Hit Me with Your Best Shot" before he could reply.

"Wonder who that could be?" Trey laughed.

I laughed too and answered.

"Hey! Where are you?"

"At the hospital in Omaha," Delilah said.

"The hospital! Are you okay?"

"Fine," Delilah said. "We brought Sarah Abrams here."

"Then you have her?" I asked. "How is she?"

"She's unconscious, but they think she'll be okay. I heard from

Dorcas too about twenty minutes ago. She and Dad found Jacob Le Roux's house empty. There was food on the table like he had sat down to lunch, but it was hardly touched. Get this! Beside the plate was a coaster with a black shark on it from some place in Belle Plage!"

I told her about our own discovery at François Muir's apartment.

"Damn!" Deliah said. "We got to Sarah's just in time to see two men trying to carry her out the front door. They dropped her and ran when we went after them. Rico chased them down the street. They jumped into a car at the end of the street and took off."

"What did they do to Sarah?"

"Doctor said they probably gave her chloroform or something like it," she said. "It's taking a while to wear off. The doctor couldn't say much because of HIPAA laws, but I got the impression she doesn't tolerate anesthesia well. Makes sense she would struggle with the chloroform."

"What are you planning to do?" I asked.

"We'll hang out here a little longer to see if she comes around," Delilah said. "Maybe she can tell us something helpful."

"Sounds good. I owe you an apology, Delilah."

"Well, this should be good," she said. I could hear the grin in her voice.

"I should have understood better what you were saying about getting wrapped up in Lucille's world again," I said.

"You don't have to apologize for that, Di," Delilah said. "I get why you feel a responsibility here. It's just . . . we worked so hard to get free of their bullshit! The exorcisms! The stupid rules and authoritarian religious dogma! The tragic fashion choices! I'm glad to help do some good here if that's what needs to be done. But there's no way in hell I'm getting sucked back into their dysfunctional demon drama!"

"I'm with you," I said. "Always. Let's keep each other sane through this."

"I'm always with you too. Thank you, Sis."

My heart melted. She'd only called me that once or twice in our lives.

"So sweet and totally moving," Trey whispered, grinning. He didn't whisper quietly enough.

"Tell him I'm going to smack the crap out of him next time I see him."

"I think he received the message," I laughed as Trey rolled his eyes.

"So, what's next?" Delilah asked.

"I don't know," I said. "Why did they kill the others and kidnap these last three? And how did they know who the students were and where they were? There's obviously another copy of that list out there somewhere."

"The others died early in the week," Delilah said. I heard muffled conversations on the other end.

"What? Speak up! Because the emergency room is loud," I told her and waited patiently.

"Rico says he thinks they were doing cleanup early in the week," Delilah said. "Trying to get rid of anyone who knew about the chest and whatever secrets are connected to it. He has . . . experience."

Who the hell did we let into our living room?

Instead of voicing my thoughts, I said, "Why did they change their plan?"

"They expected to recover the chest or what was in it," Delilah said. "We stopped them. Now they're trying to adjust."

"Rico thinks they're using Lucille's students as leverage now?" I asked. "Like a bargaining chip?"

"Or as bait," she said. "All three of us agree. That coaster looks like both a threat and an invitation."

My eyes met Trey's. He nodded.

"All roads lead to Belle Plage," I said.

"Looks like it," Delilah said. "Want me to call Dor?"

"Definitely," I said. "We're going to need our translator."

"We'll text the details. Meet you there. Be careful."

"You too," I said. "Love you."

"You too, Di."

I hung up. Trey watched me expectantly.

I raised my glass again and said, "Fancy a trip to France?"

CHAPTER SEVEN

MAY 2, 1995

"How would you like to take a trip to France today, *mes jolies filles?*" Aria's eyes sparkled. She held a large coffee table picture book. The Eiffel Tower adorned the cover. We gathered around her on the couch. Angélique sat on the far left, letting all of us close to her mother so we could see the pictures better.

"Can you really see the Eiffel Tower all over Paris?" I asked.

"No," Aria said, "not everywhere. But you can see it from many places. You can see it especially well from here." She flipped several pages over. Dinah and I leaned closer to examine the beautiful picture that covered both pages. Intricate greenery adorned a lavishly landscaped garden punctuated by majestic fountains.

"Where is that?" Dinah asked breathlessly.

"*Le jardin des Tuileries,*" Aria said, "the Tuileries Garden, in English. It is a beautiful garden in the heart of Paris' historic district. It was built for Catherine de' Medici, one of the most powerful queens in French history. There were several royal palaces there at different times. The French royal family was forced to live in one of them during the first revolution."

"Why isn't it in the picture?" I asked. Delilah was sitting beside me trying to pretend like she wasn't interested. I noticed she was covertly listening for the answer too.

"It was destroyed," Aria said. "Revolutionaries attacked it in August 1792 and murdered the royal family's Swiss Guards. They moved the royals to the Temple, a drafty old medieval castle. So many beautiful landmarks and historic structures were destroyed over the course of France's many revolutions."

Momma emerged from the office and stood listening to Aria's narration. Her mouth turned upward slightly, indicating she was enjoying our fascination. Some days, that expression was the closest she got to a smile.

Aria turned the page. Dorcas, who was sitting on Dinah's lap, shrieked with glee.

"A pyrmid! Look, Momma! I found a pyrmid!"

"Very good, Dorcas," Momma stepped closer. She exchanged a genuine smile with Dinah and patted Dorcas on the shoulder. "Remember, it's a pyr-a-mid."

"What is that?" I asked.

"It is beautiful, *no?*" Aria gushed. "I. M. Pei designed it. He is an architectural genius. We call it *La pyramide du Louvre*, The Louvre Pyramid. It stands over the underground entrance to the Louvre, one of the grandest museums in France."

"What is it made of?" Dinah asked.

"Glass panels and steel," Aria said. "It was first opened in 1988. What do you think, Lucille?"

Momma had stepped closer to Aria and was studying the picture of The Louvre Pyramid with intense focus. Another smile, two in two minutes, spread across her face. That smile puzzled me. It was the kind of smile she allowed herself when she was taking satisfaction in some task completed or celebrating an accomplishment.

"Much better," Momma said with satisfaction. Dinah raised her eyebrows and gave me an amused sideways glance. Momma acted as if she had sat down with Pei and drawn the design for him.

"You know what we should do?" Dinah said.

"What?" I asked.

"We should plan a Paris party. With a night in Paris theme. We could get the artificial greenery we used in the Easter program at church."

Dinah carefully used the word "program." Church theatricals were called "programs" in the Hebert household. "Plays" were those "worldly" things they did at school. Although Dinah had shined as Liesl in her high school production of *The Sound of Music*, Momma, in Delilah's words, shut Dinah's budding theatrical career down afterward. The only opportunities Dinah got to pursue her theatrical interests now were planning dramatic programs at church when they let her and enlisting us to put on amateur plays at home.

"We could make fountains with Daddy's water hoses and those old birdbaths we have in the barn," I said.

"I'm not sure I like the word 'party,'" Momma said.

"Shocker," Delilah muttered.

"What was that?" Momma demanded.

"Soccer," Delilah said. "Like on Angélique's shirt." Angélique had traded Brazil for Argentina.

Momma studied Delilah for a moment, deciding whether it was a battle worth fighting. She opted to let it go.

"We're not talking about a huge party, Momma," Dinah said. "Just us and Trey. And Angélique, of course." We planned little events like that often when Momma and Daddy were gone. Those tiny celebrations gave us an opportunity to stretch our imaginations, relieve our boredom, and spend a little time in an alternate reality far away from the demon-infested horrors of our family's "ministry."

"And no alcohol?" Momma asked.

"Really, Mom?" Delilah said. "The closest thing we have to alcohol here is rubbing alcohol. And Dorcas' nasty fermented apple juice when she leaves it on the table too long."

"I like to drink it all day!" Dorcas said, spreading her arms wide to indicate "all day."

"We plan them all the time, Momma," Dinah said, rolling her eyes.

"I wasn't aware," Momma said.

"You're not usually here," Dinah replied.

Dinah's rebuke was mild, but Momma's expression showed that it hit home.

"I guess that will be okay," Momma said uneasily.

"I will . . . help you," Angélique said. "Help you make it look . . ." She gestured with her right hand, searching for the word. We all jumped at the sound of her voice. No one expected to hear it.

"Holy hell! You talk?"

"Delilah!" Momma shouted. "Watch your language!"

"I'm watching hers," Delilah said.

Angélique blushed.

"You're going to help us make it look real?" Dinah asked.

"Yes!" Angélique nodded furiously, excited to be understood and included. "It is *très*, very, beautiful."

Aria smiled affectionately at her daughter.

"Angélique loves to decorate," she said. "She is very artistic."

"Me too!" Dinah said. "It's going to be so much fun!"

"I suppose," Momma sighed. She looked at her watch. "I need to go pick some things up from the store. Your daddy should be back tomorrow. Things cleared up there faster than we expected. I need groceries if we're going to feed this whole crew."

"Have you heard back from them?" Aria asked.

A frustrated look flashed across Momma's face.

"Not yet," Momma said. "Let's keep those questions behind closed doors."

"*Pardon*!" Aria said. "I just want to be sure they're safe."

"There's no reason to assume they're in danger yet," Momma said. "You may have jumped the gun." At Aria's confused expression, Momma clarified, "A figure of speech. Acted before there was a good reason."

I could tell Aria wanted to argue with Momma. She decided to cut her losses and turned back to her picture book.

"Can we go to the store too, Momma?" I asked.

"I could probably use some help," Momma said.

"Me too?" Dinah asked. "I'm ready to get out."

"If Aria can agree to keep herself here without supervision," Momma said.

"I think I can manage that, Lucille," Aria said, frost in her voice.

I saw the look on Angélique's face and felt sorry for her. She was feeling cooped up too.

"Can Angélique come too?" I asked.

Momma hesitated. I could see her internal gears whirring. She studied Angélique for a minute.

"Angélique, can you understand me?" Momma asked.

Angélique nodded. Her eyes were hopeful.

"If you go with us," Momma said, "you can't tell anyone where you're from or why you're here."

I was thinking that would be pretty easy since none of us, including Angélique, seemed to have any idea why they were here. Momma and Aria had spent hours inside the office using the phone and talking secretly since Aria and Angélique arrived on Saturday. When Momma had announced Saturday night that we were not going to church the next morning, we'd glanced at each other in wide-eyed astonishment. Dinah was expected to dress us and carry us to church even when Momma and Daddy were gone on deliverance and paranormal investigation trips. Momma dropped a further bombshell Sunday night when she announced we would stay home from school for "a couple of days." It sounded great at first. By Tuesday afternoon, the novelty had worn off.

"You're worried about her talking too much?" Delilah said with a smirk.

"Delilah," Momma's tone carried a warning. "The same thing goes for all of you girls. It's very important that people not know Aria and Angélique are here."

Dinah and I exchanged another quick glance. *What is this all about?*

"Go get ready," Momma said. "We're leaving in fifteen minutes."

She didn't have to tell us twice. We rushed upstairs to get our shoes. Delilah slathered some makeup on her face. I resisted the urge to make a clown joke. No need to start a fight when we were finally on the verge of liberation after two long days at home.

We piled into our brown station wagon. Dinah drove while Momma rode shotgun. The rest of us were jammed into the backseats. Our sardine tight situation worked as long as we were still, but Dorcas never stayed still.

She bounded around the backseat the whole way, provoking grouchy complaints from Delilah. Momma deployed the "we will stop this car" threat twice before we got to the store.

Dinah and I peeled off from the others when we got there. We went to the baking aisle to look at cake mixes while everyone else followed Momma and the buggy to pick up essential groceries.

"What do you think?" Dinah asked. "Chocolate or strawberry?"

"I like strawberry, but more of us like chocolate," I said.

"You're probably right," Dinah agreed. "The French have so many desserts with chocolate too."

"Hello, Dinah." The voice was flat and cold. We turned to see a woman with curly gray hair standing by the frosting section. She was dressed in stylish white slacks and a silky red button-up blouse.

"Miss Bernadette," Dinah said. "How are you?"

"Fine. Is it someone's birthday?"

I shifted uncomfortably as her eyes traveled up and down me. I felt examined, assessed, and judged.

"No, Ma'am, just a little treat for us," Dinah said. "We're trying to decide on chocolate or strawberry."

"That's nice. It's good to have choices."

"Sure is," Dinah said. I could tell she thought the situation was awkward too.

"It's my daughter's birthday next week," Bernadette said.

"Oh, that's nice," Dinah said. "I didn't know you had a daughter."

"She passed away a long time ago," Bernadette said.

Awkward!

"I'm so sorry," Dinah said.

Bernadette looked past us with a steely expression. I followed her gaze and saw Momma pushing our buggy with Dorcas sitting in it. Delilah and Angélique must have discovered some curiosity to check out.

"Hello, Lucille," Bernadette said without warmth.

"Bernadette," Momma's greeting was equally cool.

"I was just telling your girls that Tamera's birthday is next week," Bernadette said.

"I doubt they would be interested in hearing about that," Momma said. You could cut the tension with a knife. Bernadette's face reddened at Momma's response. She stared at Momma for a moment, but Momma returned her gaze, unblinking and unintimidated.

"Well, I guess I should finish my shopping," Bernadette said.

"Probably," Momma said. "You here by yourself?"

"Raymond brought me. He's over there."

Her son was standing at the far end of the aisle looking at milk and cheese in the cooler. He turned slightly when he heard his name. His expression morphed into a scowl when he saw us.

"Why are those people always so rude?" Dinah whispered to me.

I barely heard her. The sight of Raymond caused my stomach to twist. I prayed Raymond hadn't brought his daughter.

Momma says there are three ways the Lord answers prayer. He says yes, wait, or no. When he says wait and no, it means he wants to test our faith. I didn't have to wait to hear the response this time; my faith was about to be tested.

"Well! Look who's here! Goodwill closed, Hebert?"

I closed my eyes, said another prayer for patience, and turned to face Bernadette's granddaughter.

"You would be the first to know if it was, Crissy," I said.

"Not my crowd, Hebert," Crissy Hines said. Her penetrating blue eyes roved up and down me with the same analytical judgmental gaze Bernadette used. "You doing okay, Dinah? Miss Lucille?" Her syrupy tone made me want to vomit.

"We're fine," Dinah said. Dinah's tone was friendly enough, but Crissy never fooled Dinah. She knew full well what a bully Crissy was.

"We were just saying hello to your grandma," Lucille said, beckoning us to move on.

"Just move on and forget the past!" Bernadette said. "Wrap yourself up in your little holy roller fantasy world! Maybe we should entertain these girls with some memories?"

Momma had turned away and started to lead us down the aisle. Bernadette's words turned her around again. Her eyes were blazing.

Delilah and Angélique walked up at that moment.

Delilah leaned over and whispered to me, "I have no idea what's going on, but that old woman is about to get shut down."

"Let's tell them the story of a sad vain woman who only had time for high society and a lonely little rich girl who had everything but love," Momma said. "Stop embarrassing yourself and let this go, Bernadette. I was there. When she needed me, I was there. Where were you?"

"She left me," Bernadette said. "She left me because of you."

"She left you because of you," Momma said, stepping so close she was in danger of invading Bernadette's personal space. "She left looking for a better life."

"Is that what she found, Lucille?"

"No," Momma said. "She made her choices. I'm making mine and walking away before I say or do something I'll regret. Say hello to your mother for me, Crissy."

Crissy nodded, speechless for once.

Momma turned her back on Bernadette. She continued down the aisle with Dorcas.

Bernadette called after her, "It's not so easy, Lucille. Being there. You're already failing your daughters too! You'll know what it's like to live with this pain every day!"

"Grandma," Crissy said. "Maybe you should go see if Daddy needs any help."

Crissy's words brought Bernadette back to the present. She processed through her mental fog of rage and pain how much she was embarrassing her granddaughter. She nodded and looked like she was going to say something to Crissy. Instead, she turned and walked down the opposite end of the aisle.

Delilah hurried after Momma.

"You should have decked her, Momma," Delilah said.

"We should turn the other cheek, Delilah," Momma said.

Crissy's eyes narrowed.

"Thank you, Crissy," Dinah said. "Sorry about Delilah."

"I didn't stop her for you," Crissy said, her eyes flashing. "She's too good to tangle with fanatical white trash like your mother!"

Dinah's mouth drew into a tight line. My sister had her own "shut it down" look.

"Let's go, Debbie," Dinah said.

I was very happy to comply. Crissy and I exchanged a bitter look. Hers promised retribution. Mine communicated I was ready for whatever she could dish out. Crissy Hines moved through life as a perennial bitch in the best of circumstances. I didn't expect this encounter to sweeten or sour her more than usual.

Angélique couldn't follow the flurry of agitated English, but she got the gist. She sensed the gravity of it all.

"*Désolé*," Angélique said to Dinah.

Crissy was watching us walk away. I looked back to see her staring at Angélique with intense curiosity.

"What did she say?" Crissy asked.

"Nothing," I said.

"Where is she from, Hebert?" Crissy said.

I ignored her, hurrying to catch up with Dinah and Angélique. Momma and Delilah had checked out and were waiting for us with Dorcas at the door.

We piled into the car in silence. Dinah steered us out of the parking lot and started toward our house. After about five minutes, Dinah quietly asked, "What was that about, Momma?"

"It doesn't matter, Dinah," Momma said.

"It seemed to matter a lot to both of you," Dinah said.

"Old business from another life," Momma said. "There's been too much of that this week. We need to settle it so we can get back to the Lord's work. Don't worry. It's fine."

Dinah gave me a helpless look through the rearview. Momma's secrets were impenetrable.

CHAPTER EIGHT

BANQUE GENÈVE

Reference # 12181991

Manuscript Held In Trust For Boxholder 763

An Excerpt from

DARK CONFESSIONS (1975)

By Lucille A. Broussard

Lucy breathed a relieved sigh, thankful she didn't have to navigate the bustling Paris Montparnasse train station alone. Alexandre strolled through the terminals with the practiced confidence of someone who'd taken these trains all his life. They reached their platform with ample time to spare.

"Ah, Lucy!" Alexandre said dramatically. "You now get your first introduction of the day. What does your American singer Johnny Cash say? The man in *noir*? We have our own man in black."

Lucy blinked in astonishment. One of the largest men she had ever seen was standing in front of her on the platform. He wore a black suit and shiny black loafers. Someone had worn out several brushes shining those shoes. The man clutched a newspaper under his left arm. He looked their way and snorted derisively at Alexandre's description.

He said something in French so fast Lucy couldn't translate it.

"English please, Robert," Alexandre said. "Cousin Lucy speaks our language a little, but she is still learning."

Robert gave Lucy a condescending look as if lacking fluency in

French constituted a fundamental human flaw.

"I said I wear it better than you could, Little Man," Robert repeated in English. His voice rumbled like thunder echoing from mountain peaks.

Lucy decided Robert could call anyone "Little Man" and it would fit. He was at least six three. Possibly a little taller. His substantial bulk wasn't formed by flab. Far from being obese, Robert rippled with muscle in all the strategic places an athlete needed to develop for maximum performance. Lucy had seen pictures of Alexandre's family when he stayed in Picardy. She knew Robert was a big man, but the pictures hadn't prepared her for the intimidating effect Robert produced in person. He resembled their father while Alexandre and Jean-Paul, the youngest and oldest, looked like their mother.

"Robert Broussard," Alexandre said with a dramatic sweeping motion, "Lucy Broussard."

Robert extended his enormous paw. Lucy felt like a child again when her hand disappeared into the massive cavern of his palm. He shook her hand gently. That gentle shake was born of caution, not chivalry. Lucy could tell he was holding her hand like fine china because any real pressure he exerted could snap it like a twig.

"Nice to meet you," Lucy said.

Robert grunted in response. She noticed his black hair was thinning already in his mid-twenties. His hairline was receding in front. Lucy guessed his crown was showing signs of hair loss too, but no one was going to verify that without a stepladder. Alexandre followed her glance.

"Robert is like Papa. He is doomed to misplace his hair."

Robert glared at Alexandre. "I will wear that better than you too, Little Man."

Alexandre raised his hands in mock surrender and winked at Lucy.

They stood on the platform making small talk, mostly Alexandre and Lucy with an occasional grunt from Robert, for thirty minutes before boarding their train to Brittany. Robert led them to a large richly furnished private car. Lucy settled onto the ornate red cushioned seat in their car and gazed with wonder at the furnishings around her.

"What do you think?" Alexandre asked.

"Beautiful," Lucy said. "I'm not used to fancy treatment like this."

"Your fancy is our normal," Alexandre said. "It's good to have the finest. A great recipe for happiness."

Lucy nodded, biting her lip.

"What is it, Lucy? I see the storm clouds in your eyes."

"I'm sorry," Lucy said. "I couldn't help thinking that Tamera always had the finest too. At least, the finest material things. Those things didn't fill the hole in her heart. I think, in some ways, they may have made it worse. Her parents thought if she had all the material things she wanted all her needs were met. I'm sorry, Alex. I don't mean to keep bringing it up."

Alexandre patted her hand.

"Grief is a journey, Lucy. One where we don't get to set the stops along the way or how long it takes for us to arrive. If we ever arrive. You do not need to apologize."

Robert peered over his newspaper, showing mild interest for a moment before returning to his reading. The train rolled out of the station with a shriek of its shrill whistle and a powerful surge from its engine. Lucy watched buildings sweep by her window at increasingly high speeds. Once beyond Paris' outer suburbs, the train glided at full speed across the bright green countryside.

"What is more interesting than us, *mon frère*?" Alexandre asked.

"Many things," Robert said.

Alexandre shook his head. "I mean, what specifically is so important in the pages of *Le Monde* that you are willing to miss our company?"

Robert unleashed a stream of French that clearly expressed frustration.

"Robert?" Alexandre said, nodding toward Lucy as a reminder. "Be polite to our guest."

"I am sorry," Robert said to Lucy. "For some reason my little brother thinks it is necessary for me to inform you that the French government is full of spineless little whores!"

"You said bastards the first time," Alexandre said.

"They are whores and bastards!" Robert said.

"Thank you for the update," Lucy replied.

Alexandre laughed. Robert rewarded Lucy with an annoyed stare.

"You are still mourning the fate of Paul Touvier?" Alexandre asked.

Robert nodded. "He is still in hiding. After years of public service, who are these weaklings to cast infamy on him? To question his character? What even is a 'crime against humanity'?"

"The last day of Paris fashion week," Alexandre said, tossing a grin at Lucy.

"You do not take important matters seriously enough!" Robert thundered. "What could this secularist scum do to other faithful Catholics if they can tarnish the reputation of a man like Touvier?"

"The Roman Catholic Church has done quite well for itself over the centuries," Alexandre said. "I am sure this too shall pass."

"You are a Broussard!" Robert snapped. "You have a responsibility to protect the reputation and influence of this family. But instead of working alongside Papa and Jean-Paul to protect our legacy, you waste time drawing pretty pictures!"

Alexandre's face flushed. He replied in agitated French. Robert responded in kind. Lucy was treated to a five-minute exchange in feverish angry French that left her grasping to identify words. The one she was sure she heard several times was "*Merde!*"

Robert finally rose and stalked out of the car. Lucy understood just enough to gather he was going to get a drink in the dining car. Alexandre shook his head.

"I see what you meant yesterday," Lucy said.

"He is the quiet one," Alexandre said. "Wait until you meet Papa."

"Who is Paul Touvier?" Lucy asked.

"You Americans really do live in your own world," Alexandre said. "It is unpleasant business left over from the Second World War. During the Vichy era. The man is accused of committing atrocities against Jewish prisoners. My limited understanding of the situation comes from Papa and Robert's rants about it. Touvier was sentenced to death *in absentia* shortly after the war. He hid and evaded capture for decades. Touvier employed skilled lawyers. His death penalty sentence expired in the late sixties. President Georges Pompidou pardoned Touvier in 1971, but a public outcry led to further investigations. A complaint was filed charging him with 'crimes against humanity' last year."

"Did he go to prison?" Lucy asked.

"No," Alexandre said. "He disappeared again. No one knows where he is. As Robert said, many traditional Catholics are angry about his treatment. They see him as one of them and the attacks on him as an attack on the conservative religious establishment."

"Traditional Catholics?" Lucy asked.

"Very conservative old money Roman Catholics," Alexandre said. "What survives of the old aristocracy. Some of them are frustrated with Vatican II and all the changes it has brought to the church. They are scandalized by the English masses and Bibles. And the limited acceptance of Protestants and the Eastern Orthodox the church has adopted."

"Is the man guilty?"

"Which man?"

"Touvier, of course."

"Does it matter?" Alexandre said.

"It might. If it's true. His crimes sound horrible!"

"Dear Lucy," Alexandre said. "You always want to fix everything and everyone. This ugliness does not concern us. Our job is to mold fortunate young people into successful adults. Focus on that. Leave the rest to the politicians and the priests."

Robert returned an hour later. He settled into his seat and glanced at Lucy.

"I am sorry to disturb our journey," Robert said.

Lucy nodded, "Thank you."

"The Americans say it takes a big man to admit when he is wrong," Alexandre said. "It is very true in your case, Robert. *Très grand!*"

"I am sorry also that my little brother is a pretentious little ass," Robert said. "But you will learn to endure him as all the rest of us have."

"*Bien vu*, Robert!" Alexandre said.

Lucy felt a surprising ache in her heart. She missed Etta. She could hear her sister putting her in her place with just the right mixture of severity and affection. They rode in relative silence for the next couple hours. Lucy read passages from the little red Bible for an hour and then dozed for a while. When she woke, she stared out the window, watching the lush emerald hills. Occasionally, the train stopped at a village station to take on and release passengers before rumbling on to the next stop. Each kilometer was taking them further from the bustling commercial and political center of France to the beautifully wild Celtic fringe nestled on the rolling coast of Brittany.

A voice came over the intercom system. Lucy heard the sounds of people moving outside. Alexandre and Robert rose.

"We are entering the station, Lucy," Alexandre said.

Lucy gathered her things and followed them out to the platform. About fifteen people were exiting with them. The train corridors appeared empty.

"Where is everyone?" Lucy asked.

"We are the last stop because of the coast," Alexandre said. "Everyone else has already departed the train. They will take on more people here and start back to Paris."

Robert led them through the small station with its tiny ticket office and three benches for waiting passengers. They stepped outside on the edge of a parking lot. A young man stood beside a sparkling black limousine. He was dressed in a very official looking gray chauffeur's uniform complete with a sharp-billed gray cap.

"Alejandro!" Robert said. "Papa sends his own chauffeur! We are honored!"

Even if his name had not already revealed his Spanish descent, Alejandro's dark complexion, chiseled face, and even darker hair confirmed it.

"This is Cousin Lucy, Alejandro," Alexandre said. "She is joining us as a teacher at the school."

Alejandro took Lucy's suitcase and bowed.

"Pleased to meet you," he said in tentative accented English.

"Pleased to meet you too, Alejandro," Lucy said.

Robert settled into the seat beside Alejandro while Alexandre and Lucy took the backseat. The limo pulled away from the station. Within two minutes, they were rolling through a vibrant seaside village. Lucy lowered her window slightly so she could hear the cries of the seagulls swooping overhead. The beach was visible through the buildings to their right. The sound of waves breaking on the rocks was audible even from that distance. A sign proclaimed the village name in large block letters.

"Welcome to Belle Plage," Alexandre said.

"It's very nice. Why do you spell the name without a hyphen?"

Alexandre threw his head back and laughed. "Once again, when confronted with incredible beauty, Lucy Broussard focuses on the dull details. I think the name had a hyphen at one time when it was just a little fishing village. Our family made it a tourist destination right before and after the war. We like the more modern spelling."

"It looks better and fits better on merchandise," Robert said.

"So, you've basically created what Americans call a tourist trap," Lucy said.

"Not at all," Alexandre said. "Belle Plage is a beautiful town with a long history and deep Celtic roots. Paleolithic remains have been discovered in the caves below our estate. People were living here when Julius Ceasar conquered Gaul. It served as an important outpost for the French navy in our wars with the British. We have beautiful beaches, beautiful customs, and beautiful women. Why shouldn't we invite the world in to share our good fortune?"

"How charitable," Lucy said.

The village's main street radiated French provincial charm with businesses and shops extending from a town square with a stone fountain in the center. A beautiful gray stone church towered behind the fountain. Lucy noticed a modest brick building on the edge of the square with a brown wooden sign hanging above the door. The sign carried the name *Le Requin Noir* with a simple black shark image below it.

"That is where you go to have a good time and an even better drink in Belle Plage," Alexandre said.

Lucy saw villagers milling around the fountain. Children were splashing in its sparkling waters. She noticed three of the children had red hair.

"Those children have such bright red hair. I haven't seen many people with red hair since I got to France."

"This is Celtic country, Lucy," Alexandre said. "People in this region cherish their deep Germanic roots. It's where the name 'Brittany' originates. They have their own language, which still survives, and their own customs."

"It is one thing that gives us some trouble sometimes," Robert said. "Some of these people think we are too French for them."

"There is some resentment toward us," Alexandre agreed. "We are an easy . . . how do you say? The goat people blame when things go wrong."

"A scapegoat," Lucy said, smiling.

"Yes," Alexandre said. "Things go wrong, and it is the Broussards' fault whether it is the weather turning bad, the crops withering in the summer sun, or the farmer's daughter getting in the family way."

Robert laughed, a harsh gravelly sound.

"Jean-Paul?" Lucy asked.

"Always Jean-Paul!" Alexandre laughed.

The village fell behind them. The limo followed a twisting curvy road that gradually started uphill. The ascent grew steeper until they rounded the crest of the hill. A breathtaking sight filled Lucy's vision. The road ahead led through two elaborate black iron arches. The name "Broussard," itself also forged in iron, was fused into the metal ironwork, centered in the middle and spilling over onto either side.

The massive chateau beyond the driveway was the most elegant house Lucy had ever seen. She'd toured beautiful plantation houses with her schoolmates growing up, but the European models imported by Louisiana Creoles had not prepared her for the epic old-world reality. Chateau Broussard stood three stories. It was built of creamy white limestone. Lucy observed that the white stone gave the building a glistening effect during the day and, she learned later, it produced an ethereal ghostly effect at night. Pedestrians approaching the chateau on foot at night described it as a white ghost rising from cliffs, reflecting the moonlight like new fallen snow. Elegant iron grillwork framed the shutters on the massive windows and the fence that ran the perimeter of the property. The grillwork reminded Lucy so much of New Orleans. She felt that momentary pang of homesickness again. The windows were about seven feet tall on the ground floor and were placed symmetrically on each floor from the bottom to the top of the structure. A turret stood attached to the house at a strategic point in the middle rear of the chateau. Another smaller one was perched alongside the western back edge of the house. Blue slate tiles adorned the roof, complimenting the limestone walls well. Eight peaked gables, three on the front, three in the back, and two positioned on each end of the house gave the roof an angular look. A conical roof capped the two turrets, covered with the same blue tile.

A flagpole extended from the larger turret flying two flags. One was the easily recognizable tricolor French flag. The other flag resembled the American flag by general design, but with nine horizontal white stripes and five horizontal black stripes. The canton field in the left corner was white dotted with eleven black symbols that looked to Lucy like eleven brushes with a cross or a fleur-de-lis rising from the top of each one.

"What flag is that?" Lucy asked.

"The Gwenn-ha-du," Alexandre said, "the official flag of Brittany."

The limousine pulled into a spacious circle drive. Servants ushered the passengers into an elaborate outer hallway while Alejandro directed the remaining staff to unload their luggage. Lucy experienced sensory overload, her gaze dancing from velvet red tapestries to the ornate crystal glass sparkling from the chandelier. Massive paintings were placed at equidistant points along the hallway, giving visitors a look at the lords and ladies from every era who'd called Chateau Broussard home.

A young blonde woman in a maid's uniform drew close to Alexandre and whispered in his ear.

"Ah! Excellent!" Alexandre said. "Monique says Maman wants to see you in her salon, Lucy. She wishes to greet you personally. Monique will take you."

"You're not coming?" Lucy asked.

"No," Alexandre said. "I will make sure our rooms are prepared and freshen up a little. We will meet before supper. I will escort you to the dining room personally."

Lucy swallowed, surprised at how nervous she suddenly felt.

"It is okay, Lucy," Alexandre said. "It is true that Maman is a feral feline, but she has not devoured anyone yet."

Robert raised an eyebrow, indicating he doubted that was true.

Lucy followed Monique down the lavishly decorated central hallway, then up a winding staircase to the second floor. They passed several closed doors before Monique guided her into a large ornate room with a beautiful view of the ocean through the central window.

"Please wait here," Monique said.

Lucy paced the room nervously. Two soft cushioned settees, both royal blue with gilded gold frames, sat in the center of the room. Bookshelves lined three of the walls. They were filled with books of every genre and language. Lucy noticed that historical works predominated in the nonfiction category while romance and classics comprised the majority of the fiction works. Open brown paneled spaces in between each bookshelf held decorative works like family crests and framed embroidered nature scenes.

Lucy stepped closer to one of those open spaces. A large portrait dominated the space, covering most of the wall. A middle-aged woman with chestnut colored hair and a golden tiara emblazoned with jewels stared back at her. Her dress identified her as someone from the past, but Lucy wasn't familiar enough with the history of fashion or art to place her in time.

"Catherine de' Medici. Queen, mother, and defender of France."

Lucy started and turned to face the woman who'd quietly slipped into the room.

"I'm sorry, *ma chère*," the woman said. "I was quietly examining you while you were examining her."

"No," Lucy stammered. "I'm sorry. I didn't hear you."

"I pride myself on my discretion," she said. "I am Madeleine."

Lucy remembered Alexandre's "feral feline" description. It seemed very appropriate now. As Madeleine moved toward her with her hand outstretched, Lucy got the impression of an elegant Persian cat gracefully and stealthily slinking across a room. Her bright green eyes peered into

Lucy's with the same feline effect. There was something welcoming and curious, but also hungry and sardonic in those eyes. Lucy couldn't decide if she felt more like the cat's new favorite possession or its next meal. Or both.

Madeleine's hair was tinted a beautiful auburn color. She had it bound up in a tight bun, revealing a slender white neck as elegant as her dress and bearing. Lucy wondered how long her hair was when it was fully released from its bonds. Her emerald frock complimented her eyes and hair well. Lucy knew from Alexandre's age and description of his family that Madeleine had to be approaching her late forties. She didn't look her age at all. Her face was mature, but no wrinkles or lines marred her complexion yet and no gray infiltrated her hair. Madeleine's contribution obviously gave Jean-Paul and Alexandre their lighter look. Lucy guessed those Breton Celtic roots Alexandre mentioned accounted for Madeleine's appearance. The Broussards may have been "too French" culturally, but Madeleine's genes were forged in the Celtic coastlands.

Madeleine gripped Lucy's hand with a firm shake.

"I understand Americans greet one another this way," Madeleine said. "Perhaps one day we will know each other well enough for me to give you a proper kiss on both cheeks."

"Of course," Lucy said. She willed her voice to be steady.

"Calm yourself, *ma chère*," Madeleine said, wrapping her left arm around Lucy and giving her a tight side hug. "You must be at ease with me. No one is more excited that you are here than I am. Well, maybe Alexandre. But I believe my need for skilled teachers outweighs his need for a companion. Come, sit."

Madeleine gestured to the two settees. Lucy settled on the one facing the window while Madeleine sat across from her, leaning forward and cupping her hands in her lap.

"I started a preparatory school for three reasons, Lucy. First, I think I can prepare our local young people for university better than other options in this region. You are impressed with my English?"

"Very," Lucy said.

"I had the best teachers here and in Paris," Madeleine said. "I traveled the world for two years as a young woman before I married Henri and settled here. I've continued to study educational methodologies around the world. We can do it better here." She said it not as a boast, but as a simple matter of received fact.

"Second, I believe we can do a better job with children from this region because we understand the culture that has shaped them. Most of these children are destined to work the same trades as their parents and grandparents before them. There is nothing wrong with that. It is what makes the world go round, as you say in your country. But there are an elite few who are capable of something more. I want to help the best of Brittany shine at university and around the world." Madeleine stopped and looked at Lucy expectantly.

Lucy took the bait. "And what's the third reason, Madame Broussard?"

Madeleine laughed. Her laughter was full, rich and deep.

"You will call me Madeleine, Lucy," Madeleine said with a twinkle in her bright green eyes. "The third reason is because I was bored and going out of my damn mind!" She laughed again. This time Lucy felt comfortable enough to join her.

"God has blessed me with three sons like my inspiration, Queen Catherine," Madeleine said, nodding to the portrait. "They are now young men finding their way in the world. They still need their mother, but not as much or in the same ways as before. A woman of my gifts and interests needs something important to occupy her. A way to make a difference and serve. This school is my way."

Madeleine leaned forward further.

"You are a writer, Lucy?"

"I write a little. Mostly short stories. I would like to write something longer someday."

"I have no doubt you will," Madeleine said. "I need someone to teach my students literature and English."

"I'm not a certified teacher," Lucy admitted. "I've only completed one year of college."

"The lessons are outlined for you already," Madeleine said. "I taught them myself for a while, but the administrative and practical needs of the school are growing. They demand more of my attention every day. You're a native speaker. See how I use your contractions? Learning the nuances of the language, the way people actually speak it, is just as important to me as cultivating understanding of the formal rules and structures of the language. You will teach two or three classes, but much of your influence on the students will flow naturally from the caretaking you do in residence with them. You will share a room with another teacher on the same second floor wing where the girls are housed so that you can help with their practical needs. Alexandre and another male teacher live on the third floor with the male students in a similar arrangement."

"I think I can handle that," Lucy said.

Madeleine reached out and cupped her hands over Lucy's.

"I know you can. We'll build something beautiful here, Lucy. I am so excited to get to know you. Alexandre said wonderful things about you when he returned from Louisiana."

"He's a wonderful person," Lucy said. "He became one of my best friends during a very stressful year."

"Where would we be without good friends and family?" Madeleine said. She spread her arms wide and clapped her hands together. Madeleine stood and motioned for Lucy to join her.

"Let me introduce you to the teacher who will share your room."

Lucy followed her down the hallway. Piano music met them along with a soaring soprano voice singing in French. The music grew louder as they drew closer to a door at the end of the hallway. Lucy thought she recognized the melody, but she couldn't quite place it. Madeleine paused at the door and waited until the voice subsided and the piano music ceased. She rapped on the door and opened it.

"*Excusez-moi*," Madeleine said. "I would like to introduce you to our new teacher."

Lucy entered behind Madeleine. A young woman about Lucy's age rose from her seat at the piano. Her lustrous raven hair spilled down the back of her red dress in flowing rivulets. Her blue eyes swept from Madeleine to Lucy. A young girl with black pigtails and a bright yellow dress stood beside the piano. Lucy guessed she was the source of those soaring vocals.

"Lucy Broussard," Madeleine said, "this is Aria Fournier. Aria is our music teacher and your fellow resident assistant."

"*Enchantée*, Lucy," Aria said, bowing slightly.

"Very nice to meet you too, Aria," Lucy said.

"Lucy is still learning our language, Aria," Madeleine said.

"I will try to remember," Aria said. "I am excited to get to know you, Lucy. I cleaned your side of the room this morning. You should have plenty of room for your things in the wardrobe and desk."

"Thank you so much," Lucy said.

"And this little treasure is one of our very best," Madeleine said, circling the girl and placing her hands on her shoulders. "Say hello to Lucy, my sweet little songbird."

The girl's sweet smile warmed Lucy's heart. Lucy could see her concentrating, striving to get her English words right.

"My name is Sarah. I am very happy to greet . . . meet . . . you." Sarah reddened, embarrassed at her slight mistake.

"I'm very happy to meet you and be greeted by you," Lucy said. "Your voice is so beautiful."

"*Merci,*" Sarah said.

"You have practiced well today, Mademoiselle Abrams," Aria said. "You may go rest a little before dinner."

"*Merci,* Mademoiselle Fournier." Sarah performed a perfect curtsey for her teacher then swiveled and did the same for Madeleine and Lucy.

"Amazing child!" Madeleine said when Sarah had gone. "You are doing well with her, Aria."

"Thank you, Madeleine," Aria said. Only her brightly shining eyes revealed how much she reveled in Madeleine's praise.

"How old is she?" Lucy asked.

"Only nine," Aria said.

"She's an amazing talent already," Lucy said.

"Absolutely!" Aria said. "Think what she will do when her talents are fully disciplined."

Madeleine clapped her hands together and said, "I have matters to attend to before dinner. Aria, could you show Lucy to her room? Your suitcase and bag should be there already. I will see you at dinner, Lucy."

Lucy thanked Madeleine and followed Aria back down the hallway. Aria was describing the storage spaces in the room when a girl's voice called her name.

"Just a moment," Aria said to Lucy. She hurried to a nearby open door and entered. Lucy heard her ask in French, "What do you need, Estelle?"

Lucy stood waiting in the hallway. She was studying the floral-patterned wallpaper when she heard a rustling behind her.

"Have you come to help us, Mademoiselle?" A pre-teen boy with untamed brown hair was poking his head around another doorway.

"Yes," Lucy said with a smile. "I'm here to teach you English."

The boy shook his head. His lower lip trembled. A tear trickled down his cheek. "Please don't let them take me."

"Let who take you?" Lucy asked.

"The devils. They took Jacques and Avery."

Lucy crouched to put herself on his level.

"God is more powerful than any devils," Lucy said. "He will protect us always."

The boy shuddered visibly and shook his head.

"God does not live here, Mademoiselle," he whispered. "Only the devils do."

Lucy tried to find a response, but she was too shocked to think clearly.

"François? Do you need something?" Aria had returned.

"No, Mademoiselle Fournier," François said. "I am fine."

His head slipped back around the corner and the door shut gently.

Lucy stood straight, still shaken.

"Are you well?" Aria asked.

"Yes, I'm fine," Lucy said. "Who is that boy?"

"François Muir," Aria said. "He is a nice boy. Very smart. He is a little nervous sometimes. Do want to see our room?"

"Yes," Lucy said. "Lead on."

Lucy tried to recover the blissful excitement she'd been feeling only five minutes before. Instead, two chilling sentences kept running through her head.

God does not live here, Mademoiselle. Only the devils do.

CHAPTER NINE

I RETURNED TO CONSCIOUSNESS, ROCKED by a sudden jerk. Trey's left arm was wrapped around me. My head had been resting on his chest while I slept. Trey was reading a book on his tablet. He gripped me tighter as another jolt shook us.

"What kind of track is this?" Dorcas said.

"We're rolling on a track?" Trey asked.

Daddy chuckled and went back to studying his gigantic old-school paper map of Brittany. Dorcas was sitting on the far edge of their seat to avoid the huge map spilling out in both directions.

"Doesn't feel like it," Dorcas agreed.

"How long have I been out?" I asked groggily.

"About two hours," Trey said. "I think we're almost there."

Delilah poked her head over the pair of seats three rows in front of us.

"You've obviously never ridden on a tour bus," she said.

"And now I have no plans to," Dorcas said.

I sat up and tried to rearrange my messy hair. Trey handed me a bottle of water. I accepted it gratefully and doused the bitter taste of sleep from my mouth.

"She awake?" Delilah called.

"Maybe." Trey said.

"Why do you have to be evasive, T?" Delilah said.

"Because I love updating you on her status every five minutes," Trey said. "What is this? Update twenty?"

Delilah stood and made her way back to the seat we occupied across from Daddy and Dorcas. When she arrived, Delilah stood expectantly with her arms folded. Trey tried to pretend he didn't see her for a moment and then looked up with a teasing smile.

"Can I help you?" Trey asked.

"Go get some air. Check out the bathrooms. I hear they're awesome."

"Not unless you composed some new graffiti since last time I went," Trey said.

"Which one of us is going to endure this standoff longer?" Delilah asked.

"Probably the one who is a certifiable psychopath," Trey said. He patted my leg and said, "Want anything from the snack car?"

"No thanks," I said.

He rose, grinned at Delilah, and dramatically gestured to the empty seat. As he walked away, Delilah called after him, "I've never been officially certified."

"You'd probably blow the scale wide open anyway," Trey called back.

"That's probably true," Delilah said.

Delilah settled in the seat next to me and looked at me expectantly.

"Just ask," I said. "I'm getting the idea this is going to be a heavy conversation, and I'm not awake enough for it yet. Rip the band aid off."

"What are we going to do with her?" Delilah gestured to the seat beside her own a couple of rows up. She lowered her voice as she said it, a rare move for Delilah. A short woman with salt and pepper graying hair was gazing out the window watching the landscape sweep by. Her sweet oval face radiated curiosity and kindness with an undercurrent of nervous energy.

"Watch her and protect her at all costs," I said. "I can't believe you brought her!"

"She insisted," Delilah said. "She would have been on the next flight behind us if I'd said no. I decided she'd be safer with us. What if those kidnappers decided to try again after we left?"

"If I had my way, she'd be hidden somewhere safe like that chest," I said. "I don't like the idea of bringing her back here."

"She might be able to help us," Dorcas said. "At least, that's what she said."

"She said she doesn't remember much," I said. "Not much about that night anyway."

"It might come back to her." Dorcas said. "We can at least get the parts she does remember once we get settled tonight. Besides, those men they took were her friends. The women who were killed were too. She has just as much right as us to see this through."

Sarah Abrams glanced back at us and gave us a tentative smile. She knew we were discussing her. We returned her smile with three reassuring fake smiles.

"You feel like a trio of mean girls gossiping about a classmate?" Delilah asked through her fake smile.

"I was wondering if this is what it feels like to be Crissy Hines," I agreed, feeling my own twinge of guilt.

"Feeling like Crissy Hines these days means the pleasure of showering in an open cellblock with twelve angry women staring at you," Delilah said.

"I'm trying to decide if you think that's a bad thing or not," I said.

Delilah gave me an "I'll never tell" grin and stood up for Trey.

"We're pulling into the station," Trey announced.

"Did you get me anything from the snack car?" Delilah asked.

"Is that the reward for seat theft now?" Trey said, sliding back beside me.

"You need to keep working on this one, Di," Delilah said. She went back to her place beside Sarah. On the way, she gently slapped a sleeping Ramona on the back of the head. She and Rico were nestled on the pair of seats across from Delilah and Sarah.

"Delilah!" Ramona complained groggily. Rico snickered and began preparing his things for the train's arrival.

I'd been marveling off and on at the beautiful landscape once we left

Paris. I stared out the window for two hours before I drifted off to sleep. The sights, sounds, and smells enchanted me again as we stepped off the train onto the platform. I could hear the surf washing against the beach even though we were still a couple of streets away from it. The calls of seagulls brought back so many memories of beach trips past. The air was tinged with that tangy salty smell you only experience near the ocean.

Angélique waved to us from the edge of the platform. She kissed each of us on both cheeks in turn and shook Trey's hand when I introduced him. She looked a little apprehensive as she did the same with Rico and Ramona.

"Angélique," Delilah said, "this is Sarah Abrams."

Angélique's eyes widened. The look she gave me promised a conversation when we were alone similar to the one I'd just had with my sisters. Her hand trembled as she extended it to take Sarah's. Sarah was gazing at Angélique in awe. She had the same reaction when they stepped off the plane at Charles de Gaulle and she saw Dorcas standing with us. Delilah and I had always looked more like each other and my dad's side of the family. We'd also changed our look enough over the years that we'd muted our physical similarities to Lucille. Dorcas, however, still looked so much like Dinah and Lucille. Sarah had started weeping and threw her arms around Dorcas.

"I'm sorry," Sarah said, "I know you're not her, Sweetheart. But you look so much like her. She was so special to me."

Dorcas put her arms around Sarah and started crying too. They'd held each other for several minutes while the rest of us stood awkwardly silent.

Sarah held Angélique's hand and placed her other hand on top of Angélique's.

"Your mother was an incredible woman," Sarah said, tears moistening her cheeks again. "She helped me discipline my voice and gave me a desire to use my gifts to bless others. I think of her every time I sing."

"Thank you for sharing that," Angélique said, tears welling in her own eyes. "I am planning to spread her ashes on the beach at sunset tonight. Would you like to join me?"

"I would be honored," Sarah said.

"Would all of you join me tonight as well?" Angélique asked.

Delilah's expression announced pouring ashes on a beach wasn't at the top of her itinerary.

"We would be honored," I said with a sideways look at Delilah.

Angélique nodded. "Thank you. I've arranged rooms for all of you at *La Brise Atlantique*. It's a beautiful little inn. Jacques and Enora Kerouac, old family friends, have owned it for years."

"Kerouac?" Delilah asked. "Like the *On the Road* guy?"

"Yes," Angélique said. "At least, I think so. Kerouacs were Breton nobility back in the medieval period. Not so wealthy or influential now."

Delilah grinned at me. "This trip is getting better already."

I moaned on the inside. *On the Road* won the distinction of being the only book Delilah enjoyed reading in high school. I absolutely hated it. Memories of our arguments over the book surfaced in my mind.

"How can you not appreciate that kind of freedom!" Delilah had said. "They're riding the open road owing nothing to anyone."

"They're a bunch of rootless dope fiend idiots roaming the country literally dependent on the charity of everyone," I'd countered with all my teenage wit and wisdom.

"They're living the dream," she insisted.

"They treat women like disposable garbage!" I proclaimed.

It went on like that for an hour before we declared a truce to sneak downstairs and treat ourselves to Blue Bell ice cream. The Homemade Vanilla disappeared in thirty minutes. Our disagreement over Jack Kerouac's adventures lives on.

We piled into Angélique's rental van and drove through the quaint seaside village of Belle Plage to *La Brise Atlantique*. I noted the umbrellas that dotted the beach. Tanned bodies of all varieties and ages splayed along the beach or frolicked in the rolling blue waves. According to Angélique, Belle Plage catered to tourists during the summer months. Residents of Belle Plage made most of their yearly income from those visitors, most of them from Paris, who swarmed the beaches to soak up the sun and surf. They dined in three or four restaurants the town boasted and shopped in the little stores that lined the main street. Angélique pointed to several nicer homes on the clifftops.

"Those belong to Parisians," Angélique said. "They are what you call vacation homes. People use them for the summer season and return to Paris for work the rest of the year. The population of Belle Plage is artificially inflated by at least a thousand people in the summer. It shrinks to under two thousand during the off months. Businesses transition from serving tourists primarily to taking care of locals. They enjoy the summer boom and then relish the quiet the rest of the year."

As evidenced both from the number of people on the beaches and the people strolling along the main street, we had clearly arrived at the onset of tourist season.

"Are those fishing boats out there?" Dad asked, spotting a small harbor in the distance.

"Yes," Angélique said. "Fishing is their other major industry. Not as big as tourism now, but there are still families who make their living harvesting fish, oysters, and lobster."

We drove down the main street toward the town square, little seaside shops beckoning us with their signs to buy souvenirs. Trey grabbed my arm and pointed. A wooden sign hung outside a building on the edge of the town square. The black shark from our coaster grinned back at us over his lowered sunglasses.

"The Black Shark," I said.

"That's the most popular local tavern," Angélique said. We hadn't had a chance to show her the coaster yet.

I marveled at the Catholic church's gothic architecture. It looked particularly old-world European with the fountain set in front of it.

"Are most people here Roman Catholics?" I asked.

"Cradle and cultural Catholics," Angélique said. "I am not sure how many people actually practice their faith beyond baptisms, christenings, and Easter, but it still serves as a cultural hub for the village. They sponsor public events and hold village meetings there. They have a small parochial school. A very small one. But they are not alone; your American evangelicals have a little mission church here in town too. It does not run most of the year. Not enough people. But they always have a visiting minister and a couple of missionaries here in the summer to evangelize the tourists."

We pulled up to a modest two-story establishment with a bright blue and pink sign identifying it as *La Brise Atlantique*. We wrestled our luggage into the small lobby. The inn reflected the architecture of the early seventies with lime green and beige colors, but obvious attempts to update the décor and facilities were scattered around the lobby space as well. The Kerouacs were trying to keep up with the times as best they could. A tall woman with gray hair hurried around the front desk to hug Angélique. I listened to them greet one another in French. Angélique gestured to us, explaining who we were. The woman nodded eagerly and greeted each of us in turn. She stopped when she reached my dad.

"I am so sorry for your loss, Monsieur," Madame Kerouac said. "I did not know your wife long, but I know she had a good heart. She rests with the angels now."

Dad nodded, obviously trying not to choke up. "Thank you," he said.

"And you, little one," she said to Sarah, "do you remember riding to Paris with your little head in my lap?"

Sarah's eyes widened. "That was you?"

"Yes," Madame Kerouac said. "We were the ones who met your boat down the coast."

I exchanged curious glances with my sisters. We needed to get the rest of that story as soon as possible.

"We will get you checked in and then you will rest."

"Thank you, Madame Kerouac," Dorcas said.

"You will call me Enora."

"Thank you, Enora," Dorcas corrected.

"Jacques will be so excited you are here!" Enora said, hurrying around the desk to get our room keys.

We separated to check out our rooms, which were quite nice. Not overly spacious, but they contained all the modern conveniences along with a small television, microwave, and mini fridge. Trey collapsed on the bed while I unzipped our suitcases.

"Paris looked really amazing," Trey said.

"We didn't get to see much," I said. "I promise we'll spend a few days exploring, just the two of us, when this is all done."

"Sounds like a date, Doctor," Trey said. He reached over and pulled me down beside him. We cuddled on the bed for a few minutes. I savored his nearness and the scent of his cologne.

"Know what I'm thinking?" I asked.

"How much you wish you hadn't agreed to go up to the chateau first thing?" he said into my hair.

"I was actually wondering how soundproof these walls are," I teased. "But, yeah, that was on my mind too."

"You want me to go up with you?" Trey asked.

"No. Better just the three of us and Angélique. We don't want to overwhelm her. And Angélique knows her."

"That may or may not be a good thing," Trey said. "It doesn't sound like they get along. And Madeleine doesn't sound like someone easily overwhelmed."

I sighed. "There's a lot that doesn't really add up. Maybe talking to Madeleine will give us some answers. What are you going to do?"

He grinned and rolled over. I heard him fishing in his backpack. Trey rolled back with a miniature shortwave set like Chip's in his hand.

"I'm going to see if I can talk to my boy," Trey said. "Then maybe I'll ask your dad if he wants to walk down to the docks."

"Why am I feeling like we're drawing the short straw?" I said, leaning in to kiss him.

He kissed me back and said, "Anything for the cause."

"Have you ever read *Rebecca* by Daphne du Maurier?" I asked Delilah.

"If it doesn't have panels, pictures, or audio, no," Delilah said.

"It's a little more elegant than your Beatniks," I said. "A gothic suspense novel. This place reminds me of it."

"I've read it," Dorcas said. "And I agree. The whole estate gives me major *Jane Eyre* vibes."

Chateau Broussard loomed ahead of us. The intricate ironwork arched across the drive with the family name clearly scrolled in the center. I gazed at the limestone walls and blue tiled roofs. We were approaching the front, but I could make out the two turrets beneath their conical roofs as we circled the main drive. I noticed that the blue tile was wearing and even missing in a few places. The majestic tall windows reflected the sun, as did the limestone walls, giving the building a luminescent effect.

An elderly maid introduced herself as Monique and ushered us through the impressive main foyer and up the stairs. A few young staff members passed us along the way, but I was struck by how few we saw compared to the size and complexity of the chateau. I tried all along the way to check out the paintings that adorned the walls. We were moving too fast for me to get a detailed look at them. I was pleased when Monique finally left us in a second floor sitting room with an impressive view of the ocean out the picture window.

"Madame will join you shortly," she said, covering her mouth as she coughed.

"*Merci*, Monique," Angélique said.

Monique glared at her and left without a response.

"Hospitality is a bit thin," Delilah said.

Dorcas and Angélique took seats on one of two blue settees in the room while Delilah and I explored. I gazed in fascination at the collection of books on the bookshelves. Whoever compiled them enjoyed history, classical works, and a good trashy romance. The collection spanned several decades before thinning over the last decade. Either the reader was reading less or moving into digital and audio editions.

"What was that?" Dorcas asked.

"What was what?" I said.

"Listen," she whispered.

All four of us listened attentively. A sound issued from above us. It sounded like a long moaning wail. None of us dared to breathe. The mysterious moan resounded two more times before it stopped. We listened for a few more minutes, but whatever was causing it had subsided.

"Maybe just the wind," I said. "These old chateaus must have a million open spots where the wind can sweep through the upper floors."

"Sure," Dorcas said. I could tell she wasn't convinced. Her ghosthunter brain was already scanning the walls and ceiling. If she and Dad had their way, they'd be up here with EMF meters before all this was over.

"How long has this place been here?" Delilah asked.

"Different pieces were added at different times," Angélique said. "I think maybe the earliest parts were built in the seventeenth or eighteenth century. Before the revolution."

I pulled out my phone to check Chateau Broussard's actual birthdate. Dorcas noticed my furrowed brow.

"What's wrong?"

"I'm not getting any signal at all here," I said. "Nothing. It's like we've stepped into some kind of communications blackout."

Dorcas raised an eyebrow and widened her expressive eyes.

"Don't say spirit entities block cell phone signals," I said, heading off her pending observation.

"Of course not," Dorcas said. "But they do." She grinned at my exasperated head shake.

"Who is this chick?' Delilah asked, staring up at a painting of an early modern French woman in royal robes. A thin gold crown glistened from her brow.

"Catherine de' Medici," I said. "She was queen of France from 1547 to 1559 and then the power behind the throne during the reigns of all three of her sons. Catherine exerted powerful public influence pretty much from 1547 until her death in 1589."

"I do not know how you do that," Angélique said. "I struggle to remember family birthdays, much less birth and death dates from five hundred years ago."

"She's been a storehouse of useless trivia willing to share freely all her life," Delilah said.

"And you love it," I said.

"Don't know how we would live without it," Dorcas said, winking at Delilah.

"I love it better now that I don't have to share a room with you," Delilah said. "Good luck, Trey."

Delilah continued studying Catherine's image. I thought I heard a slight thump behind us. Before I could look, Delilah rendered her verdict.

"She looks frustrated," Delilah observed.

"Her life was tragic in so many ways," I said. "She had a lot of reasons to be frustrated."

"And what were those, Professor?"

The gravelly feminine voice startled us all. I jumped and turned to face the ghostly gothic presence looking back at me expectantly. I'd done my research and recognized her from her photographs online. Madeleine Broussard bent slightly forward, taking several inches off her tall stature. She rested her weight against a black cane gripped in her right hand. Her complexion was chalk white and dotted with freckles. Those freckles were the remaining trace of the once lustrous auburn hair I'd seen in the internet photos. Her auburn locks had surrendered their color to the advance of time, transforming into a grayish white swirl. She was approaching ninety and her body, despite the lingering evidence of her former self in her frame, looked frail. Her eyes told a very different story. They still blazed with fierce light. I decided anyone would be foolish to underestimate Madeleine Broussard even in her twilight years. She was dressed in black from head to toe. Her black dress was complimented by a thin black veil pulled back from her face. I got strange reverse Miss Havisham vibes. Instead of being a bride frozen in time like Dickens' famous character, Madeleine Broussard looked like a mourner or widow frozen in time. I thought of Queen Victoria, mourning Prince Albert for the rest of her days by wearing black. Who or what was Madeleine Broussard mourning?

"Continue, Professor Chambers," Madeleine said. "I'm interested to hear about the tragedy of Queen Catherine."

I didn't like the very familiar way she addressed me and looked at me. I felt like a specimen she'd been observing at a distance for years suddenly presented to her for closer inspection.

"Excuse me," I said. "Have we met, Madame Broussard?"

"Call me Madeleine, Diana," Madeleine said. "No. We've never met. You could call me a fan if you like. Or an interested observer. I've always been closer than you could possibly imagine."

I felt a chill ripple through my entire body. She smiled, sensing my discomfort.

"No need to worry, Dear," Madeleine cooed. "I have the utmost respect for you. Women need to be strong to make their way in the world. So, tell me, why do you say Queen Catherine's story was tragic?"

I was grateful to return to something more familiar and less awkward. "She lost her husband to a lance because he decided to be irresponsible and compete in a jousting tournament. Her two oldest sons died far too young. Her younger son was assassinated after a tumultuous reign. Her country was torn apart by religious wars, and her family dynasty was supplanted at the end of those wars. Her family basically brought the Valois dynasty crashing down and much of France along with it."

Madeleine pursed her lips.

"That is certainly a very . . . critical . . . interpretation," Madeleine said. As she spoke, she moved slowly to the settee opposite Dorcas and Angélique. She lowered herself onto it and peered at Angélique.

"I see you brought reinforcements," Madeleine said.

"I would not need help if you would speak with me like an adult instead of hiding behind your son and your servants," Angélique said, steel in her voice.

"No one here owes you anything," Madeleine said.

"You owe us all an explanation and an apology at the very least!" Angélique said.

Madeleine responded with a stream of French. Angélique answered with equal vehemence.

"Let's please try to be civil," I said. "I know Aria frustrated you with her visits. I'm sorry about that. We can talk this over calmly."

Madeleine's head whipped toward me. "What do you mean-Aria's visits?"

I looked at Angélique. Her face was set and expressionless.

"Aria's attempts to investigate your new primary school," I said. "Angélique told us you had her escorted off the estate twice."

Madeleine threw her head back and laughed. It was a full minute before she recovered.

"Is that what you told them?" Madeleine said in English.

"What the hell is going on here?" Delilah demanded.

"You're here at the invitation of a cunning little liar, Delilah," Madeleine said.

I exchanged startled looks with both my sisters. None of us had introduced ourselves. Madeleine seemed far too familiar with all of us.

"Aria Fournier has not set foot on this estate since she left my employ in 1974," Madeleine continued. She pointed at Angélique. "This woman has made a habit of trespassing off and on for the last two years. And we are getting tired of it! If you hadn't brought the Heberts with you this time, I would have had you thrown in jail!"

"You can have me thrown wherever you want!" Angélique shrieked. "I will still get to the truth no matter what!"

My mind was swirling. I looked towards my sisters, but they both seemed as stunned and disoriented as I was.

"Let's back up a step or two," I said. "Madeleine, can you tell us why our mothers left here so suddenly?"

Madeleine looked genuinely sad.

"I think the bizarre stories village gossips told got in their heads," she said. "Your mother came here from Los Angeles full of horrible fantasies about demons and devils. I think she had a friend who died of a drug overdose just before she came here. I loved Lucy so much! I wanted to mentor her and help her hone her incredible talents. She broke my heart when she and Aria left. We were relocating some of our students to a better facility. Our room on the estate was limited, and we had entered into a partnership with another preparatory school in Nice. Your mothers imagined something sinister in that. They took the opportunity provided by a costume gala we were hosting on the estate to sneak five of our students through the tunnels beneath the chateau to the coast."

"On the same night your son was murdered," I said.

"Yes."

"Were those two things connected?" I asked.

"The same enemies who planted those wild ideas in Lucy's and Aria's heads were responsible," Madeleine said. "Influential people like us have many enemies waiting in the shadows. They took advantage of the distraction Lucy and Aria created to kill Jean-Paul."

"You sound like you know who killed your son, but the murder remains officially unsolved," I said.

"I never said we knew who killed Jean-Paul," Madeleine said. "We know the dark powers that motivated them. And we will have justice. We command powers of our own at Chateau Broussard."

"Maybe we can help solve the mystery behind his death," I said.

"It has been a long time, and many have tried before you," Madeleine said. "But we would be grateful for any help you can give us."

"She knows who killed Jean-Paul because she ordered his death!" Angélique said.

Madeleine's face twisted into an angry snarl.

"How dare you accuse me of killing my own son!"

"Please calm down, Angélique," Dorcas pleaded, resting a hand on her arm.

Angélique ignored Dorcas, continuing to stare at Madeleine. When she spoke, Angélique was still looking at Madeleine, but her words were directed at us. "Ask her what they did with Alexandre."

"Who?" I asked.

"Her youngest son, Alexandre. Ask her where he is."

Madeleine was still trembling with rage. "How dare you insult me like this in my own home!"

"Who is Alexandre and where is he?" I asked.

"Alexandre is my youngest son," Madeleine said. "He studied in Louisiana for a year in high school and grew close to your mother. I learned about her from him. He is the reason she came here to teach for us."

"And where is Alexandre now?" Dorcas asked.

Madeleine lowered her eyes for a beat. When she looked back at us, I could see deep pain and loss in the depths of her eyes.

"He left us not long after Aria and Lucy did," Madeleine said. "They poisoned him against his family. I don't know where he is now. I wish I did. There is so much I wish I could say to him."

She seemed very sincere to me. I could feel the weight of the gulf between Lucille and me in her words. All the conflict and pain. That need to detach yourself because you are so toxic to each other. A tale of family dysfunction as old as families.

"Convenient," Angélique muttered.

"Angélique," I said, hoping my tone carried enough warning to stop her. She got the message.

"My own life is a bit like your tragedy of Queen Catherine," Madeleine said to me. "God blessed me with a handsome husband and three sons, each of them very different. One was murdered in cold blood. Another disappeared. Their father died. Only Robert remains to give me comfort and manage our family affairs."

A sudden thought struck me. "How long has it been since your husband passed away?"

"Henri died of heart failure in 1995. Almost thirty years."

"I'd very much like to meet Robert," I said. I'd seen pictures online of him and his son, Carlton. Together they had expanded the Broussard family business from a focus on real estate and investments to tech and social media holdings over the last decade. Carlton and his assorted tech bros launched *Unis* in 2021. Still a smaller upstart in the world of social media, *Unis* was gaining ground due to Carlton's innovative strategies and the struggles experienced by other platforms. From what I could see surveying the grounds of Chateau Broussard, Robert and Carlton were keeping the Broussard fortune on life support two hundred characters at a time. I was eager to see Robert in person. An examination of his images online reminded me of the driver we chased in Picardy.

"He is away on business at the moment," Madeleine said. "But I know he would be very happy to meet you if you could schedule a return visit. Preferably without her in tow." She tossed that last sentence at Angélique. Angélique started to reply. Dorcas clasped Angélique's hand and shook her head.

"We're looking for two of the students who disappeared from your original school," I said. "Two of the five students who left here with Aria and my mother were killed recently. Their names were Greta Rosenberg and Estelle Martin. François Muir and Jacob Le Roux were abducted at their homes in Boston and Houston. We have reason to believe they were brought here."

"To Chateau Broussard?" Madeleine asked.

"To Belle Plage, at least," I said.

"We've had no contact with those students since they left in 1974," Madeleine said. "They are not here at Chateau Broussard. I noticed you neglected to mention one of them. Is it possible that Sarah Abrams was brought here too?"

Madeleine stared straight into my eyes. Her grin widened as she read my body language. She knew Sarah was in Belle Plage and wanted me to know she knew. No point in trying to deny it.

"You do know that Aria Fournier was murdered in New Orleans?" I asked.

"I heard," Madeleine said. "A tragic accident." She offered no condolences to Angélique.

"I witnessed it," I said. "There's no doubt in my mind she was intentionally run down."

"You didn't see the driver?" Madeleine asked.

"No," I said. "Their windshield was damaged, and it happened too fast."

"They didn't look like," Madeleine said slyly, "a crazed middle-aged woman trying to get revenge because mommy didn't love her enough?"

"You manipulating mentally unstable witch!" Angélique screamed.

"Okay," Delilah said, "maybe it's time to go."

I agreed. We'd hit diminishing returns a long time ago.

"Thank you for your time, Madeleine," I said. "We would like to visit again if you would permit us to."

"I would like that," Madeleine said. "It would be nice to talk with you more about your mother and her time here. I'd like to hear more about her life in Louisiana also."

We said our goodbyes. Angélique followed us sullenly, refusing to look Madeleine in the eyes. We filed outside and followed Monique down the main staircase without speaking. Monique stopped in the lavish main foyer.

"I will ask Reginald to bring your car around," Monique said. "Please wait here."

Monique walked out the front door, leaving us standing in the foyer.

"We will be lucky if they don't murder us in . . ."

Angélique's sentence was cut short. Delilah grabbed her with lightning fast reflexes, lifted her off her feet by her shirt, and slammed her against the ornate front door.

"What the hell kind of twisted game are you playing, Bitch?!" Delilah demanded.

"Not here, Delilah," I said.

Delilah ignored me.

"Why did you lie to us, Angélique?" Delilah said.

"I didn't lie to you," Angélique said, her eyes round with fear.

"Not the way it sounded to me."

"You believe her?" Angélique pleaded.

"I sure as hell don't believe you," Delilah said.

"I didn't think you would come if you knew it was me trying to get answers," Angélique said. "My mother always lived in fear of the evil here, but she never had the courage to do anything about it."

"She was doing something," I said. "She came to find me. What about it, Angélique? Who do you think killed your mother? What was she really trying to tell me? And, come to think of it, how did you get to New Orleans so soon after it happened?"

"You cannot let her get inside your head," Angélique said. "I told you I followed my mother because I was worried about her. This is what she does. Madeleine is a master manipulator."

"You don't seem so bad at it yourself," I said.

Footsteps approached the door. Delilah let go of Angélique and allowed her to step away from the door.

"We're not done, Angélique," Delilah said.

Angélique smoothed her shirt. Her eyes flitted to each of us. "Please believe me. I only want to do what is right for all of us."

I wanted to believe her. But I couldn't.

Jacques Kerouac greeted us warmly and settled us comfortably around the living room he shared with Enora. He was an energetic little man with a rugged complexion and gray hair. Their house stood behind their little inn. With several tourists still using the hotel's common area, Enora decided to invite us all back to her home to give us some privacy.

The night started surreal and continued that way. After dinner, we all walked down to the beach and found a quiet place. No small feat during vacation season. Angélique recalled fond memories of her life with Aria growing up in Paris. She spoke for about five minutes and then took the little black urn with Aria's ashes to the edge of the beach. Angélique removed the lid and poured the ashes along the beach. A strong sea breeze whipped our hair, causing the ashes to dance and scatter. We stood watching as the tide rolled closer to them. When the water reached them and began to pull them out to sea, Sarah started singing spontaneously. I was startled when the first notes rippled from her mouth. Then I settled into the melody. I knew the tune well. Sarah's beautiful voice rang across the cliffs and over the waves singing "Amazing Grace." The professor in my head pondered what Aria would think given her attraction to Wicca. The pragmatist in my head told me to shut up and enjoy the music. The pragmatist won this round. I felt a hint of moisture on the edge of my eyes as Sarah poured all she had into one last musical salute to her teacher.

Those powerful images and sounds still filled my mind as we settled onto the Kerouacs' couches and armchairs to hear Sarah's story. Sarah was seated in the comfiest of Enora's armchairs. Before she started, Trey and Daddy said they had something to share.

"We walked down to the docks today to look at the boats and get some air," Trey said.

"You like what you saw, Daddy?" Delilah asked.

"They had some nice little ships," Denny said. "Not bayou quality. But you can't expect that everywhere."

Delilah grinned at his assessment, which was exactly what we'd all expected.

"We saw a little pharmacy on the way back," Trey said. "I had a hunch, so we stepped inside. The pharmacist spoke great English. We asked him if the Broussards shopped there. He was wary of sharing information at first. The longer we talked, and the more we bought, the more he loosened up."

"He was a boat guy too," Daddy said. "Didn't take long before he was sharing local gossip. Said the Broussards don't come into town much. They mostly send their servants in to buy anything they need from the village stores. He had all kinds of great ghost stories about the chateau." He glanced at Dorcas with an unspoken promise to tell her more later.

"That's interesting," I said. "Tells us a little more about their relationship with the people of Belle Plage."

"There's more, Di," Trey said, his voice rising with excitement. "He said two servants came down from the chateau a few days ago and purchased some items. One of them was a cane."

"Madeleine has a cane," Dorcas said.

"They also purchased some medications," Trey said. "A big supply of medication."

"Could have been for them," Delilah said.

"I got the names of the medications from the pharmacist," Trey said. "I called Gladys in Boston and had her go up to François' apartment to check his medicine cabinet. Di, three of the five medicines they bought are prescribed to François. I'm guessing we'd find the other two in Jacob Le Roux's bathroom."

We sat in stunned silence.

"They are here," I finally said. "She lied to us."

"Or she doesn't know," Trey said.

Angélique rolled her eyes but didn't say anything. No one spoke for a minute.

Sensing it was her turn, Sarah's cup of tea trembled slightly as she began her story. All eyes turned to listen.

"I was orphaned when I was three," Sarah said. "My parents were killed in a car accident. They worked for Madeleine at the chateau. She arranged to place me with another family in the village and helped pay for my expenses. When I turned eight, Madeleine persuaded my foster family to send me to her new primary school. They were excited, and so was I. I'd started showing musical ability early, and my foster parents knew what an incredible opportunity it was. One they could never afford on their own."

Sarah looked at Angélique and smiled.

"Your mother started just a short while after I came. She was a marvelous teacher. Everything I've learned since was built on the foundations she laid. I enjoyed it so much . . . at first."

I leaned forward. "At first?" I prodded.

"Yes," Sarah said. She took a nervous sip of her tea. "It's hard to describe. The curriculum at the school was harsh."

"Challenging?" Trey asked.

"Brutal," Sarah said. "I remember the day I first realized something was very wrong. It was about two months before Lucy came. Two boys named Jacques and Avery started fighting in the dining hall. They turned tables over and scattered chairs everywhere. Alexandre came in and told them to stop. They didn't listen to him. They were both bloody and bruised by the time help arrived. Jacques had Avery on the ground! He was pummeling him with his fists. Then Jean-Paul and Robert came into the dining hall. Everyone froze."

"They stopped the fight?" Delilah asked.

"Alexandre thought they were going to," Sarah said, shuddering. "I could see his relief when they came in the room. Robert even walked over and grabbed Jacques' arm. He said, 'Remember Little Man, I am northwestern France's regional wrestling champion. Do not fight with me.'"

"You remember the exact words after all these years?" I asked.

Sarah groaned and shook her head. "Robert said that all the time to everyone. It was his way of intimidating people before they had a chance to start something. He was always bullying someone. Jean-Paul told Robert to let Jacques go. He walked over to one of the tables and picked up a knife."

Her voice cracked, and she took a longer drink of her tea. Delilah reached into her pocket and produced a silver flask. She screwed the top off, reached over, and poured a generous helping into Sarah's tea. Sarah gave her a grateful smile and took another deep sip.

"Jean-Paul handed Jacques the knife and told him to finish it," Sarah continued. "We were all staring in absolute horror. Jacques too. Jean-Paul told him if he was a real man he would finish it now. No one spoke for several minutes. Jacques looked down at Avery. I just knew he was going to kill him right there in front of us! But he didn't. Jacques dropped the knife and stood up. He reached his hand out and helped Avery stand."

"Sounds like he learned something valuable at the chateau," I observed.

"Diana," Sarah said, "Jean-Paul grabbed Jacques by the arm and forced him over to the table. He had Jacques spread both hands out on the table. Jean-Paul gave us all a lecture about how weaklings will never get anywhere in this world. All the while, he was stabbing the knife into the table between each of Jacques' fingers. It went on for at least ten minutes. Every time the knife went down, we all thought he was going to cut Jacques. Each time, the knife hit the wood between his fingers. When he finished his lecture, Jean-Paul asked us if we would all remember what he said. We all nodded. Anything to make it stop! He said, 'You probably will not, but you will remember this.' He raised the knife and brought it down one last time right into the center of Jacques' left hand! Jacques screamed. We all screamed. Then he pulled the knife out and handed it to Avery. 'You know what to do,' he said. Avery took the knife and stabbed Jacques' right hand. Jean-Paul made us all stand there watching and left Jacques sitting there bleeding until he finally called Monique to take him away. We stood there at least five minutes before Jacques got any help."

None of us knew what to say. I finally asked, "Didn't the other brothers try to stop him?"

"Robert was, probably still is, a sadistic bully," Sarah said. "He was enjoying it more than Jean-Paul. Jean-Paul did terrible things because he thought they were necessary. Robert does them because he enjoys hurting people. Alexandre never had the courage to stand up to them. I think he had a kind heart, but he was afraid of them too. He just watched. I think it made him sick too, but what could he do?"

"Tell Madeleine," Dorcas said.

"If you think Madeleine would care, you were not paying attention today," Angélique said.

"I grew very close to François," Sarah said. "We would go for walks on the cliffs. When we were far enough out not to be overheard, he would tell me about the terrible things they were teaching the boys. He was terrified. A week after the fight between Avery and Jacques, he woke up in the middle of the night. There was noise in the hallway on the boys' third floor wing. François looked out his door and saw four monks in red robes dragging Jacques and Avery down the hallway. Both boys were screaming and crying. They went up a stairway at the end of the hall and disappeared. François wanted to follow, but he was too scared. The house shuddered and trembled right after they went upstairs. François heard a strange whirring noise after they left. It woke Jacob up. They huddled in their room until the sun came up. There were fifteen of us at the beginning of the year. Thirteen were left after Jacques and Avery disappeared."

Monks in red robes! I glanced over at Dorcas. She raised her eyebrows and shook her head.

"There are so many more stories I could tell you leading up to the night we left," Sarah said. "Things started to change when Lucy came. She wasn't afraid of anyone. Even Robert and Madeleine didn't intimidate her. They recognized she was a problem. One night, she and Aria gathered us all in their room. It was packed with all thirteen students there. They told us they were worried about us and wanted to get us out of there. By then, no one argued with them. We all saw it. They told us we were leaving in five days in the early morning. They told us to be ready with only what we could carry."

"And that's what happened?" I asked.

"Not quite," Sarah said. "The Broussards hosted a masquerade two nights before we were supposed to leave. People milled around the lower grounds in costume, but only a few were permitted inside. We'd settled into our beds while the party was still going on outside. About two o'clock, our door slammed open. Aria woke us and told us to hurry. Estelle and I followed her into the hallway carrying our little bags. We saw two men in red robes dragging Jacqueline and Marie down the hallway. They were both crying. Another one came out of Greta's room dragging her too. Aria screamed for him to stop, but he ignored her. He'd just reached the bottom of the stairs leading to the third floor when Lucy appeared out of nowhere with a cricket bat. She smashed him twice in the head with it. Lucy hit him so hard his hood slipped down. He panicked. I'm not sure whether he was more afraid of Lucy or that we could see his face. He released Greta and ran for help."

Sarah's adrenaline rose, and she allowed the blanket to drop from her knees as she continued the story. I had no doubt the part with the cricket bat was true. Lucille's ability to swing with fury and power lingered in my memory too well.

"Lucy had François and Jacob with her. She told Aria the other boys were already gone. One of the other kids must have betrayed us. They were taking us away earlier than planned. Lucy had the bat in one hand, François' bat, and a brown satchel slung over her shoulder. She hugged it protectively the whole time like there was something of immense value inside. They led us down two flights of stairs to the cellar. We all knew there were underground tunnels all over and beyond the property. You could see where one of them came out on the beach below. But we had no idea there was an opening inside the house. Aria and Lucy shoved a bookcase aside to reveal the opening. We plunged into absolute darkness. François held my hand and guided me in the dark. We walked for what seemed like forever. I could tell we were going down. We finally reached the end and came out on the beach."

"There was a boat waiting for you?" I asked, remembering what Enora said when we arrived.

"Yes," Sarah said. "The Broussards always had several small boats with oars and a small motor for personal use. Aria and Lucy loaded us into one. They looked up then and realized that the beacon was dark."

"The beacon?" Trey asked.

"A miniature lighthouse," Enora said. "One stood at the top of the cliffs on the Chateau Broussard property. It was mounted on a large wooden platform that extended over the ocean. The Broussards would light it when ships were coming in so they could avoid the rocks along the coast. We have another one further down the cliff now outside the Broussard property line."

"You said this one 'stood' on the Broussard property," I said. "Past tense?"

Sarah nodded. "I'm getting to that."

"They needed the light of the beacon to navigate around the coast safely," Enora explained. "Without it, they risked coming to shore too soon and hitting the rocks."

"Why was it out?" Dorcas asked.

"It ran automatically most of the time," Sarah said. "Even in the seventies, computers could perform most of the basic functions. They booted and rebooted the system when needed. But the power source for the whole complex fed off the Chateau Broussard power grid. They could stop it at the chateau by flipping a switch on the fuse box."

"Which is what they did that night?" I asked.

Sarah nodded. "Lucy told Aria to get us in the boat and set out. She went back into the tunnels to see if she could turn the beacon back on. Before she left, Lucy handed the brown satchel to François and told him he must protect it at all costs. Jacob and Aria rowed us out. We floated for a bit, waiting for the light to come on. Aria was about to give up and start the engine when the platform erupted in flames."

"The light came on?" Delilah asked.

"No," Sarah said. "The entire platform was burning. I guess Lucy couldn't turn it back on, so she lit the whole thing on fire. An instant later, the other half of the wooden platform collapsed against the cliffside. We were too far out, and it was too shadowy to see it well. It hung there for a while, but pieces of it were falling every few minutes. We could see them falling and hitting the beach. François was screaming for Aria to go. She couldn't do it. Aria didn't want to leave Lucy. Finally, she had no choice. We could see flashlights blinking on the cliffs. They were climbing down. They'd have boats in the water coming after us soon. Aria started the motor. We started moving down the coast. We went a little down the coast and then we stopped. Aria killed the motor. She was still looking for signs of Lucy. That's when we heard them."

I knew what she meant, but I wanted to hear her say it. "Heard what?"

"The gunshots," Sarah said, "the ones that must have killed Jean-Paul. They rang out one after another. At the time, we were afraid they had shot Lucy. Aria started the motor again and headed for the coast. François was pleading with her to keep going out to sea, but I think the shots must have made her fear for Lucy. We reached the point where we had to stop the motor again. Aria had just shut it off when Estelle yelled and pointed. We saw someone walking along the beach. It was Lucy. She waded out to meet us and got into the boat. Aria started the motor again. We sailed down the coast. We rode for about ten minutes and then rowed into a small cove. That's where they were waiting for us."

Sarah nodded toward the Kerouacs.

"We had grown close to Aria, and we adopted Lucy too when she came to Belle Plage," Enora said. "They came to the inn a week before and asked if we could meet them at a particular cove down the coast and then give them a ride to Paris in our truck. They told us the children were in danger. We believed them. They were so sincere and looked so afraid. We got a call in the middle of the night from Aria. She had just enough time to tell us that the timeline had moved up before the connection was cut off. We got dressed and drove to the cove. We waited for three hours. They finally arrived looking exhausted and in shock. We bundled them into the truck and drove through dawn toward Paris."

"What happened when you got there?" I asked.

"We separated," Sarah said. "The boys left on a train immediately. I don't know where to. Lucy had connections with someone who was going to find them a place to stay. They told us that it was dangerous to go back to our old lives. That we were going somewhere safe. Aria promised to get in touch with my foster family and tell them I was okay. Lucy left that afternoon too. We took her to Gare du Nord. She told us goodbye. She made us promise to do whatever Aria said. She and Aria were so sad. They hugged, and Lucy got on the train. She still wore the same clothes from the night before. They were dirty and the sleeves of her shirt were torn like she'd ripped them on purpose herself. She carried the brown satchel with her."

"Where was she going?" Dad asked.

"I don't know," Sarah said. "I didn't see her ticket. I did notice the train was eastbound."

"Geneva," Dorcas said. The rest of us nodded. Based on the timeline the documents in the chest gave us, it made sense that Lucille went straight from Paris to Geneva.

"I thought that was the last time I would see her," Sarah said.

"It wasn't?" Delilah asked.

"No," Sarah said. "We stayed with Aria in Paris for a week. Then Aria took me to Omaha to meet my new family. They were amazing. I was homesick for a while, but I had a great life in Omaha. It finally started to become home. I'd been there a few months. It would have been early 1975. Around March or April, I think. One of the first warmer days that year. I was at school eating lunch outside with friends. They got up to go inside. I was about to follow them when I noticed someone sitting on a bench across the street watching us. I couldn't believe it! It was Lucy. I ran across the street to see her. It was her, but it wasn't."

"What do you mean?" I asked, giving my sisters a curious glance.

"She was still kind, but so solemn," Sarah said. "Very serious. She was never a fashionable person, but she'd worn trendy clothes in Brittany. That day, she was wearing a plain white blouse and a blue skirt. She asked me how things were going. About my music. My family. We talked until the recess bell rang. When I told her I had to leave, she took my hand and prayed for me. She was religious before, but I never remembered her doing that in Brittany."

The woman Sarah described may have been unfamiliar to her, but she was intimately familiar to me. The version Sarah encountered in Omaha sounded much more like my momma than the person Sarah had first met in Brittany. I looked over at my dad. He smiled back at me. He was thinking the same thing. Based on the time Sarah placed their last meeting, Lucille was probably on her way back to Louisiana the long way around. Possibly checking on each of her former students as she traveled back. Within four months, Etta would drag her to the parish fair one night where she met a lanky shy boy with messy black hair and a booming voice. To Etta's absolute shock, Denny Hebert broke through the shell around Lucille Broussard's heart like no one else ever had or could. They married one year later and welcomed their first daughter, Dinah Lucille Hebert, in 1977.

We sat quietly for a while, no one daring to break the silence.

"What does all this mean for today?" Trey asked. "Why would they come after all of you now after all this time?"

"I don't know," Sarah said. "They never told us why we had to start over. Nor why we were not allowed to contact each other or see each other."

"I do want to know what happened then," I said. "I need to know what happened in the past. But I think our priority should be freeing François and Jacob. The rest will fall into place while we're doing that."

The others nodded in agreement.

"How did you manage to get on the property without their permission?" I asked Angélique.

"Like I said," Angélique said, "I had a childhood friend who helped me get into the chateau."

"You said your childhood friend got your mom onto the grounds," Delilah reminded her.

"I lied, okay," Angélique said. "I was doing it for a good reason. I am sorry."

"Let's table that for now," I said. "Can your friend get us back in?"

"No," Angélique said. "They fired her last time she let me in."

"Way to go," Delilah said.

Angélique glared at her.

"What about the tunnels?" I suggested. "Or the cliffs? Could we sneak in through one of those routes?"

"Maybe," Enora said. "No one goes up on the cliffs much anymore. Especially not near the Broussard property. They have become very private over the years."

"No local guides could take us up there?" Daddy asked.

"None willing to risk the wrath of the Broussards," Jacques said. "Even the local police bow to them."

"And the tunnels?" Dorcas asked.

"The problem with the tunnels is that it is easy to get lost in them," Angélique said. "They run through the cliffs like an anthill. Some go up to the cliffs, and some go down to the beach. I have tried to get an ordinance map of the area. There are none. The Broussards brag about how they supported the Resistance during the Vichy era by allowing Resistance fighters to use the tunnels. But no one can get access to any maps of the area, either historical or contemporary. It seems the Broussards have worked very hard to keep the exact contours of the tunnels a secret to everyone but them."

"You weren't able to find any maps at all?" I asked.

"I came close to one," Angélique said. "It was a medieval drawing of the village and future grounds of the chateau. The drawing shows the tunnels as they were then. It was housed at the Sorbonne for a while. I checked. The Broussards donated it and set up strict guidelines for who can view it. They've put a ban on any digital reproductions or online versions. Unfortunately, it is on loan right now to an institution in the United States."

"Where?" I asked.

"The Minneapolis Museum of Art in Minnesota," Angélique said.

Excitement raced through me.

"I might be able to get access to it," I said.

"Really?" Angélique said in amazement.

"Possibly," I said. "I'll see if I can call in a favor."

"I was thinking about the cliffs too," Enora said. "There is someone who might be able to take you up there. His name is Michael Latimer. He has been the visiting pastor at the little mission church by the beach for three summers. Michael comes by and drinks coffee some mornings with the guests. We talk often. He loves to hike. He is not from here, so he is not intimidated by the Broussards. He explores the cliffs often."

"Would he be willing to take us up there?" I asked.

"You will have to ask him. But I would think so. He is a very kind man. Always willing to help. If he is not at the mission, you can find him most days on the beach or visiting with people at The Black Shark."

"We'll try to find him tomorrow," I said. "I will also get the ball rolling in Minneapolis."

"Thank you," Sarah said. "All of you. I haven't seen François and Jacob in fifty years. But the bond we share doesn't erode with time or distance. Please help them."

"We will," I said. I hoped it was a promise we could keep.

CHAPTER TEN

THE BLACK SHARK EXUDED COZY CHARM. Even in the early morning, about twenty people were gathered around the bar and the tables. A quaint stone fireplace in the corner conjured images of a crackling fire warming villagers as they consumed their drinks during frigid winter nights. I could almost feel the chilling sea breezes blowing through the streets, driving everyone inside their favorite watering hole to sit by the fire and tell stories into the early morning hours. The crowd looked mostly local with only one or two tourists evident among them. Maybe the tourists came later in the day.

I navigated through the wooden tables with my sisters. Trey had stayed at the hotel with Dad and Jacques to go over maps of the area. He would join us later if we succeeded in convincing Pastor Latimer to take us up into the cliffs. Rico and Ramona were assigned to twenty-four seven Sarah guard duty. All three were making the best of it. Sarah had started to treat Rico and Ramona like adopted grandchildren as they followed her around. To our surprise and delight, they were enjoying it. I guessed it was the first time either of them had that kind of relationship with a mother figure.

Delilah pulled her baseball cap lower as several patrons looked our way. She'd been recognized twice in Paris. It was less likely she'd be known to the typical resident of Belle Plage, but the abundance of tourists meant she still needed to keep a low profile if she could.

I realized when we arrived at the Black Shark that we'd neglected to ask Enora for a description of Pastor Latimer.

"Anyone know what this guy looks like?" I asked my sisters.

"We should have asked," Dorcas said.

"Our choices seem to be fishing village chic, mid-life crisis day drinker, and wizened clone of Gandalf the Grey at the bar," Delilah said. She was right. Most of the patrons were men, and the majority of them looked like fishermen coming in from their early morning catch. Or early morning bust.

"Of course, you also have hipster chic over there," Delilah said, nodding toward a younger man seated at a table in the middle of the room. The man appeared to be in his early thirties, skewing young for the Black Shark late morning demographic. He sported a well-trimmed black beard and full shoulder-length black hair that curled at the back of his neck. His plain green t-shirt, tennis shoes, and brown shorts contrasted with the fisherman's gear worn by most men in the room. Delilah's hipster looked small-framed, but very athletic and fit. He was carrying on an animated conversation at the center table with an older man wearing a fisherman's vest and cap.

We surveyed the room helplessly.

"Any of these guys look ministerial to you?" Delilah asked.

"I guess pick one and ask them if the pastor is here, Dor," I suggested.

Dorcas nodded and started toward a table with two fishermen. She changed direction when the fisherman at the center table stood up and hugged the young hipster guy. They said their goodbyes and the older man stepped away, leaving the younger man alone. Dorcas seized the opportunity. She glided past the tables and stepped up to his table just as he was sitting back down.

"*Pardon, Monsieur,*" Dorcas said. "*Je m'appelle* Dorcas Hebert. *Nous recherchons* Michael Latimer. *Pouvez-vous nous aider?*"

The man looked up in surprise. He started to say something, but he seemed at a loss for words.

Dorcas decided she must have made a mistake with her French.

"Désolé, peux-tu me comprendre?" He started to speak again. This time he was cut off by Delilah. We'd reached the table by then, and she couldn't resist the urge to "help."

"She's asking if you understand her," Delilah said, shouting over the din. "We . . . are . . . trying . . . to find . . . a pastor dude." Delilah said each word at peak volume and separated each one like you would for a toddler you're trying to help pronounce their first words.

He grinned at Delilah's performance, totally immune to her usually irresistible shock and awe approach. Even as she spoke, his eyes kept traveling back to Dorcas. She smiled timidly back at him.

Finally, he looked up at Delilah and shouted, "Of . . . course . . . I . . . understand."

I laughed at Delilah's shocked expression.

"After all," he said with a strong American accent, "nothing helps people understand a language they don't know better than shouting it at them."

"You're American," Dorcas said.

"That's what my birth certificate says. Issued by the great state of Texas in the tiny hamlet of Dallas. It also tells me my name is Michael Latimer."

"You're the one we're looking for," Dorcas said.

"Then I'm a very lucky man," Michael said.

I watched him as he gazed at her. There was something different in the way he looked at her. Nothing lustful or creepy. His eyes seemed full of wonder and awe. I'd been struggling to put a label on it. The word "enchanted" floated to the surface. I thought I saw Dorcas' cheeks flush slightly when Michael said he was a "lucky man."

"I'm sorry I assumed you were French," Dorcas said.

"No apologies necessary," Michael said. "I love the French. Besides, I found your French very charming, Dorcas Hebert."

Dorcas' cheeks flushed a very deep crimson this time. Her wide brown eyes were sparkling. Delilah noticed it too. She gave me a covert sideways look that said, "What is happening?" I winked at her.

"These are my sisters, Diana and Delilah," Dorcas said. "We'd like to ask you for a favor if you don't mind."

"Absolutely," he said.

Michael gestured to the seat across from him and rose to drag two more chairs from a neighboring table. Once we were seated, he said, "How can I help?"

"We need to explore the cliffs above Belle Plage," I said. "We're staying with the Kerouacs. Enora said you were the best person to guide us up there."

It was the first time I had spoken. Michael did a double-take, studied me for a moment, then smiled at me.

"I knew you looked familiar," he said. "You're the professor who helped take down the Emerson Network. I've seen your interviews on YouTube and heard you on a couple of podcasts."

"Guilty as charged," I said. "Hope they weren't friends of yours."

"Not at all," Michael said. "I don't mix with authoritarians, racists, and sexual predators. Emerson got what he deserved. They were giving Christianity a bad name and harming a lot of people. Thank you for exposing them."

Not something I got to hear often. I didn't know what to say, so I just nodded and smiled back. Delilah looked slightly irritated. She was the family celebrity always recognized by strangers and the glamorous sister who got the lion's, or lioness', share of male attention. Our superstar sister wasn't sure how to process her sisters soaking up the adulation.

Michael's mental gears were turning. Apparently, the revelation of my own identity linked other threads in his mind too.

"Hebert," he said. "You're the sisters from that demonologist family, the ones in the movies."

"That's us," Dorcas said.

Another thought occurred to him, and his eyes softened. "I heard about your mother. I'm very sorry."

"Thank you," I said.

Delilah nodded.

Dorcas tried to thank him but couldn't speak. Tears pooled in her eyes and trickled down her cheeks. She managed to smile at him through her tears and mouthed the words, "Thank you." I decided I liked Michael Latimer at that moment. I could see in his eyes that he would give anything to take her pain away.

"I can help you," Michael said, turning back to the topic at hand. "I spend a lot of time hiking those cliffs during the summer. I'll take some of the college students that come to worship at the mission with me sometimes. So, I'm used to guiding people up there. You do know the Broussards are very private? They don't always like it when people go up there. I try to be careful not to cross their property line."

"We're aware," I said. "They're actually our cousins. Hopefully that will buy us some goodwill."

"One can always hope," Michael said with a smile. "Things are light at the mission today. I'm free until sunset worship tonight."

"Sunset worship?" Dorcas asked.

"We gather on the beach at sunset and sing," he said. "I do a short devotional. We visit afterwards and sort of talk about our day together."

"That sounds nice," Dorcas said.

"You should join us tonight if you're free," Michael said eagerly.

"Thanks," Delilah said. "Not my thing."

"I'll take a pass too," I said, "but thank you."

Dorcas looked disappointed.

"You should go, Dor," I said.

She looked surprised. "Well, I'm not sure I want to go alone."

"I could come by and pick you up," Michael said. "Maybe we could get some dinner and then head over to the beach."

Dorcas' eyes were giving off that sparkling effect again. She looked uncertainly over at me.

"Sounds great to me," I said. "We've got everything covered tonight. You should go."

Dorcas looked at Delilah. Delilah grinned and nodded.

"Okay," Dorcas said. "It's a date. I mean, you know, it's a plan."

"Sounds great," Michael said. "Looking forward to it. Everyone will enjoy meeting you. How soon will you be ready to climb the cliffs?"

"Can you give us about thirty minutes?" I asked.

"Can do. I'll meet you at the inn."

We thanked him and headed back there.

"Hey Di, what's the difference between a date and a plan?" Delilah asked, grinning mischievously.

"I always say it's what happens afterwards," I teased.

"You don't think he thinks I expect something from him?" Dorcas asked anxiously.

"I think he hopes you do," Delilah said.

I smacked her on her right arm.

"Ow!" she said.

"Stop pretending," I said. "You know that didn't hurt."

"It's a matter of principle," Delilah said.

"I hope it goes okay," Dorcas said. "I haven't . . . had plans . . . in a long time."

I wrapped my arm around her and pulled her close.

"Don't be nervous," I said. "You're just going to a worship service together."

"That would make me nervous," Delilah said.

I laughed and said, "Just enjoy getting to know someone new. No expectations. Just have fun."

She nodded and returned my hug.

Trey met us in the lobby.

"Any word from Minneapolis yet?"

I held up my phone for him to see my text exchange with Aidan Carlisle.

Trey laughed. "He really doesn't bow to text lingo, does he?"

"Not at all," I said. "He still insists on writing grammatically pristine paragraphs. What none of the kids are doing these days."

I'd explained, in abbreviated format, why we needed to see the medieval map of Belle Plage and the complications we faced in getting access.

Aidan replied:

FRANKLIN CENTER DOESN'T HAVE ACCESS, BUT I HAVE A FRIEND AT THE ART INSTITUTE. I WILL SEE WHAT I CAN DO.

"Franklin Center?" Trey asked.

"That's his version of what Aubrey wants me to do at Tulane," I explained. I'd mentioned Aubrey's offer in my messages to Aidan too.

He responded:

OF COURSE, I HAVE THOUGHTS. I WILL SHARE SOON.

In one small step for communication and one giant leap for Aidan Carlisle, he'd actually shared a winking face emoji.

"A graduate student must have convinced him to try emojis," I said. "Hopefully we'll have an answer soon."

Michael arrived right on time. We introduced him to Trey, gathered our things, and headed up the trail to the cliffs.

Michael and Dorcas walked ahead of us carrying on a nonstop enthusiastic conversation. Delilah took the middle with Trey and I bringing up the rear. Trey stopped at one point to help me over a particularly steep rise on the cliffside.

"Dor seems to be having a good time," Trey said with a knowing smile.

"You think?" I said, returning his conspiratorial grin.

"Does this mean we get to return all her matchmaking energy over the years?" he asked.

"With interest," I said.

A breathtaking view greeted us when we reached the summit of the cliffs. The ocean filled the horizon as far as we could see. Azure blue rippled with glistening white waves.

"It still takes my breath away," Michael said. "No matter how many times I see it."

I breathed in the briny air. The gentle Atlantic winds massaged my face. So different from the intense humidity in Nashville and Picardy this time of year.

"How high are we, Michael?" Trey asked.

"About seventy to a hundred feet," Michael said. "Not the highest on the Breton coast. There are places near the English Channel where the cliffs rise to two hundred thirty feet."

"It's beautiful," Dorcas said.

"Absolutely," I said.

For once, Delilah had nothing to add. She seemed as awestruck by the view as the rest of us. I turned slightly and looked toward the looming silhouette of Chateau Broussard nestled on the edge of the cliffs.

Michael followed my gaze.

"They've gained the whole world," he said. "But you have to wonder what they've lost along the way."

I noticed a figure standing in the distance. Nearer to us than the chateau, but still beyond the Broussard property line. The black dress and veil were unmistakable. Madeleine stood on the edge of the cliff, facing out to the sea. Something wooden or cement extended for a foot beyond the cliff edge where she stood.

"What's she doing?" I whispered.

No one answered. We all watched quietly as she continued looking toward the horizon, totally oblivious to our presence. The wind whipped her dress and veil.

"What's that in front of her?" Dorcas asked.

"That's what's left of the old beacon that used to be up here," Michael said. "The village old timers have told me about it. It was built with a big wooden platform around it. The one that collapsed the night Jean-Paul Broussard was murdered."

Madeleine raised her right hand. I could barely make out the yellow rose in her grasp. She held it over the cliff and released it. We watched it spiral through the air toward the beach below.

"What are you doing here!"

We all jumped at the harsh bellow.

I looked to my right. Robert Broussard stood glaring at us just beyond the Broussard property line wearing a black button-up shirt and jeans with his arms folded. He looked just like his pictures.

"Well?" Robert said. "Why are you spying on my mother?"

His English was good.

"We're just out for a hike, Robert," Michael explained. "We don't mean any harm."

"What you mean and what you do are two different things," Robert growled.

"We're just enjoying the scenery, Robert," Michael assured him. "We'll be gone soon."

"It would be good if you and your perverted religion were gone from here for good," Robert said. "If only the popes had exterminated your bastard religion five hundred years ago."

"But you have to ask yourself, Robert," Michael said, "could the Catholics have given us VeggieTales?"

Robert's expression clearly communicated he wasn't a fan of VeggieTales or Michael's sense of humor.

"You seem pretty eager to pick a fight, Friend," Trey said. I grabbed his hand and squeezed.

"Be careful who you challenge, Little Man," Robert said dismissively. "You are talking to France's northwestern regional wrestling champion for six consecutive years."

"Why couldn't you win a seventh?" Trey asked mildly.

Michael tried to suppress his laugh; it slipped through anyway. Robert was not amused.

"You think you can mock me on my own land!" Robert roared.

Seizing the opportunity, I said, "We're more interested in what you were doing on our land. I think we've met before, Robert."

"I don't know what you mean," Robert said. His discomfort was palpable.

"He doesn't remember, Delilah," I said.

"I wouldn't want to remember either," Delilah said. "That was pretty uninspired driving."

"I always drive amazing!" Robert screamed. I didn't know whether to be afraid or amused. It sounded so ridiculous coming from a middle-aged man.

"Not always, Rain Man," Delilah said. "My little sister drove your ass into the ground in Louisiana."

Dorcas gulped.

"You will leave now," Robert said, abruptly changing the subject. "My mother wants her privacy."

"We'll go," I said. "Just one more thing. We're looking for two men named Jacob Le Roux and François Muir. They were abducted in Boston and Houston in the States. Do you know anything about them?"

"Why should I care about the whereabouts of two old men?" Robert thundered. "I don't have time to concern myself with the welfare of cripples."

He realized his mistake when he saw the triumphant expression on my face.

"Who said one of them was a cripple?" I asked.

"You will leave now!" Robert screamed.

"Let's go," I said to the others.

As we started to walk away, Michael paused for a moment and turned back to Robert.

"Just remember, Robert," he said, "Goliath was a big man too. It's a dangerous game to elevate yourself above others. Sooner or later, someone's going to knock you down."

"Let them try," Robert said.

We spent about fifteen minutes walking around to get a sense of the topography before we started back to Belle Plage. I looked back and saw Madeleine watching us descend the cliffs from her perch beside the old beacon.

Around six that evening, I slipped into the room Dorcas and Delilah were sharing. Dorcas was sitting in front of the mirror wrestling with a tangle in her hair. Delilah was lying across the bed on her stomach watching Dorcas.

"I told her I would help with her makeup when she gets done with her hair," Delilah said, "But that seems to be taking a while."

"I just can't get it right," Dorcas moaned. "I really shouldn't care anyway. It's not officially a date."

I took the brush from her. "Let me help you, Sweetie."

I slid the brush through her thick black hair, smoothing it like fine silk. She started to calm down a little.

"It's been a long time since we've done this," I said.

Dorcas smiled. "I always loved it when you fixed my hair."

As I stroked her hair, images from the past floated through my mind. I saw myself sitting in front of the mirror in our room getting ready for prom. Delilah had already dressed and gone downstairs. I was sixteen and preparing for a night I'd been anticipating for years. I stared at myself in the mirror, admiring my beautiful red dress, which complimented my dark hair so well. I was fine until I reached for my brush and started fixing my hair. That was when I broke.

Delilah came back upstairs to find me face down in my dress sobbing into my comforter.

"Hey," Delilah said. "What's wrong? I can help you with your hair and makeup. No big deal."

"It's not that," I sniffled.

"What," Delilah tried to joke, "you afraid I'm gonna outshine you?"

I wanted her to make me feel better. But I was breaking too much inside.

"I want Dinah," I said, dissolving into heaving sobs again.

Delilah looked hurt, but she understood. Every version of this night I had imagined included Dinah sharing it with us. She never would. It was one of the few times Delilah broke her no contact rule as a teenager and pulled me into a hug. Somehow, we managed to pull it together and make it to prom. It was a great night in so many ways. But I couldn't help feeling Dinah's absence so much that night.

"What's wrong, Diana?" Dorcas asked.

I realized tears were trickling down my cheeks.

"Nothing, Sweetie," I said. "It's just . . . I'm so sorry I wasn't there to do this for you all those years."

Dorcas reached up and took my hand. Her eyes were teary now too. Her voice quavered slightly when she said, "You're here to do it now. That's all that matters."

"Okay, people," Delilah said. "No painter wants to work with a wet canvas. Dry it up so I can work my magic."

Dorcas and I exchanged a grin, wiped our eyes, and made room for Delilah.

We watched Dorcas and Michael stroll out of the inn and down the street from our second story window half an hour later.

"She looks beautiful," I said.

"We do good work," Delilah said. "Of course, we had a perfect subject."

"I hope they have a good time," I said.

"You think he looks a little bit like Dad when he was younger?" Delilah said. "You know, with that black beard and all."

"Let's not unpack that," I said, rolling my eyes. My phone buzzed in my pocket. I pulled it out and saw Aidan had sent an update.

MAP IS ALREADY ARRANGED FOR RETURN TRANSPORT. THEY COULDN'T GIVE US ACCESS TO IT HERE, BUT THEY DID ACCEPT OUR HELP TRANSPORTING IT BACK TO PARIS. IF YOU CAN BE AT CHARLES DE GAULLE IN TWO DAYS AND FIND A PRIVATE PLACE TO LOOK AT IT, OUR DELIVERY PERSON CAN LET YOU EXAMINE IT FOR A FEW MINUTES BEFORE WE RETURN IT TO THE SORBONNE.

It wasn't ideal, but it could work. I quickly texted a response, thanking him and promising to be at Charles de Gaulle in two days to intercept the map. As an afterthought, I reminded him about Aubrey's offer. His response came a few minutes later.

I'M SENDING MY ANSWER WITH THE MAP.

That's cryptic. Aidan enjoyed his riddles.

"What's up?" Delilah asked.

"Looks like we're heading back to Paris for a day or two."

We met Trey and Daddy downstairs, and I shared Aidan's message.

"We need it," Trey said. "There was no sign of an opening for those tunnels on our side of the line today. The opening must be on the Broussard side. We're going to have to find some kind of guide to get us in."

"And, just as important, get you out," Daddy said. "If everything goes right, you're going to be coming out with two frail men who have spent days as prisoners. They're not going to be able to move fast. You need to know exactly where you're going."

"I don't know if we can put that kind of confidence in a medieval map," I said, "but it's better than no map at all."

"Sounds good to me," Delilah said. "Rico and Ramona can stay here with Sarah. They can keep laying low until we get back."

"There's one more thing," I said. Looking at Dad and Trey, I warned, "You're not going to like it."

"What's that, Angel?" Dad said.

"I've been thinking about the satchel Momma took from Chateau Broussard," I said. "Sarah said she still had it with her when she left on the train."

"You think that's what she left for us in Geneva?" Trey asked.

"Yes. I'm sure of it. I think we need it."

"Okay," Daddy said. "We'll go get it."

"You need to go get it," I said.

"She left the note for you, Angel," Dad said.

"Yes," I said, "but you're the official next of kin. All my official documents have got a different name on them. They're going to be more likely to release whatever is in that box to you. You need to go get it for us."

"Okay," Dad said. "No problem. I guess Dorcas and I can head that way from Paris in a couple of days."

"We're going to need Dorcas to help us with any French translation challenges," I said.

"Hold on a minute," Trey said. "If you think there is any way we are leaving you three alone, you can forget it."

"Sounds like the boys don't think we can handle things without them," Delilah said sarcastically.

"That's not it and you know it," Trey said. "I can't leave you, Di." Trey rose and walked out of the room.

"Give us a minute," I said to Dad and Delilah.

I caught up with Trey in the hallway.

"You can't ask me to leave you, Di," he said. "Especially with creepy characters like Robert stalking us."

I cupped his face in my hands.

"Trey, you have to do this for me," I said. "We need whatever Lucille left in that bank. I can feel it. Dad has the best chance of getting it for us."

"Then send Delilah," Trey insisted.

"I need to know he's safe," I said. I felt myself starting to cry. I didn't want to. I didn't want to guilt him into doing it in any way. Trey wrapped his arms around me and pulled me close.

"I can't lose him, Trey," I said. "Not so soon after Lucille. You're the one I trust to get him back safely. Please."

Trey knew my logic was irrefutable and my emotional appeal irresistible.

"You will promise not to take any unnecessary risks until we get back?"

"Absolutely," I said.

"You will keep your sisters with you at all times?"

"Definitely," I promised.

"You will let me win all arguments for the next year?"

"Why start now?" I said, burying my face in his chest.

The paths forward lay, at least for now, in Paris and Geneva. Two lives depended on us. Maybe many more.

CHAPTER ELEVEN

MAY 3, 1995

"You're hoarding those M&M's like your life depends on it," Trey complained. "Give me a couple."

"You took forever separating all the greens," I said through a mouthful of chocolate. "I think you touched every single one."

"My fingerprints give it flavor, Sweetheart," Trey said, snatching the pack back.

"Gross," I said. "I like my M&M's with the color still on them. How long are you going to keep quoting that old movie?"

"Pretty good, huh?" he said. "I think I sound just like that dude. My dad says I do too."

"Is he a voice expert now?"

"It's his favorite actor and his favorite movie," Trey said. "Who knows better than him? I might just quote it forever."

"Just a phase," I said, rolling my eyes and snatching the pack back. "You miss having all the M&M's to yourself?"

"No!" Trey said emphatically. "You're not allowed to miss any more school for the rest of the year. I listened to Kevin go on and on at lunch about the rabbits they're raising to show this fall. Who cares about rabbits?"

"Warner Brothers?"

He laughed and handed me the remainder of the M&M's. I tried not to show how pleased I was that Trey missed me. I glanced down the sidewalk to see if Dinah was coming. Trey and I were sitting on the bench outside the school beside the bus drop-off area. Everyone but the kids in detention or band practice were gone.

"What's she doing?" Trey asked.

"I don't know," I said. "She just said she had a meeting after school. Delilah rode home with Tianna and her sister, and Momma picked Dor up in Aria's rental car."

"What's it like having her around for a change?" Trey asked. He was genuinely curious. Trey's dad Jerry worked as an accountant. His mom Mary taught second grade at Picardy's elementary school. And, yes, everyone absolutely had maximum fun with the "Jerry" and "Mary" rhyming thing. They returned home most days in time for family dinner, but we never knew when Momma and Daddy would be back after they left for an investigation.

"I don't really know," I said. "I mean, she's there. But so are those other people too. It's not normal."

"Heberts and not normal?" Trey grinned. "That's new."

I laughed and shoved him playfully.

"If I fall off this bench, you may never get fresh M&M's again," Trey said.

"I'm sure there'd be someone to throw me a pack and quote some fossilized movie," I teased.

"Not like me, Sweetheart," Trey said, winking at me.

I smiled back at him. He rose and walked over to the trash can to deposit our spent wrapper. As I watched him, an unexpected wave of emotion swept over me. In spite of what I said, a conviction nestled deep in my heart that no one ever could or would fill Trey's place in my life. The depth and strength of my feelings surprised me. And scared me a little too.

"Sorry it took me so long," Dinah said as she hurried down the sidewalk, her keys jangling in her hand. She was carrying three intimidating books.

"Are those dictionaries?" I asked.

"No," Dinah said. "Just extra studying."

"I thought the whole point of graduation was to escape studying?" Trey said.

"You're in for a rude awakening," Dinah said. She guided us to our brown station wagon, and we set out for home.

My heart leaped when I saw the big brown truck parked in our front yard.

"Daddy's home!" I said.

Dinah smiled beside me. Trey leaned forward in the backseat. We glided down our little dirt and gravel driveway past our blue barn. Dinah eased us into the faded spot in our tall grass where the station wagon usually rested from its labors.

Daddy met us at the door with Dorcas already wrapped around his neck and back. He hugged Dinah and me fiercely. After he released us, he thumped Trey on the back and shook his hand.

"It's so good to see you kids," he said. "Missed you."

"Did Momma tell you what's been going on?" Dinah asked.

"A little bit," Daddy said. "They seem pretty happy today. Got a couple of phone calls from the people they've been trying to get in touch with."

"Good," Dinah said. "It's been a little tense around here."

"Your momma's been tense?" Daddy said, trying his best to sound astonished. He was rewarded with resounding laughter. "I think they're almost done. That Aria lady said something about how they might be able to pick up and leave by early next week."

"Early next week!" I said.

Dinah regarded me with a smile and a raised eyebrow.

"Which is great," I said through slightly gritted teeth. "We love having them here."

"Not what you said this morning," Trey said.

Daddy laughed and said, "Any of you want to go down to the river and throw a line in? I think they might be bitin'."

"Sure," I said. Trey nodded.

"I can't right now," Dinah said. I noticed she was holding her books slightly down so they wouldn't draw as much attention. "You should take Angélique."

I wasn't thrilled with the idea. I wanted Daddy to myself for a little while. Well, myself and Trey.

"She has been kind of moping around today," Daddy agreed. "Might be good for her."

We tramped through the living room. I went upstairs to change into shorts and a t-shirt. I grabbed a pair of Trey's old shoes we kept in my room for these occasions and hurried downstairs. I heard Momma's voice as I passed the office. She was talking with someone on the phone. Her voice carried a sentimental tone I rarely heard.

"It's so good to hear from you, François," Momma said. "How are Evelyn and the children? Another one! When?"

I hurried past the office to the kitchen. Dorcas was standing on a chair by the sink wrestling with a jar of peanut butter.

"What are you doing, Dor?" I asked.

"Dinah said she was going to fix me a peanut butter sanditch," Dorcas said, "but she's still upstairs."

"It's sandwich, Dor," I said.

"I'll take one of those, please," Dorcas said. "With peanut butter and jelly."

"You'd be annoying if you weren't so cute," I said, unscrewing the peanut butter jar.

"Momma's friend said I was cute too," Dorcas said.

"Aria?" I asked absentmindedly while I opened the bread.

"No. The lady who gave me this by the barn."

I looked over my shoulder. Dorcas had just pulled a Tootsie Roll out of her pocket and was unwrapping it. Something about the situation rang alarm bells in my head. After all, I was a nineties kid living in the shadow of the eighties. Not to mention my parents were obsessed with Satan. We knew all about what happened when you took candy from strangers.

"What lady?" I asked.

"I don't know," Dorcas said. "The lady with the red and gray hair. By the barn."

I set the peanut butter jar down and crouched to Dorcas' eye level.

"What did the lady say, Sweetie?"

"She said she was momma's friend and that I was very cute," Dorcas said. "I asked her if she wanted me to get Momma. But she said she would see her later. I think maybe she was looking for somethin' in the barn."

My heart raced. Something felt wrong.

"Sweetie, can I have this?" I asked, gently taking the candy from her. I didn't really think there was anything wrong with it, but you could never be too careful.

"But she gave it to me, Deborah!" Dorcas said crossing her arms and giving me a sour expression.

"Debbie," I said. "And I'll trade you some M&M's for it when Trey gets a new pack."

Delayed gratification didn't exist in Dorcas' world. She nodded, but her frustration was written all over her face.

"Come with me," I said. I led her to the office. It was quiet inside. I looked through the door and saw Momma sitting at the desk with her face buried in her hands like she was resting. I knocked on the door. Momma raised her head and attempted a weary smile when she saw us.

"What is it, Deborah? Everything okay?"

"Momma," I began. "I don't know if this is anything important. But I thought . . ."

"Debbie took the candy your friend gave me," Dorcas blabbed. *Little tattletale!*

"Aria knows she shouldn't be handing out candy without permission," Momma said.

"Not Aria," Dorcas said, waving her hands in frustration at this world of silly adults who just don't get it. "The red-haired lady by the barn!"

I'd tried to repress memories over the years of sitting in the backseat of our car while my momma stood outside facing down a man having what my parents called a "full-on demonic attack." He screamed, raved, and threatened Momma while she stood boldly staring him down with nothing more than a crucifix and prayers. Whether it was the prayers, as Momma claimed, or Daddy's timely arrival, as he claimed, we survived the encounter. It was one of the last times our parents took us with them before they started leaving us in Dinah's care. I'd seen my momma face all kinds of terrors with barely a flinch, but the sight of her at that moment terrified me. The color drained completely from her face, and her hands visibly trembled. She rose from her seat and circled the desk to place her hands on Dorcas' shoulders.

"What did this lady say to you, Dorcas?" Momma's voice was steady despite her body language.

"She said I was cute," Dorcas said with pride. "And she said she was coming to see you soon, Momma. Won't that be fun?"

Momma pulled Dorcas to her, hugging her fiercely. She looked up at me.

"Thank you, Deborah," she said. "You did the right thing."

"Do you want me to tell Daddy?" I asked.

"No," Momma shook her head. "Let's just keep it between us for now. I will take care of it. Are you going fishing?"

She'd noticed my clothes.

"Yes, Ma'am."

"Be sure to leave Dorcas with Dinah and tell Dinah to watch her closely," Momma said.

"I will."

We left Momma in the office, looking more concerned and tired than when we found her. I led Dorcas up the stairs to Dinah's room. Dinah was spread across her bed on her stomach, one of the enormous books opened in front of her.

"Dinah, can you watch Dorcas for a bit?" I asked.

Dinah tried not to show her frustration. "Momma can't do it?"

"She said for you to," I answered apologetically.

Dinah patted the bed beside her, and Dorcas scrambled up by her side.

I left Dinah's room, stopped by mine for a minute, and started for the stairs. I passed the guest room where Aria and Angélique were staying together. I noticed Aria sitting on the bed, gazing down at her chest. As I continued watching, I realized she was staring at the silver pendant she always wore around her neck.

"Hello, Deborah," Aria said without looking up. "Curious?"

"I'm sorry," I said, feeling my cheeks burn bright.

"Not at all, *ma chère*," Aria said, beckoning me to come closer.

I walked into the room, my eyes analyzing the silver pendant and the exotic shape at its center.

"It's called a pentagram," Aria explained. "It's an ancient symbol."

"Momma says it's the devil's symbol," I said automatically in obedience to a lifetime of programming.

Aria smiled sadly. "Some say it is. Some may use it that way, but most who do are just pretending. I don't worship the devil. I don't believe in the devil."

"But who tempts us to do bad things if it's not the devil?" I asked, genuinely curious.

"Unfortunately, there is more than enough bad in all of us for us to do terrible things," Aria said. "Unspeakable things. At least, that is what I believe."

"Momma wouldn't like that," I said.

"No," Aria said. "Your momma and daddy have their own beliefs. I respect them. I just don't share them."

"But she's your friend," I said. I knew the statement was obvious. But to me it was also revolutionary.

"Yes, we are."

"How?" I asked. "I mean, Momma says we have to be careful about mixing with folks who don't believe or who believe other things. I think that's why she disapproves of Trey. Because his parents don't go to church."

"You might be surprised," Aria said with a twinkle in her eyes. "Lucille is very grumpy sometimes. Well, most of the time, I think. But she loves Trey more than you think. She loves you all more than she can show. She has never been good at that."

"What are you doing with that, Aria?" I pointed to the pendant.

"Do you pray, Deborah?" Aria asked.

"Sometimes," I said.

"That's what I was doing," she said. "Praying. Meditating. Reflecting."

"Praying for what?"

"For my sweet Angélique. For you and your family. For our friends so far away. That we will all be safe."

"Who do you pray to?" I asked.

"We call them the goddess and the god, the lady and the lord," Aria said. "They represent different things to different people. To me they represent the elemental forces of nature. The balance that unites us all. Your momma and I chose different paths years ago. She follows the teachings of Jesus and believes she must confront the powers of darkness in his strength. My path led me to embrace Wicca, a religion of the earth and sky. A belief in the magical elemental forces that bind us all together."

"Do you have rules like we do?" I asked.

"An' it harm none, do what you will." Aria smiled at my confused expression. "It means do no harm to others and you may do what you like. It's a way of freedom and love for others. You would say, 'Do to others what you would have them do to you.'"

"That's what Jesus said," I said, stating the obvious again.

"Very true," Aria said. "We may not all follow the same paths or believe the same things. But the intended destinations are the same. I believe there are fundamental needs in every human heart for purpose, love, and grace. I may not find them fulfilled in the same way your momma does, but I can respect her way and, maybe someday, she can grow to respect mine."

She placed the end of the necklace in my hands. I ran my fingers over the silver pentagram, noting its smooth texture and ornate design.

"I gave one of these to your mother years ago," Aria said. "I told her to show it to anyone who knows me, and they would always be her friend. I make the same promise to you, *ma petite*. You will always have a friend in me. When you see this symbol, know that there is someone who will stand beside you no matter what."

"Thank you," I said, not sure what else to say. Aria studied me as I studied the necklace. She smiled at me.

"There was a Wiccan teacher named Doreen Valiente who wrote a poem in 1964 expressing fundamental ideals commonly held by Wiccans,"

Aria continued. "We call them our 'Rede' or wise counsel. A verse of her poem reminds me so much of you, Deborah. 'Light of eye and soft of touch, speak you little, listen much.' Your loving heart and curious mind will serve you well. Hold on to them both. Never lose them. Or yourself."

"Debbie!" Trey called from downstairs.

Aria patted my hand. "Go and enjoy."

"Thank you," I said. I wasn't sure what I was thanking her for, but I felt grateful deep inside. As we parted and I started down the stairs, I knew I would be thinking about our conversation for a long time to come.

Angélique, Trey, and I followed Daddy down to the riverbank and set up in an area near some old fallen trees resting in the water. Daddy hoped the fish would be gathering near the limbs. He baited our hooks with worms and placed each of us strategically along the bank.

Trey and I each got a bite after about twenty minutes. Trey wrestled with his fish for several minutes before it escaped with his worm. I managed to lift mine out of the water into my daddy's waiting hands. As Daddy swept my catch off the hook, he reached over and pulled me close for a hug.

"Good job, Angel," Daddy said. "You guided him in like a pro."

I noticed Angélique watching us. Something about her expression made me curious. She looked longing and sad. Angélique showed in her handling of the fishing pole and the awkward stance she adopted that she had no fishing experience. At one point, she tried to cast and tangled her line in the thick tree branches sticking up out of the water. Angélique tugged helplessly at the line trying to free it.

"Looks like you're stuck," Trey said.

"Obvious much?" I said.

Angélique turned red and continued tugging, finally stomping her foot in frustration.

"Hold on, Angélique," Daddy said. He hurried over and grasped her pole. "If you keep jerking on it, it'll just get more tangled." He patiently worked the line until most of it was free. He pulled it back in.

"Now," Daddy said. "Let's see what we can do." He reset Angélique's line and cupped his hands over hers as he guided her to cast it out. This time, her bait hit open water. He stood for a while beside her, giving her instructions on how to adjust for the current.

We kept fishing without another catch until dusk began to creep over the river. Daddy mentioned that we should probably collect our gear and head back for supper. I was pulling my line back in when I heard a shout beside me. Angélique's pole was shaking in her hands. Daddy raced to her and helped her steady it.

"Pull!" Daddy said.

Angélique pulled the line toward her with supreme effort. I saw the fish rise to the surface, bucking and pulling against her line. Angélique spun her reel with Daddy's guidance. The fish came flopping to shore.

"Look at that!" Daddy said, clapping Angélique on the back. "You did amazing, Angélique."

Trey and I gathered to admire the catch.

"Good job, Angélique," I said.

"This one is destined for the dinner table," Daddy said.

Angélique beamed with excitement as she looked at the fish flopping at her feet.

"I'm proud of you, Angélique," Daddy said.

I saw the emotion rippling through every inch of Angélique's face before the tears burst forth. It surprised us all. She began sobbing and heaving, her breaths coming in quick gasps.

"Hey, what's wrong?" Daddy asked. He hesitated for a moment and then decided it was better to risk a hug than leave her sobbing without comfort. Daddy pulled Angélique into his massive arms. She buried her head in his shoulder and sobbed for a couple more minutes. When she finally recovered, Angélique said, "*Merci, je suis désolée.*" She turned and hurried back toward our house.

The rest of us collected our things and the two fish. As we walked back, I let Trey get ahead of us.

"Daddy, what was wrong with her?" I asked.

He rested one hand around my shoulders as we followed the darkening trail.

"Angel, I don't think she's ever known what it's like to have a daddy," he said. "I might be the first man who's ever said he was proud of her."

"That's awful," I said, suddenly realizing how lucky I am.

"It is," Daddy said. "I'm glad we took her today."

"Me too," I said.

It was fun gathering around the table with everyone that night. Momma served a generous meal of fried chicken, mashed potatoes, and green beans. We enjoyed the meal along with a peach cobbler and a rare indulgence of ice cream. Afterwards, we all played board games in the living room until bedtime when Momma sent Trey home. It was a rare night of no drama in the Hebert house.

I settled into bed and looked across at Delilah's empty bed. She was staying at Tianna's house for the night. Momma agreed on the strict condition that they get to school on time the next day. I laid long odds on them actually making it to school. Momma could be a little too trusting when she was distracted with other things.

I rolled over and slipped into a deep sleep filled with dreams of flopping fish and gleaming pendants. Something woke me a few hours later. I rolled over and saw it was 3:30 on my alarm clock. I stumbled out of bed and went to the bathroom. After I finished, I filled a cup of water at the sink to wet my parched throat. I walked down the hall toward my room carrying the cup of water. I'd just reached my door when I heard someone moving quietly downstairs. I slid up to the banister that lined the edge of our stairs. My position gave me a perfect view of the hallway and our front door. It also hid me perfectly from people looking up. We'd often used that convenient hiding place to our advantage.

Momma was bending over beside the door, slipping her black ankle boots on. She was dressed in what Delilah called her "battle gear" behind her back. Momma wore her typical long skirt and white blouse with her hair pulled back into a tight bun. Something bulged slightly underneath the skirt at her hip. I had always wondered what it was but never worked up the courage to ask. Momma stood straight and patted her blouse around her waist and then her skirt just below her waist. It looked like she was checking to make sure something was fastened well underneath. Last of all, she raised her right leg and felt for something near her ankle. Evidently satisfied that all was in place, Momma slid out the front door and closed it quietly behind her.

I wanted to follow her, but I could imagine the fury that would greet me if she caught me. I padded back to my room and looked out the window. Momma was walking past the barn toward the woods. She crested the hill overlooking our house and stood still for a moment. I wasn't sure if it was a trick of the light or my imagination. For a second as the clouds rolled away and the moon shone brighter, I was sure I saw two silhouettes of my momma standing on the hill. At least, the silhouettes were so similar they looked like the same person. I realized there were slight differences as I continued to stare. The momentary moonlight gave way to clouds again, and I lost them in the gathering darkness. I waited patiently for the moon to reappear. When it did, the two silhouettes were gone.

I returned to my bed, resolved to check again in a few minutes. That resolve drifted away as sleep claimed me once again.

CHAPTER TWELVE

BANQUE GENÈVE
Reference # 12181991

Manuscript Held In Trust For Boxholder 763

An Excerpt from

DARK CONFESSIONS (1975)

By Lucille A. Broussard

Lucy woke every morning of the first two weeks not knowing where she was. It took a moment for her to run her eyes over the ornate furnishings of her room before she realized they were the walls of Chateau Broussard. She'd then glance over to see Aria sleeping soundly still, her chest rising and falling beneath her white comforter. Lucy was accustomed to early mornings from her years on the family farm. She would throw off her blanket and start getting ready. Aria replaced her at the sink after she stepped into the bathtub. They had settled into a well-oiled routine by the end of the second week.

Aria, Lucy, and Justine, the math teacher, would gather the girls on their floor and guide them downstairs each morning for breakfast. All students, boys and girls, were seated at a long wooden table in the chateau's dining area. This plain room stood in sharp contrast to the elegant family dining room on the other first floor wing.

Lucy had shared an awkward dinner there with Alexandre's family her first night at Chateau Broussard. Madeleine continued to welcome her warmly, serving as a delightful hostess and aspiring mentor. Alexandre helped Madeleine carry the conversation. Henri, their father, sat watching everyone with hawkish interest while Robert imitated his silence, choosing to focus on his food throughout most of the meal. Father and son were alike in their dark hair and bulky physique as well.

Jean-Paul sat at the head of the table. He contributed to the conversation occasionally. Lucy also felt him studying everyone at the table, but in a different way than his father. Henri seemed to survey them like a lord taking stock of his kingdom, savoring the fact that he was master of all he surveyed. Jean-Paul's watchful eyes analyzed others with Machiavellian calculation. Lucy felt like a pawn on Jean-Paul's chess board, a piece to be played or discarded depending on his needs. He exuded a rugged handsomeness and invincible confidence to go with it. His general attitude could better be described as arrogance rather than confidence. Lucy could tell that Jean-Paul was the kind of man who knew he was handsome and considered himself entitled to everyone's admiration. She'd known boys like him in Picardy too, though those Louisiana boys boasted far fewer reasons to consider themselves superior than Jean-Paul could. Lucy found it amusing that Jean-Paul couldn't conceive of a world where anyone found him less than irresistible.

Aria fit very well into Jean-Paul's universe of admirers. She tried not to show it, but Lucy could see it. Aria would glance down the table toward Jean-Paul only to avert her eyes when he turned his own blue ones in her direction. Lucy saw him smile knowingly a couple of times. When Aria asked him to pass the bread and butter, Jean-Paul was deliberate and very flirtatious in the way he slowly rose and walked around the table to deliver it to her.

Lucy broached the subject while they were getting ready for bed.

"I noticed Jean-Paul stopped by the classroom today to talk with you," Lucy said. "Anything important?"

"No," Aria said, a slight blush coloring her cheeks. She folded her pants and shirt, placed them in her drawer, and slipped a faded Beatles t-shirt on before she slipped under her covers.

"Nothing to do with classes?"

"Lucy, you are a clumsy detective," Aria said with a smile.

Lucy considered her words carefully. "Aria, I'm starting to consider you a friend. A good friend."

Aria propped herself up on her left arm.

"*Moi aussi*, Lucy," Aria said. "I feel you are my friend too."

"And, though I don't know him well yet, Jean-Paul is my cousin."

"Lucy, will you be getting to your point soon?"

"Be careful, Aria," Lucy said. "I'm still getting to know Jean-Paul, but I've known boys like him all my life."

"Jean-Paul Broussard is hardly a boy, *ma chère*," Aria said.

"All the more reason to be careful," Lucy said. "I heard things about Jean-Paul long before I met him from Alexandre. He has a reputation with women."

"I appreciate your concern for me, Lucy," Aria said. "I really do. I know what I am doing. I haven't been physically intimate with a man. Not completely. But I have had some relationships. That is new for you? *No?*"

"Yes," Lucy admitted. No reason to deny it. "I haven't really had a serious relationship."

"I promise to be careful," Aria said. "To take it slow. Now, let us talk about less serious things. Do you like Joni Mitchell? I think her voice is transcendent! How do you Americans say it? Groovy?"

Lucy assured her this American didn't, but she allowed Aria to turn the conversation to music.

Lucy thought about their conversation the next day as she sat beside her girls in chapel. Two solid oak doors formed the entrance to Chateau Broussard's chapel with elaborate stained-glass windows on each side. Madeleine had installed pews with kneeling extensions and an ornate communion table in the front. A small podium stood to the side for homilies. Both the eucharist and the homilies were delivered by Belle Plage's resident priest. Father Pasteur journeyed up the winding road to the cliffs every weekday morning to deliver a devotional homily to start the day and every evening to close the day with prayers and communion. His faithful fulfillment of those duties testified to the Broussard's local influence and generous donations to the church.

Lucy struggled with the high church ritual and abundant statues the first few days. She knew Catholics in Louisiana; some of them were good friends. Still, the liturgy rubbed her Protestant soul wrong and made her uncomfortable. She particularly resented being refused communion. Lucy balked the first evening when Aria told her she had to cross her arms, indicating that she was requesting a blessing, instead of taking communion with everyone else.

"But I'm a Christian!" Lucy insisted.

"That is how they do it here," Aria said apologetically.

Lucy was accustomed to it by the end of her second week, but she still didn't like it one bit.

Lucy was guiding her girls from chapel to class when she saw Madeleine beckon her. Lucy signaled she would return soon. She left the girls with Aria for their music lesson and went looking for Madeleine. Lucy found her standing in the main foyer. Alexandre walked up just as Lucy also approached her.

"*Bonjour, Maman,*" Alexandre said, kissing her on the cheek. He handed her a beautiful yellow rose. Lucy had witnessed this ritual every morning since she arrived at Chateau Broussard.

Madeleine accepted the rose from her son, kissed him on both cheeks, and took a deep sniff of the rose. "*Merci, mon doux garçon,*" Madeleine said. "Thank you so much, my sweet boy."

Alexandre smiled at Lucy.

"How are you this morning, Lucy?"

"That is what I was wanting to know too," Madeleine said. "Is everyone treating you well?"

"Very," Lucy said.

"*Magnifique!*" Madeleine said. "I am so very glad. You must let us know if you need anything. We need to discuss the future when we have more time. You are a remarkable young woman, Lucy. I want to see what we can do to keep you with us for a long while. Are you joining us for dinner tonight?"

"I'm not sure," Lucy said. "Aria and I are going down to the village this evening to see the Kerouacs again. I don't know if we'll make it back in time."

"A very nice couple," Madeleine said. "I think you went to school with Jacques, didn't you, Alexandre?"

"*Oui, Maman.*"

"You can let us know later," Madeleine said, patting Lucy's hand. "Alejandro can drive you down to the village if you would like. Henri doesn't need him tonight. You must excuse me now. I need to go check and see if the lunch preparations are underway. Neverending!"

"Are you bringing the girls out for recreational activities this afternoon?" Alexandre said when his mother was gone. "Maman said it would be fine for them to miss the literature lesson this afternoon."

"I'll bring them out," Lucy promised.

"*Fantastique!* I will see you then."

Lucy didn't see Alexandre when her cohort of six girls joined the other students on the lawn. She released her girls to find their preferred activities and walked over to where Jean-Paul was standing with a group of four boys. François watched her closely from among the cluster of boys. He hadn't spoken a word to her since that strange conversation on her first day.

"Lucy!" Jean-Paul called. "Come quickly. You will be perfect for this."

"For what, Jean-Paul?"

Jean-Paul grinned wolfishly and said to the boys, "Mademoiselle Lucy comes from the wild swamps of Louisiana. She will do this better than any of you."

Jean-Paul took Lucy by the hand. He guided her to a spot on the lawn facing a target set about six feet away.

"Observe, Cousin Lucy," Jean-Paul said.

Jean-Paul raised his right arm and cocked it back. The silver knife he held shone in the bright afternoon sun. His arm shot forward, and the knife whirred toward the target. It sounded like a million buzzing bees unleashed all at once. The knife embedded itself into the target's center with a resounding thud. The boys erupted in applause. Jean-Paul bowed.

"That is how it is done!" Jean-Paul exclaimed.

He offered a second knife to Lucy.

"Try, Cousin," he said.

Lucy took the knife, surprised at how light it was in her hand. She twirled the blade slowly.

"You have some experience with knives?" Jean-Paul noted.

"Just sharpening them for my father," Lucy said. "Not throwing them."

Jean-Paul stood behind her and took her right hand. He guided her arm back until it was slightly bent and poised just like his own had been.

"Focus on the center of the target," Jean-Paul instructed. "Come forward and then release the knife as your arm sweeps down. Throw it with force and intention."

He stepped back. Lucy swallowed, adjusted her arm a little, and threw the knife with all the force she could muster. The knife flew toward the target but hit it at the very bottom and bounded into the tall grass behind it. A couple of the boys snickered.

"She still threw better than most of you her first time," Jean-Paul reminded them. "Try again, Cousin Lucy."

He handed her another throwing knife. Lucy accepted the knife and twirled it, measuring its weight. When she felt ready, Lucy raised her arm again. She exhaled, gazed at the target, and threw the knife with more force. It whizzed to the target, embedding itself firmly in one of the outer circles.

"Bravo!" Jean-Paul shouted. The boys clapped with him.

Lucy allowed herself a satisfied smile.

"You enjoyed, Lucy?" Jean-Paul asked.

"I did," Lucy said. "Very much."

"I can teach you how to throw so you rival the best," Jean-Paul said.

"The best being you?" Lucy asked.

"Of course!" Jean-Paul said, with no trace of humility or irony.

"That would be fun," Lucy said. After ignoring her for a few days, Jean-Paul had started trying to win her favor in subtle ways. Lucy guessed he saw her growing friendship with Aria and hoped she would become an ally in his pursuit of her. "Do you know where Alexandre is, Jean-Paul?"

"The dreamer?" Jean-Paul said, rolling his eyes. "He is over there scribbling by the signal platform."

Lucy found Alexandre sitting on the edge of the wooden base, resting his back against the metal beacon with its powerful strobe light. On previous occasions, she'd found him facing the ocean, sketching images of the waves and horizon. That day, he was turned instead toward Chateau Broussard. Lucy could see the roof and turrets of the chateau taking shape on his pad.

"Will you paint that, Alex?" Lucy asked.

"Maybe," he said. "I hope Papa will buy me more canvas when he and Robert go to Paris next week. You can have the drawing when I am done if you would like. To remember Chateau Broussard always."

"I don't think I will ever forget Chateau Broussard," Lucy said. "It's an amazing place."

He smiled and continued sketching. Lucy sat beside him for a few minutes, relishing the fall breeze in her hair, the sun on her face, and the gentle sounds of the tide washing in below. She closed her eyes for a few minutes. When she opened them, Lucy noticed a flurry of activity near the chateau's main entrance. She couldn't see clearly from that distance, but it looked like the servants were moving furniture outside.

"What are the servants doing?" Lucy asked.

Alexandre frowned. "I am not sure. They are taking some kind of household inventory. I saw them checking the living room furniture earlier. I believe it may be why Maman wanted us to have an outside day today."

"Strange," Lucy said. "They do that often?"

"Not ever that I can remember," Alexandre said.

Lucy's curiosity grew when she entered the chateau an hour later to gather her things and meet Aria. Servants were moving from room to room on the second floor. She stood in her doorway watching them. Monique was directing the second-floor crew. Lucy heard Monique read instructions from a notepad she was carrying. The other maids scurried down the hallway and through the rooms looking for the objects Monique requested. When they located them, the maids took them to Monique, who would make a notation on her notepad, then call for something else. Lucy heard the French words for lamp, chair, and chest among the items on Monique's list.

Monique noticed Lucy watching them.

"Can I get you something, Mademoiselle Broussard?"

"No," Lucy said, suddenly embarrassed. "I was just curious."

Monique frowned and nodded. She said nothing to satisfy Lucy's curiosity.

"I guess I'll be going," Lucy said.

"*Bonsoir*, Mademoiselle," Monique said.

"Good evening to you too, Monique."

Monique watched closely until Lucy walked down the hall and descended the stairs.

Lucy and Aria enjoyed a relaxing night with the Kerouacs. Enora's quick wit reminded Lucy of Etta. She felt that aching homesickness again for a few minutes before she lost herself in the comfortable warmth of being among friends. They played games and told stories around the fire. Jacques entertained them with stories his father had told him about life in Belle Plage before the war. Soon the conversation turned to more harrowing stories about life in occupied France.

"The Nazis used the ports and caverns along the coast as naval bases," Jacques said. "The Resistance was active in this area, spying on them and trying to undermine them every way they could."

"It sounds so dangerous," Lucy said.

"It was," Jacques said. "The Nazis discovered some of the leaders not long before the Allies liberated us in 1944. They arrested my grandfather and several other Resistance leaders and took them to Paris. If the war had not ended when it did, they might have gone to German prison camps across the border."

"They were relocating people?" Lucy asked. "Taking them out of the country?"

The Kerouacs nodded gravely. Aria shivered and pulled Enora's blanket closer around her shoulders.

"Especially the Jews," Jacques said. "There were several families who took refuge here. They escaped the Nazis in Germany only to find themselves under German rule again with the Vichy regime."

"That's horrible," Lucy whispered.

"Maman told me stories about seeing the families waiting in the streets while the Nazis pillaged their homes," Enora said. "The Abrams family was living in a nice home on the cliffs when they came. Those were your pupil's grandparents."

"What happened to them?" Aria asked.

"The parents and the children were deported to Germany," Jacques said. "The parents died in the death camps. So did one of the children. The other two survived and made their way back to Belle Plage after the war."

"Couldn't the Broussards do anything to protect them?" Lucy asked.

"They tried," Jacques said. "Henri's father allowed the Resistance to use the caverns beneath the cliffs until the Nazis seized them. They tried to bribe the Vichy officials to return the Abrams, but it was too late. The Broussards kept their place as Belle Plage's most influential family because of their resistance during the Vichy years. So much pain and so many lives lost in this area and on that estate. That is why there are so many ghosts."

"These girls do not need to hear your scary stories," his wife insisted. "Especially when they are on their way to sleep in that haunted place!"

Jacques laughed and turned the conversation to more pleasant topics.

Later as Alejandro drove them back to Chateau Broussard, Lucy couldn't shake the image of the Abrams being herded to the train station like cattle. She gazed at the darkness outside her window, noting the barely visible motion of the waves in the distance. *How could people be so hateful to one another? What is evil?* The question troubled her once again.

Lucy saw the library lamp shining through the windows when they pulled up the drive. Alexandre often sat in there before bed, reading or drawing. When they strode into the hallway, Lucy told Aria she would join her soon. Aria went upstairs while Lucy walked toward the library. She peeked through the barely cracked door and saw Alexandre through the opening. He was bent over a large brown volume at the desk, the short lamp shining over him. Lucy was just about to knock when the library's other door across the room slammed open.

"Where is it?!" Henri Broussard demanded.

"Where is what?" Alexandre asked, clearly as startled as Lucy was at his father's sudden appearance.

"The chest from your room," Henri said. "The one with the silver lock and inscription."

"How should I know?" Alexandre said. "I have an over-abundance of old chests. You should stop stuffing them in my room if you want to keep up with them."

"This is no joke!" Henri seized Alexandre's book and threw it across the room.

"Papa!" Alexandre shouted. "What is wrong with you?"

"Where is that chest?!" Henri shouted again.

"I don't know!" Alexandre insisted.

Henri stepped toward Alexandre, towering over his son despite Alexandre's own considerable height.

"God help you if you are lying to me!" Henri shouted in Alexandre's face.

"I am not lying, Papa," Alexandre said.

Lucy gripped the doorknob. She wanted to intervene. Henri stepped even closer to Alexandre. Lucy started to ease the door open. Henri was focused so intently on Alexandre that he didn't hear or see her, but Alexandre saw her out of the corner of his eye. For a fleeting second, fast enough that his father wouldn't catch it, Alexandre sent Lucy a clear message with his eyes. *No!* That look was so desperate, so urgent, that Lucy obeyed without thinking. She eased the door back to its original position and continued to watch.

"You know something," Henri demanded. "What is it?"

"Henri!"

The sound of Madeleine's voice caused relief to wash over Lucy like a refreshing waterfall.

"You should go to bed, Henri," Madeleine said as she entered the library.

"I am not tired!" Henri growled. "I will get the truth from him!"

"I will talk to him," Madeleine said. "You are only making things worse. Leave us."

Her tone left no room for argument.

Henri gave Alexandre one last glare and left him with his mother.

Mother and son stood in silence for a moment.

"*Merci, Mam . . .*"

Lucy didn't see Madeleine's hand move until it struck Alexandre's face. The crack of palm on face boomed through the silent chateau. Lucy felt herself gasp despite her determination to stay quiet.

Alexandre's jaw blazed red even in the weak light of the lamp. His eyes expressed total shock. His brothers and father bullied him all the time, but Lucy could see that Madeleine's betrayal cut deeper than all of it combined.

"Why are you . . ."

Madeleine's hands flashed twice more, striking Alexandre on the opposite side and then again on his right cheek.

"Where the hell is that chest, Alexandre?!" Madeleine hissed. Lucy's blood froze in her veins.

"It is safe, Maman," Alexandre said. "That is all I can say."

"You will say much more," Madeleine said. "You have no idea the sacrifices the rest of us make so you can live in your fantasies!"

"I am sorry to disappoint you, Maman," Alexandre said.

"You disappoint yourself," Madeleine said. "You will go upstairs and think about what you owe this family. You will tell me tomorrow where that chest is. Do you understand?"

"Why does it matter, Maman? It is just another piece of furniture."

"You let me worry about why it matters," Madeleine said. "Tomorrow, Alexandre. You will tell me."

Madeleine shook her head and started for the door where Lucy was standing. Lucy scurried from the library door to the darkened conservatory. She hid around the corner while she listened to Madeleine's firm footsteps clattering on the marble floor of the hallway. When she was sure Madeleine was gone, Lucy peered around the corner of the conservatory door. Alexandre was walking toward the stairwell.

"Alex," Lucy whispered.

He turned. Lucy could see the tear streaks running down his face and the already visible swelling around his jaw.

"I'm so sorry," Lucy said. "Why didn't you tell her?"

"You must not tell her, Lucy," Alexandre insisted. "Something is not right. I do not know what. I am afraid for you if they know. Please promise you will not tell."

Lucy couldn't speak. She nodded her assent.

"Thank you," Alexandre said.

He turned and continued the journey to his room.

Lucy leaned against the wall, her knees threatening to give out. What had she just witnessed? Why this fuss over an old chest, no matter how beautiful or valuable?

Lucy remembered the first time she'd seen it. She and Tamera were visiting Alexandre at his host family's house in Picardy. The Hightowers had allowed Alexandre to pile his possessions in their second guest bedroom. He was searching for a particular canvas to show Tamera when Lucy spotted the chest in the corner.

"What is that?" Lucy asked.

Alexandre looked in her direction and snorted.

"An irritation is what it is!" he said.

Tamera tossed her blonde curls and patted her foot impatiently.

"You found that picture yet?"

"No," Alexandre said. "Lucy is distracting me with the annoying chest."

Lucy squatted beside the antique oak chest, running her hands over its wooden surface. A sterling silver band encircled it. A heavy locking mechanism framed its cover. Lucy leaned closer to read the inscription on the lid. *L'obscurité fuit devant l'aube.*

"Darkness flees before dawn," Lucy read aloud.

"You are doing well with your French lessons, Lucy," Alexandre said. "You are fascinated by my chest?"

"She likes older things," Tamera said. "Just not older boys."

Lucy paused long enough to give Tamera an eyeroll before returning to her examination of the chest.

"It's so beautiful," Lucy said. "Nobody makes things like this anymore."

"You need something pretty to put your crap in, Lucy?" Tamera teased.

"Imagine the places this has been," Lucy continued. "The stories it could tell."

"It could tell you the story of how it became the annoying chest," Alexandre said. "Maman has dropped all her spare furniture into our rooms since we were small. I asked for containers to store my canvases and paints when I was fifteen. This showed up in my room along with about five other worthless pieces of furniture. Does this look good for storing canvases to you?"

"No," Lucy admitted. "That's way below its pay grade. Your mother just gave this to you?"

"I think she told the servants to find me containers," Alexandre said. "They put it there. She just never bothered to remove it."

"How'd you get that on the plane? Tamera asked.

"Ah!" Alexandre said with a dramatic flourish. "The servants strike again! I came with two bags on the plane. They were supposed to send my canvases and paints by special delivery to the Hightowers'. Three weeks after I got here, this arrived! My canvases and paints were not in there. Just a few brushes and old drawings. We had to pay again to get the canvases sent!"

"Poor little rich boy," Tamera purred. "You could have just bought more in New Orleans."

"I wanted mine," Alexandre said. "The brushes at least. I can work on any canvas."

"You feelin' sorry for him yet, Lucy?" Tamera said.

"I don't feel sorry for either one of you," Lucy said, still examining the chest. "You're both spoiled rich kids."

"You like the chest, Lucy?" Alexandre said.

"Very much."

"Then it is yours," he said.

"What?" Lucy wasn't sure she'd heard him right.

"It is yours," Alexandre repeated. "Keep it and enjoy it."

In Lucy's experience wealthy people could be miserly or extremely generous depending on their personalities. Alexandre dispensed lavishly. He considered possessions mere objects to be acquired and discarded with ease because he'd never had trouble getting them. He made friends fast in Picardy giving gifts and picking up the occasional tab for his rebellious friends. Giving Lucy a possibly priceless chest on a whim fit his outlook on life like a glove.

"That's too much, Alex!" Lucy said. "I can't take this."

"If you do not, my family will have to pay to transport it once again when I'm finished with school," Alexandre said. "What a waste! It does not hold what I need well. Take it, Lucy. A beautiful gift for my beautiful cousin to remember me when I am across the sea."

Lucy looked questioningly at Tamera.

"Don't look at me," Tamera said. "I ain't carrying it."

"Do you think I should take it?" Lucy asked.

"I think you already want to, and you need me to give you permission," Tamera said.

"And?"

"You need to learn to treat yourself, Lucy," Tamera said. "Take it."

Tamera did help carry the chest and complained all the way to Lucy's car and all the way from her car to her house. It was still sitting in her bedroom at her parents' house in Picardy.

Lucy remembered and agonized while standing in the darkened hallway of Chateau Broussard. She wanted to tell Madeleine. But not the Madeleine she had just encountered. Lucy wanted to tell Madeleine her mentor. Madeleine the educator. Madeleine the devoted mother and wife. She hadn't recognized the person she just saw attack Alexandre. Why did Madeleine want this chest so much, and who was the real Madeleine Broussard?

CHAPTER THIRTEEN

"WE'LL SEE WHO THE REAL MADELEINE Broussard is now," I said.

"You think?" Trey said.

"I think I have a better chance one-on-one and without Angélique around," I said.

Trey steered Jacques' truck down the long drive and parked beside the massive doors of Chateau Broussard.

Two messages had arrived at the hotel desk that morning. One was anonymous and dropped on the desk sometime in the middle of the night. Terse and to the point, it read:

IF YOU WANT THE OLD MEN ALIVE, BRING THE CHEST TO BELLE PLAGE WITHIN THE WEEK.

The second message came from Madeleine, inviting Dr. Diana Chambers to visit her at the chateau around ten o'clock. We were leaving for Paris shortly after noon. I decided to accept the invitation, curious to see what Madeleine wanted. We left the others making final preparations for our quick trips to Paris and Geneva.

I was surprised when Monique led us past the main staircase and down the hallway toward a heavy wooden door with ornate stained-glass windows. She opened the door and ushered us inside. I was amazed to see a fully furnished chapel with a table for eucharistic services, statuary, and more stained glass. Madeleine was seated at the front gazing at a copy of Michelangelo's Pieta standing behind the table. The Virgin Mary's head was bowed in prayer or contemplation as she held the lifeless crucified body of her son.

Madeleine rose to greet us.

"*Bonjour*, Diana. It looks like you brought a friend."

"Madeleine, this is . . ."

"No introductions are needed," Madeleine said. "It is nice to formally meet you, Trey."

"Formally?" Trey said. "Have I seen you before?"

"No," Madeleine said. "But I've seen you."

I could tell her familiarity unnerved Trey as much as it had the rest of us.

"Nice to meet you," he said carefully.

"My invitation was to Diana alone," Madeleine continued, "but I'm not surprised you didn't want her to come by herself."

"I hope I didn't offend you," Trey said.

"Not at all," Madeleine's admiration seemed genuine. "Would that we all had a white knight or two. There are far too many of the other sort. You are a lucky woman, Diana."

I grinned at Trey's embarrassed expression. "Thank you, Madeleine."

"Would you be willing to wait outside for a few minutes while I speak with Diana?" Madeleine said. "There is a chair in the back. You can drag it outside and position it where you can see through the stained glass. I promise I mean her no harm. Quite the opposite."

Trey glanced at me. I nodded reassuringly. I wanted to hear Madeleine out.

"Okay," he said. "I'll be right outside if you need me."

"Would you like Monique to bring you something to drink?" Madeleine asked. She laughed when she saw how much Trey was debating the question. "Really, Trey. You give me much more or much less credit than I deserve. I promise no one is going to slip you a sleeping potion. Your beautiful princess is safe with me. I promise."

"Thanks," Trey said. "I appreciate the offer, but I'll skip the drink. I'll be outside, Di."

Madeleine smiled when the door closed behind him. "A rare breed. Just like you, Diana. You complement one another well."

"I'm glad you approve."

Madeleine linked her arm through mine and together we walked around the perimeter of the chapel.

"I thought you would appreciate this room given your academic and personal interests," Madeleine said.

"It is quite impressive. Do you use this for the school?"

"I think Angélique may have exaggerated how far along we are in establishing the new school," Madeleine said. "I have only four students. Like the students in our previous school, most of them are orphans or foster kids from this region. Kids who could never afford an elite private education, but who have the gifts and determination to benefit from it. But, yes, we did use it every morning for chapel services. I think your mother found our Catholic rituals challenging."

"I'm sure," I said. "The statuary and furnishings are beautiful."

"Thank you," Madeleine said.

We walked along the eastern wall, which was adorned near the ceiling with oak carvings depicting the stations of the cross.

"Does the local priest perform mass for you?" I asked.

"Yes. The Latin Rite in the original Latin."

I raised an eyebrow.

"You're not a fan of Vatican II?"

"Sometimes the church makes mistakes," Madeleine said. "I consider that one of them. Or several of them if you take each decree separately."

"Interesting. I would love to sit in sometime. I enjoy hearing the Latin cadences."

"Can you speak Latin, Professor Chambers?"

"No," I said. "But I can read medieval Latin. I can pick phrases out because I know the English liturgy."

"We would be delighted to have you," Madeleine said. "In fact, I would be delighted to have you with us all the time."

"All the time?"

"I don't have many years left, Diana," Madeleine said, turning to face me. "Even in the best-case scenarios my days are numbered. I'm fortunate to still have good health and an intact mind. I want to ensure my final legacy while I still can. Your mother was a woman with extraordinary gifts. It crushed me when she decided to leave. I believe we could have built something amazing here. I still think we can. You are even more talented than she was. And more experienced. You've lived and worked long enough in this world to appreciate the fact that the world is not a perfect place. Sometimes we must make compromises to build something good. I think Lucille was too young and idealistic to understand that when she was with us."

"You might be surprised how well she internalized those ideas later," I said. "She would have given me the same speech coming from a different angle."

"I know," Madeleine said. "I spoke with her a few times over the years."

I finally had the answer to a question that had been bothering me since Angélique first told us about Madeleine.

"It was you, wasn't it?" I asked. "You were the lady Dorcas saw at the barn in 1995. I saw you with Lucille late that night."

"Yes," Madeleine said. "Henri had just died. And there were other circumstances that had changed as well. Lucille and I needed to renegotiate things between us."

"What circumstances? What was there between the two of you?"

"More than you want to know," Madeleine said. "We've maintained a tenuous understanding for fifty years. A balance. A sort of détente, if you will."

"You and Lucille have been engaged in a cold war for fifty years?"

Madeleine smiled bitterly at the ironic description, "You could say that."

"What's changed?"

"You're very perceptive, Diana. Two things. Lucille's death has left certain items that she was keeping private in play again. I want to reacquire those items if I can."

"The chest?" I asked.

Madeleine nodded. "And other items too."

"Where are François and Jacob?"

"I honestly don't know, Diana," she insisted. "I did not authorize their kidnapping or Aria's murder. That's not how I like to handle things."

"What about members of your family? Robert and Carlton, for instance?"

"They wouldn't act without my permission," Madeleine said. Despite her assurances, I sensed a slight hesitation. She wasn't as sure of their discipline or obedience as she pretended.

"You said there were two things that changed."

"Angélique," Madeleine said, shaking her head. "She insists on dredging up the past. I'm sorry I lost my temper when you were here with her. She . . . how do you say in the States? She pushes my buttons. Aria also picked at things in a way your mother never did. She finally let it go as Angélique grew and consumed more of her attention. Then, two years ago, Angélique started pushing. Your mother's death has only intensified her efforts. I don't think Aria was coming to see you because she wanted you to investigate us. I think she was coming to warn you about Angélique."

"What does she want?" I asked.

"Something I can't give her."

"You know it would be easier to settle all this if you were more transparent," I said.

"I'm being as transparent as I can be right now," Madeleine said. "I promise to tell you more as we continue. I want to put all this behind us as much as you do. More. I want it settled before I die. My family is rebuilding our influence after decades of setbacks."

"*Unis?*" I asked.

"*Unis* is part of it. Social media and AI are the wave of the future. Carlton has positioned us well. Do you use *Unis?*"

"I've logged on a few times."

"What did you think?" Madeleine said.

"A fetid swamp of racism, pretend white grievance, and baseless conspiracy theories," I said honestly. "Plus, I don't think you can convey many profound truths in 200 characters."

"This is why I like you," Madeleine said. "Noble and no pretense. We may not like it, Diana, but today's world runs on such things."

"A very sad and sick subset of today's world runs on such things," I countered.

"Don't you believe in free speech?" Madeleine asked.

"Absolutely," I said. "I also believe in using that freedom responsibly. Spreading lies and baseless propaganda, especially when those lies are calculated to hurt other people, violates and undermines free speech."

"We'll agree to disagree for now," Madeleine said. "I understand you have a train to catch?"

I looked at her helplessly, speechless. *How did she know these things?*

"Information is power," Madeleine said. "I have my sources. Or maybe I just gaze into my crystal ball. I wanted to give these to you."

She reached down to one of the pews and picked up a small sheaf of items. I took them from her.

"Your mother left them in her room when they fled," Madeleine said. "You might find them enlightening. Especially the one from her minister friend in Los Angeles. You know the kinds of supernatural obsessions your mother had. She was paranoid by the end of her time here. No doubt encouraged by her evangelical friends in the States. Lucy transformed an innocent service here in this very room into a satanic rite in her fevered imagination. She interpreted a simple student transfer as mass kidnapping by a satanic cult. We're not bad people, Diana. You and I could do so much good together. Please consider it."

Dismissed, I found Trey sitting in his chair by the chapel door. He looked relieved to see me.

"You okay?"

"Doing fine, my white knight," I said, kissing him on the cheek when he rose.

"Please don't let that become a thing," Trey groaned.

"Oh, it's become," I said.

Monique reappeared and led us toward the front door. We thanked her and walked to our waiting loaner truck.

"Have you noticed the phone signals here?" Trey asked. "Or lack of phone signals?"

"We did," I said. "Dorcas said ghosts were interfering with the signals."

"More like a jamming device," Trey said. "Remind me to try it again when we're further out."

We drove to the arched gateway at the end of the drive. We both checked our phones again.

"No signal," I said.

"This thing is massive enough to black out the entire property," Trey said grimly. "What are they up to?"

We were rocketing back the way we had come an hour later as the high-speed train bore us toward Paris.

Delilah, Trey, Dorcas, Daddy, Angélique, and I were gathered around the items Madeleine shared with us.

Delilah held a picture of three high school students. Lucille sat on a bench dressed in a simple blouse and bell-bottom jeans. Her wavy auburn hair reminded me of Farah Fawcett. Farah Fawcett's hair at least. Her face bore a hauntingly close resemblance to Dinah's. The girl beside her was dressed in a turtleneck and stylish skirt. Her curly blonde hair fell just below her shoulders. The bookish boy next to them was tall, thin, and had curly blond hair. A scribbled notation on the back of the photo read, "Tamera H., Lucy B., Alexandre B."

"Momma looks so much like Dinah," Dorcas whispered.

"You remember that day Momma almost had to bitch-slap Bernadette in the grocery store?" Delilah asked.

After chewing on that incident for days afterwards, I hadn't thought about it again in thirty years. Now it came roaring back.

"You think that's her daughter?" I asked.

"Yep," Delilah said. "Would have been Crissy's aunt if she had lived.

I'm guessing she's the one Madeleine said died of a drug overdose."

"At UCLA," I said.

Neither of us said it in front of Daddy, but we exchanged a knowing look. Lucille's paranoia about higher education surely had some roots in Tamera's self-destruction.

"The letter is exactly what Madeleine said," I told them. "We don't have Momma's side of the conversation, but the pastor is confirming her belief that a ceremony she witnessed in the Broussard chapel was similar to satanic rites he claims to have witnessed in Los Angeles. She'd shared quotes with him taken from the ceremony and from the curriculum they were teaching the students. He claims some of it was similar to ideas he'd read in Anton LaVey's *Satanic Bible*."

"Then we are dealing with something supernatural," Dorcas said.

"I'm not so sure," I said. "The quotes Lucille shared aren't direct quotes. They read more like loose paraphrases from the writings of the German philosopher Friedrich Nietzsche. LaVey was obsessed with Nietzsche's philosophy. Some critics have said LaVey's Church of Satan is just Nietzsche's authoritarian ideas combined with candles and carnival tricks."

"Anton LaVey founded the Church of Satan," Dorcas said. "If they're quoting the same philosopher, doesn't that mean these people worshipped Satan too?"

"The Church of Satan doesn't worship Satan," I said. "They were and are a collection of skeptics using satanic imagery and the black mass as a way to make a point. It's an unusual and eclectic mix of ideas. A bunch of counter-cultural rebels elevating Satan as the ultimate symbol of rebellion against the system. They got more than they bargained for after the Manson murders and the beginning of the satanic panic. People accused them of plotting mass murder and satanic ritual abuse on a massive scale. Anton's daughter Zeena spent a lot of time on tv throughout the eighties and early nineties trying to convince people her father's church was innocent of those crimes."

"Were they?" Dorcas asked.

"As far as we can tell, those alleged crimes never happened," I said.

"Lots of hype and hysteria that led to almost nothing when authorities formally investigated the allegations. There was Richard Ramirez and Sean Sellers who really did commit crimes and blame them on satanic worship, but most of it was mere illusion."

"Hard to imagine they could play with those things without being possessed by demonic powers," Daddy said. Dorcas nodded vigorously.

I decided to avoid the debate for now. It was sure to come up again later.

"Maybe there is something to Momma's fears of satanic influence at the chateau," I said. "Maybe not. Just because there are some loose overlaps between LaVey's writings and the ideas at Chateau Broussard doesn't mean they're connected. They could both be drawing separately on Nietzsche's writings as common source material. It is very possible that something else was going on and Momma misunderstood it like Madeleine said."

Dorcas smiled at me sweetly. "I love to hear you call her Momma."

I smiled back. "It's getting a little easier with time."

"So what's our plan when we get to Paris?" Delilah asked.

"You need to see what Lucille hid in Geneva," I said to Trey and Daddy. "I'm guessing those are the other items that Madeleine wants to reacquire."

"We will," Trey promised.

"You two will go to Angélique's apartment and get things ready for us," I said to Angélique and Dorcas. "Delilah and I will get the map at Charles de Gaulle and bring it to the apartment along with the delivery person."

"We'll be ready for you," Dorcas said.

"Angélique," Delilah said. "I love my sisters."

Angélique looked surprised. "Of course, Delilah."

"Dorcas better be in perfect health when I see her next or you won't be," Delilah said.

"I told you that you can trust me," Angélique insisted.

"Everyone tells me that," Delilah said. "And I don't trust most of them."

"You don't have to worry," Dorcas said. "I'm tougher than you think, Big Sister."

"The real question is whether Angélique would have more to fear from Delilah or from our minister friend," I said.

My joke had the intended effect. Dorcas blushed and smiled. Michael had appeared at the Kerouacs' inn two more times in the two days after Dorcas went with him to the beach service. Always with the pretense of inviting her to some group activity that ended with the two of them strolling on the beach or getting a bite to eat. I'd slipped into the little chapel by the beach one day at noon to listen to Michael's devotional. His teaching was animated and deep at the same time. He clearly knew the Bible well and enjoyed sharing it with others. I was comforted to hear none of the rougher and more radical versions of contemporary evangelicalism. No patriarchy, conspiracy theories, or nationalism. Just a simple message of grace and acceptance.

"Does that beard tickle when you kiss him?" Leave it to Delilah to focus on the important stuff.

"Delilah!" Dorcas said, turning beet red this time. "We haven't done that yet."

"Yet?" Delilah said with a grin. She always heard the part she wanted to hear first.

Dorcas was saved by a notification over the intercom that we were pulling into Paris. We separated there. Daddy and Trey hugged us and hurried off to catch their train to Geneva. Angélique and Dorcas went outside to get an Uber to Angélique's apartment. Delilah and I bounded down the tracks to board our train for Charles de Gaulle.

I checked my texts on the way to make sure there had been no change of plans.

Aidan had sent arrival times and the flight number that morning. WE TRIED TO GET ACCESS TO THE MAP BEFORE THE FLIGHT, BUT THEY INSISTED ON DELIVERING THE MAP TO THE AIRPORT PERSONALLY TO MAKE SURE IT WAS CHECKED PROPERLY. THEY CHECKED IT; NOW WE ARE RESPONSIBLE FOR DELIVERING IT FROM CHARLES DE

GAULLE TO THE SORBONNE. THAT WILL BE YOUR OPPORTUNITY. HAVE A PLACE READY WHERE YOU CAN VIEW THE MAP SECURELY. WE'LL GET IT TO YOU AND GIVE YOU ABOUT THIRTY MINUTES TO STUDY IT. THEN WE MUST GET IT TO THE SORBONNE BY OUR DEADLINE. BEST I CAN DO.

I texted my thanks. I also tapped Delilah on the shoulder and leaned over to take a selfie of us both. I texted the picture to Aiden. Several dots appeared. I waited as patiently as I could. My heart sank when the new message arrived.

THE ART INSTITUTE TOLD US THAT THEY NOTIFIED THE SORBONNE AND THE BROUSSARD FAMILY. THE BROUSSARDS HAVE KNOWN IT WAS COMING FOR TWO DAYS. WE'VE TAKEN PRECAUTIONS. YOU SHOULD BE PREPARED FOR ANYTHING. THE MAP WILL BE AT CAROUSEL 26 IN TERMINAL 2E.

"Damn!" I said.

"What's wrong?" Delilah asked.

"The museum contacted the Broussards. They know the map is coming."

"Guess that old bitch doesn't have a crystal ball after all," Delilah said.

"She's terrifyingly well connected," I said. Madeleine's preternatural ability to anticipate our every move scared me more than I wanted to admit.

We stepped off the train at Charles de Gaulle a few minutes later. I glanced at my phone. It was already 1:45 p.m. The plane should have already landed. We started running, slipping past annoyed pedestrians. Some of them shouted words and phrases I knew I shouldn't bother to translate. We reached the escalators, taking each step two at a time. We hit the main baggage claim area and rushed down the rows of carousels. The numbers flashed by us, ticking up toward the twenties.

We stopped short at carousel 24. A janitor had spilled their cart beside the carousel. A massive pool of blue cleaning fluid oozed across the baggage claim area. Security was blocking the way while two janitors worked feverishly to clean up the mess.

I looked helplessly down the row of carousels. I could see 26. The nearness of it made our inability to get there even more agonizing. Just a few bags were left on the conveyor belt. The crowd of passengers was beginning to disperse. The only people left waiting were a young white man in jeans and a hoodie, a black businessman in a blue suit, and an elderly Indian woman dressed in a blue sari with matching head covering. I didn't recognize any of them.

"What the hell, Aiden?" I grumbled. Whatever the "precautions" were, they were good enough to fool me too.

"Di!" Delilah grabbed my arm. I followed her pointing finger. Robert was striding through the airport flanked by two imposing personal security guards in gray suits. Dressed in black from head to toe and heading straight for carousel 26, Robert looked like the grim reaper.

I looked toward the carousel again and noticed a long document tube with a shoulder strap descending to the conveyer belt. Robert noticed it too. He barked an order and made a sweeping motion with his hand. The two security guards fell back to flanking positions across the room where they could survey the crowd and guard the exits. Robert himself headed straight for the document tube.

"We've gotta get over there!" I shouted. Delilah and I started pushing through. Security was opening the way, but now the accumulated mass of people was slowing us down. I looked back at the carousel. The businessman and hoodie guy had picked up their bags and moved on. Only the elderly Indian woman remained. I blinked in astonishment as she made her way to the document tube. She walked slowly, stooped with a slight hunch in her lower back. I could see the gray streaks in her hair beneath her head covering. She reached down and picked up the document tube by its carrying strap.

"He's closing in, Diana!" Delilah said.

Robert was nearing the Indian woman.

"He's going to get there before us," I said. "The gloves may have to come off."

"They were never on," Delilah said grimly, her voice edgy with adrenaline and anticipation. I trusted Delilah's skills implicitly, but did we really stand a chance against Robert and two trained security personnel?

The Indian woman was turning to leave the carousel when Robert blocked her path. He towered over her like a mountain. My heart sank. Robert grabbed the document canister with a triumphant gleam in his eyes.

CHAPTER FOURTEEN

I'VE ALWAYS BEEN FASCINATED BY ACTORS and their craft. Their ability to channel another personality. To make fictional worlds and people real. I tried it myself a time or two in college. I was okay, but never as gifted as Dinah. She inhabited her roles. Dinah temporarily became her characters. I envied that ability to be possessed by another personality in that way, a possession so different from the demonic variety my parents feared.

The first thing I noticed was her hands. When Robert gripped the document canister, I realized her hands were unusually smooth for someone her age.

"Don't be sad, Little Woman," Robert boasted loud enough for us to hear. "You have lost to the six-time wrestling champion of Northwestern France. No shame in that."

Her response was unnerving. The hitch in her back disappeared first. Then she began rising. As she straightened, the woman gained several inches. Robert still towered over her, but she had lessened the gap. Robert stared in shock as she released the document canister. Her hands fell to her waist. She rummaged beneath her sari and produced a lipstick tube.

"We do not have time to do my makeup," Robert said, recovering a little from his surprise.

"Too bad," the woman said in a melodic British accent, "An ugly son of a bitch like you could use it." She twisted the end of the lipstick tube and jammed it into Robert's neck. Before he could react, a series of blue flashes issued from the tube. Robert Broussard screamed and tried to pull away. The Indian woman pressed the lipstick tube deeper. The document cannister clattered to the floor. Robert succeeded in breaking away and fell. Delilah and I finally arrived just in time to see Robert Broussard writhing and twisting on the floor by the baggage carousel.

The woman picked up the document with lightning speed. She turned to us and examined us closely, obviously comparing us to the selfie I'd sent Aiden. Satisfied, she motioned with her head toward the security personnel. Robert's men, drawn by his screams, were rushing to him. Rushing was relative at Charles de Gaulle that day. They were hindered by the same crowd dynamics that delayed us.

"We need to go," she said.

I nodded. "We passed another set of exits on our way. We can get out there."

I started to lead them to the exits. The woman began to follow, hesitated, and deliberately went back to give Robert Broussard a hard kick in the crotch while he continued to writhe on the ground.

"I think I've found my new crush," Delilah said, grinning in absolute delight at Robert's agonized cries.

"Sorry," the woman said, hurrying after us.

We raced back, weaving through the crowds. We hit the escalators and bounded down the steps three at a time. I spotted one of Robert's guards at the top of the escalator as we scrambled aboard the train for Paris. He stumbled down the escalator, but he stopped when our train doors closed. He pulled out his phone, spoke into it, and hurried back upstairs.

We collapsed onto our seats, all three of us panting.

"That was awesome!" Delilah said. "What was in that lipstick tube?"

"It's basically a miniature taser," the woman said. "I was afraid it wouldn't work on someone his size. Electricity wins again!"

She reached into her sari and fished for something. Removing a small object, she handed it to me. I looked at the object in my palm and laughed out loud. A Spider-Man pin stared back at me with the webslinger's unwavering stylized white eyes reflecting my own.

"Sorry," she said with an apologetic smile, "nobody ever accused us of being cool. Aidan said you would get it."

"I get it," I said. "No apologies necessary. You're the coolest as far as I'm concerned. Thank you so much for bringing this map to us. And you are?"

"Shakti Patel. I'm Aiden's associate director at the Franklin Center."

"You're a pretty versatile associate director," Delilah said.

"Other duties as assigned," Shakti said. "Researcher, therapist, sounding board, special deliveries, grave digger . . ."

"Grave digger?!" Delilah exclaimed.

"It's a long story," Shakti said. "I'm a historian by training."

Shakti passed the document tube to me.

"How long do we have?" I asked.

"About two hours total," Shakti said. "We need to set a forty-five minute timer when we get to your location and try to stick to that time frame as closely as we can."

We rushed into Angélique's tiny apartment twenty minutes later. Angélique shared a modest two-bedroom apartment in the 7th Arrondissement with Aria until her mother's recent death. The living and kitchen areas in the scandalously overpriced apartment bordered on the claustrophobic, but the Fourniers had enjoyed a nice location close to Angélique's travel agency with a decent view of the Eiffel Tower.

After we introduced Shakti to Dorcas and Angélique, Shakti asked Angélique, "Do you have a shower I can use?"

"Yes," Angélique said. "You must feel filthy after all those hours on the plane."

"I do," Shakti said. "But, more importantly, I don't want to get any of this makeup on the map."

"Of course," Angélique said. "This way."

We waited in the living room until Shakti returned ten minutes later. Her transformation was amazing. Every hint of wrinkles and gray hair was washed away, leaving behind a young woman in her late twenties, probably just a few years younger than Dorcas. Her light brown complexion, heart-shaped face, and green arresting eyes reminded me of the actress Aiswarya Rai Bachchan. Her damp hair, now jet black and straight, hung down past the middle of her back. She was dressed in blue jeans and a gray Franklin Center t-shirt, which I assumed she'd been wearing under her sari.

"Thanks for waiting," Shakti said. She produced her phone, started a timer, slid two protective gloves pulled from her pocket on each hand, and popped the top off the document tube. Shakti gingerly eased the map out of its protective container and slowly spread it out on Angélique's kitchen table.

I gasped in astonishment at the rumpled vellum manuscript emblazoned with green, brown, gray, and blue pigments. The map itself rested in the center of the manuscript while drawings and quotations drawn in beautiful calligraphy covered every inch of the border. I was scanning the map's edges. I couldn't compose in Latin, but my graduate school language requirements had prepared me to read well enough to do basic archival research.

"Most of these quotes are from the Bible," I said. "A couple of them may be from noted theologians. I think I recognize one from St. Augustine's *The City of God*."

"That's consistent with our estimates of its age," Shakti said.

"How old?" I asked.

"Definitely after the Carolingian Renaissance," Shakti said to me. Noting the confused looks on everyone else's faces, she added, "the early 800s. The reign of Charlemagne."

I smiled and shook my head at them in mock disappointment.

"It's your map, Shakti," I said. "Teach us. How new is it?"

"High Middle Ages?" Shakti said. "Maybe twelfth or thirteenth century."

Shakti pointed to the coast and the cliffs clearly illustrated at the bottom.

"That's where your little seaside town is today," Shakti said. "Notice there are very few structures on the coast at that time. Most of the settlement is on the cliffs. So is the monastery." Shakti pointed to a circle of smaller structures surrounding a gray dot with a brown top in its center.

"Is that a well?" Dorcas asked.

"Yes," Shakti said. "Looks like the main fresh water source for the village. And, if you look within the walls of the monastery, they also have one to meet the needs of their community. They're close enough to each other that they may draw from the same groundwater."

"They must have created the one we see in the village square now as a memorial to the original one," I said.

"Safe assumption," Shakti said. "Here is the part that you're interested in." She pointed to the left corner of the map, taking care not to touch its actual surface. The cliffs were transparent like someone had applied an ancient x-ray to them. A series of tunnels ran in all directions like a massive ant farm. One large artery led straight from the monastery to the coast. Shakti pointed at it.

"This one is the main section that we know is still in operation today," Shakti said. "The Broussards use it all the time."

"You got access to a spy satellite?" Delilah asked.

"No," Shakti said, "Google Earth. They've never tried to hide the fact that they use it. I'm sure that's the tunnel your mothers used to escape with the kids in 1974."

"But Sarah also said Momma took the tunnels to the top of the hill," Dorcas said.

"That's the tricky part," Shakti said. "They obviously exist. Or, at least, existed. You can see several of them branching off and twisting up to the original settlement."

"Why would monks create all this?" Angélique asked.

"Ease of transportation," I said, pointing to the main tunnel that led straight to the water. "And, also, storage and protection. They could store surplus food for themselves and the village. They could also bring the villagers into the monastery for protection behind their walls if there were ever an attack."

"Was that a real problem?" Delilah asked.

"More than you might think," Shakti said. "We're talking Norsemen in the early medieval period, wars between the French nobility, conflicts between the French and English, and pirates trying to score easy booty."

"Everyone's always trying to score easy booty," Delilah said in mock lament.

"A lame joke like that would get you sent to the back of my class," I said.

"But I would take my new seat as a hero."

"Our problem," Shakti said, clearing her throat, tapping the timer, and looking at us like disobedient children, "is that without any current maps, we have no idea how many of these tunnels are still navigable. If they are still open, they could be very dangerous. Subject to cave-ins. They could contain all kinds of creatures. Plus, the Nazis used them. Who knows what they might have left behind."

"You thinking Gestapo ghosts?" Delilah asked.

"I'm thinking unexploded ordinance, bodies, and who knows what else," Shakti said gravely.

"You're wishing we had a ghost or two to hunt now," Dorcas said with satisfaction.

I traced with my eyes one long tunnel up the cliffside where it emerged near the cliff's edge. I tried to picture what I knew of the contemporary layout.

"I bet this comes out close to where we saw Madeleine standing," I said. "By the old beacon platform."

"If Sarah remembers right," Delilah said, "that must be how Mom got up there."

"So it could still be open?" Dorcas said hopefully.

"Maybe," I said. "We're still talking fifty years. Any number of things could have happened to close it since."

"I wish I could help you with that part," Shakti said. "But the only way you're going to know for sure is if you check it out yourself."

"That could be very risky," I said. "They could figure out what we're planning. On the other hand, they probably already know since they know we wanted the map."

The timer chirped.

"Just a few more minutes and I'll need to head out," Shakti said.

"Can I take pictures of it?" I asked.

"No flash," Shakti insisted.

"Of course," I said. I moved around the table taking pictures from every angle.

Shakti started preparing the canister to receive the map again.

"Anything we can do?" Delilah asked.

"Yes," Shakti said, "as a matter of fact, there is." She produced a small bag that must have been hooked to her jeans beneath her sari. I guessed that was where she kept her lipstick taser. She pulled out a CD case barely small enough to fit in the bag. She tossed it to Delilah. Delilah grinned when she saw the words "Hostile Haircut" printed on the cover with her own youthful photo preparing to shave the mullet off a model standing in for Sampson.

"Always good to see the debut again," Delilah said. "You want it signed?"

"Yes," Shakti said. "Make it out 'To Delia' with all the appropriate metal head phrases."

"Not your jam?" Delilah said, smiling as she started writing with a marker supplied by Angélique.

"I'm more Mozart than Metallica," Shakti said.

I took the last of my photos and scrolled through them to make sure they were clear. On impulse, I selected several of them and texted them to Brandy as a peace offering.

THOUGHT YOU MIGHT FIND THESE INTERESTING. MISS YOU AND LOVE YOU. DI

I added a heart emoji and then decided to send another thank you to Aiden. He responded immediately.

GLAD ALL IS WELL AND EVERYONE IS SAFE. ALWAYS READY TO HELP. I HOPE YOU GOT WHAT YOU NEEDED.

I considered a moment and responded.

WE DID. THANK YOU. NO HURRY, BUT I WOULD APPRECIATE ANY ADVICE ABOUT THE TULANE OFFER WHEN YOU GET A CHANCE.

Three dots appeared. I waited as Shakti started rolling up the map.

I SENT YOU MY ANSWER. SHE'S STANDING BESIDE YOU. I MAY NOT BE THERE PHYSICALLY, BUT ALL THE BEST OF ME AND MUCH MORE IS THERE WITH YOU RIGHT NOW. WE DON'T JUST NEED YOU AND ME. WE NEED TO EQUIP MORE PEOPLE LIKE SHAKTI TO FIGHT THE GOOD FIGHTS IN PLACES WE WILL NEVER GO AND LONG AFTER WE'RE GONE. THAT IS WHAT YOU'RE GOING TO DO AT TULANE, AND YOU WILL BE AMAZING.

I glanced at Shakti as she slid the map back into its cannister. She looked up from her work and returned my smile, looking a little curious at what I was up to. Shakti slid the strap over her shoulder and reattached the small bag to the belt around her waist.

"Thanks for signing the CD," Shakti said, taking Delilah's hand. "Very nice to meet you. Look me up next time you play Minneapolis."

"Definitely," Delilah said. "Thank you for handling our friend so well."

"You need to get new friends," Shakti said with a laugh as musical as her accent. "Nice to meet you too," she added, nodding to Angélique and Dorcas.

"Do you need a place to stay tonight?" Angélique asked.

"I have a friend in the city with a bed and a change of clothes," Shakti said. "I'll be on an early plane to Minneapolis tomorrow morning."

"Need a ride?" Dorcas asked.

Shakti smiled and held up her phone. "Uber. It's probably best if I don't show up at the Sorbonne with any accomplices. The Broussards are going to raise enough hell as it is."

"I'll walk you down," I said.

Shakti said goodbye again. After we walked down the stairs and out into the cool night air, I stood with her waiting for her ride.

"Tell Aiden how much we appreciate it when you see him," I said.

"Will do," Shakti said. "He must think a lot of you. I don't see him go to this much trouble for many people."

"He's a good friend," I said. "We've had each other's back in the trenches over the years."

"Sounds like pretty interesting war stories," Shakti said with genuine interest. "Would love to hear them someday."

"Do you like what you do?" I asked. "Working at the Franklin Center?"

"Yes," Shakti said, displaying her musical laughter again. "Other duties as assigned doesn't begin to cover it. We get into some . . . interesting adventures sometimes."

"Your work is fulfilling?"

"The work, the opportunities to help people, and the people I work with are amazing," Shakti said. "There are a couple of guys. One is a computer whiz. The other is like a little brother to me. He's also Indian, but the Native American variety. We've got an Irish goth. She's the one who gave me the CD Delilah signed. And then there's Miss All American Girl. She's new. I wasn't sure about her at first, but she's growing on me. Aiden and Laura, she's a religious studies professor too, have sort of adopted us all. Bunch of strays pulled together by shared traumas and insane adventures."

"You make it sound like a family," I said.

Shakti looked surprised and then thoughtful.

"I guess we are in a way," she said. "Don't tell any of them I said so. I'll deny it."

A gray compact car pulled beside us. The driver confirmed Shakti's name and destination.

"Thank you, Shakti," I said, gripping her hand.

"It was an honor to meet you, Diana," Shakti said. She slid into the backseat of her Uber. Before she closed the door, Shakti said, "The answer to all the questions you just asked is yes. People like me need people like you. I don't know where I would be without Aiden. I'll deny I said that too if anyone asks. Best of luck in Belle Plage. I hope to see you again in New Orleans."

Shakti closed the car door and waved again as her Uber started for the Sorbonne. I waved back and watched until the car disappeared. I looked up and saw the Eiffel Tower. I marveled at the beauty and symmetry of Gustav Eiffel's masterpiece.

"Beautiful, isn't she?" Angélique said. "I never get tired of seeing her."

She was standing on the steps with a cigarette balanced between her long well-manicured fingers. She took a drag from the cigarette and exhaled a stream of smoke.

"I know," Angélique said, "nasty habit. I have mostly quit. Had not had one in three years. Then Maman died."

"Not my place to judge," I said. "I'm sure it's been hard."

We watched the famous landmark in silence for a few minutes.

"Angélique," I said, breaking the spell despite my wish to stay transfixed. "Why did you bring us here?"

"I did not bring you here," Angélique said. "Your mother did. Our mothers did. They discovered something that needed to be put right. It is our responsibility to do that. To finish what they started."

"Are you sure that's what they would have wanted?" I asked.

"You've been spending too much time with Madeleine," Angélique sniffed.

"Madeleine said you wanted something from her. What is it?"

"To see her pay for the murder of Jean-Paul and the exile of my mother from Belle Plage," Angélique said. "I want to see the Broussards pay for all their crimes."

"I think that's true," I said. "At least, I think you believe it's true. But that's not all. There's more you're not telling me. What do you want from Madeleine?"

"In good time," Angélique said. "You should come upstairs. It can get quite cool after the sun goes down."

I reluctantly followed her upstairs, frustrated again at the firewalls she and Madeleine maintained to hide their secrets.

My heart leaped when Bryan Adam's *Heaven* sounded from my phone shortly after lunch the next day. I excused myself and stepped outside the apartment for privacy. I accepted the video call. Trey's face filled my screen.

"Hey, Sir Lancelot," I said.

"It's become a thing," Trey groaned. "Good to see and hear you, Beautiful."

"How are you two doing?"

"Great. Your dad likes Geneva okay, but he thinks Lake Geneva is a little 'small and lazy' compared to Lake Pontchartrain. He called the jet d'eau 'just a fancy water sprinkler.'"

"Can a lake be lazy?" I asked. "I thought only rivers could be lazy."

"I'm not sure why any water has to be lazy," Trey said. "I'm just the messenger."

"Did you make it to the bank?"

"Yes," he said. "Just after we arrived yesterday and then again this morning."

"They made you come back?"

"It was close to closing time by the time we got there," Trey explained. "But we also had another problem. They had no record of a Lucy Broussard, Lucille Broussard, Lucille Hebert or any other combination we tried. The paperwork we presented matched the account number, but they said the names we kept using didn't match the name on the account. Without both, they were reluctant to let us look at the safety deposit box."

"What did you do?"

"We got a hot meal and went to our hotel to regroup," Trey said.

"It does make sense that Lucille wouldn't use her own name," I said. "I'm sure Madeleine traced her movements after Belle Plage and would have searched any place she thought Lucille would hide the materials she took from Chateau Broussard."

"That's what I thought too," Trey said. "I'm just going to pause here for a moment and ask what it's like to be in love with a genius."

"You tell me," I teased.

Trey grinned and continued, "It's funny you mentioned Madeleine. She helped us out without realizing it. While I was shaving my insanely well-proportioned rugged jaw this morning, I realized the best alias to use if you're trying to hide something is a name no one is using anymore."

He could tell by the look on my face I'd guessed it too.

"Wow," I whispered.

"We went back this morning and matched our documentation to a safety deposit box registered to Tamera Christine Hines."

I felt a twinge of emotion hearing her middle name. It appeared Raymond Hines had a heart after all. He'd named Crissy after his sister.

"How did you find her middle name?" I asked.

"They let us have access with just her first and last names," Trey said. "I saw 'Christine' on the paperwork. Di, you won't believe what we found."

I steadied myself internally, preparing for anything.

"First, we found a manuscript," Trey said.

"A letter?" I asked.

"A book," Trey said. "Maybe the first one she ever wrote. It's called *Dark Confessions*. I read the first few pages. Her voice in it is so different from her later books, Di. You can tell it's her, but it's not quite as . . ."

"Wild and crazy?"

"Yeah," Trey said. "Of course, I only read a few pages. There's still plenty of time for it to go off the rails. She talks about the pastor who sent her that letter Madeleine gave you. And about Tamera. And Alexandre. I'll try to read more later."

"You have it with you?"

"Yeah," Trey said. "They let us take it all since we had documentation of your mom's death. Thankfully, she communicated with them in 2014 and sent an additional item to be included in the safety deposit box. She had to send them an updated picture then. We showed them Lucille's photo. They were satisfied with the match."

"An additional item?"

"Yes," Trey said softly. "Letters addressed to you and your dad."

"To me?"

"We're going to leave it sealed until you can read it," Trey said. "She must have written it when she prepared the other envelope she left for you in Picardy. And there's more. Brace yourself. I'm sending you an image. There was also a folder in the safety deposit box. These old photos were in it."

I saw the text from Trey and opened it. The stark black and white image broke my heart. A beautiful young woman with long dark hair was sitting amidst a cluster of three children, two girls and a boy. The boy, about five years old, stood straight and tall by his mother's side while one sister held his hand. She looked a few years older. Her body language clearly communicated her determination to protect and comfort her little brother. The youngest girl looked about three years old. She had her head buried in her mother's lap. Her mother was resting her hand on her youngest daughter's head, trying her best to comfort her. There was something so familiar about the woman's features. Her face was weary, sad, hopeless, and desperate. Objects were stacked around them. Was it luggage?

"Here's another one," Trey said.

The second image showed the same scene zoomed out a little. With the wider perspective, I could see that the items stacked around the family were their household possessions. The front door of their house stood open behind them. Uniformed paramilitary police wearing light-colored shirts and black pants were carrying more items out. I recognized the white gamma insignia of the *Milice française* on their shirts. The *Milice française* rounded up Jews and French citizens resisting Nazi control on behalf of the Vichy government. Two officers stood beside the family, making sure they didn't interfere as the French paramilitary unit pillaged their home. Her husband was gone, probably already taken away while the rest of his family was forced to watch the dissolution of their lives.

I reached down and touched the woman's cheek on my screen. I could feel her pain, her fear, her helpless desperation to save the people she loved. I wanted so much to reach through the barrier of time and comfort her. I wanted to tell her it was going to be okay. It was best that I couldn't, however, because that would have been a lie. It wasn't going to be okay for them. I already knew their fate. I felt tears flowing down my cheeks.

Trey's voice came gently through the phone. "I'm sorry, Di. Her name was Hannah Abrams. She was Sarah's grandmother. She died at Bergen-Belsen in 1944."

That's why she looked so familiar. I could see the resemblance to Sarah. Slight, but clearly there.

"That's horrible, Trey," I said, wiping my eyes. "Did the children survive?"

"Two of them. The boy in the picture is Sarah's father. He and the younger sister survived. They came back to Belle Plage after the war."

Trey gave me a beat to process everything before dropping the biggest bombshell.

"Di," Trey said, "look what she's sitting on."

My eyes traveled to the lower edge of the photo. Grief turned to rage. There it was. Visible below the folds of her dress. Looking just like I saw it only a few days before.

"My God, Trey!"

"I know." I could hear his own fury in his voice.

Hannah Abrams was sitting on an ornate wooden chest framed with silver bands and a formidable lock. Her chest. Her possession. No doubt a family heirloom brought with them as they moved from place to place to avoid the oncoming Nazi storm. Trying to find somewhere they could be allowed to just be. To live. To enjoy the basic human right to exist.

"Are you thinking what I'm thinking, Trey?"

"Your dad and I are both thinking it," Trey said.

"She didn't give this chest to the Broussards," I said. "Did she?"

"No," Trey said. "And, thanks to your mom, I have the paperwork to prove it in my hands. This file is amazing, Di. It's the ultimate burn file. A prosecutor's dream. I don't know how Lucille got it, but she could have easily destroyed the Broussards with it. There are communiques sent from German military and Vichy political leaders to Henri Broussard's father. Inventory lists of items confiscated from Jews and the French Resistance leaders arrested by the *Milice*. Items given to the Broussards as a reward for their cooperation."

"But everyone in Belle Plage says they helped . . ." My voice trailed off. Horror rippled through me. I felt a wave of revulsion. "They were trapping them, weren't they? The Broussards offered the Resistance the use of their caverns and access to their estate so they could learn who they were and how they operated. Then . . ."

"There's a transcription here of a message sent from the chateau by shortwave radio with lists of the leaders and a location where the *Milice* could catch them meeting."

"A lot of things are falling into place," I said.

"How so? What else?"

"France held a series of tribunals to address collaboration during the Vichy era immediately after the war, but those mostly ended by 1946 with a lot of people escaping accountability," I said. "There was a renewed determination to address those crimes in the early seventies. Lots of energy was expended trying to uncover past atrocities and recover stolen property. There were prosecutions in France during the 80s of German officials like Klaus Barbie who'd committed atrocities there. The first French citizen convicted of war crimes in France was a former *Milice* commander named Paul Touvier. He was indicted for ordering the execution of seven Jewish prisoners in retaliation for the assassination of a Vichy government official."

"Why did it take so long for them to catch him?" I could see that Trey had another window open on his phone and was reading about Touvier.

"He was hidden by sympathizers, including traditionalist Roman Catholic church officials. He was arrested hiding at a priory in Nice in 1989. But, Trey, here's the interesting part. I just checked to see if my dates were right, and they are. Touvier went underground as charges were being leveled against him. That was in 1973. About a year before Lucille arrived in France. He was arrested in 1989. He was convicted in 1994. The year before Aria and Angélique showed up at our front door."

"Why would they have waited a year to come?" Trey asked.

"Because Henri Broussard didn't die until 1995," I said. "What if those two things together convinced Aria that their former students might be in danger?"

"But why?" Trey asked. "After all that time, why would the Broussards still fear them?"

Trey was right. There were too many questions still left unanswered, but the biggest one was eating at me.

"Trey, why didn't she?"

"Who?"

"Lucille," I said. "Why didn't she use the file to topple the Broussards? Sure, the French government was ambivalent still in 1974. But the damage the file would have done to the Broussards in Belle Plage alone would be enough to weaken their power. After that, it would only be a matter of time. Why would she have kept this hidden all those decades? Especially when there was a push to see justice done."

"I wish I could answer that," Trey said. "Maybe her friendship with Alexandre? Nostalgia for what she shared with Madeleine? Christian teachings on forgiveness and leaving things behind?"

None of those possible answers satisfied me. "Pedro often said he thought I got my obsession with righting wrongs from her."

"Obsession?" Trey said. "With all due respect to Pedro's counseling credentials, I think he tended to label some of your greatest strengths as weaknesses because he was incurably cynical."

"Maybe," I said. "I am very curious to find out why Lucille didn't pull the trigger by releasing this file. I need to go tell the others. Are we still good to meet at the station tomorrow?"

"Yes," Trey said. "Get our tickets for us, and we'll meet you there."

"Thanks, Trey. Love you so much. Be careful."

"You too. See you tomorrow."

When I shared Trey's news, everyone reacted with the same range of emotions I'd experienced.

Angélique's eyes gleamed. "I always knew it was something horrible. Did our mothers leave because of this?"

"It has to be part of the reason they left with the kids," I said. "But it may not be all of it."

"We need to get back there," Dorcas said with determination.

She opened her laptop and started reserving tickets.

We reached the train station early and sat waiting for Trey and Daddy. I finally got a text from Trey only an hour before our own train was supposed to depart.

SOME KIND OF MECHANICAL ISSUE SLOWING US DOWN. WE MAY NOT MAKE IT BEFORE THE TRAIN LEAVES.

I tapped my foot constantly, driving Delilah crazy, until another text came through only ten minutes before we had to board.

WE'RE MOVING AGAIN, BUT WE'RE NOT GOING TO MAKE IT IN TIME.

I texted back.

SHOULD WE WAIT?

Trey answered.

NO POINT WASTING YOUR TICKETS TOO. GO AHEAD AND WE'LL BE RIGHT BEHIND YOU. WE'LL GET THERE AS SOON AS WE CAN.

As I stepped off the platform onto the train, I felt an uneasy sensation. I looked around the platform and examined the interior of the train as we found our seats. Nothing seemed out of order. Still, I couldn't escape the feeling that we were being watched.

CHAPTER FIFTEEN

MAY 7, 1995

I dreamed someone was watching us. A shadowy figure with gnarled hands like tree branches and a skeletal face stood on the hill overlooking our house. Flames burned in their dead eye sockets as they watched and waited. Sometimes Momma was standing with them. Once, the ghostly figure grabbed Momma and snapped her neck while I watched from my window. I screamed as her lifeless body tumbled to the ground. The apparition turned its burning eyes on me, sending a clear message.

"You're next!"

I woke up screaming. Five seconds later, a pillow flew across the room and hit me in the face.

"Shut up!" Delilah growled.

I debated the ethics of using my sister as a human shield should the tree skeleton demon pay us a visit.

I'd found Momma sitting in the kitchen sipping a cup of tea the morning after I'd seen her sneak out. She pointed to our breakfast on the table and acted like all was normal. I debated asking her where she'd gone and who she'd met. As usual, my courage failed me when it came to my momma. I thanked her for breakfast, and we sat in silence until the others joined us one by one.

Later that afternoon, Daddy took Delilah and me out to an old houseboat moored on the edge of the river. Angélique accompanied us again. The houseboat was tied just above our property line. Tommy Simpson owned the property and the houseboat. He was looking to sell the boat.

"What do you think?" Daddy asked.

"Looks like a piece of garbage, Dad," Delilah said.

"You're always honest, Angel," Daddy said, laughing.

"Are you thinking about fixing it up?" I asked.

"Maybe," he said. "It's cheap. I can get a lot of parts from the landfill or wrecking yards. Would be a fun project to keep me busy when I'm home."

I could hear Momma in my head pointing out all the other unfinished fun projects lying around our yard. The old houseboat was painted fire engine red. Obvious signs of corrosion were visible on the lower deck. I hated to think about the corrosion that wasn't visible.

"You're going to have to paint it for sure," I said.

"I kind of like the red," Daddy said.

"People are going to think the fire department is coming when we float down the river," I said.

"You sound like your momma," Daddy said.

Didn't hear that often.

"We have these on the Seine," Angélique said, pronouncing each word with care. Her vocabulary was improving. I decided she must have known more than she showed at first. She'd just needed to gain some confidence to use it.

"Exactly," Daddy said. "We could be like those fancy European folks."

Angélique gave him an indulgent smile, probably not wanting to dispel his idealized visions of fancy European folks.

When we got back to the house, a blue Ford Escort was parked in our front yard. I recognized the car. It belonged to my parents' friend Sharon Thibodeaux. She and her husband Ron also attended Trinity Assembly of God. Sharon worked as a beautician while Ron served as the town coroner.

"Is that one of them?" I heard Sharon ask as we walked through the door.

I saw Momma roll her eyes in exasperation. Sharon rose from her place on the couch, her dirty blonde curls wagging as she walked toward Angélique.

"We're so glad to have you in America, Honey," Sharon said, enunciating like someone talking to a toddler.

"Thank you," Angélique said, looking uncertainly at each of us.

"Sharon came over to see our guests," Momma said. "Apparently, Beth Hines has been spreading it all over town that we have visitors from France."

Why do you have to be you, Crissy! What a jerk!

"Hope you're settlin' into life here okay, Honey," Sharon said.

"Angélique is going home soon," Momma said. "They have tickets to fly out on Wednesday."

We all looked at my momma in surprise, including Angélique. It was news to us. We were going to have to plan our little French tea party fast to meet that deadline.

"I'm sorry you have to go so soon," Sharon said. "There were so many things I wanted to ask you about over there."

"*Oui oui,*" Angélique said. "I am glad to tell you."

Sharon leaned closer to Angélique and whispered conspiratorially. "Is it true that you ladies don't shave your legs and your armpits over there? Not that I'm judging or anything."

"Maybe we should let Angélique go get ready for supper," Momma said, rising to take Sharon's arm and escort her to the front door.

We had a good dinner that night, but I sensed a palpable tension between Angélique and Aria. The adults tried to keep the conversation light, with Aria talking about all the things we would do together if we ever made it to France. Daddy left after supper and returned with some tools from the barn. To my surprise, he went into the artifacts room. He hadn't worked in there much since he put some new shelves in a year ago.

"What are you doing in there, Daddy?" I asked when he came out.

"Just a little project for your momma, Angel," he said. "I'm going to have to move some of the artifacts out while I work."

"Even Christine?" I asked. I did not want to see my nemesis demon doll leering at me from the hallway every day when I came home from school.

"Just for a day or two," he laughed. "Christine will behave herself."

I found that very unlikely.

"You think we can take Trey fishing again soon?"

"Maybe," he said. "We'll see. Your momma and me will have to get back to it after Aria's gone."

My heart sank. "Get back to it" meant going away all the time.

"We'll have to see if there are any good days for it this week," Daddy said. "The paper said we're going to have some rain. Hopefully won't be much."

I said goodnight and went upstairs to brush my teeth. I noticed Angélique and Aria's light was still on when I joined Delilah in our room. I lay there trying to go to sleep for a while before I finally drifted off. I awoke an hour later.

I couldn't understand what they were saying, but Aria and Angélique's muffled voices were loud enough to break my sleep. Their voices were raised. I couldn't begin to translate the French, but I could tell it was a heated conversation. I lay awake listening to them fight.

CHAPTER SIXTEEN

BANQUE GENÈVE
Reference # 12181991
Manuscript Held In Trust For Boxholder 763

An Excerpt from

DARK CONFESSIONS (1975)

By Lucille A. Broussard

Lucy lay awake wrestling with her thoughts. September had turned to October. Lucy had been at Chateau Broussard for almost a month. The euphoria of her first few weeks was giving way to growing dread. She looked across the room to Aria's empty bed. Where was she? They'd been downstairs playing chess with Alexandre and Jean-Paul. Angélique and Jean-Paul had taken a walk outside. Lucy had got tired of waiting for her and finally went to bed, expecting to fall asleep quickly. Instead, she lay there turning recent events over in her mind and getting worried about Aria.

Lucy had decided to read *Huckleberry Finn* with her class for two reasons. She felt she needed to give her students the benefit of hearing about an American classic from an American teacher, and it was a fun inside joke that only Alexandre could fully appreciate. However, Lucy hadn't anticipated the furor it would cause.

A teenage boy named Louis raised his hand on the third day they were reading the novel.

"Yes, Louis?" Lucy said.

"Why are we reading this, Mademoiselle?" Louis asked.

"It's an American classic," Lucy said.

"Why is this boy helping the man escape his owners?" Louis asked.

"He's helping Jim get to a state where he can be free. Where he can help his family gain freedom too."

"That is unnatural," Louis said. "The man is inferior. He should respect his master."

Several other boys nodded. The girls were silent.

Lucy had grown up hearing things like that all her life, but she hadn't expected to hear it at Chateau Broussard.

"Louis," Lucy began. "We are all created by God."

"And he created some to be inferior," Louis said. "To serve the master races."

Lucy's blood chilled at the mention of "master races."

"Who told you this, Louis?" Lucy asked.

"Monsieur Jean-Paul," Louis said. Other students nodded. Lucy noticed François looking down intently at his desk as Louis continued. "He said the African races were created when God cursed Ham in Genesis."

Lucy had grown up in a Baptist church with at least three deacons active in the Ku Klux Klan. She thought those ideas couldn't shock her anymore, but she was wrong. Louis terrified her with his nonchalant recitation. She tried to explain that the "curse of Ham" story was a racist mythology, a violence to responsible biblical interpretation. Louis heard her out, but his eyes and steadfast expression revealed his commitment to Monsieur Jean-Paul's interpretation.

François scared her more when he came to her later that day. He told a horrific story about a fight that had happened before she arrived. One boy had almost killed the other. When Jean-Paul arrived, he incited further violence and then stabbed the boy in the hand when he refused to finish the fight. Then he made the boy repeat and imitate what Jean-Paul had done. François said he was the only one willing to talk about it. Everyone else was too afraid. They'd even been warned not to tell Aria, who was working outside when it happened. These were the boys François said were later taken by "devils" wearing red in the dead of night.

Lucy had caught Sarah after class the next day and taken her for a walk on the beach. It took a lot of persuasion, but Sarah eventually confirmed François' story in tears, trembling from head to toe the entire time. She begged Lucy not to tell anyone.

As Lucy lay there thinking over the growing signs of something very twisted about the education Madeleine was offering, she heard boats below the cliffs. They sounded close. Like they were pulling into the little cove right below the chateau. Another sound teased her ears. *A helicopter?* She threw her covers off and looked out the window. Lucy had guessed correctly. A helicopter sat on the lawn below, its rotors slowing their rotation. Three people emerged from the chopper. Lucy couldn't make out any details about them in the darkness. They walked across the lawn and headed for the chateau.

Something wasn't right. Lucy couldn't contain her curiosity any longer. She slipped out of her room and started down the hallway. When she reached the first floor, Lucy heard noises coming from an open doorway behind the stairwell. She'd never been down to the basement. She concealed herself when two men in black suits came out of the open door and turned toward Madeleine's chapel. Lucy waited a few minutes. When she was sure there was no one else coming, Lucy left her hiding place on the other side of the stairs and eased the door open. A set of winding stairs led down to the basement. Lucy followed them, tiptoeing down each step in her slippers. She clutched her pink robe around her nightgown as a cool breeze flowed up the stairs. *Where was that coming from?* She was basically underground. There shouldn't be a breeze.

Lucy reached the bottom and found herself in an old wine cellar. Wooden shelves lined the walls with bottles poking out of each. She looked at some of the labels. The vintages represented were very old. Some of them centuries old. The Broussards had a treasure trove worth a fortune in their wine collection alone.

Voices teased her ears. Another breeze lifted the bottom of her nightgown as Lucy continued down the row of shelves until she reached a more open area. Two large empty rooms with heavy doors occupied the wall to her left. The doors of both rooms were standing open. Lucy slipped from one to the other, seeing nothing inside either one. Both were bare. The voices resounded again. Lucy came to a dead end and turned left. She jumped back just in time to avoid being seen by Monique.

Lucy cautiously looked around the corner. Monique was standing with a candelabra clutched in her right hand. The flames of each candle were dancing wildly, stoked by a breeze coming from an open door in front of her. Lucy noticed a bookcase pushed to one side. She guessed it usually covered the entrance. She could make out the little wheels mounted on the bottom to make it easier to move. As Lucy watched, a man dressed in a gray suit with dark slicked hair entered through the doorway.

"*Bonsoir*, Monsieur Ravel," Monique said. She reached into the pocket below her apron and produced a sheet of paper. She handed it to him.

"*Merci*," he said, bowing to Monique.

Lucy scrambled to one of the empty rooms and hid there while Monsieur Ravel walked past her and started up the stairs. Lucy guessed that the basement door Monique opened led down the cliffs to the tunnel entrance on the beach. Lucy had seen it from the other end when Alexandre took her boating one day, but she didn't realize it actually emerged inside the house.

Lucy heard a scraping noise. It took her a moment to realize it was Monique sliding the bookshelves back in place. Lucy moved quickly. Monique's steady steps resounded through the corridor, heading straight for her. Lucy hurried up the stairs, tripping twice in her haste. She made it to the first floor, but she could hear Monique right behind her. With no time to find another option, Lucy hid again behind the grand staircase, crouching painfully. She didn't dare breathe. Her legs felt like rubber by the time Monique finally satisfied herself that no one else was coming and started toward the kitchen.

Lucy rose, stretching her legs as best she could. The sounds of music rippled from the chapel. Who was conducting mass at this hour? Lucy walked cautiously down the hallway to the large doors of the chapel. She stooped so she could look through a clear panel in the stained glass. Lucy gasped and jumped back. She recovered her composure and leaned down again. She had actually seen what she thought she saw the first time. François' devils had come to life! About twenty people dressed from head to toe in red robes, hoods raised, were reciting a liturgy in Latin. Lucy couldn't understand any of the words. Standing at the front leading them, his own hood lowered to reveal his face, was Henri Broussard. The candles flickering on either side cast a ghostly psychedelic glow over the assembly.

Lucy felt sweat pouring down her body despite the chilly night. The scene looked so much like the rituals Pastor Lindell described in his Bible studies. He warned people constantly about an increase in satanic cults around Los Angeles. There'd been the Manson family in 1969, horrifically murdering the beautiful actress Sharon Tate along with her friends and unborn baby. Then Mike Warnke had appeared on the L.A. scene, a Christian comedian telling stories about his past as a satanic high priest. Now Lucy was witnessing her nightmares come to life.

The ritual was changing. The worshippers were chanting in French now. Lucy picked out a few words. She heard blood, soil, life, and rule. It was a confusing array of ideas and images.

"Lucy?"

Lucy jumped. Madeleine stood a few feet away. As always, she'd been silent in her approach. She was fully dressed in formal attire. No doubt she was expecting these visitors.

"Don't be afraid, Lucy," Madeleine said. "I can explain if you let me."

"What are they doing?" Lucy demanded.

"It's just a ceremony honoring our ancestors and our hopes for the future," Madeleine said. She reached for Lucy. Lucy flinched, instinctively shrinking away from her. Madeleine looked hurt, but she didn't force the issue.

"Lucy . . ."

"Can I return to my room, please?" Lucy said stiffly.

Madeleine deliberated for a moment. She seemed to decide it was better to discuss things in the light of day.

"Yes," Madeleine said. "We can talk tomorrow. Please don't form any opinions until you hear me out. You're very special to me, Lucy. I don't have any girls. I've come to think of you like a daughter. I want you to stay with us. To help us in our work. Please don't let this scare you."

Madeleine's words and demeanor were so persuasive. Even seductive in a motherly way. Lucy could almost forget what she'd just witnessed. Then she heard Pastor Lindell's voice in her head. *Satan disguises himself as an angel of light.* She couldn't give into the temptation. *What is evil?* It doesn't just exist in vomit-soaked dormitory rooms or dark alleys. It exists in exquisite chateaus. It exists everywhere.

"Good night, Madeleine," Lucy said, hurrying past her. She felt Madeleine's eyes on her as she hurried back to the main staircase. Aria was still gone when she reached her room. Lucy collapsed onto her bed, her body trembling with adrenaline and fear. She decided she would write to Pastor Lindell tomorrow and explain what she'd seen and heard. Maybe he would know what to do. She pulled the little red New Testament from her side table and clutched it to her chest, praying its very presence would ward off the evil cloud she felt gathering around her. She fell asleep with the Bible still against her chest.

The next morning, Lucy awoke to a quiet chateau. Since it was Sunday, there were no classes. The students were allowed to sleep in. While Lucy was dressing, she heard the doorknob turn. Aria walked in wearing the same jeans and light sweater she'd been wearing the night before. Her elegant black hair was disheveled as if she'd just woken up.

"Lucy," Aria said, blushing slightly. "I thought you would be downstairs for breakfast already."

"I didn't sleep well," Lucy said. "I was worried about my roommate."

"I did not mean to scare you," Aria said. "I did not plan to be gone."

"Where were you?" Lucy asked. The question was moot. Lucy already knew.

Aria sighed. "There is no point in lying to you. I was with Jean-Paul."

"You walked on the beach all night?" Lucy said.

Aria raised her eyebrow.

"Really, Lucy?"

"So, you . . ."

Aria nodded and sat down on her bed. Lucy didn't see what she expected to see. Aria's expression was so sad.

"Are you okay?" Lucy asked.

"*Je ne sais pas*," Aria said. "I did not plan it. He invited me up to his room. We talked for a while. We started kissing. And then, it just happened so quickly."

"Was it not . . . good?" Lucy felt very awkward asking and with the conversation in general.

"It was fine."

It was obvious Aria had been hoping for better than fine.

"It was good," Aria said as if trying to convince herself. "It was a little painful at first. Then it felt good."

"So, what's wrong?" Lucy asked.

Aria looked at Lucy with confusion in her eyes. "I just expected it to be more . . . intimate. Tender. It was over so fast. Then Jean-Paul just went to sleep. He left early this morning without saying good morning or goodbye. I felt like I was just a goal he needed to accomplish. And once it was accomplished . . ."

Lucy resisted the urge to remind Aria of her warnings.

"I'm sorry," Lucy said instead.

"Maybe I am just expecting too much," Aria said, trying to push herself out of her funk. "He is probably processing things too. We will talk today. It will just get better with time."

"I'm sure," Lucy said. She wasn't sure at all. A million warnings about the dangers of premarital sex from her parents and pastors lodged on the tip of her tongue. She decided Aria wouldn't react well to any of them and now wasn't the time anyway.

"Can I tell you something?" Lucy said. "I'm sorry to burden you with it now, but it can't wait."

Lucy told Aria the things she'd experienced in class and the stories she heard from François and Sarah.

"Why would Sarah not tell me this?" Aria asked.

"They seem terrified to tell anyone. I think I earned François' trust when I questioned Louis in class."

"There has to be some other explanation, Lucy. Can you imagine Madeleine encouraging those ideas?"

"There's more." Lucy told Aria about the argument she witnessed in the library. About Madeleine slapping Alexandre. Deciding to go for broke, she told Aria the full story of her trip downstairs including her discoveries in the basement and chapel.

Aria pressed her hands to her temples when Lucy was done. "It is too much all at once, Lucy. We need to talk to the boys. There must be things we do not know."

After breakfast, Lucy and Aria found Alexandre and Jean-Paul talking in the library. Alexandre was seated in the chair he usually occupied near the work desk. His chair was turned to face Jean-Paul. Jean-Paul was sitting behind Henri's personal desk, larger and more solid, directly across from Alexandre's smaller desk. Lucy noticed the awkward looks Aria and Jean-Paul exchanged when they entered.

"You ladies look so serious!" Alexandre exclaimed. "It is Sunday! Play day!"

"Alex, can we ask you some questions?" Lucy said.

"Absolutely!" Alexandre responded with enthusiasm. "We will answer as best we can!"

Jean-Paul didn't look interested or inclined to cooperate. He watched Lucy with cool detachment as she told her stories and asked her questions. Aria tried to make eye contact with Jean-Paul several times, but he wouldn't hold her gaze.

"It sounds to me like you are making accusations more than you are asking questions," Jean-Paul said finally.

"I don't mean to accuse anybody," Lucy said. "I just need to know if there is an innocent explanation for all this."

"An explanation for what?"

"Well, for starters, did you hurt those boys and threaten the other students to stay quiet about it?"

"Of course," Jean-Paul said.

Alexandre stared at the floor.

Lucy didn't know what to say. She'd expected an argument or at least some attempt at a defense. The last thing she expected was Jean-Paul to admit what he'd done in such a matter-of-fact tone. Lucy stole a glance at

Aria. Aria's mouth was hanging open and her face ashen.

"Alex?"

"It's true, Lucy," Alexandre said quietly.

"Why?"

"Because they were little weaklings," Jean-Paul said. "No man of destiny starts a fight and fails to finish it. That is why we sent them to Lyon. The academy there is harsher. They will learn there to be real men."

"The story about monks in red robes dragging the boys away is true?" Aria said.

"It wasn't handled well," Alexandre said. "They woke the boys up without warning. The boys were confused. There was nothing to fear."

"You have freaks running around this place in red robes terrorizing children in the dead of night and there is nothing to fear!" Lucy said. "Are they satanists, Alex?"

"They are not satanists, Lucy," Alexandre said. "They are associates of Papa's."

"Why must they hide their faces?" Aria asked.

"Why does that matter?" Jean-Paul said.

"Because I do not trust people who hide their faces," Aria said. "Such men always have something worse to hide."

"You are both being foolish," Jean-Paul said.

"I am foolish because I do not think someone should stab a little boy's hand for showing mercy!" Aria was shouting.

"They will be grateful one day when they are strong leaders," Jean-Paul said.

"I told you not to do it, Jean-Paul," Alexandre said.

"*Merde!* I do not take orders from you, Little Brother."

"Maybe you should," Alexandre said. Lucy could tell the words just slipped out. Alexandre looked shocked and terrified the moment they left his lips.

"Do you want to challenge me, Brother?" Jean-Paul demanded.

"Are you and Robert going to beat me again?" Alexandre asked. "I am used to that by now."

Jean-Paul slid open the desk drawer beside him. He reached into the drawer and rummaged for a moment. Lucy's heart skipped two beats when he raised his right hand. Jean-Paul was pointing a Browning P-35 high-powered handgun at Alexandre. The gun's black muzzle glistened wickedly in the light streaming through the windows.

Aria screamed and covered her mouth. Lucy prepared herself to dive or duck. Alexandre stared back at Jean-Paul, his face a maze of conflicting emotions one after another.

"Not such a big man now," Jean-Paul snarled.

"Papa says we are not to touch that," Alexandre said, his voice trembling.

"Papa says we are supposed to be real men who conquer worlds," Jean-Paul said. "When have you ever cared what Papa said? You know how many rounds this weapon can fire?"

Alexandre shook his head.

"Thirteen. I could put a lot of holes in you, Brother. Many holes in very little time."

All four of them remained frozen. Finally, Jean-Paul lowered the gun and placed it back in the drawer. He rose, walked around the desk, and spit at Alexandre.

"Pathetic," Jean-Paul said. He directed a disdainful stare at each of them and turned to leave. Aria rose and hurried to catch him. She followed him into the hallway.

"Jean-Paul, please wait!"

She kept calling his name until he turned to face her.

"We need to talk," Aria insisted.

"What do we need to talk about?" Jean-Paul asked.

"About everything," she pleaded. "All of this. About what we shared last night. There has to be a misunderstanding. You can't believe these things are right? That this is the way?"

Aria reached out and touched his arm. Jean-Paul knocked her hand away and grabbed her by both arms. Jean-Paul slammed Aria against the wall so fast and with such force that she gasped in mingled shock and pain. He held her there, screaming in her face.

"You do not ever presume to tell me the way, you pathetic little whore!

You think you can spread your legs once and tell me what to do! No one owns me! You disgust me!"

Lucy heard their conversation. She came out of the library just in time to see Jean-Paul slam Aria against the wall. Alexandre joined her as Jean-Paul screamed at Aria. Absolute devastation covered every inch of Aria's face.

"Alex, do something!"

"It is between them, Lucy. Not for us to get involved."

Lucy started down the hallway, yelling at the top of her lungs, "Take your hands off her!" She surprised even herself with the force and volume of her shout. Startled, Jean-Paul released Aria and stepped back. He turned, trying to stare Lucy down with his steely eyes. She braced herself, fully prepared to advance and claw those eyes out of their sockets if necessary. Jean-Paul shook his head and walked away. They heard his heavy footsteps pounding up the stairs.

Aria started crying. She slid down the wall, ending up in a sitting position on the floor, her back still braced against the wall. Lucy hurried to her and gathered Aria into her arms. They huddled on the floor together as Aria poured her heart-rending sobs into Lucy's chest. Lucy gripped her tight.

"I'm so sorry," Lucy said.

Alexandre stood watching. He put his hands in his pockets and removed them compulsively, not sure what to do.

"Why didn't you stop him?" Lucy demanded.

"It was not my place."

"What is your place, Alex?" Lucy said. "When do you decide to take responsibility for anything that happens around you?"

"You don't understand, Lucy," Alexandre said.

"I understand just fine," Lucy said, glaring at him over Aria's head. "Your brothers are right. You're just a gutless coward."

Alexandre flinched as if Lucy had physically struck him like Madeleine had. It was clear the psychological slap stung worse.

"I'm sorry you feel that way," Alexandre whispered. He looked stricken. Lucy watched him disappear back into the library. Part of her regretted what she said the moment she said it. The other furious part in her head insisted that "coward" was too kind. Besides, comforting two people at once was more social energy than Lucy had left.

Lucy managed to walk Aria up the stairs and get her into bed. She tried to think about what Etta would do to help someone in Aria's situation. Lucy stroked her hair, lost in her swirling thoughts, until Aria cried herself to sleep. Lucy was still sitting on Aria's bed when she heard a soft knock on the door. Madeleine stood there when Lucy opened the door. She looked past Lucy to where Aria lay sleeping soundly.

"Are you okay?" Madeleine asked.

"You obviously know we're not if you're asking," Lucy said. She was tired, angry, and done with being diplomatic.

"Can I speak with you for a moment?" Madeleine asked. "Out in the hallway so we don't disturb Aria."

Lucy nodded, easing the door closed behind her.

"First," Madeleine began, "I'm sorry you witnessed the ritual last night without warning. It had to be terrifying if you didn't know what to expect. Especially with your background."

"I see why the villagers tell stories about ghosts and cults in this place," Lucy said. "You know running around in red robes and saying Latin chants is not normal? It seems very satanic to me."

"*Ma chère,* we are not satanists," Madeleine insisted.

"Sounds to me like what a satanist would say," Lucy said. "What are you then?"

"We are people wanting to provide order and security for a chaotic world," Madeleine said. "You would dismiss any label I put on it because of the biased propaganda you've been taught all your life. People call evil what they do not understand and reject the very things that can bring them a better world. When I was a young woman, just a teenager, I visited these halls for the first time with Henri. The banquets his father would host! The ambitions to build a better world in the people around us. It was such a time! A time all too brief for us."

Lucy calculated based on Madeleine's age. Her breakfast returned to her throat and threatened to spill out of her mouth. Swallowing it back,

Lucy said, "How can you be nostalgic for those times?"

"You don't understand," Madeleine reached for her hand. Lucy allowed her to take it. "Stay with us and let me help you understand. Open your mind to new possibilities. Help me continue my work here."

"Madeleine," Lucy said, surprised how truly sorry she was to say it, "I can't follow you down this path. It goes against everything I believe."

Madeleine released her hand. Her disappointment filled her eyes. She sighed and stared at the floor for a moment. When she looked at Lucy again, her demeanor was gentle, but formal.

"Henri has decided for a number of reasons that we need to relocate the students for a bit," she said. "Just until some things blow over. We partner with a sister academy in Lyon that offers a strong academic program and stricter social training. Henri thinks our students will benefit from some time there."

"Relocate them?" Lucy said. "When?"

"We have a reception planned for October 31," Madeleine said. "A costume party. You and Aria are welcome to come. Special guests are attending. They will want to see the students and get a sense of their progress. Our *La Toussaint* or All Saints' Day observance will be held on November 1. Then we will transfer the students over the weekend in time to begin their classes on Monday."

Lucy tried to hide her alarm. She couldn't begin to imagine what the students would face at Lyon if it were stricter than what they'd been receiving at Chateau Broussard. Lucy wanted to protest. To argue against this course of action. Instead, she heard Etta's voice in her head. *Sometimes you catch more flies with honey, Lucy B.*

"What about the teachers?" Lucy said, forcing a steady tone.

"We'll keep all of you on," Madeleine said. "I'm hoping to bring the students back by Christmas or shortly after."

Lucy nodded.

"Please stay, Lucy," Madeleine said, determined to try again. "Take some time to think about it. We could have an amazing future."

She took Lucy's hand and squeezed it. Madeleine turned and walked slowly down the hallway to her private sitting room. Lucy thought back to their first meeting in that room just weeks ago. It seemed like a lifetime now.

Lucy eased the door open. Aria was still sleeping. Lucy slipped back into the room and leaned against the door. Two urgent thoughts filled her mind.

We can't let this happen! And we don't have much time!

CHAPTER SEVENTEEN

WE STEPPED OFF THE TRAIN AT BELLE PLAGE knowing we needed to move fast. It was only a matter of time before Robert retaliated for his humiliation at Charles de Gaulle. Unfortunately, I underestimated him.

We'd just stepped off the train with our small overnight bags. I was taking my phone out to see if Trey and Dad made their second train. I saw the alarmed look on Dorcas's face first. I felt a solid object against my back.

"Don't move," a harsh voice said.

I looked up to see Robert, his two security personnel, and a couple of reinforcements who'd been waiting for us at the platform. They were surrounding us. One of them was pressing a handgun to my back while the others were covering my sisters and Angélique. Robert glowered triumphantly at us.

"You think you can make a fool of me and just disappear?" he said. "Where is your friend with the taser?"

"Almost home by now," I said. "Did you ask your mommy if you could do this?"

I could tell he wanted to hit me. I raised my chin, daring him. Robert obviously heard mommy's voice in his head like a much less interesting version of Norman Bates. He restrained himself.

"You have a big mouth, Professor."

"So I've been told. You want to know where the last guy who told me that is now?"

"We waste time here," Robert grumbled. "We are going to the chateau. I will keep you all there until your friends bring us that chest."

"You're piling up a lot of hostages," Delilah said.

"The more I have," Robert said, "the more I can kill without losing leverage."

We rode back to the chateau in silence. Robert's men had confiscated our phones on the platform, so I hadn't had time to confirm that Trey and Dad caught their train or give them any indication we were in trouble. I searched my mind for an escape. Possibly a way to signal someone. Furtive looks at Delilah revealed she was working on the same problem and wasn't any closer to a solution. Dorcas gave me a reassuring wink. My brave little sister trusted us to come up with something clever much more than I trusted myself. Angélique sat beside her, simmering. She glared with undisguised hatred at the back of Robert's head.

We reached the chateau and processed through the hallway. Robert opened a door at the bottom of the main staircase. Our captors prodded us down a smaller set of stairs to the basement level. We entered a wine cellar stacked with vintages of every variety. Cobwebs hung from some of the wooden shelves; the standards of cleanliness were slipping at Chateau Broussard.

"Where is the other old man?" Robert said.

"We moved him upstairs," one security guard said. "He wasn't doing well with the dampness down here. The other one is still here."

Robert nodded. "We can put these in the other room for now. They do not need much space."

We passed the rows of wine bottles and entered a larger open space. Two closed doors, apparently opening to small rooms, were set in the wall across from us. At the sound of our approach, a face appeared at a small window cut into the door on the left side. An older man with gray hair looked out at us in surprise. I recognized him immediately from his pictures.

"François!" I said.

He started at the sound of his name. François looked hopeful when he saw me. Then he saw Dorcas. His eyes widened, and his expression grew even more hopeful.

"Don't talk to him!" Robert thundered. "He would not even be here if you had just let us take the chest."

"He would be dead like the others," I said. "How do you justify killing innocent people to hide your dirty little secrets?"

"We don't need to justify anything to people like you," Robert said.

"Spoken like one more rich psychopath making the world a worse place," Delilah said.

"I believe you make much money too with your singing and your silly dancing," Robert said. "Maybe a woman your age should be doing something more grown up now."

I could tell Delilah was making a mental note to make Robert pay with interest. "It's called working hard for the money, Trust Fund Boy."

"Are you out of your mind!"

Madeleine's shriek startled all of us. She swept into the basement, her black dress swishing across the floor.

"Don't answer that!" Madeleine yelled. "You clearly are and have been since you were born!"

Robert shrank back at the sight of his mother. It was like watching an elephant terrified by a mouse.

"I thought it was time to take action!" Robert said, trying to recover his bravado.

Madeleine marched straight up to Robert and slapped him.

"Score one for Miss Havisham," Delilah whispered.

"Glad you can still laugh about all this," I muttered.

Robert clutched his jaw, tears in his eyes. Instead of silencing him, Madeleine's slap made him angrier and more talkative.

"Why do you punish me?" Robert screamed. "I am trying to clean up a mess you have left us with for fifty years!"

"You are trying to clean it up in the most clumsy, brutal way possible," Madeleine said. "Just like your papa! You lack discipline still, Robert. After all these years. If only . . ."

"What?" Robert demanded.

"It doesn't matter," Madeleine said.

"No!" Robert yelled. "Say it, Maman! If only Jean-Paul were here! If only the golden boy had not gotten himself killed! Robert will never be good enough for you! You should remember how all this new trouble started! We would not be here if not for Jean-Paul's little bastard!"

"Shut up!" Madeleine hissed.

"So, it is true!" Angélique shouted, her eyes brimming with satisfaction.

"Robert doesn't know what he's saying," Madeleine said.

"You lying Bitch!" Angélique said.

"That's not a nice way to talk to your grandmother, Angélique," I said.

"How long have you known?" Angélique asked.

"I started doing the math after my last conversation with Madeleine," I said. "How long have you known?"

My sisters were staring at us in astonishment.

"I have suspected for years," Angélique said. "I have been trying to get proof for the last two. Maman would never tell me for sure. She wanted to protect me from these fiends."

"It doesn't matter how much noise you make or how many hairbrushes you try to steal," Madeleine said. "You will never be a Broussard in the truest sense."

"Then why will you not just give me a DNA sample?" Angélique asked. "What harm could it do?"

"It could give you a claim to their fortune and their name," I said. "She doesn't want to share. But, of course, you know that. That's really what this is all about, isn't it? Justice for you means getting a slice of their pie."

"And an acknowledgment of the wrong they did to my mother," Angélique said. "She deserved so much better than to be cast out and ignored."

"She left of her own free will," Madeleine said. "I'm tired of people blaming us for their poor decisions!"

"Why did you kill her, Robert?" I asked.

He started to deny it. Seeing the look on my face, he knew there was no use.

"We were trying to take the chest by surprise," Robert said. "I received a call while we were preparing to take it from your home that Aria was in New Orleans looking for you. I tried to catch her before she met you, but she found you first. I panicked. I did not know what else to do."

"That will be on your tombstone," Madeleine growled. "Robert, the man who did not know what else to do. No one has the gift for turning a small problem into a bigger one like you."

"What was I supposed to do?" Robert whined.

"Not kill her, you fool!" Madeleine shouted. "Or any of the others."

Robert's expression hardened. "We would have ended this years ago if you had sent armed men to capture Lucy that night instead of your sons. Your obsession with her has blinded you and made you weak. You never had the stomach to do what must be done. You let her hold us hostage for fifty years when we should have ended it long ago!"

"You understand nothing!" Madeleine said.

"I guess Carlton has no idea what you masterminds are up to over here," I said. "No wonder he stays in L.A. with his tech bros."

"Don't forget his meth and his hookers," Delilah said. "I've met a couple of aspiring actresses with black eyes. They were the lucky ones. The West Hollywood rumor mill says some women don't get to walk away from Carlton."

"Don't even begin to criticize my family," Madeleine said. "You two couldn't wait to leave the exorcist freak show Lucille and Denny created. Lucille neglected you in pursuit of her fanatical cause. Dinah died because of her obsessions and scruples."

"You just crossed a line, Bitch," Delilah said. "I can say that. You don't get to."

"Momma was ten times the woman you will ever be," Dorcas said.

"You're such a simple girl, Dorcas," Madeleine said. "Caught in the same drama as your mother. When will you stop chasing devils?"

Dorcas' eyes flashed. "At least I'm not a Satan worshipping Nazi."

There it was. The bomb finally dropped. The word no one had dared to say yet pushed into the open for all to hear.

"To be fair," I said. "She's not a Satan worshipper."

"But what about the red robes and chanting?" Dorcas said.

"It's based on a short-lived German occultist group called the Thule Society," I said. "I've encountered them in my previous research. I was refreshing my memory on the train. They were dissident Germans who dabbled in the occult during the early Weimar Republic. They supported the rise of Naziism and overlapped with the Nazi Party's membership. With the exception of Rudolf Hess, they weren't part of Hitler's inner circle. Nazi leaders were glad to benefit from their support and speak at their meetings occasionally, but they were embarrassed to be associated too closely with the Thule Society. They faded as a distinct movement by 1925, and they haven't existed as an organized movement for decades. Lucille saw an underground cell of rich fascists cosplaying as an ancient society and wearing red robes to conceal their identities from anyone who might happen to surprise them. They aren't satanists. Nazi, on the other hand, fits well."

"There was a time when some people wore those labels proudly," Madeleine said woodenly.

"Times change," I said.

"Yes, they do," Madeleine said. "Like a revolving wheel they recycle what has been into new forms. A wave is cresting as we speak. People are looking for authority. They want protection from the things and people they fear. We are ready to provide it for them again. We're everywhere, Diana. You know it. Leading your businesses. Influencing your churches. Infiltrating your universities. Our time is coming again."

She wasn't wrong. Anyone paying attention could see the rancid tide riding on the currents of misinformation and conspiracy. Hatred, greed, lust, and fear driving it deep into the hearts of ordinary people too busy or too afraid to ask the hard questions.

"All waves recede eventually," I said. "People have a remarkable ability to rise above their hatred when they overcome their fear. You can bet against love and courage and win for a while, but the human spirit always comes surging out of the ashes stronger than ever."

"Always the idealist," Madeleine said. "You have more in common with your mother than you realize." She turned to Robert. "Put them in the cells for now. Put Angélique upstairs with Jacob. I don't want her poisoning their minds. We'll try again later and see if we can salvage some agreement."

"Always with your agreements," Robert said.

"You blew this up by killing those women and kidnapping these men," Madeleine said. "You don't get to whine about how I fix it."

"Where did the other students go?" I asked.

"To Lyon," Madeleine said. "They were trained at another academy sympathetic to our cause. I can give you their names. Some of them are highly placed in business and politics across Europe, Asia, and the Americas. We make it our business to invest in young people who can return our patronage someday with favors. Like I said, Diana, I'm always closer than you can possibly imagine."

Madeleine and Robert left with two of Robert's men and Angélique, leaving the other men to guide us toward the two doors. We exchanged glances, none of us offering the others any immediate way out.

The security guard in front studied us and said, "Maybe we shouldn't overload the cells. Let's put the first one in with the old man."

Delilah happened to be the "first one." The guard eyed her warily as he turned his key in the door. He could tell she was a potential problem. He kept his eyes focused on her as the lock popped and he eased the door open.

The door slammed into him with such force it threw him off balance. His gun hand wavered. Delilah seized the opportunity. Moving with catlike reflexes, she kicked the gun out of his hand. It skittered across the floor. François kicked the door a second time, knocking the guard forward. Delilah kicked him in the chest.

The gun came to rest at Dorcas' feet. She scooped it up just as the second guard drew his gun and trained it on Delilah. Dorcas fell into a crouching position to make herself a smaller target, aiming the gun with a perfect stance that looked so much like my dad's she could have been his clone. Daddy always said never to point a gun at someone unless you were prepared to use it with deadly precision. Dorcas was prepared. She fired two shots. One shattered the guard's kneecap while the other hit his right arm just above his elbow. He screamed and fell to the ground. Dorcas hurried over to him and kicked the gun away from his hand.

Delilah and I were both on top of the first guard trying to subdue him. He kept struggling. Delilah finally seized his head and slammed it back on the cement floor. His eyes rolled back in his head and closed.

"Is he dead?" I asked.

"Do I care?" Delilah snorted.

"We should." I checked his pulse. He was alive.

François stumbled out of his cell, gripping the doorframe to keep himself standing.

"That was incredible, François," I said.

"Who are you?" he asked.

"We're Lucille Hebert's daughters. I'm Diana. This is Delilah. Dorcas is the one with the gun."

François smiled at the mention of Lucille's name. "How did you get here?"

"Believe it or not, we're here to rescue you," Delilah said.

Shouts and stomping feet resounded from the basement entrance.

"They heard us," Dorcas said.

"François, can you walk?" I asked.

"I'm slow, but I think so," he said.

"We've got to get out of here."

"What about Angélique and Jacob?" Dorcas said.

"We'll have to come back for them," I said.

"Where exactly are we going?" Delilah said. "They're coming from the direction of our most obvious escape route."

"We're going out the way we planned to get in," I said.

We hurried around the corner, moving further back into the basement. There it was, exactly where I hoped it would be. The bookcase Sarah had mentioned in her story. Dorcas and I pushed while François leaned on Delilah for support. The bookcase moved easily, rolling on four tiny wheels fastened to its undercarriage. The musty odor of damp packed earth filled my nostrils. The darkened tunnel extended before us. I noticed a light switch on the wall. I flicked it. A series of lights started coming on along the tunnel, illuminating the tight underground passage. A larger anteroom stood just outside the door. Boxes were stacked in one corner. A set of shelves held several flashlights and replacement gear for the boats moored on the beach at the other end of the tunnel. Beside them, a large mechanical device filled half of the wall space with a rolling chair sitting in front of it. Just beyond it, the narrow part of the tunnels began.

"What is this?" Dorcas asked.

"Wow!" Delilah said, dropping François' arm to take a better look. "This baby is vintage!"

"It's a large shortwave unit," I told Dorcas. "Trey and I never had one this nice to play with."

"I think this is a refurbished World War II era unit," Delilah said, fiddling with the dials. "It's in perfect working order."

"This is how they work around their own signal jammer," I said.

Delilah nodded. "They've probably got an antenna running to the surface."

Shouting voices and running feet brought us back to reality. Delilah moved back to the bookcase and kicked it firmly, turning it awkwardly so that it jammed the opening to the tunnels.

"Bring me some of those boxes," she said. "We'll block it to slow them down."

Dorcas and I each brought a sealed box. François helped Delilah position them against the bookcase. Dorcas picked up her third box. This one was open.

"Uh, Di?"

"What is it, Dor?"

"Is there any legitimate reason the Broussards would have boxes of Fentanyl lying around their tunnels?"

Delilah and I ran over to confirm her discovery.

"Their wealth is more precarious than I thought," I said.

"I guess *Unis* doesn't pay the bills," Delilah said.

"Don't you miss the days when they'd just marry the heir off to keep the family fortune like in Jane Austen or Downton Abbey?" Dorcas said.

"You've seen Robert," Delilah said. "And Carlton's no peach either. You'd have to pay someone to take them off your hands."

"Between the folder Trey has and the Fentanyl, I think it's safe to say the Broussards' European branch is about to go offline," I said.

"If we can get out of here," Delilah said.

We started down the lighted passageway. As we moved through the claustrophobic tunnels, we passed the side tunnels we'd seen on the map. They were pitch black and smelled even mustier than the main tunnel. I remembered what Shakti said about bodies and unexploded ordinance. At one point, several stalactites hung from the roof, almost obscuring the side tunnel's entrance. Finally, light appeared ahead. A cool breeze wafted through the earthen enclosure. The sweet sound of waves washing up on the beach massaged my ears.

Delilah left François leaning against the wall. She cautiously approached the opening of the tunnel. She stuck her head out slightly and ducked back in quickly. A bullet struck the wall just above where her head had been.

"They're out there," Delilah said when she returned to us. "About five of them. All armed."

"They've learned since 1974," I said.

We waited with bated breath for them to come into the tunnels. After about ten minutes, Dorcas said, "They're going to wait us out."

"They know you still have the gun," I said.

"One gun won't do much good against that many," Dorcas said.

"Do you know another way out?" François asked.

"We had a map that could get us up on the cliffs," I said, "but it was on my phone. I don't remember it well enough to find the right branch. I should have memorized it. I assumed we'd have the image on the phone if we needed it."

"So, we're trapped under a rock between two hard places," Delilah said. "And no one knows where we are."

CHAPTER EIGHTEEN

WE STOOD THERE FOR A FEW MINUTES considering our options. Then an idea blossomed in my mind. A wild thought at best. But the time had come for a Hail Mary.

"Delilah, can we get that shortwave transmitter running?" I asked.

"It runs fine as long as they haven't broken through the bookshelf yet," Delilah said.

"Let's get back there."

We retraced our steps. The Broussards had put all their eggs in the beach basket. No one had bothered to force the bookshelf yet. Delilah and I leaned over the shortwave set, warming it up while Dorcas tended to François. Sweat was pouring down his face. Dorcas dabbed it with her shirt and looked over at me with worried eyes. All those days of captivity and his exertions today were catching up with François. We didn't have much time.

"It's ready," Delilah said. "Are you calling Trey?"

"He didn't take his set to Geneva," I said. "He left it in the room at Belle Plage."

I estimated the time, adjusted the frequency, leaned over the shortwave radio, and hoped. I pressed the speaker button and spoke into it. "This is Diana Chambers calling user Nighthawk. User Nighthawk, acknowledge." The speakers crackled. We waited anxiously. I leaned in and repeated my query two more times. Finally, a surge of static erupted and resolved into a voice.

"Diana?" Chip sounded like an angler shocked to find a fish dangling from his hook and not sure what to do with it.

"Yes!" Relief and hope surged through me. "It's me, Chip!"

"You having fun in France?" Chip asked. We couldn't help laughing. *Sure, France is a riot right now.*

"We're having a bit of a situation right now," I said. "Is your mom there?"

"No," he said. "She went out with her friends. My sister is. And Amira."

"Please get them for me, Chip. We're stuck somewhere bad, and we really need help."

"Got it," he said.

The line went silent with just the gentle humming of the unit filling our ears. We sat anxiously. Time crawled, making minutes seem like hours.

"Diana?"

I almost sobbed at the sound of Brandy's voice.

"Yes!" I said. "It's so good to hear your voice, Brans!"

"I hear we got ourselves in trouble," Brandy said, sounding just like her mother.

"You can say I told you so later," I said.

"Oh, I will," Brandy said. "Where are you?"

"We're in the tunnels below Chateau Broussard. We need directions from the map I sent you."

"Opening it now," Brandy said. "Hey, what are you doing?"

"It's my chair," Chip said.

"Then you're going to have to hold the microphone thingy up for me."

"Not the time, guys," I said, rolling my eyes while my sisters shook their heads.

"Are those kids?" François asked.

"You don't want to know," Delilah said.

"What do you need to know?" Brandy asked.

"We need to know which tunnel leads up to the cliffs from the main tunnel," I said. "The one that goes to the beach."

"Looks like it's about five tunnels down from the entrance," Brandy said. "The entrance on the house side."

I could hear a quiet voice mumbling in the background.

"Amira wants to know if you've seen anything else unusual."

"No," I said. "Just the tunnels. Some pretty stalactites."

"What did you say?" Brandy said. "What do you mean? What's it? Come talk."

"Hey!" Chip said. "You're crowding me."

"Diana," Amira said, "the correct tunnel on the map runs below the village well."

"Of course!" I said. "Stalactites! That's why they're there and nowhere else in the tunnels."

"Groundwater depositing minerals over time," Dorcas said. "Presto! Stalactites."

"We're going to try to get out that way," I said. "Thank you! Brans, can you . . ."

"I'm already calling Dad," Brandy said. "I'll let him know where you are."

"Thank you, Brans. I love you guys."

"Me too," Brandy said.

"We love you too, Diana," Chip said. "Please be careful and come back."

"I will," I said, wiping a tear away.

We regrouped and started back down the tunnel. When we reached the passage partially covered by stalactites, Delilah took a deep breath and led us in. Grateful Dorcas had thought to grab flashlights, we turned them on now. The air was stale, and the walls were close. We stumbled several times. Dorcas caught François once just before he hit the ground. It took both of us to get him upright again.

Delilah eased around one turn and cursed.

"What's wrong?" I called.

"Check it out," Delilah said, shining her flashlight on the ground. A skeleton lay sprawled against the wall of the passage. Its clothes were tattered and decayed, making it impossible to date. An insect skittered through an eye socket and down the rotted face.

"Looks like Shakti was right about the bodies," I said.

"Let's hope she was wrong about the unexploded ordinance," Delilah said.

We felt the tunnel gradually sloping upward as we continued to make our way. I imagined Lucille climbing this path alone. Her courage was one thing I could never doubt. We continued climbing. The walls got narrower and the roof lower. The claustrophobia was getting to me.

I stopped at one point to wipe the sweat from my brow. My hand went up too far and hit the roof. Silt started raining down on us. For a terrifying moment, I expected the whole passage to collapse.

"Cover your heads!" Delilah shouted.

We ducked and covered until the silt stopped dropping. The tunnel, at least for now, held fast. We stood as straight as we could in the tighter space. Delilah exhaled, nodded, and motioned for us to keep going.

Finally, a faint light spilled from a hole overhead. François stumbled again in his hurry to investigate the opening. Delilah and Dorcas picked him up.

"Check it out," Delilah said, "but be very careful."

I nodded. I reached up and grasped the edges of the opening. With effort, I hoisted myself up. I saw the night sky above me, stars sparkling overhead. I reached up further to hoist myself higher. A hand gripped mine. Panic seized me for a moment. Then the thumb caressed my hand in a familiar pattern.

Trey lifted me the rest of the way through the hole and held me tightly to his chest, kissing my head. I buried my face in his chest, exhausted and relieved. He held his phone up behind me.

"We've got them!" Trey said, his voice breaking. "They're safe! You guys are so amazing!"

I could hear sounds of celebration coming from his phone.

"Anyone care that we're still down here?" Delilah called.

Trey laughed and released me.

"How did you get up here in the dark?" I asked.

"The nearsighted led the blind," Michael said. He clicked his flashlight on and handed a rope to Trey.

They lowered it into the opening and lifted the others out in turn.

Dorcas smiled when she saw Michael.

"Sorry, I'm looking a little rough around the edges," she said.

"You look absolutely beautiful," Michael said, pulling her into his arms.

"How are you?" Trey asked Delilah and me.

"I think we're fine," I said.

"Able to handle a little more tonight?" he asked.

"Sure," I said, curious. "What's up?"

"You'll see," Trey said. "Jacques has been busy. We're going to end this nightmare tonight."

"I'm all for that," I said. Trey kissed me and offered his shoulder to François. They started making their way down the hill. I paused for a moment as the others started down. I thought again of Lucille breaking through that opening, determined to light the way for her students. Robert said Madeleine had sent her sons to stop Lucille. He must have meant here. Was that why the platform broke and caught fire? Had there been a confrontation? How did Lucille escape? Did she face them alone? I pictured Madeleine standing about where I was standing. I saw a yellow rose falling to the beach to be washed away by the sea. I saw Lucille watching Trey and me examine the chest for the first time all those years ago. I saw drawings carefully preserved in that same chest. It was then that I knew.

My vision blurred.

"Diana!" Trey called in the darkness.

"I'm coming!" I called. I wiped my eyes and looked one more time at the rugged scar where the platform had once stood.

"I'm so sorry, Momma."

CHAPTER NINETEEN

"I should have told her, Lucille," Aria sobbed. She was sitting with Momma at the kitchen table. They were waiting for Daddy to get back so they could go searching for Angélique.

"You made the right decision, Aria," Momma said. She hesitated for a moment, then leaned over to rest a hand on Aria's shoulder. We were fixing our breakfast. All cereal today. Momma was too preoccupied with the Angélique situation to make a big breakfast for us.

"She has a right to know," Aria said.

"We both know it wouldn't lead anywhere good," Momma said.

Delilah and I exchanged an annoyed glance. It felt like sitting on the edge of a group of girls whispering about secrets you weren't allowed to know. Every word you heard confused you and just made you more curious to know what was going on.

We woke up the Monday morning after I heard Aria and Angélique fighting to Aria calling Angélique's name. Further investigation revealed Angélique's travel bag was gone along with some of our food from the pantry downstairs. We were sent to school while my parents and Aria spent the day looking for Angélique. Nothing so far. They'd even called the airport to see if Angélique had managed to book a flight home somehow.

They kept us home on Tuesday. Rain poured all night and was

forecast to continue throughout the day. The mild storm that forecasters promised was turning into a major event. No wind or hail, but rain upon rain. Water levels were starting to rise and could turn dangerous if it kept raining.

Daddy came stumbling through the kitchen door, stamping his booted feet and shaking his drenched rain slicker.

"Anything?" Momma asked anxiously.

Aria's face fell when Daddy shook his head.

"No," he said. "No news. Sam Dearman said he would close up the drug store at noon and help us look if we haven't heard anything by then. I called Jim at the police station. He said we have to wait forty-eight hours to file a formal missing persons report, but he's going to look around town himself today."

"At least that's something," Momma said.

"We'll find her, Aria," Daddy said. "Let me get a bite and some coffee. Then the three of us can go out together in the truck."

I watched them leave an hour later.

"Hope they find her," I said.

"Me too," Dinah said. "This rain is getting scary. I'm going to go read upstairs."

"Are they giving you some big final test?" I asked. "I thought seniors finished early."

"The tests never end," she said, patting my back before she left.

I sat down on our couch and retrieved my copy of Agatha Christie's *Hallowe'en Party* from the coffee table. I was deep into the story when Delilah entered the room and tapped me on the shoulder.

"What up?" I asked.

"Check this out," Delilah said. She held up Angélique's sketch pad. I'd seen her scribbling and drawing in it off and on throughout their visit.

"Yeah, so."

"Look at this drawing."

She held up a drawing of the red houseboat Daddy showed us on Sunday.

"So?"

"Think about it," Delilah said. "They haven't found her anywhere in town. She hasn't gone back to France. At least, as far as we know. Remember what I did a couple of years ago?"

After a titanic fight with Momma two years ago, Delilah had also disappeared one morning. We found her the next day sleeping in a tent in the woods only three miles from our house.

"You think she's close?" I asked.

"Maybe," Delilah said. "I wasn't really planning to leave forever. I just wanted to make a point. For people to miss me."

"I already had plans for the extra bed," I said.

Delilah punched me in the arm and shook the drawing.

"Ow!"

"I'd bet good American money she's hiding there," Delilah insisted.

I took the tablet from her and examined the drawing.

"We'll tell Momma and Daddy as soon as they get back."

"Or . . ." Delilah said. "We could go find her ourselves. Really live one of those mysteries you read instead of vegging with one on the couch."

"I don't think Dinah would like that," I said. Warning bells were sounding in my head.

"Who says Dinah has to know?" Delilah said. "It'll only take about thirty minutes to run down there and back. We might have Angélique with us when we get back."

"I don't know," I said.

"Come on, De-Bore-A," Delilah pleaded, grabbing my arm. "Give us some of that rebellious D&D energy."

Before I fully processed what we were doing, I was standing at the door with my boots and raincoat on. Delilah appeared similarly dressed. We'd just opened the door when we heard a voice behind us.

"Where you goin'?"

Delilah groaned and said, "We're going down to the river, Dor. We need to look at a houseboat Daddy wants to buy. Stay with Dinah until we get back."

"Does Dinah know?" Dorcas asked.

I exchanged a glance with Delilah.

Delilah leaned down and said, "It's a surprise for Dinah. We have to keep it secret. Can you do that, Dor?"

Dorcas tilted her head in deep contemplation.

"I don't think Dinah will like that surprise," she said. *The kid had a point.*

"What's not to like?" Delilah said. "Dinah loves the river."

Dorcas looked at me skeptically. I didn't trust myself to say anything convincing.

"We'll be back in just a bit," Delilah said. "Stay with Dinah."

We escaped onto the front porch and made our way toward the river. I started regretting our decision immediately. The rain pounded us the second we stepped off the porch. My pants were drenched before we made it out of our yard.

"We should go back!" I shouted.

"We're already wet now!" Delilah said.

We threaded our way through the woods, across the property line, and down to the river. Our boots sank deep in the muddy soil. I had to stop and pull them loose a couple of times. Finally, we saw the fire engine houseboat ahead.

"Good thing it's so bright," I said. "I wouldn't be able to see it in this rain if it was darker."

"Yeah. Momma's definitely going to shut that down if he buys it."

Something seemed weird about the orientation of the houseboat. I tried to put my finger on it, but the rain obscured it too much to make it out clearly. We jumped from the bank to the boat and skirted the deck, holding on to the rail that circled it.

"Angélique!" Delilah called as we entered the living area.

The roof provided welcome cover from the rain. I was grateful for the break, but I realized what was wrong with the boat when we stepped inside. The floor was slightly tilted.

"Delilah, is this thing . . .?"

A loud noise interrupted me. The houseboat swayed and tilted with such force we lost our balance. I tumbled to the floor and slid downward. Water rose to meet me. I felt Delilah slam into me. I started reaching for her and felt someone else. I turned to see Angélique with her head resting on the tiny wooden post that passed for a kitchen table. The water was rising, almost to the top of the table. I noticed an ugly red welt on Angélique's temple. Something had fallen from the shelves above us the first time the boat tilted.

"Is she dead?" Delilah sputtered, fighting to keep her balance.

I pushed myself toward Angélique and felt her arm. I didn't have any training in how to read a pulse, but she felt warm enough.

"I think she's just knocked out," I said.

The loud noise sounded again. The houseboat tilted even more.

"What's happening?" I cried.

"It's a good thing Daddy didn't buy this thing," Delilah said. "That rusty hull can't handle the rain or some debris ran into it. Maybe a log? Must have punched a hole in it."

"You mean . . ."

"Yeah," she said. "I think it's going down."

CHAPTER TWENTY

BANQUE GENÈVE
Reference # 12181991

Manuscript Held In Trust For Boxholder 763

An Excerpt from

DARK CONFESSIONS (1975)

By Lucille A. Broussard

The circus had come to Chateau Broussard. Lucy watched the colorfully costumed guests talking, eating, and dancing amidst the flickering kerosene lanterns Madeleine had purchased especially for the occasion. A long table covered with a black tablecloth held exquisite hors d'oeuvres and succulent meats. Fruit and vegetables occupied the far end of the table. A dessert table held frosted white cakes alongside several bowls of colorful wrapped candies.

Madeleine glided gracefully from person to person, dressed in a flowing blue Renaissance era dress with a gold crown mounted on her head. She was, of course, dressed as Catherine de' Medici. Monique guided the staff with efficiency and a firm hand. Maids and servers bustled through the crowd carrying drinks. Madeleine had pulled all the stops out for this display of Broussard pageantry.

Pleasure boats had been depositing passengers on the beach below the chateau all day. They were guided through the tunnels, up the stairs, and to a preparty reception hosted in the grand ballroom. A shuttle bus, also specially rented by Madeleine for the occasion, had picked up passengers from the train station and deposited them at the chateau. Three private helicopters had landed on the lawn just before the festivities began. Their excited occupants spilled onto the green lawn to join the festivities. Madeleine had combined a costume party and outdoor masquerade ball, which the French were accustomed to enjoying, with some American Halloween customs new to her French neighbors. The resulting potion produced a definite hit by early evening.

Lucy scratched her neck beneath the uncomfortable gingham dress she wore. She'd opted to go as Anne of Green Gables. She felt ridiculous with her hair braided in pigtails, but it seemed preferable to the spookier options. Aria stood by her side dressed as Marie Antoinette, complete with a towering white wig. Aria had added an extra grisly touch with a vivid red gash across her neck, a sobering reminder of Marie's fate. Aria sipped a svelte glass of white wine while Lucy chose a plastic cup of water.

"Madeleine enjoys playing the hostess, *no?*" Aria said.

"She's very good at it," Lucy said.

"This is the part I will miss," Aria admitted.

Lucy was trying not to think about it. She really didn't have a plan yet beyond getting the children out of the chateau. Pastor Lindell's warnings only strengthened her resolve to do something. Aria needed some convincing, even after Jean-Paul's abuse had broken her. They worked out a systematic plan to take the kids away and contact their guardians once they were settled. For the children without a place to go, Pastor Lindell had put Lucy in contact with a missionary group that specialized in relocating displaced children. Lucy feared the Broussards might accuse them of kidnapping. Jacques told them the local police were firmly under the Broussards' influence. They could hope for no help there. Still, she felt a responsibility she couldn't shake. Lucy's growing sense of God's calling on her life was still undefined, but she believed she had come to Chateau Broussard for such a time as this. Let the chips fall where they may and leave the consequences to God.

Aria had walked along the beach a couple of times and selected two boats always moored there for the Broussards' personal use. Since there was too much organizing to leave before and the chateau would be full of people on Halloween night, Lucy and Aria decided to make their escape on the evening of November 1ˢᵗ before the planned transfer on the 2ⁿᵈ. They would take the two boats down the coast to a little cove. The Kerouacs would be waiting with their truck to carry them all to Paris. They'd debated selecting a few trusted students, but they decided to take everyone. That meant letting all the students know they would be leaving in a few days. It was a big risk. Lucy watched Louis in particular as they shared the news with the students. He cast his eyes to the floor and stayed quiet. She made a mental note to watch him closely.

All was prepared, and they were enjoying their last days in the splendor of Chateau Broussard. "Enjoy" was relative. Tension filled the air. Lucy and Madeleine were cordial, but the warmth had seeped out of their relationship. Aria and Jean-Paul were not speaking. Alexandre and Lucy were hardly speaking. Robert maintained his usual custom of barely speaking to anyone and no one minded.

Lucy noticed Madeleine heading inside. She checked her watch. It was almost ten o'clock. Lucy wondered how long the guests would stay. A few had taken the shuttle back to the train station already, but most of them were still committed to the party.

"Where do you think she's going?" Lucy asked.

"To take care of some trouble with the food service?" Aria speculated.

"They should all be full by now," Lucy said.

"You are not accustomed to French parties, Lucy," Aria said.

Lucy couldn't shake her curiosity.

"I'm going to follow her," Lucy said. "I'll meet you back at the room."

"*D'accord.* Be careful, Lucy."

Lucy followed Madeleine through the foyer and down the darkened main hallway, making sure to keep a safe distance between them. Madeleine stopped outside the dining room. She knocked and stuck her head inside. A moment later, Henri emerged. He took her hand and led her to the library. Lucy slipped down the hallway to the dining room door. She peered through the slightly open door. A group of men in suits sat around the table. Smoke filled the air. Ashtrays sitting on the table were filled to overflowing with butts and ash. Lucy wondered if some of these men were the same people she'd seen wearing red robes in the chapel.

Lucy continued down the hallway. She heard Madeleine and Henri talking in the library. Lucy took the same position outside the door that she had when she'd eavesdropped on them last time. Henri and Madeleine were waiting on Monique to light a fire in the fireplace. Lucy frowned. It was cool, but it wasn't that cold.

"Make it very hot, Monique," Henri said.

"*Oui, Monsieur*," Monique said.

She stoked the fire until it was blazing.

"Thank you, Monique," Henri said.

Lucy breathed a sigh of relief when Monique started the other way. Monique bowed and exited through the opposite door.

Henri circled his desk and bent over. Lucy heard a dial turning and a safe door pop. Henri produced a file and laid it on his desk. He opened it, pulled two sheets out, walked over to the fireplace, and dropped them into the fire. They shriveled instantly.

"Monique does her work well," Henri said.

"She does," Madeleine said. "You're going to burn them?"

"I must," Henri said. "They are relocating Touvier again. These moral purists are relentless. We need to take precautions until their appetite wanes."

"What if it doesn't wane?"

"We will deal with that when the time comes," Henri said. He walked over to Madeleine and wrapped his arms around her.

"Your father should never have kept those papers and photographs," Madeleine said.

"He was a prideful man," Henri said. "And these images are a piece of history. When sanity returns someday, they could serve as a record of the fight we waged in the shadows. But we cannot take the chance of their discovery before then."

Madeleine sighed and nodded. Henri released her and said, "*Ma chérie*, the Society believes we need to move the children early."

"What? When?"

"Tonight."

"I told you I would speak to Aria and Lucy," Madeleine said. "They won't go through with their plan. They may be scared and desperate, but they will be sensible when I reason with them."

"It does not matter," Henri said. "If the purists come here investigating, they will look at everything. Including the school. The children will be better off in Lyon."

"But I was going to talk to the children tomorrow, Henri. They're not prepared. They will be terrified."

"I am so sorry," Henri said, bending down to kiss the top of her head. "I know the school means much to you. I promise we will try again when we can."

Madeleine sighed again and nodded. "Take them after the guests begin to clear. The party provides cover, but we also can't risk someone hearing them. Can you do it without the robes this time?"

"I wish we could," Henri said. "The Society members will not want their faces to be seen."

He wrapped his right arm around Madeleine's shoulders and guided her to the door. Lucy shrank back to the conservatory. She watched Madeleine and Henri walking toward the dining room.

"We will let them know they can take the children, and then you can go make arrangements with Monique," Henri said. "I will come back to finish burning the files after we inform them."

Lucy waited until they entered the dining room. Every ounce of self-preservation told her she should hurry to meet Aria immediately. Instead, Lucy dashed across the hall and entered the library. She couldn't resist. The folder was lying open on the desktop. Lucy began to leaf through the pages. She hadn't gone far before she realized the significance of what she held in her hands. Lucy was thankful for her progress in French over the last two months both to aid her ability to understand the Broussards' conversation and to read the materials in the folder. Her hands trembled as she closed the folder and hurried through the opposite door, the same door she'd followed Aria and Jean-Paul out only a few days before. She raced up the stairs. Thankfully, Aria had tired of the party and was already back in the room.

"Aria! We have to hurry! They're taking the children tonight!"

"What!?" Aria had begun to remove her costume. She hurried to finish and pull jeans and a light sweater out of her drawer. Lucy threw her own costume off and changed into similar clothes.

"Can you get to the phone downstairs and call Jacques?' Lucy said.

"*Oui!*"

"I'm going upstairs to get the boys," Lucy scanned the room. A brown book satchel sat in the corner. Lucy scooped it up and dropped the folder inside. They hurried down the hall together, separating at the main staircase. Aria rushed downstairs while Lucy climbed to the third floor. She went straight to François' and Jacob's room. They were still awake, sitting on their beds talking.

"Boys! Get your things and come with me. We have to leave early."

François and Jacob threw their clothes on and stuffed items into their pockets. Lucy watched them anxiously. Each second ticked painfully by. They had just finished when noises in the hallway confirmed Lucy's worst fears. The "devils" were at work already. She heard surprised boys protesting. Pounding feet nearby announced the arrival of François' "devils" on their end of the hallway.

Lucy looked desperately around the room. She spied a cricket bat leaning against François' desk. Grabbing it, she positioned herself against the wall. When the door creaked open, Lucy brought the bat down on the red hooded figure's head. He tried to rise. Lucy swung the bat again. He lay still.

Lucy and the boys ran from their room to the stairs. Lucy tried to close her mind and heart to the sounds behind her. There was no way they could save the other boys. She fought to concentrate on the ones she could save. They took the stairs two at a time.

Lucy stepped onto the second floor just in time to see a red hooded monk attempting to drag Greta away. Lucy raised the bat again. She smashed the bat into his head and side. His robe slipped. Realizing his face was exposed, the man panicked. He ran to the other end of the hallway to get help.

"Down the stairs!" Lucy shouted. "We have to get to the basement!"

The two teachers and five students hurried down the stairs. Lucy prayed they could get to the little door under the staircase before word spread that they were running. Mercy prompted them to take a foolish risk by telling all the students they were leaving. Wisdom kept them from sharing how they were going to do it. Lucy hoped the general confusion and crowded estate would keep the Broussards from guessing which route they were taking.

They reached the first floor. Lucy threw open the door below the staircase and ushered the students through.

"Where the hell is it?!" Henri roared from the direction of the library.

"What is he trying to find?" Aria asked.

"Don't worry about it now," Lucy said, clutching the satchel tightly.

When they reached the basement, Lucy led the students through the wine cellar. They were almost to the end when someone stepped out of the darkness. Alejandro was holding two wine bottles in his hands. He stopped and stared.

"Lucy, what are you doing?" he asked.

They all froze. Lucy felt her heart thumping. Upstairs, she could hear feet pounding. They would be coming very soon. She tried to think of a convenient lie. Nothing came to her. Aria seemed tongue-tied as well.

Alejandro tried again. "Aria? Lucy?" His brown eyes flitted from one to the other and then to the students. Dawning awareness was replacing the inquisitive look he'd given them at first.

"Please, Alejandro," Lucy said. She heard the desperation in her own voice. "Please don't tell them. Help us."

Alejandro's face showed the conflict inside, the war between his loyalty to the Broussards and the human impulses rising within him. He held Lucy's gaze for a moment. Something there seemed to reassure him. He looked at the students, trembling and shell-shocked.

"Come with me," he finally said. They followed him to the bookcase. Alejandro slid it open and beckoned for them to enter. Lucy entered last. She turned just before Alejandro closed the door.

"God bless you, Alejandro," Lucy said. "I will never forget this."

"God speed your journey, Lucy," Alejandro said.

The bookcase slid shut behind her. She heard Alejandro kicking the bookcase, jamming it to make it harder to open.

Lucy entered the pitch darkness. Aria activated the small flashlight they'd brought. The students were huddled in a circle, wide-eyed. Sarah was starting to cry. She buried her face in François' shoulder. He stroked her hair gently.

"*Tout ira bien, mon petit moineau,*" François whispered.

Lucy looked questioningly at Aria.

"My little sparrow," Aria said, smiling affectionately at Sarah and François.

"I'm sorry, but we have to keep going," Lucy urged.

All seven of them stumbled through the darkened cavern. The students tripped several times in the dim light afforded by their tiny flashlights. Lucy felt her sweater clinging to her, damp with sweat despite the chilly night. Streams of silt rained down on them when they turned the tight corners. Finally, faint moonlight appeared ahead.

Lucy wanted to get down on her knees and shout a prayer of thanksgiving when she saw the beach empty. The two boats were waiting for them. Now, they only needed one. The students clambered aboard. Jacob and Aria seized the oars, preparing to row them out far enough to engage the motor safely.

"Lucy! Look!"

Lucy followed Aria's finger to the top of the cliffs. The beacon had been shedding its welcoming light all night as boats had come and gone. Now most of them were gone. And someone had turned it off. The beacon and the coastline were dark.

"Can we go without it?" Lucy asked.

"We need it!" Aria said. "To avoid the rocks and to use as a point of reference to rendezvous with the Kerouacs."

Lucy tried to think fast. Alexandre had described the tunnels to her. He'd played in them often as a boy against his parents' wishes. She made her decision.

Handing the satchel to François, she said, "François, you must guard this bag at all costs."

He nodded.

"Lucy, you can't!" Aria pleaded. She'd already guessed Lucy's plan.

"We don't have a choice," Lucy said. "Don't wait for me, Aria. I'll try to catch up, but don't wait. Go as soon as you see the light."

Lucy took the tiny flashlight and plunged back into the darkness. She counted the tunnels until she came to the one Alexandre had described. She hoped he was right. The air was dank. The walls and roof pressed close all around. Lucy tried to regulate her breathing, feeling herself starting to hyperventilate. She gained control of her breaths and pushed on. The tunnel began to inch upward. She felt the increasing elevation in her legs and the back of her hips.

Lucy turned a corner and almost screamed. Three rotting bodies lay in a little wall recess, their clothes nearly gone. She wondered if they were Resistance members lured into the Broussards' deadly web, escapees who avoided their captors only to die trying to find their way out of the maze of tunnels. She held her hand over her nose and forced herself to keep going.

Finally, she saw an opening overhead. Lucy jumped twice before she was able to grip the opening and pull herself up. The platform sat there, dark and silent. Lucy hurried to the beacon. She searched feverishly for a power mechanism. Several minutes ticked by, each one an agonizing eternity. Finally, Lucy identified a breaker switch on the beacon's side. She reached to flip it, but it was already in the "on" position.

"We turned it off at the house," Jean-Paul said behind her. "You really think we would let you slip away so easily?"

Lucy turned to face him. He stood just beyond the platform, a mocking smile on his face. He held one of the kerosene lanterns from Madeleine's party. Its flickering light gave a ghostly glow to the space between them.

"Just tell them to turn the power back on and let us go, Jean-Paul," Lucy said.

"Never, Lucy. You are very fortunate my mother has a soft spot for you. She sent me to bring you back instead of the armed men waiting at the chateau. I would take advantage of her mercy. Come quietly. We will collect Aria and the children. All will be forgiven."

"We're not going back, Jean-Paul," Lucy said. She was trying to distract him while her mind worked feverishly to think of a way to turn the light on.

"You are, Lucy."

"Do you think you can make me?" Lucy said.

"Possibly," Jean-Paul said. "But I do not have to. I did not come alone. Fetch her, Brother."

Lucy hadn't seen Robert skulking in the darkness just beyond the glow of Jean-Paul's lantern. He stepped out of the shadows and marched to the platform.

"Come, Lucy," Robert said.

He stepped onto the platform and grabbed Lucy's left wrist. When she tried to pull it free, Robert wrenched it backwards and twisted. Lucy bit her lip to keep from screaming.

"There is more where that . . ."

Robert's words were cut off when Lucy spun herself around and punched him in the mouth as hard as she could. It wasn't hard enough. Robert barely flinched. He raised his hand and backhanded Lucy, sending her tumbling across the platform.

"You are strong, Lucy," Robert said. "I am stronger. Come along."

Lucy tasted bitter coppery blood in her mouth. She spit it out and glared at Robert.

"You'll meet someone stronger someday, Robert," she said.

"Too bad it is not tonight," Robert said, laughing.

"Secure her, Robert," Jean-Paul said, annoyed and bored.

Robert started to advance. Lucy poised to try and run past him, knowing it was useless.

"Stop, Robert!"

Everyone paused at the sound of Alexandre's voice.

"Well, look who left his sketch pad to help us," Jean-Paul said, turning to face Alexandre. "You want to carry her back to the chateau for us?"

"She is not going back to the chateau, Jean-Paul," Alexandre said, his voice quiet but intense.

"You do not get to make that decision, Little Brother," Jean-Paul said.

"As usual, we will not waste time listening to you."

"Then you will listen to this," Alexandre said. His arm pointed straight at Jean-Paul. Lucy saw Henri's Browning Hi-Power semiautomatic pistol gleaming in Alexandre's hand. The dancing light from the kerosene lantern painted fluid patterns on the black casing.

Jean-Paul laughed. A sardonic booming laugh.

"Now it gets interesting," Jean-Paul said. "Go ahead. Shoot! Shoot, you little coward!"

Alexandre stepped closer, backing Jean-Paul to the edge of the platform.

"Are you okay, Lucy?" he asked.

"I will be," Lucy said. She tried to ignore her throbbing wrist. She stood straight and moved closer to Alexandre. Robert stayed where he was, unsure what to do.

"Shoot me," Jean-Paul growled.

Alexandre was fighting to keep his hand steady. "Lucy, take the children and leave."

"We can't, Alex. They've shut down the power. We don't have a beacon."

"It seems you have a situation, Brother," Jean-Paul said.

Alexandre turned slightly to extend a hand toward Lucy. She reached for it. Jean-Paul seized the opportunity. He tackled Alexandre. Both of them crashed onto the platform, knocking Lucy down with them. The gun and the lantern both rolled across the platform. Robert, galvanized to action, dove for the gun. The platform rocked when he landed.

"Stop, Fool!" Jean-Paul yelled. "This thing is not made for this much weight!"

Robert landed just shy of the gun. His hands fumbled for it. Lucy couldn't reach the gun either. But the lantern was beside her. She rolled onto her back, gripped the lantern with her right hand, and swung it in an arc. The metal smashed into Robert's head. He yelled. Lucy drew her arm back and swung again. The second strike opened a gash on Robert's forehead. He screamed as blood started pouring down his face. He blindly groped for the gun. Lucy kicked desperately until her feet struck the gun.

It clattered to the far end of the platform.

Lucy felt a sickening swaying sensation when she tried to rise. The platform was splitting into two pieces as Alexandre and Jean-Paul struggled on the edge and Robert groped blindly. The section they were standing on was moving away from the section holding the beacon. Lucy looked down at the lantern still dangling from her hand. She made a desperate decision.

Lucy cocked her arm and tossed the lantern onto the wooden platform at the beacon's base. The glass exploded when it struck the wood. Kerosene spilled across the platform. Greedy flames licked the kerosene and blazed high.

"What the hell?!" Jean-Paul screamed. He punched Alexandre and detached himself. "Robert! Get off! Now!"

Jean-Paul stumbled off the platform into the grass. Robert tried to follow and fell again. The platform pitched and swayed. Robert rose again and stumbled to solid ground. He collapsed, unconscious, blood pouring from his head wound.

Lucy turned to check on Alexandre. Robert's last fall had destroyed what was left of the platform's support structure. Alexandre saw it coming.

"Lucy! Fall! Grab the opening between the slats!"

Lucy felt the platform giving beneath her. She fell flat and wrapped her fingers between the slats just before the platform swung downward, slamming into the cliffside. She looked down to see Alexandre hanging on close to the bottom.

"Alex!"

"Hang on, Lucy!"

Lucy could see debris raining from the platform to the beach below. Her vision blurred. She felt dizzy. Lucy willed herself to look up. What she saw filled her with fury. Jean-Paul stood at the edge of the dangling platform, looking down at them.

"Jean-Paul!" Lucy shouted. "Help us!"

"I think maybe you should hang there for a while," Jean-Paul said. "Think about what you have done. I will go check on Aria, and then maybe I will come back to get you."

Jean-Paul stopped to check on Robert. Satisfied that Robert wasn't in immediate danger, Jean-Paul grinned, waved, and walked away.

The platform shifted again so hard that Lucy almost lost her grip. Her wrist throbbed. She fought to ignore it.

"Do you think he'll come back to get us?" Lucy asked.

"It will not matter," Alexandre said. "The platform will not hold long enough. Try to climb, Lucy."

Lucy fought to ignore the swaying motion. She closed her eyes and started climbing step by painful step. The platform still swayed, but her weight didn't bring the platform closer to collapsing. She stopped and looked down.

"You try," Lucy called.

Alexandre started climbing. The swaying increased. Lucy could feel the remaining supports weakening.

"I can't, Lucy," Alexandre said. "I weigh too much. You try again."

"Okay," she said. "I'll get to the top and go for help."

Lucy started climbing, slowly and painfully. She paused once and looked out to the ocean. She saw a tiny speck moving down the coast. At least Aria and the students were free. She took a breath and tried to move again. The platform shook violently. Lucy struggled to regain her grip. Her hands ached. Her palms were raw and chaffed from the rough wood. Her wrist was screaming, sending agonized cries through her nerve endings.

"Did I move too fast?" Lucy asked.

"No," Alexandre said. "It was not you. The total weight is the problem. The platform will not hold long enough for you to make it."

"Of course it will." Lucy started climbing again.

"I found my courage, Lucy." Alexandre said.

"Yes, you did," Lucy said as she continued to climb. The platform shook again. She gasped and clutched the slats. "I wouldn't have survived without you. I'm sorry for what I said."

"I am sorry for not acting sooner," Alexandre said. The platform pitched and swayed.

"Better late than never," Lucy said, breathless.

"Lucy, you must listen to me."

"What?"

"You will want to follow me. You must not. Keep climbing."

"Of course I will keep climbing," Lucy said. "Just give me a moment to rest."

"Lucy."

Something about the way he said her name compelled her to look down at him. His earnest eyes stared up into her own, bridging the distance between them. He smiled.

"Promise me that you will write a beautiful story."

"Alex . . .?"

His eyes were growing distant. The space between them was turning into an expansive gulf. A thundering anguished scream erupted from Lucy's throat as she realized Alexandre had released his grip and plunged with the platform debris into the darkness below.

CHAPTER TWENTY-ONE

I WASN'T PREPARED FOR THE WELCOME we received when we stepped into *La Brise Atlantique*. Trey was right. Jacques had been very busy. Twenty men were gathered in the tight reception area along with my dad, Jacques, and Enora. They ranged from early twenties to late middle-aged. I recognized the gray-haired bartender from The Black Shark. Several other men were familiar from our walks around town. All of them were Belle Plage residents; the tourist set was not represented among them.

"I sent images of everything we had to Jacques," Trey said. "He spread the word while we were on our way back."

François still gripped Trey's arm.

"From what I saw, you will need every . . ." François' voice trailed off. His lips trembled. Tears filled his eyes.

I looked across the room. Sarah had just entered with Ramona and Rico. François released Trey's arm and took a step forward.

"*Mon petit moineau,*" he said.

Sarah rushed across the room and threw her arms around him. François had been incredibly composed the whole time he'd been with us. The instant he fell into Sarah's arms, he broke down into deep sobs.

"*Tout ira bien, mon ami,*" Sarah said, stroking his hair while she held him.

The bartender from The Black Shark walked up to me.

"Jacques said you have been inside the chateau. You can show us where the other man and Aria's daughter are being held?"

"Yes," I said. "Should we contact the police first?"

"A waste of time," he said. "They have ignored the problem for too long. We will make things right tonight."

He took my hand in his own calloused paws.

"Thank you, Monsieur . . .?"

I felt something cool and metallic in my palm.

"Fournier. Gerard Fournier. Aria was my cousin. We do not forget."

He released my hand. I looked down at the bright silver pentagram nestled in my palm.

Monsieur Fournier turned to Sarah. She was standing arm in arm with François. He bowed to her.

"Your family will have justice tonight."

The men around the room murmured. Some of them nodded vigorously.

Sarah's eyes flashed. She nodded her gratitude, unable to speak.

Dorcas and Michael decided to stay with Sarah and François to be sure they were settled and safe. That freed Rico and Ramona to join our group doing what they did best. The men led us outside. A collection of work trucks and vans sat waiting for us. The European variety were smaller than American trucks, mostly Citroën Berlingos and Nissan Nivaras, but they suited our purposes well. Thirty minutes later, we were packed into six trucks and winding up the road to Chateau Broussard.

I heard a helicopter veer overhead as we approached the archway gate.

"Someone's planning an exit," I said.

"We'll see who can move faster," Trey said.

Our lead truck, driven by Monsieur Fournier, smashed through the archway, sending security personnel scattering for cover. The second truck veered toward the helicopter. It had just touched down on the lawn. We could see the villagers climbing out of their trucks and clambering onto the skids. Our own truck raced to the front door.

We burst into the now familiar foyer. I directed the men up the main staircase. Servants protested, but no one was bold enough to try to stop us by force. Most of the men got ahead of us along with Rico and Ramona. I hurried after them with Trey, my dad, and Delilah on my heels. Shouts from the third floor told me they'd found Jacob and Angélique. A struggle was raging between our allies and Madeleine's remaining security personnel on the third floor. The twelve security personnel had threatened the villagers with their guns when they first appeared on the third floor, but none of them seriously wanted to shed blood. The chances of them escaping Belle Plage without retribution were slim, and they knew it. The villagers were disarming and subduing them.

We slipped through the chaos and entered the room at the epicenter of the struggle. Jacob and Angélique lay tied to two separate twin beds. Delilah and Trey rushed to release Jacob and check his vitals while my dad and I untied Angélique. The second her bonds were loosed, Angélique jumped to her feet and headed straight for the door. Jacob collapsed when Trey and Delilah tried to get him on his feet. My dad ran to help them.

"Where are you going?" I yelled to Angélique.

"I know where Madeleine is!" Angélique called over her shoulder, already racing toward the stairs.

Sensing trouble, I ran after her. I took the stairs two at a time and still didn't catch her until she reached Madeleine's private chapel.

"Angélique!" I called. "Wait!"

Angélique ignored me. She reached for the door. A hand extended from the darkness and gripped her wrist. Angélique looked up, startled. Robert twisted her arm behind her back and slammed her face into the door. Angélique collapsed, dazed.

Robert stepped over Angélique. He moved toward me with menacing determination.

"We will see if you do as well as your mother," Robert laughed. "She took her beating like a woman."

I backed away, searching for an escape. Seeing none, I closed my hands around the mace in my pocket and hoped I could catch Robert by surprise. *This is what you get for going off alone.* I took another step back.

A board creaked behind me. I might have left everyone. But everyone hadn't left me. Denny Hebert emerged from the darkened hallway. One look at his face revealed he'd heard every word Robert said.

"Well, my friend," Robert said. "You should know that you are about to face . . ."

Robert never finished. Daddy stepped forward and delivered a vicious punch to his face without pleasantries or preamble. Robert stumbled backwards. Genuine shock covered his face. He wasn't accustomed to his opponents hurting him. Denny didn't allow time for Robert to process the situation. He swung again, knocking Robert's head backwards at an awkward angle. Robert unleashed a furious yell and hammered back with two punches of his own.

Denny Hebert grew up with three brothers. He'd worked long hard hours in the fields of Picardy and the docks of New Orleans. One thing he knew well was how to handle pain. Robert looked concerned after my dad punched him. He looked terrified after he punched my dad and realized Heberts possessed a pain threshold far beyond his own. Denny shook the blows off and kept coming.

They slammed into the door of the chapel. Angélique rolled over, pushing herself out of their way. I pulled my mace out, looking for an opportunity to shoot Robert without hitting my dad. They were too close together to do it. Robert seized Denny from behind. Denny wrestled his arm loose and brought it crashing back into Robert's stomach. Robert grunted and released his grip. Denny turned and punched him again.

Angélique climbed to her feet, moving to the heavy doors again. She gripped the handle and pulled. Angélique screamed in frustration. The doors were locked.

Robert was struggling to gain an advantage using his height. For a moment, my dad seemed to be losing. He disappeared beneath Robert. I'd almost decided to attack Robert from behind. Then I saw Robert start to rise. With supreme effort, Denny lifted Robert from below, his arms wrapped around Robert's waist. Denny drove them both into one of Madeleine's stained-glass door frames with Robert absorbing the impact. The stained glass shattered into a million brightly colored sprinkles.

Robert pushed himself out of the doorframe, swaying drunkenly.

Denny kicked him in the chest. Robert fell to his knees. Denny pressed his advantage, delivering a series of punches as Robert sank lower. Robert kept trying to use the techniques from his years of training. They failed each time because Denny Hebert never attended any classes or learned formal techniques. He was drawing on years of real experience and pure refined instinct. Denny was unpredictable, and Robert had no idea what to do with that.

Angélique ran to the shattered window and forced her way through. Screams from within told me she'd found her target. I hesitated, torn between wanting to stop Angélique and concern for my dad.

There was no need. Daddy hit Robert one last time. Robert sank to the floor, his face a canvas of bloody devastation.

My heart jumped into my throat when my dad leaned against the wall, breathing heavily.

"Daddy?"

I hurried to him.

"Are you okay?"

He caught his breath and smiled at me. "Who's next?"

I gripped him in a fierce hug, relief blazing through me.

"I'll get something to tie this ox with before he wakes up," he said. "Go get Angélique."

I nodded, squeezed him tight again, and said, "I love you, Daddy."

"I love you too, Angel."

I hurried toward the shattered stained glass. Behind me, I heard my dad say to the still unconscious Robert, "How'd you like your beating?"

I grinned and pushed my way through the beautiful shards of colored glass. The scene before me was the stuff of gothic nightmares. Every candle in the place was lit. Angélique and Madeleine were wrestling over an object while the Virgin Mary watched, still cradling the lifeless body of her soon-to-be reanimated son. Angélique pulled with supreme effort and the object went flying. It landed at my feet. For a moment, I experienced déjà vu. I was back in the Picardy High School gym. Eric Dixon's gun was spinning toward my feet. I reached down and took this one like I had Dixon's that night. I felt the weight of the weapon in my hand. It was lighter than I expected.

"Yes!" Angélique shouted. "Shoot her!"

Madeleine pushed Angélique aside.

"I'm not going to shoot her, Angélique," I insisted.

"Why not?" Madeleine said. "It's what all of you want. To be rid of me."

"Yes!" Angélique screamed. "Once and for all!"

Something about Madeleine's demeanor confused me. She was more combative than usual, even with Angélique. She was goading both of us.

"Do what you need to do, Diana," Madeleine said.

She didn't bring this gun here for defense. She wants to end it. She can't do it herself. She's tired, and she wants us to end it for her.

"Yes! End it now!"

I fought to ignore Angélique.

"It's over, Madeleine," I said. "Come with us peacefully. It's either us or the authorities. No one has to get hurt."

"So many have been hurt already," Madeleine said. "So many lost. It's too late to undo that."

"Satisfy my curiosity, Madeleine," I said. "Why did you never tell the world about your son's death?"

"Everyone knows about her son's death," Angélique said. "She had my father killed."

Madeleine knew which son I actually meant.

"Henri wouldn't let us mourn him," Madeleine said. "He called Alexandre a traitor and a disgrace. How would it look if we lost two sons under suspicious circumstances the same night? We buried him quietly and told people he'd left us. After a while, it got easier to keep repeating that story. None of us wanted to remember the painful truth."

"He died saving my mother?"

"Yes," Madeleine said. "He put his devotion to her ahead of his family. What we told people was true in a way."

"Okay," I said. "We need to join the others." Angélique stiffened. I watched her for any sudden movements.

"Before we go," Madeleine said. "I have one last gift for you. I was going to leave it for you if we escaped. But now seems like the perfect moment." Madeleine reached beside her to the homily podium and produced a sheet. She took a few steps forward, stooped, and slid it toward me. I eased to the floor and picked the paper up, never taking my eyes off either of them.

I looked down at the photograph in my hand, perplexed. It showed a young Latino family. The parents were standing beside their two sons, smiling at the camera with radiant joy. It looked like it was taken at a Christmas celebration. A Christmas celebration held in the shadow of a magnificent tree standing in the grand foyer of Chateau Broussard. The parents were a picture-perfect couple. He was ruggedly handsome. She was breathtakingly beautiful. The boys looked around ten years old. I studied their faces. The oldest seemed so familiar. I looked closer, trying to balance my curiosity with the need to keep an eye on Angélique and Madeleine.

Recognition dawned. I'd seen this couple before in other pictures. I'd even met them once. I'd shared a meal with their youngest son and his wife. I'd shared everything for five years with their eldest son. My stomach lurched. My vision swam.

"I told you, Diana," Madeleine said. "I'm always closer than you think."

I fought to maintain control.

"That's Alejandro," Madeleine continued. "Henri's driver for decades. He had a sweet little family. We made sure both the boys received excellent educations. The youngest works at the Smithsonian. The oldest is an academic administrator at a prestigious university in Tennessee. Though I hear he's about to relocate. We're so proud of them. The Silvas have always been loyal and dedicated servants."

I felt my chest churning. Vomit was trying to force its way up my throat. I swallowed it back, willing myself to stay focused. The early part of my life was always the question mark. I spent so many years processing my childhood traumas. My life at Vanderbilt represented my sane life. My stable life. With one picture Madeleine had decimated that safe harbor. My mind was plunged into chaos. I found myself questioning every interaction, every decision, every intimate moment with Pedro. Five years and he never mentioned a word about Chateau Broussard, Madeleine, or that he had previous knowledge of my family before we met. The night Dinah died, I unleashed a scream of pain and loss that reverberated throughout our house. Now, an equally terrible scream erupted from my throat and echoed throughout the chapel. This time, I screamed in pure rage. In unrestrained anger. I raised the gun and aimed straight at Madeleine's heart.

"That's right! Do it!"

Angélique was making more sense.

"Do what you need to do, Diana," Madeleine whispered.

"Kill her!" Angélique screamed again. "Get justice for my mother. For your mother. For my father."

"She didn't kill your father," I said.

"Why do you say that?" Angélique demanded.

"Because I know who did," I said, feeling the trigger against my finger.

CHAPTER TWENTY-TWO

MAY 9, 1995

We bobbed in the growing pool of water. Angélique slipped from her place at the table. I hoped the water would wake her up. It didn't. She floated like lifeless driftwood. Delilah grabbed her head and pulled it above the waterline.

"Good news is the water's not that deep," Delilah said.

"What's the bad news?" I asked, afraid of the answer.

"We don't want to get trapped on a houseboat even in shallow water," Delilah said. "Help me with her."

We tried to drag Angélique up the tilted floor. We were moving, but not far enough or fast enough. Delilah gripped the cabinets lining the wall and climbed up the floor toward the entrance without us. She only made it halfway before she slid back into the water.

"Why didn't you talk me out of this?" Delilah said.

I was too scared and furious to answer. I gripped Angélique, trying with all my strength to keep her up. As the rain poured outside, I heard someone calling my name. At first, I thought I was dreaming. Then I heard it again.

Dinah appeared above us at the entrance. Her clothes and hair were completely drenched.

"Debbie! Delilah!"

"Dinah! We're here!"

"I see you, Debbie."

"How did you find us?" Delilah asked.

"Dorcas told me not long after you left," Dinah said.

"Little snitch," Delilah muttered.

"You better be glad she is," Dinah said. "What were you thinking?" Dinah was assessing our situation while she spoke. Her eyes roamed the entire room, moving from the cabinets to the walls and back to us. Finally, she said, "Hang on a minute."

Dinah disappeared back through the door. She was gone for what seemed like forever but was probably only a couple minutes. When Dinah returned, she had a rough brownish loop of rope thrown over her shoulder. She braced herself and started unrolling it.

"Where'd you get that?" Delilah called.

"It was hanging on a hook outside," Dinah said. "Good thing."

She tossed the rope and told Delilah to climb first. Delilah scampered up the tilted deck, stabilized by the rope held firmly in Dinah's hands. When she reached the top, Dinah grabbed Delilah by her shirt, her eyes blazing.

"You run, not walk, back to the house! I had to leave Dorcas alone. You stay with her. Momma and Daddy should be back soon. Send them over here. Do you understand?"

For once, Delilah didn't argue. She nodded and started for home. Dinah dropped the rope.

"Come on, Debbie."

"What about Angélique?"

"You climb up first."

I gripped the rope and pushed myself forward.

"Hold on tight!" Dinah shouted. The boat was shifting again. I clutched the rope and waited until the motion stopped. I started climbing again with renewed energy. Finally, I reached the top and collapsed into Dinah's arms. She held me tight for just a second. Then Dinah stood. She tied the rope to one of the kitchen cabinets. Then she started tying the other end around her waist.

"What are you doing?" I asked.

"I need to get Angélique before she goes under again."

The boat shifted again. We both grabbed the walls to stabilize ourselves.

When the motion stopped, Dinah finished tying the rope and started easing herself down the even more tilted floor.

"No!" I yelled, grabbing her arm.

Nightmare visions of my sister and Angélique plunging below the depths ran through my mind.

"You can't, Dinah! What if you get trapped?"

"I'll be fine, Debbie. I have to help her."

"Why?" I shouted. "This is all her fault. She's the one who ran away! She doesn't deserve it, Dinah!"

Dinah stopped and turned. She reached up and cupped my face in her hands. Her bright blue eyes peered directly into mine.

"I want you to listen to me and never forget what I'm about to say," Dinah said. "It doesn't matter what she did. Or who she is. Or what she's done to us. It matters who we are. This is what we do. We're not doing this because she deserves it. We're doing this because it's right. We're doing this because we're the people who help when someone's in trouble. No matter who they are. No matter what happens, you have to decide there is one thing you will never let people do to you."

"What's that?" I asked.

"Change who you are," Dinah said. "We are not going to let what she did make us less of who we are. Hold that rope and pull when I tell you to."

Dinah eased herself down the floor until gravity took control. She plunged into the water and surfaced with her arm around Angélique. She pulled Angélique closer and braced herself.

"I'm going to start up. Pull on the rope."

"Maybe Delilah should have stayed."

"You can do it, Debbie."

Dinah started moving forward, her progress slowed by Angélique's weight. I wrapped both hands around the rope and pulled as hard as I could. Slowly, painfully, Dinah started making progress. Halfway up, Angélique stirred. Dinah directed her to help climb as much as she could. Angélique responded groggily, but enough to help with the final stretch.

We rolled through the doorway, jumped from the deck to shore, and collapsed on the bank. The massive live oaks shielded us from the rain a little, but it still found us. The rain poured over us. None of us cared. We lay huddled together on the muddy bank. Soaked and safe.

CHAPTER TWENTY-THREE

BANQUE GENÈVE
Reference # 12181991

Manuscript Held In Trust For Boxholder 763

An Excerpt from

DARK CONFESSIONS (1975)

By Lucille A. Broussard

Lucy clutched the platform, her head resting against the rough wood. It had stopped swaying. She felt tears on her cheeks. For a wild instant, she thought about letting go too. Letting the beach have her. Letting it all be over. She wondered what it was like for Alexandre. For Tamera. Would it hurt? Then she heard Alexandre's final words echoing in her head. *You have to keep climbing.*

Lucy took a breath, whispered a prayer, and started climbing. She closed her mind to the pain in her wrist. To the blisters on her hands. To the sounds of debris still falling bit by bit below her. The ruined platform shook a couple of times, but not as violently without Alexandre's weight. Lucy finally reached the top and pulled herself onto solid ground.

Robert still lay unconscious on the ground beside the platform's remnants. He was breathing heavily, but he was breathing. Jean-Paul hadn't made it back yet. If he even intended to return. Lucy assumed he cared enough about Robert to send someone. That fact motivated her to keep going. Someone would be there soon.

Lucy plunged into the tunnels and made her way back to the beach.

It was easier this time. She was going downhill and she knew the way. Lucy finally reached the beach. The other boat still sat there. She might be able to take it and catch the others. Lucy looked down the coast. She could barely make out the distant outline of Aria's boat in the moonlight. They were sailing around the bend just below Chateau Broussard. *Why hadn't they gotten farther?* They must have waited for her. Deciding she could catch them faster by land, Lucy started walking along the beach.

Lucy arrived at the debris from the platform in a couple of minutes. While she was descending through the tunnels, the last piece of the platform had plummeted to the ground. It lay there smashed to bits. Nearby, a body reposed partially covered by boards. Lucy wanted to keep walking, but she couldn't ignore one last spark of hope. She knelt beside Alexandre, surrounded by fallen boards.

Lucy couldn't look at his face. It was obvious that he'd struck the rocks below the cliffs before rolling onto the beach. His skin was cold to the touch. His limbs were rigid. His pulse was gone. Lucy wanted to cry. She thought she should cry. For her friend. Her unselfish friend who died for selfish Lucy Broussard. She couldn't cry. There were no tears left. Her heart ached with a dullness she feared might never end.

"What a mess, Lucy. I hope you're happy."

How can I ever be happy again?

Instead of voicing her thoughts, Lucy said instead, "You could have helped us, Jean-Paul. He would still be alive if you had just helped us."

Jean-Paul's thick hair was disheveled. He stood only a few feet away. Lucy could see dried blood where Alexandre's punches split his lip.

"Aria's boat is rounding the bend," he said. "We will get boats after them soon. Maman is going to be furious with you, Lucy."

"Furious with me!" Lucy couldn't believe her ears. Jean-Paul's depravity knew no bounds. "Don't you care that your brother is dead?"

"He proved a coward and a traitor," Jean-Paul said. "I am ashamed to call him my brother."

Lucy crawled backwards, disgusted. She wanted to put distance between them. Her hands felt boards, chunks of fallen soil, and screws. Then she felt something else. Everything on the platform had fallen to rest here beside Alexandre.

"I am going back to the chateau," Jean-Paul said. "You can stay here and cry over this traitor all damn night if you want."

~~Lucy~~

~~Jean-Paul~~

~~The light~~

~~She thought~~

I've been trying to write this in third person all night. I can't do it. By now, you know these dark confessions contain the truth about the horrifying legacy of Chateau Broussard. May that truth one day be known to the world. I can't make it known myself as much as I want to. My own sin and the safety of those I've sworn to protect prevent me from disclosing it. Because the darkest confession is yet to come. The darkest confession is my own. May God forgive me.

I try to imagine he made a sudden motion. That he started toward me. That, somehow, he threatened me. I may be trying to imagine it for the rest of my life. I know it's not true. He was standing there. Mocking and arrogant. About to leave me alone on that beach with Alexandre's broken body and ruined face. His cruelty enraged me. His dismissive arrogance and the injustice of it all burned my soul. Why should he get to walk away?

I rose and pointed Henri Broussard's gun at Jean-Paul's chest. He laughed at me again. Just like he laughed at Alexandre. Like he laughed at every human pawn in his hedonistic pursuit of pleasure.

I pulled the trigger. I will never forget the shocked look on his face when the first bullet struck him. That should have been enough. I should have been done. I wasn't. I kept firing. The papers later said I hit him five times. I have no idea if I only fired five times or if I only hit him five times. Either way, he collapsed onto the sand, his blood mixing with the white silt borne across the Atlantic. Maybe in the interlocking network of oceans some of that silt had found its way from that first beach where I sat watching a baptism only a couple months before.

The echoes from those shots continued resounding in my ears long after the last one was fired. As I stood there, I knew that they might echo in my head for the rest of my life. So far, they have. Every time I try to sleep, I wake up hearing them. I also knew in that moment that this one impetuous act forever bound me to that place and that moment. For a moment of vengeance, I'd traded my agency. My freedom to expose the Broussards. That awareness was confirmed when I looked up to the cliffs and saw Robert Broussard looking down at me. He was still dazed and confused, but Robert had seen the whole thing.

I looked up at him one last time. I tossed the gun beside Jean-Paul's body. Then I turned and made my way down the beach. I caught up with Aria and our students further down the coast and hopped in their boat. Jacques and Enora met us at the designated place. We crowded into their small truck. I rode in the bed with Jacob and François. As we rolled across the beautiful French countryside and the sun broke over the horizon, Jacob and François talked excitedly about seeing Paris, their young minds and hearts so resilient even in the face of trauma. I tried to listen as best I could. It was hard to concentrate with the sound of those shots reverberating in my own head and heart.

CHAPTER TWENTY-FOUR

"SO, YOU KNOW THE TRUTH," Madeleine said.

"I do," I said. "I realized it when we came through the tunnels. Based on where everyone was that night, only one person could have shot Jean-Paul if Alexandre was dead. Lucille."

Angélique's eyes widened in confusion and shock.

"What?" Angélique said. "Why would she do that?"

"Because your biological father was an A-1 bastard, Angélique," I said. "Stop obsessing over the fantasy that he would have cared about you or Aria if he had lived."

Madeleine's mouth spread into a grim smile. It spoke volumes that even she didn't defend the memory of her eldest son.

"You kept Lucille's secret, and she kept yours," I said to Madeleine. "That was the deal?"

"I believe they called it mutually assured destruction during the Cold War," Madeleine said. "We promised not to pursue prosecution. Let her live in peace chasing her demons and raising her family. We also pledged to let the students live their own lives without interference."

Madeleine looked at Aria. "We gave the same promise to you and your mother. I have no doubt you really are my granddaughter. But Jean-Paul fathered several illegitimate children. We spent money and influence to keep them from filing claims. Recognizing your claim would unleash a storm of similar legal challenges."

"In return, Lucille promised not to release the files?" I asked.

"Not in her lifetime," Madeleine said. "We hoped she would return the files and the chest eventually. They were the last two things linking us to the Vichy confiscations. We sold the rest in the early seventies when Paul Touvier's case raised the possibility of further investigations. We lived with the constant fear that your mother would have a change of heart and torpedo us all or do exactly what she did. Which was leave you the tools to destroy us."

"Kill her!" Angélique screamed. "You see what a monster she is!"

"We can't," I said. But my words didn't match my posture. I was still aiming the gun at Madeleine.

"You want her dead," Angélique said. "I saw it on your face when you looked at that photograph. You know you want to make her suffer!"

I did. Very much.

Madeleine stared at me. Calm and expectant. Wanting me to end it.

"Your mother would have finished it!" Angélique screamed. "She did what she had to do. Now you should too! Honor the one who raised you! Honor her legacy!"

My thoughts swirled with a kaleidoscopic range of emotions. Fear, anger, sadness, betrayal, hurt, and longing consumed me all at once.

"Hear her voice and do what she would have done!" Angélique screamed again.

Time stood still. That chapel and all three of us seemed frozen in an eternal instant. Angélique's words soaked into my mind.

Then I heard her. In my heart. In my mind. Embedded there for all my days. The one who raised me. The one who always did what was right no matter the cost. The one whose legacy I would always honor. Her voice came to me accompanied by the sound of raindrops.

It doesn't matter what she did. Or who she is. Or what she's done to us. It matters who we are.

"Do it, Diana!" Angélique insisted.

We're not going to let what she did make us less of who we are.

I could feel strength rising within me. Dinah's strength. There was no question what she would do.

We're doing this because it's right. We're doing this because we're the people who help when someone's in trouble. No matter who they are.

I dropped the gun.

"What are you doing?!" Angélique shrieked. She charged for the gun. I punched her as hard as I could. She fell against the pews and lay still.

"I wish Delilah could have seen that," I said.

"I did."

Delilah and Trey were pushing their way through the stained-glass window.

"Your dad came to get us," Trey said.

Madeleine stood looking at us impassively.

"We're done here," I said, crumbling the photograph and stuffing it into my jeans pocket. "Get Angélique and let's go."

"What about her?" Trey asked, nodding toward Madeleine.

"That's up to her," I said.

Trey and Delilah knew me well enough to know this was something I needed to do myself. They lifted Angélique and carried her out of the chapel, opening the doors wide this time.

"The cycle is broken," I said to Madeleine. "I'm not staining my hands with your blood. We're all done servicing you. We have your son outside. You can come with us now or with the authorities later. You're welcome to come join us if you want."

I turned and walked out of the chapel.

Our group was gathering in the foyer. Jacob leaned on one of the villagers. He looked gaunt and tired, but he would survive. Angélique started to revive. Robert lay bound on the floor of the grand hallway like a Thanksgiving turkey.

"Where's Madeleine?" Daddy asked.

Before I could reply, a single shot boomed down the hallway. It echoed throughout the haunted halls of Chateau Broussard. One more ghost added to the collection.

"She's reunited with her other sons," I said.

CHAPTER TWENTY-FIVE

TREY TRIED TO JOIN ME. I appreciated his support and his anger on my behalf. In the end, I convinced him it was something I needed to do alone.

The Zoom window opened.

"I was afraid we'd be having this conversation soon," Pedro said. He looked like he always had. Clean cut, handsome, and affable. His face once the face of a trusted friend. Until now.

"Why did you lie to me, Pedro?"

"It wasn't so much a lie as an omission," Pedro attempted half-heartedly.

I didn't want to ask the obvious question. It seemed childish. It didn't even matter anymore. But I still needed to know.

"Did you ever really love me?" I asked.

"How can you ask that?" Pedro said. "Of course, I loved you. I still love you. It ripped my heart out when you chose Trey over me." I wanted to see the face of a brazen liar. Instead, Pedro looked very sincere.

"Was I your 'assignment'?" I asked.

"My assignment, so far as I had one, was to report on your work at Vanderbilt. To keep Madeleine updated. Falling in love with you was never part of the plan. Madeleine wasn't happy about it at first. But she accepted it. She even hoped that someday our relationship might help her convince you to come teach at Chateau Broussard."

"But she couldn't do that as long as Lucille was alive to tell me the truth about her," I said.

He nodded. "I hoped we could get married and then I could tell you the truth about my background. But Trey was always there. In your heart. In your memory. I shouldn't have been surprised when your feelings for him rekindled last year. Diana, this doesn't change anything between us."

"It changes everything!" I said. "You hid a secret part of yourself from me. You passed personal details about me and my family to these people whose life mission goes against everything I believe. Everything you led me to believe we shared. Do you even care what their ideas could do to people?"

"Of course I care!" he said.

"And?"

"I owe them in a way you can never understand."

"That's hypocritical doublespeak and you know it!" I said. "You encouraged me to go help my family last year hoping for what?"

"That you would settle the past and be done with them," Pedro said. "Open the door for us to have a future. It obviously didn't work."

"A future serving the interests of Madeleine Broussard? No thanks." Another thought occurred to me. "Did you have anything to do with Eric Dixon?" I demanded.

"No," Pedro said. "Nor did Madeleine. We had no idea how Dinah died until you uncovered the truth. Eric Dixon was an evil little man acting entirely on his own."

"Be careful, Pedro," I said. "You don't want to get into a philosophical discussion about good and evil with me right now."

"Maybe we can meet and talk in person," Pedro said.

"Go to hell, Pedro," I said. "I'm leaving Vanderbilt for an offer at Tulane. You will stay away from me and everyone I care about. You will behave yourself and in no way further the interests of the remaining Broussard family or enable them to harm anyone. If you do, I will come down on you so hard your head will never stop spinning."

"I'm leaving Vanderbilt too," he said. I remembered Madeleine's reference to Pedro's pending change of location.

"Where?"

"UCLA."

"You wouldn't happen to owe Carlton Broussard for your good fortune?" I asked.

Pedro was silent.

"He needs you closer in case he has errands for you to run," I said. It wasn't a question.

"Diana, you have your happy ending," Pedro said. "Go enjoy it. Forget about what I may or may not be doing for Carlton. I take your warning seriously. I know you. You're formidable. Smart. Determined. But remember one thing. I am too. And I really do know you. Maybe even better than Trey. I can predict your every thought. Your every mood. Your highest ideals and darkest temptations. You don't want to duel with me."

"I'm not the same person I was when we were together or even the same person I was a year ago," I said. "I may have a few surprises for you. I can't believe you're okay enabling these people."

"I disagree with a lot of what they're doing and saying," Pedro said. "But they're powerful and influential. Right now, the cultural tides are flowing their way. You can't fight the future, Diana."

"Watch me."

I closed the Zoom window. Trey was waiting outside the door. He opened his arms wide. I gladly walked into them.

"I'm so sorry, Di. It's going to be hard not to kill him if I ever see him."

"He knows better than to cross my path anytime soon," I said. "I'll be ready for him if he rears his head."

"We'll be ready for him," Trey said.

"He's the past," I said, lifting my head to kiss Trey. "You are my future. And I'm so glad. What do you say we find a nice little place in New Orleans and grow old together?"

"Sounds like a plan, Sweetheart," Trey said.

I packed our things and descended the stairs to the little hotel's foyer.

Someone called my name.

Sarah came over to hug me. "Rico and Ramona are taking us to the train station. I wanted to see you before we left. Thank you for everything, Diana. You are your mother's daughter."

Sarah could read the look on my face. She touched my arm gently.

"I'm sorry she hurt you," Sarah said. "She was a complicated person. We're all complicated people. Hang on to the good and forgive the bad."

"Thank you, Sarah," I said. "You have any plans?"

"Going back to Omaha," she said. "I can't wait to see my daughter and grandchildren. I'm planning to take a trip to Boston in October."

"Boston," I said. "Going to see anyone I know?"

Sarah blushed slightly. "Now that it's safe, I'm going to spend a few days with François. We'll see."

"All the best to you all," I said, hugging her again. I watched the three of them drive away with Rico and Ramona.

I went in search of Trey. I found him outside the hotel talking to Dorcas. She grinned ear to ear and hugged him. It reminded me of when they were cooking up some devious scheme when she was little.

"What are you two whispering about?" I asked.

"Nothing important," Dorcas said, giving me a hug. "I'm on my way to the chapel to see Michael."

"Give him my best," I said. "I'm guessing this is not the last I'll see of him?"

Dorcas smiled, her eyes sparkling with excitement. "He's going to come see us in Picardy after he finishes here in August."

"I'll look forward to seeing him then," I said.

We loaded our luggage into the waiting trucks. Angélique passed us and settled into her seat, sullenly avoiding eye contact. Delilah smirked and winked at me. "Not saying I'm gonna miss her ranty personality."

When Dorcas returned, we climbed in and got as comfortable as we could for the ride to the train station. My last view of Belle Plage from the train window was the somber dark outline of Chateau Broussard standing on the cliffs, guarding its ghosts and its secrets.

CHAPTER TWENTY-SIX

MAY 13, 1995

"Stop fidgeting, Debbie. We're almost done."

Dinah ran the brush through my hair again.

"Can I see it yet?" I asked.

"Just a minute," she said.

When she finished, Dinah turned me toward her mirror. I barely recognized myself. She'd rolled my long dark hair and styled it into curvy waves. I wore her bright blue dress. She'd applied makeup to accentuate my features. Not a lot. Just enough to bring out my eyes and lips.

"You look so beautiful, Sweetie," Dinah said.

I stared at my reflection. I looked so grown up.

"You don't think it's a little much?" I asked.

"No, I don't," Dinah said. "I'll do this someday for your prom. And later, for your wedding."

"Who says I'm getting married?"

"You're such a little nonconformist," Dinah said, squeezing my shoulders. "Let's go see if the others are ready."

Dinah was dressed beautifully too in a green dress with a matching bow in her perfectly styled hair. We discovered Delilah and Angélique were still dressing. Angélique was leaving tomorrow. We'd barely had time to get our little party together. Whatever disagreement she'd had with Aria, it seemed to be fine now. She apologized when Aria returned with my parents. Aria was just glad to have her back. The last few days had been like an actual visit. We had fun. I was almost sorry to see them go. Almost.

Dinah and I decided to go check on our handiwork in the barn while the others got ready. We both smiled with satisfaction when we walked into our version of the Tuileries Garden. Greenery festooned the walls and areas around the table. We'd cleaned up three birdbaths. Water hoses hooked up to them emitted streams of trickling water that mimicked the fountains we'd seen in the pictures.

"We do good work," Dinah said.

"Do you think we'll get to see the real gardens someday?" I asked.

"Of course," Dinah said. "That would be amazing."

The scene was lit by the glow of fake electric candles we'd borrowed from Tianna's family. No point risking a fire for a private party. We stood together savoring the moment.

"I'm going to see what's keeping the others," Dinah said. "Be right back."

I stood alone after she left, watching the flickering candles. Listening to the soothing trickle of simulated fountains. A sense of peace washed over me. It felt like a special slice of time borrowed from a realm of epic fantasy. Like every dream could come true here.

"Debbie?"

"Hey, Trey," I said. "You made it earlier than all the people who actually live here."

I turned and faced him.

"Your mom drop you off?" I asked.

"Yeah . . . my mom . . . she did."

Trey's expression had been the same as always when I first turned to him. It changed instantly when he looked at me. It was a funny expression. He'd never looked at me like that before.

"You okay?"

"Yeah," he said. "I'm great. Looking forward to the party."

"Me too. I like your suit."

"Thanks," Trey said, looking down at his gray suit. "Mom calls it my special occasion suit."

"You look nice," I said.

"You look . . ." Trey seemed to be searching for a safe word, "great! Very great!"

His hesitation made me worry.

"Do you not like it?" I asked.

"Are you kidding?" Trey said. "You look amazing! I love . . . your dress and your hair."

"Thanks," I said, relieved. "I was afraid I looked like a total freak. It's very girly."

"You'll never look like a freak," Trey said.

"You want to check on the others?" I asked.

"Definitely," he said.

"You can lead the way since we are in France," I said with an airy fake accent. I held my hand out to him.

Trey had grabbed my hand a thousand times and pulled me from one adventure to the next. Tonight, something felt different. The choreography had changed. When he took my hand, he held it gently. He looked at me again with that mysterious expression I couldn't quite understand.

"Let's see what surprises are in store for us in the Tuileries Garden tonight," I said in my exaggerated accent.

CHAPTER TWENTY-SEVEN

WE RETURNED TO PARIS. Our group went their separate ways with Daddy and Dorcas taking a flight back to Louisiana while Delilah and her entourage flew directly to L.A. We made plans to meet up in Picardy in August to finish the work we started with Lucille's belongings. Trey and I decided to stay in France another week so I could fulfill my promise to show him my favorite Paris attractions.

I opened Lucille's letter our second day in Paris while Trey was out "taking a stroll" around Paris. I knew he just wanted to give me some privacy. Trey didn't take random strolls without me. I broke the seal and opened the envelope. Trey and Daddy found two of these notes when they visited the archives. Both written in 2014, one for Daddy and one for me. Daddy had read his already and kept its contents to himself. I respected his wishes despite my curiosity. I'd spent the afternoon reading Lucille's *Dark Confessions* manuscript. I almost decided to save the letter for another day. The manuscript alone felt like it was too much for one day.

The first surprise when I unfolded the letter was the name at the top. Not "Deborah."

Dear Diana,

If you're reading this letter, I'm no longer with you. Please be there for your daddy and your sisters. I assume you've also read the Dark

Confessions manuscript. There are so many things I want to say to you. I hope I got the chance to say them in person. The most important thing to say is that I love you. I wish we were closer. I hope someday we can be. I'm sorry for my part in the things that divide us.

The contents of this safety deposit box will give you everything you need to expose what happened at Chateau Broussard. I feel like a coward sometimes for not exposing it all sooner. I thought I might for a while after that last night at Chateau Broussard. I returned to Louisiana and had almost decided to turn myself in and share the folder. Then I met your daddy. After we spent that first night walking and talking, getting to know one another, I went home and went to sleep. I woke up that morning to an astonishing realization. I'd slept the entire night without waking up. When I woke up, all was quiet. The echoes were gone. Those shots that had haunted me since that night on the beach were stilled. Maybe I could be happy again. Maybe I could love someone with my whole heart. Maybe I could find forgiveness and purpose. Maybe I could write a beautiful story like Alexandre said. I wanted to live and not be chained forever by one mistake. I've spent my life working to atone for that mistake.

Our story isn't perfect. Far from it. It's got tragedies and blemishes and loss and terrible mistakes. But it's ours. It also has happiness and celebration and purpose and, most of all, four beautiful girls that I cherish more than I can ever say. I hope I did some things right. I know I did one thing right for sure. And that was helping bring the four of you into this world.

Thank you for doing what I couldn't. I know you will because I know you. I hope you will always feel loved. You are loved by me more than you know. I hope you will always be brave and strong. Most of all, I hope you will let yourself be happy. You deserve to be happy always and for your days to be long and fruitful. Until we meet again.

All My Love,
Momma

CHAPTER TWENTY-EIGHT

NO SIMULATION COULD COMPARE to the beautiful reality of the Tuileries Garden at dusk. Trey and I strolled along the pathways admiring the beautifully maintained grassy areas and majestic fountains. I gazed in fascination at the intricate stonework adorning each fountain. The crystal exterior of the Louvre Pyramid sparkled as the city lights started to pop on one by one. It was that time before dusk settled in. Light enough to see, but dark enough for the coming night to announce its presence. The sky ahead was fiery red. The Eiffel Tower stood against it like an elegant sentinel. I expected its sparkling lights to come on at any moment.

"You want a snack?" Trey asked as we arrived at the Bassin Octogonal, the impressive oval fountain at the center of the Tuileries.

"Sure," I said settling into one of the portable chairs by the fountain. As he rummaged in his pocket, I took a deep breath and looked out at the Place de la Concorde with the Eiffel Tower standing in the distance beyond it. My eyes swept forward and peered into the watery jet rising and falling in the center of the fountain. I could see the Roue de Paris, the city's Ferris wheel, in the distance behind the watery plume. I caught a glimpse of someone for just a second on the other side of the fountain. A young girl with long brown hair leaned against the fountain with her back to me. She had a red beret balanced crookedly on her head.

"It's so beautiful and peaceful," I said. "I wish we didn't have to go back."

Trey produced a familiar black packet. I grinned and extended my hand. He tipped it toward me. We'd performed this ritual a million times over the years. Tonight, something was different. The choreography had changed.

First, I felt something odd in my palm. Instead of the candied M&M shells, I felt something hard, sharp, and metallic tumble into my hand.

Second, Trey always bent a little to pour the M&Ms in my hand. This time, he kept bending until he was on one knee. It took my mind a beat to catch up. To process what was happening.

"Diana Chambers and Deborah Hebert," Trey said. "You are my oldest friend, my best friend, and the love of my life. I want to spend every day of the rest of our lives showing you how much I love you. I can't wait to find a little place in New Orleans and grow old with you. I've loved you since we were young, and I'll love you until I die. I want you to share my life. I want you to be my wife."

I looked down at the sparkling diamond ring in my hand and into his earnest eyes. There was no more doubt. No more fear. No more hesitation. *Give yourself permission to be happy.*

"There is nothing I want more than to be your wife, Trey Laurence," I said. "I've loved you always, and I will love you for the rest of my life. Yes! Yes! Yes!"

Trey slipped the ring on my finger. It felt cool and solid and right. He stood and swept me into a passionate kiss. I floated in the sheer euphoria of the moment. I almost didn't hear the shouts and clapping coming from the other side of the fountain.

Trey and I separated. I looked over to the fountain and laughed with joy. Brandy was perched on the edge of the fountain, her red beret so askew it looked like it would tumble off her head any moment. Chip was beside her clapping furiously. Dorcas stood behind them, wiping her eyes and smiling radiantly. Michael stood beside her. He smiled, waved, and passed another tissue to Dorcas.

Brandy cupped her hands over her mouth and shouted.

"Congratulations! We love you!" She paused and added, "Told you I would make it to Paris!"

I grinned and turned back to Trey, resting my forehead against his. The couples walking the trails and people relaxing in the green spaces were hearing the commotion and starting to figure out what was going on.

People started clapping and shouting.

"*Félicitations!*"

Our lips met again. I felt my feet leaving the ground as Trey lifted me in his warm embrace, applause and shouts of congratulations ringing in my ears.

YOUR REVIEW MATTERS

Thank you so much for taking the time to read *The Demonologists' Legacy.* I hope you enjoyed exploring Brittany and wandering the haunted halls of Chateau Broussard. Please leave an honest review of the book on your favorite platforms to help other readers discover the story. Just a sentence or two goes a long way to help raise awareness of the book and supports the creative work of independent authors. I appreciate it so much.

If you want to see how the Heberts' story began, check out *The Demonologists' Daughters.* Available in print, digital, and audio formats.

Legacy always gives birth to legend. Whose versions of the story are "true?" Who gets to define the past and the future once and for all? Those questions await in Book Three, *The Demonologists' Reckoning.*

HISTORICAL NOTES

The Broussard family, their chateau, and the seaside village of Belle Plage are fictional. Belle Plage is based on many charming French coastal villages in Brittany. The Broussards are inspired by real life French families with old money and aristocratic lineage. While the specific setting and citizens of Belle Plage are fictional, I've tried to represent Breton cultures and peoples as accurately as possible.

The information about Paul Touvier and his prosecution is accurate. Touvier was accused of the crimes discussed in the book and spent the years from 1973-1989 evading capture. He was assisted by traditionalist elements within the Roman Catholic Church who offered him sanctuary and support. The official Roman Catholic Church hierarchy insisted that officials linked to Touvier were acting in an unofficial capacity against the wishes of the church and its leaders. France's Vichy era offers a complicated historical case study of how human nature collapses or endures living under occupation. Julian Jackson's *France: The Dark Years, 1940-1944* offers a compelling historical narrative of the occupation and quest for accountability for those of you interested in more information. Jean Guéhenno's *Diary of the Dark Years, 1940-1944: Collaboration, Resistance, and Daily Life in Occupied Paris,* translated by David Ball, provides a searing primary source account of those devastating times.

While the tunnels below Chateau Broussard are my own creation, the information about coastal French ports and how the Nazis used them is based on historical fact. David Luhrssen's *Hammer of the Gods: The Thule Society and the Birth of Naziism* chronicles the shadowy and controversial group that inspired the Broussards' theatrical rituals.

I am fascinated with the history of Wicca and the emergence of pagan religious traditions in the contemporary world. I deeply appreciate the kindness and openness of practitioners who welcomed me to events in Minneapolis and assisted me with my research. Pagan practices are diverse and very individualized. Aria represents one path among many. I hope she represents those paths in a way that practitioners recognize and appreciate. Two great sources for those who want to know more are Ronald Hutton's *The Triumph of the Moon: A History of Modern Pagan Witchcraft* and Margot Adler's *Drawing Down the Moon: Witches, Druids, Goddess-Worshippers, and Other Pagans in America.*

I am very familiar with the evangelical cultural matrix that shaped Lucille and the Heberts. It shaped me, for better and for worse, in my early years too. Like Diana, my own relationship with those traditions and cultures is complicated. I can still be enchanted by the beauty of their ideals and cultural contributions while being repulsed by their tendencies toward anti-intellectualism, inhumane treatment of outsiders and dissenters, and willingness to sacrifice spiritual integrity for political influence. Readers wanting to learn more about the evangelical world that shaped Lucille should consult Larry Eskridge's *God's Forever Family: The Jesus People Movement in America,* Leah Payne's *God Gave Rock and Roll to You: A History of Contemporary Christian Music,* and Kristin Kobes Du Mez's *Jesus and John Wayne: How White Evangelicals Corrupted a Faith and Fractured a Nation.* Du Mez's work also provides historical context for the issues of abuse within churches discussed in *The Demonologists' Daughters.* I'm indebted to all these scholars for their work and am hoping to eventually add a nonfiction work of my own to the list chronicling the relationships between American religious traditions and the satanic panic that features so prominently in both *The Demonologists' Daughters* and *The Demonologists' Legacy.*

DISCUSSION QUESTIONS

1. The Hebert family includes several characters with strong personalities and distinct traits. Which character do you identify with or find compelling?

2. Complicated family dynamics are central to the Hebert saga and appear from the very beginning of this story. What complications and fault lines exist in the family circles that we meet early in the book? What strengths and positive benefits do the characters draw from their family bonds?

3. How would you respond to Lucy's questions about the nature of evil? What do you think of Alexandre's responses?

4. How does the quartet structure of the book with its shifts in time and perspective serve the story?

5. What aspects of French and Breton culture fascinated and surprised you in the story? Which do you find most appealing? Which would be most challenging for you?

6. Madeleine exerts a powerful influence over her family and the world around her. What do you think of Madeleine as a character, an educator, and a matriarch? Do you find her logic and appeal tempting at any point in the story?

7. What are your thoughts about the relationships between the three Broussard brothers? Can you relate to any of them? How?

8. How do you feel about the allied quests to hold Nazi collaborators accountable for their crimes in the decades after World War II? How long should we pursue justice and to what lengths should we go?

9. Discuss the influence of religious beliefs in the story. What are the differences and similarities in the ways that characters view faith and the obligations it places on them?

10. How have Lucille's past choices and influences shaped the woman we and her family know in the recent timelines? What do you think about her choices and commitments?

11. What are your thoughts about Dinah's lesson for Debbie on the houseboat? How do we resist the pressure to let other people define who we are and what we do?

12. How do the characters grow and what do they learn by the end of the story?

13. The story leans heavily into the concept of legacy. What does the term "legacy" mean to you? How are we shaped by the legacies of the past? What kind of legacies do we want to leave for future generations? What insights did you gain from the story about the influence of legacies in our lives?

ABOUT THE AUTHOR

K. Scott Culpepper is an author, historian, and speaker creatively exploring the history and mystery of human experiences. He holds a Ph.D. from Baylor University and specializes in the history of the early modern Atlantic World. *The Demonologists' Daughters*, his debut novel, was published by Scotland Publications in 2024. His nonfiction book *Francis Johnson and the English Separatist Influence* was published by Mercer University Press in 2011. He teaches courses in history and religious studies at a private university in Iowa where he lives with his wife, Ginger. He loves history, spooky tales, reading, writing, swimming, and spending time with his amazing family.

For more on K. Scott Culpepper's writing and other projects, you can visit his website, sign up for his newsletter, and find links to his social media at https://kscottculpepper.com/

ACKNOWLEDGMENTS

The English poet John Donne observed in his 1624 poem "Meditation XVII" that "No man is an island." Humanity lives as part of a collective whole. What we do or leave undone affects the whole human family. We all matter, and we carry responsibility because we matter. What Donne says about humanity rings true about writing and producing books as well. While a book is born as the product of one author's imagination, the process of refining and presenting that vision in physical form for others to enjoy is always a collaborative effort. I'm blessed to have amazing collaborators in my author journey who inspire me along the way, offer crucial feedback, and give generously of their time and talents to help me bring stories to life.

Scott Sontag contributed his time, editorial skills, and expansive knowledge of French language, customs, and cultures acquired from a lifetime of study and living in France. I first met Scott in high school when he performed at our local Baptist church at the invitation of our pastor, Lamar Skinner. I got to know him better while attending Louisiana College, where Scott was a campus favorite leading the musical ensemble *Common Good* and providing music education for students and local churches. Scott has lived much of his life in France, continuing to share his talents with others. His editorial insights and inside knowledge of French language and cultures were invaluable. Scott saved me from cultural and linguistic *faux pas* while helping ensure that I represented France and the French accurately. Any remaining errors are entirely mine, and there would be many of them without Scott's capable assistance. I'm grateful for his contributions and the gift of his friendship through the years.

Once again, my amazing cover designer Brandi Doane McCann created a stunning cover that captures the heart of the story. Brandi's designs immerse you in the setting. I wanted to jump on a plane to Paris immediately after seeing her haunting image of the Eiffel Tower and the Seine with the Heberts gazing into the future while their shadows tell the story of their past. I got many comments from readers about how much they loved the cover design for *The Demonologists' Daughters*. Brandi has done it again for *Legacy*. I appreciate her work and how enjoyable it is to work with her.

The same can be said for Hayli Henderson. Hayli narrated the audiobook version of *The Demonologists' Daughters*. I can't imagine anyone else doing it and certainly not as well as Hayli. She captured the heart of the story and the personalities of the characters so well. Hayli was suited perfectly to narrate the story not only because of her amazing acting skills, but also because of her own interests in art, history, and religion. She understood the story and its central themes in a way few others could. I've enjoyed working with Hayli and am excited about future collaborations.

Thanks also to the libraries, bookstores, and book festivals that have invited us to host signings and author talks over the last year. People's response to *The Demonologists' Daughters* has been gratifying and humbling. I appreciate the support and am so glad that other people find entertainment and insight in these fictional stories that are so much fun for me to create.

The book is dedicated to two men who left a lasting legacy that continues to make the world a better place. I will always be grateful to my parents, Kenny and Ann Culpepper, for the home they made for me and my sister Mandy and their encouragement for us to learn and grow. Mandy is a very gifted and successful nutritionist today with two amazing children and a brilliant husband who works as a medical doctor with expertise in infectious disease research. I teach, write, and have an awesome family. There are a lot of things that made us the people we are and chief among them is the credit we owe to our parents who encouraged us to be different when different is good and look beyond the borders of our small town to the larger world waiting out there. So many of the good things I am as a husband, father, educator, and leader are based on the example my dad set for me every day of his life. We miss him so much, and I'm so proud of the way my mom continues to live fully and energetically, working to make the world better for families struggling with a cancer diagnosis through her work fundraising for St. Jude's Children's Hospital. My grandfather, Grady Culpepper, served in World War II and raised his family well. Despite losing so many of his family too soon over the years, he continued to maintain a positive attitude and left a legacy of integrity, honesty, and love for his friends and family.

Chief editorial and design credits go once again to my amazing wife, first reader, chief collaborator, and skilled professional editor Ginger Culpepper. Our publishing journey would be more complicated and costly without her incredible talents. She edits the manuscript for grammar and style, offers feedback on the story, looks for any inconsistencies, and designs the internal pages of the book. All credit for the polished look and layout of *The Demonologists' Legacy* goes to her. I never tell her where the story is going until we get there so she can experience it like other first-time readers. Her reactions and attempts to guess where things are going add so much to the experience of writing and keep me hopeful that other people will want to read the Heberts' adventures too. It's probably no surprise to anyone who knows us that our life and love inspire many aspects of Diana and Trey's relationship. We will celebrate thirty years of marriage this year. It has been an amazing journey filled with adventures, challenges, and the joys of sharing life together. I would never have believed thirty years ago that it was possible to love her more than I did then. One of the most amazing discoveries you make when you share a lifetime with someone is how your love for each other can grow to depths you never imagined. Nothing is worth doing without you, *mon amour!* I'm so glad we get to share this project and all of life together.

I'm also grateful once again for our amazing family. They've all contributed in one way or another to the publishing and promotional process. Hannah Culpepper skillfully designed and maintains my website as well as guiding my social media outreach. She's a capable leader, skilled administrator, and gifted educator working as director of a private preschool. Josiah Culpepper creates my book trailers and edits videos for me. He does amazing work filming weddings and other events through his videography company, Culpepper Films. Micah Culpepper offers feedback and support as a fellow writer as well as assisting us with book promotion travel plans through his travel agency, Chickadee Travel. Our family has grown with the addition of our kids' three amazing partners who we love like our own kids. Our bonus daughter and Josiah's wonderful wife Maggie Culpepper read *The Demonologists' Daughters* early and has been a source of constant encouragement. Hannah's incredible fiancée, Hunter Van Beek, is always encouraging and willing to help with promotional efforts in any way. Micah's amazing partner, Andrew Austin, provides professional advice on promotion and travel through his shared ownership of Chickadee Travel. We're looking forward to two weddings in the coming year and are so proud of our growing family. I couldn't do life or writing without all of you.

An ancient curse addresses the perils of living in "interesting times." I like to say that it is much more fun to study and teach history than to make it. I sometimes tell my students that historical irony is hilarious as long as it's not happening to you. These are desperate and confusing times that call for our very best. Sadly, what we are seeing instead are often people giving their very worst. I still believe in the power of stories to help make the world a better place. May this story contribute to that end. The ideals that Diana voices that people are the point and that the human spirit always rises out of the ashes are still bedrocks we can hold on to. Night never lasts forever. The darkness flees with the dawn. Authoritarians and their paper empires always end up on the dustbin of history sooner or later. May we continue to live fully and love generously, refusing to let anyone change us or make us less of who we are.